MORODA

WORLD OF LINARIA: BOOK 1

L.L. MACRAE

Never give up
on your dreams

7.7.23

First published in Great Britain in 2022.
No part of this publication may be reproduced, stored in a retrieval system,
or transmitted, in any form or by any means, without the express written
permission of the publisher except for the use of brief quotations in a
book review.

Edited by: Olivia Hofer
Cover by: Holly Jameson
Map by: Domino44maps

Printed and bound in Great Britain by Clays Ltd, Elcograf S.p.A

www.llmacrae.com

For Pipkin, who brought me out of the darkness and gave me the confidence to follow my dreams.

ALSO BY L. L. MACRAE

WORLD OF LINARIA

NOVELS

Moroda

Palom

Amarah

Isa

NOVELLAS

Rise of a Sky Pirate

DRAGON SPIRITS

NOVELS

The Iron Crown

The Shadow Gate

NOVELLAS

The Citrine Key

ACKNOWLEDGMENTS

Olivia has my eternal gratitude.

When I wanted to burn the manuscript, she kept me going, both with feedback, reassurance, and encouragement. She was able to pick at the holes, push for character development, and build the world when I could not. She has given up far too much of her life on this book, and I'll never be able to repay that level of dedication and support.

This book would also not be what it is without my unflappable beta readers: Ian, Josephine, Laura, Maxine, and Ellie, who helped me see the wood in the trees, confirmed when I was steering things in the right direction, and were a supportive team that gave me confidence and motivation.

To anyone who reads this book, I am eternally grateful. It would mean the world and more if you would be kind enough to review *Moroda*.

THE REALM OF LINARIA

DOMINO44 MAPS

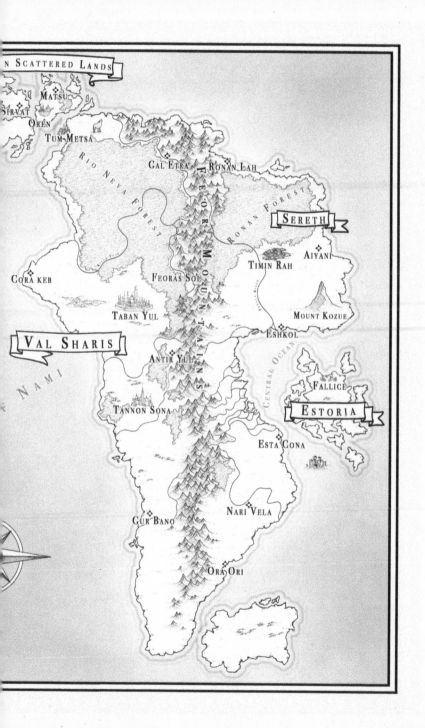

1

Morning dew flavoured her skin with the taste of autumn. Pale sunlight filtered in through the narrow, steel-barred window, and Moroda shivered in the cold cell of Rosecastle Dungeon.

She shifted her position to ease the cramp developing in her aching back and legs. She was not in chains, thank Rhea, but that didn't bring much comfort to the fear and uncertainty which plagued her.

Surely the threat of beheading had been an idle one? Something to keep the crowd from retaliating at her sudden arrest?

Only murderers and traitors to the crown were beheaded.

She'd just voiced an opinion. She didn't *really* believe they'd kill a woman for that.

Would they?

Before she could further consider her mortality, the door to the dungeon rattled and Moroda's stomach tightened. Muffled shouts and grunting carried from the other side, then a shrieked curse ripped through the air as the heavy oak door shook.

She backed away from her cell gate, the cold stone floor sending goosebumps rising on her arms and legs. She flinched, and something metallic jingled within the folds of her skirt. Reaching into her pocket, she pulled out three silver coins, a set of scales emblazoned on each.

She'd forgotten about the florins—the only money she had left—and another stab of panic pierced her.

Eryn would be so angry with her if she lost them.

Desperate, Moroda looked for somewhere to hide her treasure. If she put the coins back in her pocket, they'd jingle when she moved. She considered the window, before realising they would be seen between the bars. Dragons above, what was she going to do?

She let out a distressed whimper, then she spotted a cracked floor slab.

Outside her cell, the steel hinges of the oak door creaked as it was heaved open, and she knew she had no time to look for an alternative hiding place. Shuffling over on her knees, one fist clenched around the coins, she wedged the fingers of her free hand under the stone slab. It was rough against her skin, but Moroda lifted it just high enough to slide the florins into the gap. The dungeon door slammed shut, the slab dropped into place, and the new prisoner entered the chamber.

The same guard who'd brought her to the cell barely an hour ago now wrestled with another woman—lowborn, from the rasp in her voice and the insults she hurled at him. She spat and kicked, even tried to bite the guard as she fought to free herself from his grasp.

Moroda pressed against the wall, equally terrified yet curious, and watched the guard frog-march the new prisoner towards her cell.

Pressing the woman against the bars, he took the keys from his belt, unlocked the gate, and threw her inside.

Blood spattered the floor from an open gash on the woman's shoulder, bringing a splash of colour to the grey dungeon. She immediately whirled around and threw herself at the gate, reaching between the bars and scrabbling for the guard's face with chipped nails. 'You *pig*! Bastard! Get this gate open now or I swear to Rhea herself, you'll pay!'

'Amarah, you're done. No threat will change that.' He shrugged. Beyond the reach of her flailing hands, she was no threat.

She snarled at the guard, animalistic in her fury. 'Morgen, I'll kill you for this!' She covered the wound on her left shoulder with one hand. Blood trickled through her fingers as she tried to stem the flow. 'At least get me a medic! You don't want me to bleed to death in here, do you?' Amarah's eyes narrowed as the young man glanced at her wound.

He sighed. 'You aren't going to die. Calm down and I'll see what I can do, all right? Try not to cause too much trouble while I'm gone.' Morgen walked towards the door.

'What about *Khanna*? You ain't gonna destroy my ship are you? She's faster than anything the Imperial fleet has!' Amarah followed Morgen and walked along the bars, reaching through them at the edge of the cell. 'Be of some use, won't she?'

'I don't know. It isn't my decision. She's locked up safe and sound, just like you.' Morgen ignored her glare as he left the dungeon, slamming the heavy door behind him.

As the sound of his footsteps faded, Moroda held her breath, keeping herself as still as possible. Amarah hadn't noticed her, and she was keen to keep it that way until the other woman calmed down. She'd never coped well with conflict. Who knew who Amarah was, or what she had done to warrant being locked up.

Moroda slid down the wall, until she was half-crouched

3

on the floor, heart racing as she watched the uncouth woman. Perhaps if she stayed quiet enough, Amarah wouldn't spot her before Morgen returned to take one of them away.

After a moment, Amarah turned and looked around the cell, pausing to scowl immediately at Moroda. 'What do you think you're looking at, girl?'

Moroda was taken aback by the harshness in Amarah's voice. 'I—I didn't mean—'

'Good. Shut up and keep out of my fucking way.' Amarah strode past Moroda, looking over the rest of the cell. Her scowl deepened. 'Damned if I'm staying here long enough to be executed.'

Moroda watched her carefully and said nothing.

Amarah released her shoulder and grabbed the bars, giving each a short pull, leaving the metal slick with blood. 'Damn.' Amarah shook her head and leaned against the metal gate, her hand returning to cover the wound on her shoulder.

'What happened?' Moroda allowed her curiosity to get the better of her, and braced for another insult.

Amarah shrugged. 'Too much haste. Got sloppy. Made a mistake. Never again, I tell you.' She closed her eyes, allowing silence to fill the cell.

Moroda took the opportunity to study Amarah's face. Her hair was short, dark, and roughly cut. She wore no powders on her face or oils in her hair. A thin scar lined her left cheek, just below her dark brown eyes, pale against her tanned skin. Mostly, she looked grubby, as though she hadn't bathed in months.

She guessed the injured woman to be in her late thirties, but wounds and dirt did a lot to age a person, so she couldn't be sure. Moroda hoped Amarah kept her distance while they were locked up together.

4

'Morgen's a fool. He ain't fit to be in here. Neither are you,' Amarah said, her sneer shifting into a lopsided grin. 'I heard what you did this morning. Standing up to that foreign bastard.'

Moroda flinched as Amarah swore again, even as relief flooded her—her deed that morning had not gone unnoticed. Then again, she *had* been arrested publicly, so she supposed word of her actions—a Goldstone's actions, no less—would spread like wildfire. Not that she was really a Goldstone anymore. Her heart sank as she thought back to the three florins she'd hidden. It was all that remained of a vast inheritance that should have ensured she and her sister were well kept until the end of their days.

Moroda had wanted to leave. Run away from the debtors.

Eryn had convinced her to stay. They *could* survive without their father and his money. They'd *make* it work. After all, Niversai was their home. Leaving the only place they'd ever lived was not only foolish, it was childish.

Moroda forced a smile, unwilling to show Amarah any vulnerability. 'Thank you.'

'That the only reason you get arrested? Or you do something else? Sleep with some other Goldstone you shouldn't have, or something?'

'What? No! N—nothing like that! I would never!'

Amarah's cackle filled the dungeon, echoing off the stone. 'Ah, you Goldstones are all the same, ain't you? Little goody-goody rich girls who never get in trouble or do anything wrong.'

'I'm not a Goldstone...not anymore.' If only she'd left after her father had died...

'Yes, well I can see that, can't I?' Amarah grinned, licking her lips. She shifted her hold on her injured shoulder. 'Can't buy yourself outta this one, can you?'

Heat flushed Moroda's cheeks and her stomach roiled. 'Do you want me to help with that?' She nodded towards Amarah's shoulder, eager to turn their conversation away from her shame. 'I can use some cloth to stem the blood? Won't be permanent, but it should hold until help comes?'

Amarah paused for a moment before dropping her hand from her shoulder. 'Yeah, if you can.'

Moroda tore a strip of fabric from the thick, dark cotton at the bottom of her skirt and wrapped the length of it around Amarah's wound as best she could, tying it off with a secure knot. 'There. That should help.' She wiped her bloodied hands on her skirt, satisfied she'd done something useful.

Amarah inspected the makeshift bandage for a moment before approving it with a sharp nod. She glanced at the dungeon door through the cell bars and sighed. 'I ain't sticking around here. Neither should you, if you know what's good for you.'

Moroda knew the woman was right. She didn't *think* she'd be executed, but she didn't want to wait around to find out. She'd never been in trouble with the Imperial Guard before, let alone arrested, and she didn't have the first idea how to get out of her situation. Would there be a trial? Would she be allowed to plead her case? Beg forgiveness?

She chewed on the inside of her cheek, trying to think. She'd never been any good at planning ahead. Her sister was the brains of their duo. Moroda just dreamt up the ideas.

She didn't know how her sister managed.

'Oh great, not a Varkain, too.' Amarah's harsh voice cut through Moroda's thoughts.

'But I'm not...?' Moroda followed Amarah's gaze to the back corner of their shadowed cell. Puzzled, she looked

6

from Amarah to the corner, squinting in the darkness as she tried to make out what Amarah could see.

Her heart raced when she spotted the silhouette of another person sitting in the shadows. How hadn't she noticed them after all this time? She'd been in the cell for almost an hour!

'I do love the sound of a panicked heartbeat.'

The smooth voice from the shadows set every hair on edge, and Moroda was on her feet in an instant, breath quickening as Amarah's words resounded: *Varkain*. Someone *was* there. Someone who was mocking her fear.

A Varkain was far more of a threat than Amarah could ever be.

She could have been attacked—killed!—at any moment. Had he just been playing with her?

Stumbling backwards, Moroda tried to put as much distance between herself and the Varkain as she could. She couldn't even see him, yet her heart thrashed in her chest, as if desperate to flee.

'Ah yes. And there is the accompanying scent of fear... such a nectar.'

'Shut up you filthy creature.' Amarah hadn't moved, but she glared at the corner with such venom that Moroda thought she'd burn a hole through the stone floor. 'Why are we in the same cell as you? What in Rhea's name happened to enforced segregation?'

'Perhaps they forgot. Being invisible *is* our speciality.'

Moroda's heart thudded painfully. She couldn't quite make out the Varkain's features—the cell was too poorly lit and he was too still. She could have sworn she'd checked the cell over when she'd been thrown inside, and found it empty.

Then again, she'd never come across a Varkain before. She'd grown up on stories of brutal Varkain killings and had

7

no desire to be in the centre of the next one. Moroda couldn't even think straight, the fear gripped her so tightly. She was lucky he hadn't slaughtered her while she'd panicked about being beheaded.

'Come out from the shadows, Varkain. Show yourself,' Amarah ordered, her hand returning to her wounded shoulder.

Moroda wanted to object, but her voice fled.

'No. I am chained.'

Amarah's shoulders relaxed and Moroda followed suit, happy to take the other woman's lead. The Varkain's chains had to explain why she hadn't been attacked earlier.

She swallowed and tried to calm her breathing.

'Ah, well you're just a worm then, ain't you?' Amarah cackled, wandering to the edge of the shadow. 'Tied up and left for dead. It's all you're worth.'

'Be quiet.'

Amarah crouched and sneered. 'I don't think so. I don't take orders from anyone, not least the likes of you. Tell me, Varkain, were you given a name at birth? Or just abandoned in a nest somewhere?' She tilted her head to one side. 'Dumped in a hole in the ground and left to rot like the maggots you are.'

Moroda didn't know what might come of taunting such a dangerous creature, but Amarah clearly thought he posed no threat.

'Sapora,' he answered, voice barely more than a hiss. 'I know you are a sky pirate and thief, Amarah. And a murderer, just as I am. The scent of blood runs deep in your skin.'

Amarah snorted and straightened. She ignored the Varkain and paced the cell, clearly shaken. With her good hand, she grabbed one of the bars on the gate and furiously shook it. 'Morgen! Where is my medic?'

Silence answered.

Amarah grunted and paced again, fingers tapping against her arm. It didn't take long for her to notice the cracked stone slab.

'Oh? What's this?' She dropped to one knee and picked at the cracked stone. Within seconds, she'd lifted the slab and was rewarded with the glint of silver. 'Every cloud has a silver lining.' She snatched the coins and grinned. 'Three florins. Perfect!'

Amarah pocketed them as quickly as she'd found them, and Moroda clenched her fists in response. She couldn't bring herself to challenge Amarah, despite those coins being the only thing of worth she had left.

Especially not if she was a murderer as the Varkain claimed.

All her fight had gone out of her earlier that morning.

Moroda didn't even know why she'd got involved. She'd been berating herself about it since she'd been arrested, in between panicking about whether or not she'd actually be beheaded.

She'd been taken aback by the shift in behaviour of the townspeople after Aciel—a foreign dignitary—had arrived in Niversai some days previous. Even the Imperial Guard who'd been nothing but fair towards them had suddenly turned aggressive towards the populace. Eryn had said they were stressed about the visit.

Moroda had been convinced that something else drove the shift in behaviour. There had been visitors to the capital city that morning.

And Aciel's speech that morning had been the last straw. The injustice of it.

A guest of the city. Invited into Rosecastle. Given an address to the gathered townspeople. And yet she couldn't accept the words Aciel spewed, the condescension in his tone, the disgust with which he'd stared at her and the people of her city.

As far as she was concerned, he was a pompous, arrogant bully who delighted in war-mongering, and she wouldn't stand for it. Eryn had told her to leave it alone, but Moroda had lost too much too quickly to put up with more patronisation, and refused to be silenced. She hated conflict, had never learned how to deal with it properly, and she'd exploded.

Despite having his own soldiers, the city's Imperial Guard had leapt to apprehend her when she'd spoken out.

Her immediate arrest only proved she'd touched a nerve.

Scare people enough, and no one will stand against you.

The thought made her sick.

Closing her eyes, Moroda exhaled, resigning herself to her situation. An hour ago, she'd been worried about being beheaded. Now, she was stuck in a cell with two murderers. She shook her head, wondering which fate was worse.

It took only a few minutes before the dungeon door was forced open again with another loud creak, but it wasn't Morgen who walked down the corridor. It was a young woman clutching a ring of bronze keys close to her chest as she tiptoed across the stone floor in soft leather shoes.

Moroda couldn't believe her luck.

'Eryn!' She jumped to her feet and clutched at her sister's hand through the bars. 'What in Rhea's name are you *doing* here? How did you get into the castle?'

'Sshh, never mind that. I'm getting you out!' Eryn glanced over her shoulder.

Amarah approached the gate and elbowed Moroda out of the way. 'Get on with it, then. Hurry up!'

Eryn tried each key quickly, breathing a sigh of relief

when the successful one clicked and the latch lifted off the lock.

Before Eryn could move, Amarah wrenched the door open and shoved past. 'Get out now if you know what's good for you!' She raced down the corridor and disappeared from sight.

Clearly unfazed by Amarah's brusqueness, Eryn turned to Moroda. 'You heard her! Let's go!'

Moroda faltered, peering back at the corner of the cell. She dreaded the Varkain's wrath if he ever got out on his own and hunted her down. 'Ryn? Do you have all the keys? There's someone else back there...chained up.'

'Moroda, this isn't a jailbreak! I'm here to get you and get out!' Eryn whispered through clenched teeth. 'The guards'll be here any minute, and I'll be locked up too! Come *on*!'

'I can't. He's a Varkain!' Moroda grabbed the keys from her sister and ran to the dark corner, hesitating at the last moment. It was too late for second thoughts, now.

'There's a *Varkain* in there? We should be *locking* the gate, not letting him out!' Eryn cried, incredulous.

Moroda felt it best to address him by the name he'd given to Amarah. She took a deep breath and ignored Eryn's frantic whispers. 'Sapora? You...you won't attack me if I let you out?' Her voice was as meek and small as she felt.

'No.'

She took another step closer, trying to make out his features in the poor light. 'How do I know I can trust you?' Moroda crouched down and thumbed through the keys.

'The promise of a Varkain is known throughout Linaria as truth.'

She could feel him smiling in the darkness, and it fuelled her unease.

'Strange you choose to ignore your sister. You wouldn't be the first to leave a chained Varkain.'

His words cut deep, and she faltered. 'I...I can't leave someone behind.'

'How noble.'

Moroda shuddered. 'I'm leaving the keys with you. You can reach them?'

'Yes.'

She dropped the ring of keys and bolted back to Eryn. When Moroda looked back, Sapora had unlocked himself and was on his feet, racing through the open gate faster than she could follow.

'Thanks very much.' Sapora grinned. Both rows of dagger-like teeth flashed white as ivory from his dull, grey skin. He was thin, shorter than a grown man, but lean and supple. Dried blood covered his clawed hands—from what, or who, Moroda couldn't guess. He watched Moroda with vertical pupils dilated in the dungeon's dim light.

Then raced off without another word.

'Ugh, those creatures are vile.' Eryn shivered. 'Come on, before that guard realises what happened! He's the only one on patrol, and it won't be long before he's back!'

'How did you get rid of him?'

Eryn grabbed Moroda's arm and led her out of the dungeon and into the lower halls of the castle, forcing them both to run.

'Ryn...What did you do?' Moroda was breathless, adrenaline filling her as she ran a few steps behind her sister.

'Chased a goose into the castle and let it into a room. I'm amazed *you* didn't hear anything when it knocked over a suit of armour! With the guards distracted, grabbing the keys was easy.'

Moroda stifled a laugh.

'There's a servant's entrance just along here, at the back of the kitchens. If we get outside quickly, they'll never be able to find you again!'

Moroda's heart soared as they ran down the empty corridors, amazed at how few guards patrolled the castle. They were lucky the airship races were underway and more guards were needed in the city, otherwise they'd never have had a chance.

She couldn't help but feel bad for Morgen, the young guard who had been responsible for her, and who would no doubt be reprimanded for her escape, but she pushed the feeling away.

She could practically smell the sunlight bursting through the windows. Thank the dragons above for the resourcefulness of her sister!

The scent of baked bread was thick in the air, and her mouth watered.

'Kitchens are on the other side of this wall!' Eryn panted, evidently smelling the same thing. 'The way out is just...at the end of...this corridor!'

'If we'd left the city, we wouldn't be going through this now!'

'This isn't the time for that argument, Ro! Don't you dare start it again!'

Moroda readied herself for a final sprint when a door to their right flew open and Morgen hurtled through it, tackling both of them to the floor, his armour clanging against the stone.

'Not so fast!' Morgen grabbed at Moroda's legs as she tried to get back to her feet.

Any sympathy Moroda felt for him evaporated, and she pushed at his hands but he held her fast.

'Get off her!' Eryn kicked him, one shoe landing solidly against his wrist. It crunched.

Letting out a yelp of pain, Morgen's grip loosened, and Moroda shoved him away.

Without pausing for breath, the two sisters sprinted to the end of the corridor and into the bustling street.

The afternoon sunlight was dazzling after so long in darkness, and Moroda raised an arm to shade her eyes.

'Stop right there!' Morgen shouted, already racing down the passageway towards them.

Moroda and Eryn slammed the door behind them and darted into the crowded market streets.

2

Amarah navigated the busy streets of Niversai. Each market stall was less appealing than the one before. Shouts of fresh fruit and vegetables, floral perfumes, bags of coffee beans, sacks of potatoes, strips of cloth and jewels of every colour were directed her way, but she disregarded them.

It was a shame she couldn't indulge herself. She had come to the Corhaven capital this time of year specifically to finance her way through winter, but her arrest and the seizure of her money, weapons, and airship had put her plans on hold.

She had to get *Khanna* back.

But she was vulnerable without a weapon. And rearming herself was the first thing she needed to do.

The airship races would be on for another few days—with any luck, she might have time to win a bit of coin from arrogant pilots.

Lucky for her it was Morgen on duty. Lad had a good heart, but he was a pushover. If anything, he'd be better suited to farming fields than being part of the Imperial Guard.

She left the busier inner market and started to peruse the smaller stalls offering steadily more exotic goods and spices. Finally, she found what she was looking for: a weapons trader.

'Finest weapons in Linaria,' the vendor called, when she stared at a short sword with a glittering blue and silver hilt. His accent was thick and he swallowed words. Definitely not from Corhaven. 'None better.'

Amarah glanced up at him and smiled. The man was huge, bordering on seven feet tall, with broad shoulders, bald head, and hands that looked like they could crush boulders. Despite his imposing physique, his eyes were a soft brownish-orange, gentle and smiling, which matched the rich baritone of his voice and his deeply tanned skin. He was an Ittallan trader, no doubt about that. They hailed from Val Sharis, a country of enormous wealth which lay east across the sea; neighbours to the Varkain homeland and always at odds with the snake-people.

Amarah had dealings with the Ittallan before, and had learned quickly that they were formidable fighters who never shirked on quality.

But they often had a stubborn streak that made negotiations tricky.

'The best in Linaria? That's quite a claim.' Amarah rested a hand on her hip and played along.

'Yes. But it is *true* claim.' He selected a dagger with an ornate silver handle from the selection of blades laid out on a silken cloth. 'You see work here,' he pointed with his little finger—which was as big as her thumb—'detail in hilt is by Anahrik.' He gestured to a second man behind him, his top half hidden in a barrel at the back of the stall.

'Silver?' Amarah took the offered blade to examine it more closely. It was not something she had seen on a real blade before—usually silver, gold, or precious metals were made for display in the homes of Goldstones and royalty. They weren't put on fighting weapons.

'Yes, silver. For beauty. For strength. And is our trademark. No one else does this design for their weapons or armour.'

Amarah returned the knife to its place and stepped aside to get a better look at the rest of their wares. 'I don't see my weapon here, though.' She narrowed her eyes.

'What you want? We have blades of all shapes and lengths; we have axes, longbows, crossbows—'

'None of those,' she said, folding her arms. 'But it *is* long range, if you use it well.'

'Throwing blades?' Anahrik piped in, having resurfaced from the barrel with arms full of arrow points. He, too, was an Ittallan, though younger than the other trader by several years, and not nearly as well-built, with bright blue eyes, pale blond hair, and an even paler complexion. He had mastered the common tongue of Corhaven and spoke clearly, with no trace of the accent from his homeland. He flashed a lopsided smile and walked around the stall to Amarah's side. Though he was almost a foot shorter than her, he raised his chin confidently.

Amarah laughed and shook her head. 'No, not those. I use a scythe. You got one?'

'Only the finest! We keep them off display as they're so popular, only on request do we show them as they're so beautiful...' Anahrik began, but Amarah had stopped listening and focussed her attention back on the older Ittallan.

The larger trader turned to a heavy wooden trunk behind the stall, lifted the thick metal lid, and reached within. He carefully brought out a long package, well wrapped in soft, red linen. 'This is weapon we have for you,' he said, swallowing more words. Gently, he rested it on the counter of the stall and unwrapped it, showing off the dark ebony handle first, smoothed and carved to look like marble. The silver inlay wound around it like rope, culminating in an insignia—a tiger and falcon's head bowed together. Amarah's mouth watered at the flash of silver.

The blade at the head of the weapon was curved, serrated at the end, and glistened in the late afternoon sun.

It was no display scythe. This was better than anything she'd ever used.

She noticed the silver insignia dotted around their other weapons; inscribed into arrowheads, carved into the hilt of a battle-axe, fully covering one side of a crossbow stock.

These traders were not to be sniffed at.

'Three florins,' Amarah said, after looking back at the scythe and taking a moment to deliberate.

'Three florins? An insult,' the trader spat. 'It is worth two *crowns* at least. But to you, I can sell for one crown. No less.'

'One crown would buy all your weapons,' Amarah replied, shifting her weight to her other hip. It was a lie, but she didn't have much to bargain with, so she dug her heels in. 'Three florins is my offer.'

'Three florins wouldn't cover the silver that went into that,' Anahrik leaned forward and picked up the scythe nimbly. He caressed the handle and ran a finger along the length of the blade. 'See the precision here, that's from Ittallan forges, as someone who knows weapons would *realise*.' He turned it over carefully, allowing the gleam of the low sun to run along the blade and catch the sparkle in the silver insignia.

'Silver makes it weaker. Yes, it looks very pretty, but I'm no Goldstone, dazzled by something shiny but worthless. Do you wanna sell the weapon or not? Day's getting on and trading'll finish soon. Imperial Guard here don't like people trading after first moonrise.' Amarah pushed a loose strand of hair behind her ear. 'Cut the hogshit. Scythes ain't popular, everyone knows that. You could get rid of two dozen daggers as often as one scythe, and here I am, right now, ready to take it off your hands.'

'Palom...?' Anahrik glanced at the larger trader.

'Three florins is *not* enough,' Palom retorted, shaking his head and folding his arms to mirror Amarah's stance.

Neither was willing to budge.

Amarah exhaled, annoyed. She *needed* a good weapon, and this was, by far, the best she was going to find in the city at such short notice. Perhaps she could try and release *Khanna* without weaponry, win enough in the races, and buy the scythe with the winnings.

Stealing from Ittallan was rarely worth the risk. And these weaponsmiths looked like they knew how to handle everything they'd made.

Anahrik shook his head and handed the scythe back to Palom.

'If you can't afford it, stop wasting our time. The beggars in this city, I swear—'

Amarah's backhand came so suddenly, Anahrik was knocked to the floor before he could so much as yelp. She refused to allow *anyone* to speak to her that way—even an Ittallan. 'Watch your mouth, you damned pig!'

Palom responded by laughing, the roar of his voice shaking the stall. 'He is young, I am sorry for any offence. But if you cannot afford the weapon, I cannot sell it to you.'

Anahrik staggered to his feet, one hand on his red cheek. 'Maybe you should save your coin for a damned bath instead, you filthy—'

'Anharik, hold your tongue.' Palom held the smaller man by the shoulder. 'No need for insults.'

'I'm gonna win so much gold in the races I'll buy *your entire fucking shop*!' Amarah continued, eyes locked on

Anahrik, rage and indignation fuelling her. He'd called her a *beggar*!

'You race?' Palom asked, his eyebrows raised in interest.

Amarah turned to him with a scowl. 'I do.'

'I race, too.' Anahrik shoved Palom's hand away and shifted his weight. 'But not in those bulky airships, they're too slow.'

'You ain't never seen a real ship then.' Amarah disliked Anahrik more with each passing moment.

Palom stepped forward.

'You have both hurt another's pride, why do you not instead race? If you win, you get weapon for three florins. If Anahrik wins—'

'Deal,' Amarah replied.

'I did not finish.'

'Don't matter. I'll beat anyone. I'm the fastest thing in the skies. Even dragons can't keep up with my *Khanna*.' Amarah clenched and unclenched her fists.

Anahrik laughed. 'Ah yes, but how many Ittallan have you raced in their true form? I chase airships for fun.' Lifting his arms from his sides, he leaped backwards, and in a flash of dazzling white light, a grey falcon flew away from where a man had stood a moment before.

'Anahrik likes speed more than anything. I have not known an airship to outfly him.' Palom grinned at Amarah. 'You have agreed. You can choose. When do you wish to race?'

Amarah took a step back, annoyed with herself for agreeing to the deal so quickly, but she was equally stubborn, and backing out would show weakness. With a grunt, she slammed the three florins on Palom's counter. 'The main arena. Sundown. Bring my weapon, and I promise not to slice that bird's head off.'

With a snort, she headed back through the city towards

Rosecastle, Palom's bellowing laughter following her every step of the way.

~

AMARAH IGNORED the irony of returning to the place she'd only just escaped from. At least this time she wouldn't be thrown into the dungeon.

And Rosecastle *was* the last place Morgen would think to look for her. He was probably still fruitlessly searching in town. It would be a lesson he deserved.

Thankfully, the castle was quiet—the majority of the Imperial Guard were on duty patrolling the streets, or stationed at the city gates to monitor the crowds entering or leaving Niversai. Any other time of year, she wouldn't have had the chance.

Rosecastle's vast inner dock housed the Imperial Fleet— class one warships ready to be deployed at a moment's notice, a handful of cargo ships, and dozens of smaller vessels used for scouting or as couriers for more urgent supplies.

She ran a hand along the smooth, varnished panels of the warships as she walked past them. Most had been painted white, red, and gold—Imperial colours—and their large sails, though folded while docked, were bright scarlet with gold highlights.

She narrowed her eyes. Those colours meant danger. Prison. War.

They left a bad taste in her mouth.

Amarah slipped between the rows of docked ships, heading away from the Imperial fleet and towards the salvaged ships where she presumed *Khanna* was being kept. She checked over her shoulder, ensuring no soldiers came through on a patrol of the hangar. But other than her own barely-there footsteps, the castle was quiet, like it held its breath.

Used to keeping silent—she *was* a sky pirate, after all—Amarah left the last of the Imperial ships behind and found herself among a plethora of ships from across Corhaven. A few were even from across the ocean, if she correctly recognised the sail fabrics.

Ignoring her desire to give them a thorough look—and see what people had left lying around for the taking—she headed down another line of docked airships, hoping to spot her own, familiar sails.

'Amarah, I did not think we would meet again so soon.'

She froze, her heart thundering at the words from the shadows of the ships. She wouldn't soon forget that voice.

How could the damned Varkain be here?

That soft-hearted Goldstone had to have released him. Silly woman.

Amarah didn't have time to deal with Sapora, not when *Khanna*, money, and her pride were on the line. She pushed down her fear of him and focussed on the task at hand. 'Nor did I wish to.' She hurried along the line of ships, looking for *Khanna's* dark sails. She refused to let the Varkain's presence throw her off.

'Your movements are not random. Are you searching for something, my sky thief?'

His voice was further to her left than before.

'*Khanna*,' Amarah replied.

'A quick escape? Are you running away from Corhaven?' Sapora's voice was closer now.

Swallowing her disgust at the snake creature, she changed direction again and headed south, down a line of narrow scouting ships in various states of disrepair. 'Yes. I've had enough of this fucking pit.' She reached the end of the line and paused, glancing from side to side. 'I'm gonna get some gold and get outta here.'

'Sounds like an excellent idea.'

Suddenly, the Varkain appeared in front of her, hunkered down, a grin on his face.

She wasn't the least bit surprised—they were known for their quick movements—and sidestepped to continue along the line of ships, looking left and right with growing irritation. 'What are you doing here, anyway?'

'The same as you. I am done with the people here and seek passage across the sea to Val Sharis.' Sapora trailed several paces behind her.

'Not on my fucking ship, you're not.' Amarah glared at him. 'Having you...*things* aboard will bring nothing but misery.'

'I am deeply offended. You're more dangerous than I, pirate.' He dropped back, suddenly coming to a stop and tilting his head like a dog listening.

Leaving him to whatever he was doing, Amarah picked up her pace. She'd spotted her sails.

At the end of the row, near the entrance to the hangar, *Khanna* lay waiting. Her own airship was a class four—a fifth the size of an Imperial Warship, built for speed, not power—sleek, smooth, and heavily varnished in black and grey.

'Ah, here she is.' Relief flooded her as she clambered up the narrow steps carved into *Khanna's* side. She walked along the deck, checking her sails for rips or tears, and her propellers for signs of damage. Aside from a small scuff on the bow, *Khanna* was in the same condition as she had left it, and she could have kissed Morgen for that.

Clunk.

Clunk.

Clunk.

Armoured footsteps.

It had to be a patrolling guard. Amarah suppressed a curse.

Her joy short-lived, she raced to the side of the deck, trying to peer over the docked ships to see them. They were too far away to spot details, but their build was tall and heavy-set. Not Morgen.

She couldn't talk her way out of this one. 'No, no, no! Not now!'

'Can you not fly away?' Sapora asked from the ground.

'Of course I can! I just need a minute to get her running.' Amarah was already away from the edge of the deck. She needed to start *Khanna's* engines before it was too late.

The Varkain hissed. 'If I give you the time you need to start, will you take me across the sea?'

Amarah paused, one hand on the trap door that led into the bowels of her ship. The idea of a Varkain onboard made her skin crawl, but without a few minutes to spare, she would be discovered, unarmed, and nothing would matter.

Of course, if he wanted to cross the sea, he probably *wouldn't* attack her. At least until they arrived. And she would have her scythe from the Ittallan traders soon enough. She would be able to hold her own against one Varkain in the place she was most at ease.

'I don't have time to waste, Amarah,' Sapora called. 'And neither do you.'

The guard's footsteps grew louder, echoing off the docked ships.

'Yes, yes, fine, fine, but *don't* kill him. I don't wanna give 'em *more* reason to follow us,' she conceded. Turning away from him, she raced below deck to give life to *Khanna*.

It took her less than a minute to start *Khanna's* engines and get back on deck. Sapora was already on board, a smear of blood at the corner of his lips and a smirk on his face.

She glared at him in disgust and an old scar on her leg twitched in remembered pain. She forced the sensation away. Striding to the spoked wheel, she grabbed hold with one hand, the worn wood against her skin bringing a sense of calm despite the tense situation.

Amarah took a moment to breathe in the smell.

Khanna lifted gently off the ground, as eager to fly as she was, the propellers churning as quietly as ever. The perfect ship for silent, stealthy flight.

Grabbing one of the levers in the control panel, she unfurled *Khanna's* sails and raised the ship higher.

Now she was airborne, she was safe. She'd *always* been safe in the sky.

She turned to the Varkain, fought not to glare at him. 'Before we cross the ocean, I have a race against an arrogant Ittallan to win. You've been at odds for centuries ain't you? I think you'd like to see me knock him down a peg or two.' Amarah pushed the four engine throttles slowly forward to give her ship power, turned the wheel to port, and faced *Khanna* towards the hangar entrance.

Sapora approached her and leaned on the side rail, his smirk deepening. 'Yes, I would enjoy that very much indeed.'

'Let's get this done.' Amarah engaged the throttles fully and powered along the hanger, past the docked ships, and out into the deep orange skies above the city of Niversai.

3

M oroda and Eryn sat at an empty table, heads low. They'd ducked into a small tavern at the back of the marketplace and kept cautious eyes locked on the nearby window. It gave them an excellent view of Rosecastle and its grounds, and provided much needed sanctuary.

They had been born and raised in Niversai, and knew the western part of the city like the back of their hands. When they'd been growing up, Eryn had always wanted to visit the tavern famed for its hot cherry wine, though she'd been too young, and Moroda had been hesitant. Somehow, Eryn had convinced her sister to bring her here once she'd turned fifteen, and it hadn't taken long to become one of their most frequented haunts.

'That guard won't even realise there's a tavern here,' Eryn said, once she had her breath back. She rested her arms on the table, and put her face into them. 'It still looks like the old blacksmith's place from outside.'

Moroda couldn't share in her sister's smug jubilation. She was too sombre. 'If it weren't for you, I'd have died.' Now the adrenaline had faded, the gravity of what had happened was beginning to weigh on her, leaving her cold and numb. 'Even if you thought the beheading was just a threat, there were two *real* criminals in there with me.' She shook her head and thought back to her cell mates. 'That Amarah is obviously a thief and a fighter, and has her own airship to boot...and the Varkain, Sapora...I don't even want to *think* about him.'

She had to hope the Varkain really was a man of his word.

She'd helped him. That *had* to ensure he wouldn't hurt her if their paths ever crossed again.

Lifting her face from the table, Eryn furrowed her brow, studying Moroda for several seconds. She shrugged. 'Bit of an exaggeration. You probably weren't going to die—probably would have just been locked up for a few days, that's all. And anyway, *nothing* happened! You need to bring your head out of the clouds, that's all.' Eryn kept her gaze on Moroda. 'Don't worry, we'll be fine. We just have to lie low for a bit. I'll get us something to eat. That'll make you feel better.' Ever positive, she got up and made her way past the other patrons to the bar.

Moroda watched her sister weave through the crowd with confidence. Every step planted, as if she belonged there. Perhaps if she had some of her sister's tenacity, she'd have been able to get out of the cell herself. Or even better, never would have been arrested in the first place.

For all her brave talk, Moroda was the same helpless child she'd always been. She'd always needed someone to look after her, and a year of forced independence hadn't changed a thing.

Scowling, she decided to take better notice of her surroundings so as not to be caught unawares again. She might not come upon another Varkain for years, but anyone could be dangerous if you got on the wrong side of them.

And even if she *was* vulnerable, she didn't want to show it.

Eryn managed.

Moroda should be able to as well.

Eryn wanted her to keep her head out of the clouds, fine. She'd pay more attention. Shaking her head clear of doubts, she observed the other patrons and tried to figure out who might be a threat. Or at least, who she ought to be wary of.

The tavern was at least three-quarters full, with people standing in the spaces between tables, jugs of mead and tankards of ale clutched as they spoke loudly about the airship races. Coins changed hands, the clank of metal on wood providing a backdrop of noise against the hubbub of conversation. Grey smoke drifted lazily from a dozen cigars and pipes, forming a dark cloud that hovered just below the crooked ceiling beams.

The wooden floor creaked as people shifted their weight or crossed the room, and Moroda relished the occasional burst of fresh air that rushed in through the door whenever anyone left or arrived.

Pilots and their crews flew from all over Corhaven to the capital for the annual races. It was an event that drew in crowds, swelling Niversai almost to bursting. As a child, Moroda had always been swept up in the excitement, enjoying the spectacle. It was so wild and free, so different from the rest of her childhood where decisions had been made for her.

But even the races felt muted this year.

She chewed her lip as the door opened, and another group of half-drunk youths stumbled in, one of them holding up a heavy purse in triumph.

There must have been a good race out there.

Scratching her nose, Moroda looked away. Everyone here seemed...*normal*. How had Amarah been able to tell who was dangerous so quickly? What was she supposed to be looking for? She'd been impressed that Amarah had spotted the Varkain after only a minute or two of being in the cell, and admired the woman's observation skills—she'd even managed to find the hidden florins.

A chill raced through her at the memory of her stolen money.

That had to be her next move. Try to find that sky pirate and demand her florins back. She *had* helped Amarah with the injury, after all, and they had only escaped thanks to Eryn. Surely one good turn deserved another? And what were three florins to a notorious pirate, anyway? Amarah probably had entire chests full of silver florins and gold crowns hidden away somewhere.

Moroda's gaze fell on a cloaked man sitting alone at a tall table near the window. The thick glass was dirty, letting in only a weak shaft of light that highlighted his face. Scars lined his pale cheeks and lips, criss-crossing each other, as if he'd been carved up by an enthusiastic child who'd found a butcher's cleaver. He was hunched over a bowl of soup, his heavy brown travelling cloak fell to the floor, covering his limbs.

Suddenly, he blinked and turned, his bright grey eyes meeting hers.

Caught staring, Moroda hurriedly looked away, relieved when Eryn returned to the table a moment later with two steaming mugs of tea and a small bowl of cloudberries.

After several seconds, Moroda risked another glance at the man, who had thankfully returned his attention to the window.

In the busy tavern, one man alone stood out—even to her.

'What are you staring at?' Eryn asked, looking over the

other tables in the tavern and handing her sister one of the mugs.

Moroda took it, careful to take her time before glancing up again. 'That man at the table by the window...No, no, don't look now. He's...a bit odd.'

'Odd?' Eryn popped a cloudberry in her mouth and chewed, trying to look over her shoulder inconspicuously. It didn't take her long to pick him out, and she whipped back round to her sister. 'I'll bet he's an Ittallan!' Eryn grinned, her eyebrows raised. 'The airship races bring all sorts. He's not a trader or a pilot, he can't be, otherwise he'd be out there with the others. Maybe he's supporting someone? I wouldn't worry. Eat!' Her haughty tone belied her concern for her sister. Eryn shoved the bowl of food towards Moroda. 'Just think how close we are to the castle! We're hiding right under their noses and they'll never realise!'

Moroda smiled at Eryn's words, and drank deeply from her cup of honeyed tea. Tea usually settled her nerves, but her doubts lingered. Her world was unravelling and she wasn't sure she could put it back. 'I'm not worried about that guard.'

'Good.'

'But I *am* worried about my arrest this morning. Some stranger from a foreign land who can treat the townsfolk as though they were all beneath him, make our own Imperial Guard behave so...so unjustly! I *had* to say something. If he's going from city to city doing this...soon, all of Corhaven, all of Linaria, might be following him! I don't like it.'

'With everything else going on, Ro, I think you need to stop worrying about Linaria's politics.'

'But didn't you hear what he said?'

'Of course I heard. A load of twaddle if you ask me.' Eryn sipped her tea with a derisive snort.

Moroda frowned and stared into her mug. The drink

was dark, sweet, and steaming. But another chill ran up her spine as she thought back to that morning. Everyone had been staring up at that man, almost as if unable to look away from him.

Aciel.

She'd thought the crowds' rapt silence had been out of respect at first. But something about their reactions had been...peculiar. She'd left Eryn to walk among the crowd and get a closer look.

And it had grown cold the closer she got. So very cold.

Her limbs had stiffened, making it hard to walk, hard to think. As if something else had control of her body and mind.

And when the dignitary had spoken of taking people away from the city, of joining his cause, Moroda had cried out in defiance—her voice the only sound among the crowd.

'You go and get yourself arrested like some common criminal the moment my back is turned.' Eryn interrupted her thoughts. 'I'm sure *I* should have been the older sister!'

Moroda remained quiet as the two resumed their meagre meal, a far cry from the fine meats and cheeses they had grown accustomed to in their youth, while they observed the comings and goings of the tavern.

She tried to put that morning out of her mind, but her mistakes kept resurfacing.

She wasn't ready for this life.

She couldn't cope.

Moroda took a deep breath, bracing herself for her sister's wrath. 'I also lost the coin I had.'

'What?'

'In the cell. I tried to hide the florins under a loose slab, but that woman, the other prisoner, Amarah? She found them.' Moroda pressed her face into her folded arms on the

31

table. 'Today has been so awful. Can't even look after myself, can I? Look what happens the moment I get into trouble. I lose our money, and you have to save me. You're always saving us.'

Eryn shook her head. 'Dragons above, it wasn't your fault. All that could have just as easily happened to me!'

Moroda shook her head. 'Aciel showed up. That's when it all started. I *knew* we should have left Niversai after father—'

'Ro, stop it,' Eryn said sharply. 'It's nothing to do with that dignitary! Just your bad luck, that's all. We'll get through this! I have a crown saved and a few half florins, too. Winter gowns will be in demand soon, and we have a few left that we can dust off and sell. With all the trade going on right now, I'm sure we'll be fine. No more worrying about Aciel or politics. Agreed? It has nothing to do with us, and he's already left the city anyway, so stop thinking about him.'

'No more worrying about Aciel or politics,' Moroda echoed, feeling stupid. 'I honestly don't know where I'd be without you, Eryn.'

'Back in that dank cell with a dirty snake, I expect.'

Moroda laughed. It was the first time she'd smiled in as long as she could remember, and coupled with the honeyed tea warming her belly, she allowed herself to relax. She'd always been the dreamer. The wanderer. The one with silly ideas and lofty goals.

Eryn was the sensible one. Resourceful. She could get things done and was never fazed if something went wrong.

'I know it's been hard since we had to sell your books and those trinkets you loved so much.' Eryn sighed, frustrated.

The mention of the loss almost brought tears to Moroda's eyes. She'd loved reading, learning, and she'd had an entire room dedicated to treasures from across Linaria. A real dragon tooth from Val Sharis. Glassware that glowed in rainbow colours from the mage cities of Ranski. A three hundred year-old atlas. Flowers that never wilted. Even a bejewelled fish hook from the distant island nation of Estoria. She'd adored everything, and the books most of all.

But keeping a collection when they had no coin was foolhardy, as Eryn had rightly argued.

One after another, they sold their valuables. Luxuries. Eryn had sold all her jewels.

Soon enough, they were getting rid of essentials.

'Once the airship races finish, we'll see what we can trade with the silk merchants. And there's still a little jewellery left in a pinch.'

'Mother's jewellery.' Moroda didn't want to think about the last of their possessions going to some greedy traders just so they could buy food. She'd tried to tell Eryn they had nothing left here, that staying in Niversai was the same as a drowning swimmer refusing to get out of the lake. All they needed was an opportunity to *leave*.

But Eryn was having none of it.

'We'll manage. Forget about Aciel, okay?' Eryn leaned forward and squeezed Moroda's hand.

Movement caught Moroda's eye and she twisted in time to see the man by the window push his chair back as he stood. The scrape of wood on wood caught Eryn's attention, too, and she lowered her mug to watch him.

He walked towards the door, a slight limp in his stride, hat clasped in one hand, mug in the other.

A cold breeze fluttered over Moroda as he approached them, and goosebumps immediately rose on her arms. She shivered, rubbing her shoulders, unsure whether she should be afraid.

He looked at her, halting a few steps from their table and swayed once, unsteady. The man practically loomed over them. Taking a final swig from his mug, he wiped his mouth with the back of his sleeve and placed the empty container on the sisters' table. 'Aciel should be the least of your concerns. You wanna worry about something? You ought to worry about the dragons.'

'You were listening to us? How rude.' Eryn put her palms flat on the table and rose to her feet, her voice sharp. 'What makes you think you've any right to eavesdrop on *our* conversation?'

Moroda narrowed her eyes. Up close, she noticed a chunk of his lip was missing, twisting his mouth into a permanent grimace. Coupled with his scars and his height, he looked positively fearsome.

He placed his wide-brimmed hat on his head, the edges sagging with age.

'What about the dragons?' Moroda asked, half getting out of her seat to address the man, emboldened by Eryn's action.

'Speaking as a dragon hunter, you see. You ought to take shelter if you know what's good for you. And soon.' He tapped the edge of his hat and headed out into the late afternoon sun.

Anahrik's constant pacing and huffs of frustration were getting worse as the sun inched towards the horizon. 'Scared her off, didn't I? Typical. Guess she had *some* sense in that thick head of hers.'

Palom sat on the bottom step at the edge of the stone arena, oiling one of his broadswords with a heavy, blackened cloth, half-listening to the complaints.

He was used to his comrade's moods. Anahrik could switch between excitement and boredom in a heartbeat.

'Anahrik. Sit down. Save your energy.'

'Save my energy? For what? She's scared of me.'

Palom chuckled. 'You insulted her. She will come.'

Anahrik huffed and cracked his fingers.

If they'd been back in Taban Yul, Ahnarik could at least keep himself entertained. Here, in the capital of Corhaven, rules were stricter. They couldn't trade once the moons had risen. Couldn't enter certain parts of the city during the festivities. Couldn't drink or eat while moving around in the streets.

And everyone stared at the pair of Ittallan as if they had two heads.

A handful of tourists loitered in the arena, staring up at the enormous oval structure or pointing at the courses the airships had taken in earlier races. But most people were eager to be inside with a hot meal, not lingering in an empty arena without anything to entertain them.

Waiting had never bothered Palom.

Waiting meant time to think, plan, and prepare.

But for Anahrik, waiting was a waste of time.

'Why don't we just keep the florins *and* the scythe? After what *she* did.' Anahrik pressed a hand against his cheek, still slightly pink from where Amarah had struck him earlier.

Palom shook his head. 'That would be dishonourable. And when do you *not* take chance to race when it is given to you on plate?'

Anahrik huffed again and continued pacing.

'Come on, no more sulking like child because she is late. Focus on what is happening next. The air is thinner here. Colder. It will be good for her ship.'

Anahrik folded his arms across his chest. 'I'll be fine.'

'Is getting dark. Are you worried?'

'I'll be *fine*.'

'A falcon's eyes are not so good in dark.'

'Palom!' He whirled around, lips pressed into a thin line.

Palom bit back his laughter. Anahrik really didn't want his feathers ruffled now.

They'd been watching the sun slowly descend and the first moon rise. The second moon was soon to follow, and as the last rays of sunlight coloured the sky, the third moon's outline could just be made out among the stars.

'I don't think she's coming.' Anahrik scoffed.

'She will not have left three florins,' Palom replied without looking up. 'Little bit of light is still here. There is time.'

Anahrik snorted in response, folding his arms and

36

kicking at the loose stones on the edge of the dusty racing arena. Airships had already retired for the evening—night races were not popular in Corhaven. Most captains' poor vision warranted too many torches to be set up across the length of the arena, and audiences would miss most of the action when the race went higher.

There was no point in arguing with Anahrik when he was like this. If anything, the encroaching darkness was putting him on edge more than anything else. Sunset gave him enough light to fly by. Once it dipped below the horizon, Anahrik would be at a disadvantage. Incredible speed or not, if he couldn't see where he was going, he wouldn't be winning any races.

But Palom knew Anahrik couldn't resist showing off, whatever the situation.

Back in Taban Yul, Anahrik had kept Palom grounded. Taught him about the city, about trading and selling, and all manner of people that flooded the capital. He was never ruffled, even during the busy season.

Here, Anahrik was off-balance, and Palom was the one supporting him. Reminding Anahrik why they were there and holding him back from causing trouble.

Not that Palom was fully at ease, either. The language here was peculiar on his tongue. The climate, colder than he was used to. The stars were different, even the *grass* was different. It was the first time he'd been away from Val Sharis, and though he prided himself on his adaptability, he missed home.

But travelling across the sea to Corhaven had been an opportunity he'd not wanted to miss out on. Not to mention the fact the streets of Taban Yul had been in some turmoil, and getting out before the fires raged had been the smart thing to do.

And it was what Lathri had wanted.

His stomach clenched at the thought of her.

'Ittallan! Ready to show me how slow you are against my ship?'

In the failing light, and with his mind elsewhere, Palom hadn't seen or heard *Khanna* float towards the arena. It was only at Amarah's insult that he noticed she had arrived at all.

Both he and Anahrik glanced skywards, and Palom narrowed his eyes when he spotted the craft. It was not a long-haul vessel, and even without any engineering experience, he could see the airship was built for speed. Her side sails were angled and half folded, like the wings of a dragon in full stoop. Others were tucked at the back and against the vessel's underside, yet to be opened. The engines, one on either side, two at the back, were mounted low and seemed nothing special, but were silent as they ran.

A fast ship built for stealth.

Amarah wasn't a regular airship captain.

He had a sneaking suspicion she was actually a sky pirate.

He'd have to keep a close eye on her.

'Looks like good race, Anahrik.' Palom folded his cloth away and sheathed the sword. 'I will get scythe and meet you back here when you have finished.' He offered his colleague no more support or words of wisdom as he stood to leave the arena.

'Don't bother getting the scythe. There's no chance she'll win.' Anahrik leapt into the air, transforming as he did, and climbed to meet the ship's altitude.

'Just in case.' Palom gave Anahrik a nod before leaving the arena.

~

IT WAS strange that Amarah hadn't backed out of the bargain once she'd learned Anahrik was an Ittallan. Most people with any common sense would have changed their mind and apologised. Compared to most, the Ittallan were faster, stronger, and more formidable.

Amarah was either very stubborn, very stupid, or very brave.

As yet, Palom wasn't sure which.

Admittedly, Anahrik embodied those same three traits as well, so the duel was well-matched.

At the very least, he would bring the scythe. Perhaps a handful of other weapons as well, in case things went sour. Though far from a warship, her airship looked like it had a handful of guns, and it was always better to be prepared.

Palom made his way down the darkening streets of Niversai and to the room he had rented with Anahrik for the racing season. This city wasn't as old or large as Taban Yul, and certainly not as wealthy, and it reminded Palom of the quieter country towns of his homeland. It was unnatural for so large a city to be so quiet.

Niversai was a city of stone. It looked like it had been ripped from the ground, unmoving and ugly. Taban Yul, the capital of Val Sharis, was an artist's sculpture in comparison. White spires and gold filigree were always going to win against an ugly block of grey stone.

There was far less diversity here, too. He could count on one hand the number of other Ittallan he'd seen since they'd arrived at the start of the airship races.

Palom scoured the dwindling crowds as he made his way through the city, always on alert for trouble. As he reached their rented room—on the ground floor of a shoe-maker— he paused. One man stood out among the others; taller than most, cloaked, and with a large hat that covered his face.

Palom watched him for a handful of moments before the man disappeared down a side street.

Foreboding slowly crept up his spine, raising the hairs on the back of his neck.

There was no mistaking what that man was.

Arillian.

Palom would never forget that scent of storms and ice, and already his hackles were rising. Arillians usually meant trouble.

Quickly, Palom entered the room and sorted through their stocks. Most of their better swords and blades had been sold already, but there were a handful of weapons that could be useful. Even their cheaper stock was of far greater quality than anything he'd seen in this country so far. He picked out Anahrik's favoured twin daggers, his own longsword—which he sheathed at his back—and the scythe that Amarah wanted. After debating for a moment, he also packed a crossbow and bolts, three short swords of differing lengths, several daggers and a handful of arrows—though they no longer had any bows for them.

He briefly considered heading back to the arena, but seeing the Arillian had got his back up, and he didn't want to take any chances. He couldn't think of any good reason why there'd be an Arillian here, especially *alone*, and he needed to find out why.

If there was a storm coming, Anahrik had to get out of the sky.

Shouldering the heavy satchel, weapons safely wrapped within, Palom made his way back onto the streets, following the smell of crackling electricity and frost. It was almost full dark, but his keen eyesight worked equally well at night, and it didn't take him long to spot his target several streets away.

Pressing himself against a wall, he kept one eye on the Arillian—who didn't so much as glance in his direction.

The Arillian kept his hat low, and Palom struggled to see the man's face. If anything, the Arillian seemed as unwilling to be noticed as Palom, which only fuelled his suspicions. While there was no specific law forbidding Arillians from being on the mainland, they'd been exiled for good reason.

And with no Imperial Guard anywhere near, Palom took it upon himself to follow the stranger.

It wouldn't be long before the race was over, depending on how long Amarah and Anahrik spent insulting each other before starting. A storm would be devastating for Anahrik, and Palom had to stop the Arillian before he caused any carnage.

After a few minutes trailing his quarry, Palom found him standing in an empty square, the surrounding stalls long since closed for the evening. The wind picked up, sending a chill across the flagstones and making the colourful bunting across the buildings flap.

A small group of people were leaving the square on the opposite side, leaving Palom alone with the Arillian.

A spark of electricity burst from the Arillian's hands, though it was swiftly extinguished.

Resisting the urge to draw his sword, Palom stepped into the moonlight and approached cautiously, keeping his head low. The Arillian seemed to have his attention elsewhere, he didn't even turn at Palom's approach.

It felt peculiar to be ignored. Wrong, somehow.

And Palom wasn't going to allow Anahrik to get hurt in whatever this man was scheming.

He came to a halt a handful of paces away and raised his chin. 'You. Arillian. Are you calling lightning to destroy Niversai, perhaps?'

The Arillian spun around, pale grey eyes wide in surprise. He adjusted his hat and tucked a lock of blond hair behind his ear, recovering himself. 'Excuse me?'

'I saw lightning.'

He shook his head. 'Just getting rid of some excess. Nothing is damaged, is it?'

Palom wasn't convinced. 'What are you doing, prowling streets in dark?'

'I could ask the same of you! There is no curfew in this city. I may roam the streets whenever I wish.' His voice belied indignation, but he wasn't as aggressive as Palom had expected.

Still, there was something about the lone man that didn't sit right. Palom's lip curled, the beginnings of a fang poking out. 'This I do not believe. Where are your friends? Is there storm coming tonight?'

'A storm? Most definitely. But not the kind you're thinking of, I'm afraid. At any rate, I'm going to stop it.'

'Arillians *make* storms. They do not stop them.'

'Well you're entitled to believe whatever you want to believe.' He shrugged. 'If you don't want to be part of it, I suggest you get out of the city while you can.'

'I can fight.'

'I'm sure you can, my Ittallan friend.' The Arillian glanced away and pale light from the three moons lit up the scars across his face, different shades contrasting on his skin. 'But not this one.'

Palom scowled before looking up as well. The sky was dark blue, inky patches smearing away starlight as clouds passed in front of them. He inhaled deeply, but no scent of danger reached him.

And then...

Movement.

A silhouette in the darkness, almost invisible were he not looking for it. His first instinct was an airship until shadowed wings beat the air, destroying that notion. Its shape was instantly recognisable. One of the many creatures that made Val Sharis their home; sacred to those in other parts of Linaria. Fire flickered in its jaws—a moment of light, then it was gone.

'Is that...?'

When he looked back, the street was empty.

A rush of freezing air covered his skin and Palom looked up again, just in time to see the Arillian's shadow disappear into the night sky.

Adrenaline surged through him as the gravity of what was about to happen dawned. 'Anahrik!'

Palom bolted towards the city gates.

5

Y ou took your time. Thought you were going to forfeit,' Anahrik said, voice pitched higher than before.

Amarah didn't hide her smirk. She'd ruffled his feathers alright. It was the best way to meet an opponent—put them on the back foot.

She watched the Ittallan glance around *Khanna's* deck with a frown. When he spotted Sapora lingering near the stern, Anahrik scowled and folded his arms, but otherwise ignored the Varkain. 'What course do you suggest? I'll leave it up to you so there can be no doubt of *my* superiority.'

Amarah laughed, 'You're so easily riled. I'll have a lot of fun with this.' She walked to the bow of her ship as it hovered in place and gazed out over the empty arena. The few remaining airships from the day's racing were already grounded or heading into secure hangars to be docked, ready for the morning. The usual course markers had all been removed leaving the sky a blank slate.

It was ready for them.

'Let's keep it simple,' she said, after thinking about her options for a few moments. 'We'll race from here to the one league marker, circle Niversai and return to that marker. A clear finish line. Can fly as close or far from Niversai as we want, but we can't fly over the city's outer wall.'

'That's too far,' Anahrik replied immediately.

'Oh really? It's about the same length as a regular course, maybe a bit shorter. We'll just use the trees, valley and hills surrounding the city as our circuit. Besides, I've got a big, bulky airship, remember?' Amarah rested one hand on her hip. Despite her bravado, she knew it would be hard work, particularly with her shoulder not yet healed, but she had no qualms about winning.

With *Khanna's* colouring, she doubted Anahrik would easily be able to spot her, so she could cut a couple of corners without her opponent realising. 'I've circled the city a hundred times before, it'll take about two minutes, flat out.'

'Fine, let's get this sorted.' Anahrik shifted back into his true form and glided to the bow of the ship, where he landed and ruffled his feathers impatiently.

Amarah grinned, manoeuvring *Khanna* to the starting position. She readied her sails, ensuring those she didn't need were properly tucked away to keep *Khanna* as streamlined as possible.

Once at altitude, she took in a breath to ready herself. Glancing along the deck from her position behind the wheel and the control panel, she caught the falcon's eye and held up a clenched fist to signal her readiness.

She mentally counted to three, then brought her arm down as Anahrik leapt from the deck, straight into a dive.

Lurching into motion, Amarah followed Anahrik's descent, starting the race with an almost vertical nose-forward drop.

As *Khanna* built speed, Sapora gripped the sides of the

ship, digging his claws into the wood to stop himself sliding towards the nose. 'Amarah, you will crash!'

She disregarded Sapora's protests. She dug her heels into the rough wooden floor and braced for the speed and angle of descent. Her eyes were solidly fixed on the grey falcon as he gained more speed in the dive, distancing himself from *Khanna* and outpacing the ship in seconds. 'Perhaps you *are* quicker in a dive, but there's more to a race than that.' She pulled back on the wheel to lift the nose, fanning her side sails to give the ship extra lift as her trajectory flattened out.

Khanna careened across the arena, over the city walls, and out above the darkening forest surrounding the city. She would reach the league marker in a few moments, just behind Anahrik, but with enough of the course left, she was confident she'd be able to overtake and stretch out a lead in the twists and turns, where *Khanna's* speed would seal her victory.

Anahrik, too, had stopped his descent, and was now flying over the city walls a short distance ahead of *Khanna*.

'I don't see how...your ship can be faster than a falcon. An *Ittallan* falcon,' Sapora hissed, having slowly made his way along the deck to where Amarah piloted.

'Quiet, I'm bringing this pig's ego down a few notches. I might do the same to *you*, snake.' Amarah's gaze was locked on the marker as she turned hard, opening one of her starboard sails to make the turning angle more acute. Snapping back the power and opening the sails on the port side to hastily straighten, Amarah pushed all four engines to full power. Swooping round the torch-lit marker, she levelled out *Khanna* as her circuit around the city began.

Her first, immediate obstacle was the large forest which surrounded Niversai. Huge conifers erupted from the canopy of younger trees, causing her to veer sharply to avoid them, while banking left along the curve of the high stone wall marking Niversai's limit.

But speed and manoeuvrability were her ship's strengths. *Khanna* was fast, even on the twistiest course.

In the darkness of the trees, she lost sight of Anahrik, only glimpsing a flash of grey every so often when he appeared between the branches. If he were alone, Amarah wouldn't think twice about shooting him down, but she didn't want to risk harming him with Palom nearby, so she dug deep and focussed.

She'd have to win this the old fashioned way.

'You *sure* you can fly this thing?' Sapora hissed.

She daren't take her eyes off her route. 'Shut up. I'm trying to concentrate!' Amarah veered sharply to the right, avoiding a particularly large tree.

Sapora crept closer, clutching the side of the deck with every step, until he stood beside her. 'It would be easier, would it not, to fly *above* the trees?'

'No, I wanna keep close to the wall. And *Khanna's* agile enough to avoid 'em,' Amarah replied through gritted teeth, a bead of sweat running down her forehead despite the chill wind.

The violent turns shook *Khanna*, and Amarah's arms ached from where she gripped the wheel, but she wasn't going to let that arrogant Ittallan get the better of her.

She needed to save face and she *needed* her weapon.

'I think you should—'

'*I* think you should shut your mouth while you still have breath! Gonna throw you overboard otherwise. Trying to concentrate here.'

'No need to be so dramatic, pirate.'

Amarah snorted. 'Keep quiet! I know how to fly my ship.'

'Doesn't look like it to me...'

Although he grumbled, he grew quiet, and Amarah focussed on the race.

In spite of her perseverance, she could not stay ahead of the falcon. They overtook one another countless times as they wound their way through the trees, and she'd bet any amount of gold that he was struggling as much as she was.

They had to at least be halfway round the city, with neither appearing as the clear victor.

What was she going to do if it was a draw?

She'd just assumed she would win, take her weapon and move on.

She didn't want to hold back and lose, nor push *Khanna* too hard and end up damaging her, not if she wanted to win more coin in the remaining days of the races.

Clouds shifted, blocking out starlight and moonlight both, bathing the city in darkness. Within the city's walls, small dots of light appeared as fires were lit; a sea of stars in their own right. Amarah exhaled slowly, trying to focus in the poor light. If she got too worked up, there was no chance of winning.

She would lose both face and the weapon, and the pirate didn't know which was worse.

The trees thinned around the city's southern side, and *Khanna* was flanked only by the grey stone wall marking the city limits. This was it. She had to go full tilt, otherwise there was no clawing victory from the bird. Unfurling all sails, she pushed her engines to full thrust.

Anahrik hadn't been lying about his speed.

The falcon soared past, inching ahead slowly, his own wings spread for maximum speed and lift.

Amarah concentrated on her own course, focussed on getting every inch of speed from her ship as she flew along the wall, until her engines whined in protest.

It was only at Sapora's sharp cry that she pulled away.

A plume of fire suddenly enveloped both ship and falcon from above.

The ferocity and surprise of the attack meant both Amarah and Anahrik reacted instinctively, folding their wings and diving out of the way of the smoke and flame, back into the trees.

Letting out a scream of fright, she looked up, eyes wide as a dragon descended from the clouds with a roar of fury. 'A dragon? A *fucking* dragon?' Amarah cursed her luck as the creature swooped over the city wall in a wide arc, the dry trees below consumed by flame. The beast turned after igniting the foliage and headed back towards *Khanna*.

'What in Rhea's...?' Amarah gasped, realising *they* were under attack.

She pulled her ship up and out of the trees, trying to get out of the thick, black smoke rising from the burning branches.

'A dragon?' Sapora crouched down below the ship's controls, trying to shield himself from the heat of the flames. 'With no warning?'

Burning embers blazed on deck where the wood was alight. 'Sapora, get those flames out now or we won't be in the air much longer!' Amarah pulled *Khanna's* nose up as steeply as she could, gaining height and leaving the smouldering treeline far below her. She searched desperately for the incoming threat as she flew into the clouds, all thoughts of Anahrik and the race forgotten.

In the darkness, she could hardly see a thing.

Fuck.

Khanna was on fire. Where the damned dragon had come from, Rhea only knew.

Amarah adjusted her hold on the wheel and turned hard. She couldn't let panic get the better of her. She'd lose more than the race, if she did.

49

She'd lose *Khanna*.

Sapora covered his mouth and nose with his cloak and shuffled along the deck, towards the fire. Just before he reached it, the dragon's roar stopped him in place. It dived towards them, breathing another column of fire as it did, tinting the clouds in dredges of red and orange heat. Keeping well below the side of the deck, Sapora hissed, narrowly avoiding the scorching heat from overhead.

The dragon's aim may have been true, but *Khanna's* agility kept them out of immediate incineration as Amarah fought to keep her ship out of harm's way.

'You told me you could outfly a dragon, Amarah! Get away from *this* one!' Sapora cried, stamping out the flames building at the bow of the ship. 'Your hull may be alight. I am *not* going into the hold to look!'

'We won't be in the air for long if you don't!'

Amarah snapped, risking a glance at him but unwilling to tear her gaze from the sky for more than a moment.

The Varkain bared his fangs at her. 'I am not your crew to order about as you please, thief!'

Amarah gritted her teeth and said nothing. She was so used to people on her ship doing as they were told. But he was a guest, and a Varkain to boot. She had no authority over him. 'Just get what you can under control! Unless you wanna burn to death tonight!'

'I think flying *away* is a good idea, Amarah!' Sapora snapped as the silhouette of the dragon passed over them again.

Bright white light burst on deck to her left, and Amarah flinched, thinking the dragon had managed to sneak up on them—but when she looked, she let out a relieved sigh. It was Anahrik. He'd landed on deck and transformed from falcon to man. The Ittallan had ash in his hair and had been scalded along the backs of his arms but otherwise appeared in one piece, if somewhat out of breath. 'Where did *that* come from?' He shakily got to his feet. 'Who ever heard of a dragon attacking unprovoked like that?'

'Damned if I know. Just fighting here, trying not to go up like a match! You okay?'

'In one piece. No chance of flying away from that thing!'

'Means I win the race, right? If you've given up? Hope you got my scythe ready!'

Even in the chaos, Anahrik bristled. 'This is hardly the time!'

Amarah cackled.

'Has anyone ever told you that you're too stubborn for your own good? Get away from the dragon and continue this argument when we *aren't* in danger of being incinerated!' Anahrik took a step back and stared up at the dark sky. 'Incoming!' He hurled himself to the deck floor and covered his head with his hands.

Khanna baulked under them as Amarah turned to avoid the next swathe of dragon fire, the ship's mobility and her swift reactions saving them from the core of the attack yet again.

'I think you're just annoying it!' Anahrik called to Amarah. 'Head back to the city. It might stop attacking with that many people in one place?'

With no better plan, and no way to counter the dragon's swift attacks, Amarah turned *Khanna* around without argument. Putting her engines back on full thrust now that tight turns and manoeuvres were no longer an option, Amarah charged back to the city, believing in *Khanna's* outright speed and hoping she would be able to keep ahead of the dragon's breath until she was too close to the city for it to attack again.

The dragon followed like a cat chasing a mouse. It let out a snarl that set Amarah's teeth on edge.

She hoped it would leave them alone, that it might be afraid of so many people, of the lack of clear weakness in a stone city. She hoped it would find some other, easier prey.

And she was almost right.

Once over the city wall, the dragon ignored the ship and veered away.

But instead of retreating, the dragon turned its attention to burning the bigger target below, swooping low over the buildings and roaring out a challenge as flames danced in its jaws.

'Guess it ain't afraid of the city.' Amarah breathed deeply, allowing herself a momentary respite. '*Khanna's* hull is on fire. I need to get clear. Get out the sky. And I need water,' she said to Anahrik and Sapora. 'Jump off if you want, or knuckle down and stay.' She wiped sweat from her forehead and cheeks. 'I ain't sticking around for that thing to attack me again.'

The makeshift bandage on her shoulder was slick with sweat and smoke, and began to peel away. With blood trickling down her arm and a stitch in her side, Amarah was nearly overwhelmed with exhaustion. But she couldn't give in. She and *Khanna* weren't out of danger yet.

Her hands trembled as she grabbed the wheel again and turned, pushing her ship forward, heading away from the burning city.

oroda and Eryn strolled down the emptying streets, arms linked and bellies full. The cool early evening air was heavenly after a morning locked in a dungeon and an afternoon cooped up in a smoky tavern, and Moroda took a deep breath. Eryn had finally convinced her that Morgen *wouldn't* find them, and despite the scarred man's cryptic warning, she had actually enjoyed herself.

It was almost as if they were in the "before times" again, enjoying an afternoon together without a care in the world. Before their father had died and their small family's money had disappeared.

Before debtors, Aciel, Amarah, and half a dozen other problems.

'Strange. I thought the races were all over,' Eryn mused.

Moroda twisted around at her sister's words to watch a dark ship flying towards Niversai. She studied it as it grew closer and closer, more detail coming into focus. A name was written on the side of the ship, and there was no doubting what it said: Khanna.

Moroda's heart skipped a beat. 'Wait...Eryn, does that... does that say Khanna?'

'Yes.'

'Oh, dragons above, that's *Amarah's airship*!'

'That woman you were in the cell with?' Eryn asked, astounded. 'That's quite some ship, look at the speed of it!

But...who is she racing? I don't see her opponent?'

'I don't know. We'll get a better view from the top of there.' Moroda pointed to a marble fountain at the end of the street, carved in the shape of a dragon and set on a small rise, water spouting from its open jaws.

She sprinted over the cobblestones, past closed shops and stalls, trying to reach the vantage point quickly enough to watch the rest of the race.

'Ro! Wait a minute!' Eryn called.

Scrambling up the cold marble and narrowly avoiding falling into the fountain itself, Moroda pulled herself up onto the dragon statue. It was almost ten feet tall, but any fear of heights was pushed aside in the wake of adrenaline. The same adrenaline as that morning—fuelling her to act when she should have stayed away.

'Dragons above, what's the *matter* with you?' Eryn said, finally catching up to her sister. Though her words were sharp, her voice didn't carry any fury. 'You have wine instead of tea earlier?'

Keeping one eye on *Khanna*, Moroda offered her sister a hand.

They locked fingers, and Moroda heaved Eryn up, helping her find a foothold between the dragon's marble spines. Eryn huffed and patted down her skirt. 'Is this really over those florins?'

Moroda didn't reply as her excitement faded. There was no other ship. No race to watch.

Just the realisation that a sky pirate had jumped into her ship with all the coins she had left.

Moroda could barely see the dark ship against the inky sky, though it hurtled towards the city. She sank back, hardly realising how tense she'd been while straining to watch.

She sighed, frustrated with herself and her silly, childish behaviour. She half-wondered why Amarah wasn't *leaving* Niversai.

It would certainly be the smart thing to do.

Moroda wasn't sure how long *she'd* have to hide from the Imperial Guard. Getting arrested was bad enough. But escaping? She'd be in a world of trouble if Morgen or his colleagues found her.

Her breath caught.

She'd wanted to leave Niversai after her father's death, but Eryn had convinced her to stay. And now? Could they even go home? What if Morgen had been there all day, waiting for her? What if he was waiting for her right now? And Eryn would be in just as much trouble for breaking her out.

Moroda kept her attention on *Khanna* for as long as she could. Flying away on a ship seemed so...easy.

She stared at Eryn. The sensible one. Perhaps if *she* came up with a solution for once, Eryn wouldn't have to rush in to save the day.

Before she could give more thought to her situation, fire burst through the clouds behind *Khanna* and lit up the sky.

'Ro!' Eryn clutched her sister's hand, squeezing tightly.

Moroda's mouth fell open. 'It...it...'

'Dragon.' Eryn spoke the word in a hushed tone.

'Oh no...'

Dumbfounded, Moroda watched the dragon swoop low, attacking the ship with breaths of fire, silhouetting *Khanna* against the roaring flames.

'She's leading it back to the city!' Eryn tugged at her sister's sleeve, trying to pull her down.

The forest just outside the city's northern wall burned, flames licking up and embers spilling into the sky.

It all happened so quickly that Moroda hardly had time to register the danger. Though shocked at the sudden arrival and attack of the dragon, she was transfixed by it. Never before had she seen a dragon so close, let alone seen its raw power.

In days gone by, she had sat atop hillsides outside Niversai on warm summer afternoons and watched them circle many leagues above, lazily gliding on thermals and allowing the current of the wind to carry them far and wide.

They had always seemed such gentle, intelligent creatures, unafraid of people, and decidedly uninterested in their affairs. She had heard of dragon attacks, of course, but they were mostly in self-defence.

Attacks were never unwarranted.

'Why is it attacking the ship?' Moroda muttered, clambering down the statue at her sister's insistence.

'Maybe it's angry?'

Moroda shook her head.

'Who cares what the reason is? Maybe the races upset it? Maybe the ship flew too close to it? Get down!' Eryn succeeded in pulling Moroda completely off their fountain viewpoint. 'If we stay any longer, *we're* going to go up in flames! We need to move!'

'Eryn, she's in danger. We should help...and she has my florins!' Moroda replied, finally turning to look at her sister as she spoke. Even as she said it, she knew it was a foolish argument. 'We *need* that money!'

'Didn't I tell you to seek shelter?'

Moroda looked up at the voice and immediately recognised the scarred man from the tavern. 'It's you!'

'Kohl.' He tapped his hat in greeting. 'The dragon will be upon the city in moments and it won't stop.' His attention was locked on *Khanna* and the approaching dragon, the creature's bronze-red scales glowing from the raging fires below. 'These streets will go up in smoke and flame. You *don't* want to be here when that happens. Get away now, while you have the chance.'

Moroda was unwilling to hide again, not when Amarah was caught in the conflict. And the dragon. She wanted to know why it was behaving like that.

Had it something to do with Aciel? Or was it to be a day of coincidences?

With another deafening cry, *Khanna* and the dragon were upon them. The airship raced over the heart of the city and flew over Rosecastle, wheeling around as the people in Niversai realised what was happening and cries of shock rang out.

Whatever the sky pirate had planned didn't seem to work. The dragon drew breath, the hiss of brewing flames setting Moroda's teeth on edge. She knew what was going to happen.

Panic burst from the streets as fire rained down from above.

'Ro!' Eryn shoved her away from the fountain and Kohl. 'I'm not telling you again!'

Already, people were piling into the streets, screaming in terror. Fires jumped from thatched roof to thatched roof, burning timbers and spreading as quickly as any of them breathed.

Smoke began to choke out the sky.

This time, Moroda didn't protest. With a final glance at Kohl, she left.

Pushing through swathes of people, the sisters raced along the streets, heedless where they went, as long as it was away from the commotion. Darting down alleys and around corners, they hurried away from the chaos, arms covering their faces from the thickening smoke.

When they reached the city's outer wall, they skidded to a halt, both panting heavily. The Imperial Guard were on patrol here, the city gates well guarded by armoured officers. Most were distracted, staring at the dragon overhead and barking confused orders at each other, while others shuffled uncomfortably, clearly keen to get away but without the bravery to do so.

'Kohl said we should *leave*, Ryn. I think he meant we should leave the city.' Moroda wiped her face, a smear of ash colouring her arm.

'Leave? Not that again! And just *where* would we go? Ro, don't be silly.'

'Home's on the other side of Niversai. I don't know about you, but I'm *not* fighting my way through those people to get there. Half the buildings are on fire!' Moroda leaned against the stone wall and looked up, afraid the dragon would swoop overhead and burn this part of the city too. But the smoke was so thick in the air she couldn't even see the moons.

What were they supposed to do?

Something roared from further up the street, and Moroda could have sworn there was an enormous beast prowling nearby. She shivered, peering around the corner for a better look. Her eyes widened at the sight of an enormous man looming over three members of the Imperial Guard.

'I cannot leave? My trading partner is on airship! I *must* leave Niversai. I must help! Stand aside!'

She frowned at the man's words. He knew who was on the airship. But trading partner? Interesting name for a sky pirate...

Moroda shuffled along the wall to get a better look.

'You have too many weapons, it's forbidden,' the guard replied, voice trembling in obvious fear.

'Ro!' Eryn hissed.

Moroda waved her sister over as she peered through a stone archway that led to one of the city gates. The men of the Imperial Guard stood side-by-side, blocking the gate at the Niversai's west entrance. All around them, townsfolk screamed, trying to flee the flames and get away from the danger from above. Ash littered the streets, kicked up by the chaos of fleeing citizens.

The man who spoke to the three guards towered above them by at least two feet. He was broadly built, with a bald head, boiled leather armour, and carried an enormous satchel—no doubt full of weapons: the centre of the guards' ire.

'I am trader. I am weapon smith. It is my *job*!' The huge man barged his way past the first guard only to be held up by the pair in front of the heavy iron gates.

'I don't make the rules. I can't let you leave so heavily armed,' the second guard replied, holding out his arm across the man's chest, preventing him from taking another step. 'The city is currently trying to deal with the rogue dragon. I'm sure your colleague will be safe.'

'Leave it to the Imperial Guard, Ittallan.' The other guard widened his stance.

'Keeping the gate shut will keep the fire contained. Can't have it spreading to this side of the forest too.' The first guard gestured towards the city wall.

'Ryn...' Moroda kept her gaze on the gate while reaching out for her sister. Finding Eryn's hand, she grabbed hold, locking their fingers together. 'Ryn, I think...we can get out of the city this way.'

'What in Rhea's name are you *talking* about?' Eryn snapped. 'You *cannot* be thinking what I think you are...!'

'We need to get out of Niversai. So does that Ittallan. Sounds like he might know Amarah, too. Come on, Eryn. Be brave.'

'You're the one telling *me* to be brave! We have no idea who he is!' Eryn was incredulous.

Moroda stared at her sister. 'You want to stay in a burning city with the Imperial Guard after you? Fine. *This* is the opportunity I talked about. I can feel it. Come on!'

She didn't give Eryn time to argue. For once, *she* was going to take the lead. Bursting out from where she'd been crouched, she sprinted towards the Ittallan and the officers. 'Apologies, we're late!' Moroda skidded to a halt, Eryn only a few paces behind. 'We're travelling with him. Apprentices.' She glared at the guard, daring him to challenge her. She ignored her pounding heart. 'The other weapons are ours, you see.'

'With all of us, we're within the rules for weapon numbers. There's no need for trouble,' Eryn said, glancing at the Ittallan with a forced smile.

Moroda was glad her sister slipped into their act. It would have been worse for them if she hadn't.

'But now we're here, we ought to go. We should have left this afternoon, but we were held up by the races.' Moroda kept her voice clear and direct. She hoped that in the darkness of the night and with so much smoke in the air, the guards wouldn't recognise her from that morning. She had no way of telling if those stationed on the gates would even be aware of what had happened at the castle, but she had to hope. Regardless, her upbringing had made her used to giving orders, and her tone made the guards hesitate.

Even the trader stared at them, his eyes narrowing.

Moroda gave him the briefest of nods as the soldiers

shared a look. They ducked when the dragon roared from somewhere above and a chunk of burning debris rolled past them. The Ittallan trader didn't even flinch.

'Look, we need to sort this dragon out, with three of them it's only a few weapons each,' the third muttered to the other two.

'I'm sure you have a more pressing threat to deal with,' Eryn said, evidently putting words to what they thought. 'We aren't here to cause trouble.'

The first guard turned back to the Ittallan and the women, holding each of their gazes for several moments.

'Alright. Just this one time. Go on. Off with you, quickly!' He turned the chain winch to raise the gate for them.

Without waiting for anything else to be said, Moroda and Eryn rushed through the open gate and stone archway on the far side, the Ittallan close on their heels. They hurried down the wide walkway, until the trees framed their path and the air was blessedly clear of smoke.

Once out of earshot, the Ittallan grabbed onto Moroda's elbow. 'Wait, you...are who? What...?'

'I'm sorry. We needed to get out of the city, and it looked like you did too. That was the quickest way we were going to get the guards to open the gate.' Moroda offered an apologetic shrug. She could hardly believe it had worked.

'It is okay...I did not expect...help.'

'We really *do* know someone on that ship,' Eryn added, 'we weren't lying!'

The Ittallan frowned, and Moroda realised his eyes were orange, the pupils vertical. She was reminded of Sapora, and had a sudden tremble wrestled through her.

'You...know sky pirate?' he asked, cautious.

Moroda glanced at her sister. '*Know* is a strong word. We're...acquainted with Amarah.'

'Hmm.'

'She has something of ours. We want it back,' Eryn said, determination clear in her voice.

'Yes, and we're running out of time.' Moroda looked towards the dirt path which wound its way through the forest. Thankfully, these trees weren't on fire, but she didn't know how long it would remain safe to travel.

The flames were spreading quickly, and every second that passed, Amarah got further away.

This was her perfect chance to get away, too.

Palom frowned, then nodded to himself. 'This is rough territory. I am not sure I like you two alone in it with dragon and pirates around. For helping me leave city, I will help us all catch up with ship and my trading partner.' He dropped his satchel of weapons on the ground with a heavy thud. 'I am faster in my true form than now. If you will hold weapons, I will track ship. We will catch them before dragon can do more harm.'

Moroda and Eryn looked at each other, both sharing the same nerves. Moroda swallowed, suddenly unsure of what she was getting them into, her earlier confidence evaporating.

'Father had some Ittallan business partners, didn't he? In his trades from Val Sharis?' Eryn said, though it sounded like she was trying to convince herself as much as Moroda.

'We have no time to discuss. I will chase ship. Will you come with me?' the Ittallan asked, pushing for an answer.

Moroda glanced back at the city. Her home. Now it was simply a place full of unfriendly eyes. She had no desire to return to prison.

Clearly sensing their uncertainty, the Ittallan said,

'My name is Palom. I am trader and weaponsmith from Val Sharis. On that ship is my trading partner, Anahrik.' He rolled his shoulders, eyes locked on the brief patches of sky showing through gaps in the canopy.

'I'm Eryn, and this is my sister, Moroda,' Eryn said, though Moroda thought she introduced them more out of courtesy than a desire to continue helping him.

But Moroda knew they couldn't back out now. 'We will come with you, Palom.'

'Good. Hold weapons tightly, please.' The Ittallan closed his eyes and turned his face towards the stars. In a flash of burning light, his features elongated. Fur sprouted through his skin and clothes as he transformed.

The sisters took a step back. Moroda dropped to the ground to pick up the satchel, watching him with a mixture of fascination and fear.

It took several breaths for the man to shift into a tiger—eighteen feet long, nose to tail, with a broad chest and muscled shoulders. Pressing his ears back, the tiger bared his canines in a growl, then lowered his head and crouched down.

'Oh dragons above, he means us to ride on his back,' Moroda whispered.

'I'm with you, Ro.' Eryn squeezed her sister's hand to offer support. 'Like you asked.'

Knowing she couldn't hesitate any longer, Moroda stepped forward. Both women clambered onto the massive cat's back, weapons held securely between them.

Once the two were settled, Palom stood to his full height and glanced around, ears and whiskers twitching. He let out a low snarl as he stared back at the western gate of Niversai, which was opening behind them.

Moroda followed the tiger's gaze, flinching when hooves charged down the cobblestones towards the gate.

Her breath caught as she recognised the man atop the horse. 'It's Morgen! He must be after us!' Moroda cried out. 'Palom, we have to go now, or we'll be caught!'

Palom didn't hesitate. He sprang forward and raced

through the trees, immediately settling into a long, loping run. Branches flashed by faster than she could blink, and tears came to Moroda's eyes almost instantly. Despite the tiger's massive paws, Palom made almost no noise as he tore through the forest.

Moroda chanced a look back, but even the fastest of horses had no hope of keeping up with an Ittallan tiger at full sprint.

As Palom cleared the last of the trees, farmers' fields opened up wide in front of them, the horizon running as far as the eye could see.

'Ro! Up there!'

Moroda looked skywards at her sister's words. Much farther ahead, in the inky blackness of the night, she could just make out the silhouette of *Khanna*, illuminated every so often as the dragon flying behind unleashed another plume of fire.

But that was not what had caught her sister's attention— it was a figure much closer to them.

Floating several feet above the ground, he was following the airship and the dragon, that much was certain.

As the wind rippled through the air, the man's heavy travelling cloak whipped around, away from his body. In the moonlight, the scars on his face were clear, and Moroda saw his misshapen lip as clearly as if he were right in front of her.

'Ryn...that's...he's no Ittallan.' Moroda's voice was small amid the rushing wind as Palom ran over open ground. 'He...'

Kohl rose gently, as if pulled upwards by something invisible. His arms and legs were limp under him as he raised his creamy-brown feathered wings from underneath the cloak. A strong, cold wind picked up around him, ruffling his hair and sending his cloak waving in all directions.

'Kohl's a...he's an Arillian!'

With one powerful beat of his wings, Kohl flew after the airship and dragon, and the temperature around them plummeted.

'There's too much fire!' Anahrik screamed over the rushing wind.

Amarah didn't need him to tell her that. Flames devoured part of her airship's hull and heat washed over her in waves. Smoke plumed behind them and the wheel trembled in her grip. One of her sails was alight and *Khanna* was losing power fast.

'Amarah!' Anahrik called again.

Amarah gritted her teeth. She had her hands full enough without reassuring the Ittallan every few seconds.

Khanna descended in sporadic lurches, trees rising around them as they cleared the farmlands and open fields west of Niversai, and approached nearby woodland.

She fought to keep their descent smooth, but she couldn't defeat the fire, and they were running out of time. 'Just do what you can to hold it back! I'm gonna put *Khanna* down or she'll be in pieces!'

'*I'll* be in pieces if I go near it!'

Amarah desperately tried to control her shaking airship as another sail ripped away, incinerated in dragon-flame. *Khanna* dropped violently, the wooden hull groaning.

Somewhere in the dark sky behind them, the dragon's roars carried above the crackling fire.

Amarah bit back another curse-laden snarl and looked for somewhere to land among the trees.

Sapora hunched low, arms protecting his face from the flames licking the deck, and shuffled over to where Anahrik cowered near Amarah. 'I'd prepare yourself for a fight, Ittallan.'

Anahrik glared at him. 'Palom does most of the fighting, and I don't have any weapons.'

'If I can get one, clean strike, that might bring it down.' Sapora stared into the darkness. 'Of course it might be immune to Varkain venom.'

'Brace yourselves!' Amarah called. *Khanna* didn't land so much as smash into a large clearing, throwing up chunks of soil and bending the surrounding trees in the resulting shockwave. The lower leaves caught alight and part of the hull splintered on impact, letting out a mighty groan as wood bent and broke.

Amarah cringed at the noise, but whirled round to her two passengers and shouted, 'You don't have any weapons at all?'

Anahrik edged to the side of the ship and waved smoke away from his face. 'I didn't pack them for our race, no.' His lip curled. 'Guess it's too late to regret *that* mistake.'

Thick, dark smoke rose from *Khanna's* side and the surrounding foliage as it burned. Even the nettles which grew high and proud between the dew-covered trees had been ignited from the explosion. They ringed the clearing and lit everything beneath the trees, the contrast making the night seem all the darker. Amarah couldn't see anything beyond the tree line, though her stomach churned with apprehension.

She clambered overboard, hurrying down the steps

carved into the ship's side. If she was going to fight a dragon, she'd at least keep it away from *Khanna*.

Sapora leapt over the side and landed heavily on the soft earth, his face betraying no emotion bar grim determination.

Though she couldn't stand the sight of the Varkain, at least he wasn't an imminent threat.

'Moss is damp.' Amarah glanced at her hand where she'd touched the trunk of the nearest tree. 'Good thing it ain't dry, or we'd all be up in smoke.'

'Where is the dragon?' Sapora asked. 'It was right behind us.'

A flash of lightning lit up the sky, leaving it bright as day for several seconds. A gust of icy wind accompanied it, and the dragon came soaring into view, a large tear in one of its wings.

'An Arillian?' Sapora backed away from the clearing into the shelter of *Khanna*. Anahrik, who had not yet disembarked, poked his head over the side of the ship.

The dragon landed with a thunderous crash, trees uprooted in the force of its arrival. Debris filled the air along with the deafening groan, and Amarah dropped to her knees, hands covering her head.

There was no chance she'd die like this.

Not now.

Not to a *dragon*.

Before she could think of a plan, another gust of freezing air snapped around the clearing, extinguishing the flames and sending goosebumps rising on her skin.

'Wait a second...' Sapora had said "Arillian," hadn't he? Amarah narrowed her eyes, letting out a yelp of surprise when she spotted a cloaked, scarred man gripping onto the dragon's neck.

Was one of those storm-bringers really fighting a dragon?

Ignoring the creature's roars, the Arillian raised his right palm to shoot another gust of freezing wind into the beast's other wing. As the moving air caught the thin, leathery skin, it tore through the membrane as easily as a dagger through flesh.

Roaring in pain, the dragon lashed out with its tail and thrashed its body, retaliating violently to the attack. When it brought its spiked tail round, the Arillian leapt into the air and opened his own feathered wings. Avoiding the attack, he sent out another blast of freezing, razor sharp air, blasting the dragon's eyes and nose.

'Should we help?' Anahrik called.

Amarah was too transfixed to reply, watching the dragon and Arillian fight each other from the shelter of the airship.

A dragon attacking was rare enough. And seeing a lone Arillian in Corhaven was also unusual, let alone one *fighting* the dragon...

None of it made sense.

Easily twenty-five feet long, not including its tail, which swung furiously at the Arillian, the dragon's bronzed scales were blackened slightly from the flame and smoke it breathed. Narrow, brown spines ran along the length of its back, almost black at the tail. For a creature so huge, it moved quickly; lunging and swiping, never still for a moment. With golden eyes tinged red, it watched the Arillian as he continued to avoid its lunges.

'Didn't think it'd be as much of a threat on the ground,' Anahrik said.

Amarah wished the Ittallan would shut up. She didn't need a running commentary. Besides, if this Arillian couldn't kill the dragon, they'd all be in a world of trouble. 'Shoulda given me that scythe when you had the chance!'

Her gaze roved over the dragon's long, serpentine neck and powerful spiked tail, and she swallowed hard. The creature's spines were vicious, the largest of them three feet long. They might as well have been standing against a battalion of spearmen with the amount of damage those things could do, and she couldn't fly away.

And of course, it could breathe fire.

Amarah ducked as a wayward blast of flame shot towards her. Branches bowed in the wind, leaves and debris sent flying from the Arillian's wind and ice attacks.

Despite the incredible weaponry and natural scale armour of the dragon, the Arillian did not seem at all fazed. He was fast enough to avoid teeth and claws, and had the ability to fly out of range of both flame and tail.

And he was keeping its attention off *Khanna*.

As long as it continued that way, her ship would be salvageable.

The Arillian continued to avoid the worst of the dragon's strikes, rolling in the air and diving out of range, and it did not take long before the fight began to tip in his favour. A combination of torn wings and light wounds on the dragon's slightly softer underbelly began to weaken the beast—its attacks coming slower, without the fury from the start of the fight.

Letting out another snarl, the dragon lunged, faster and farther than before. Diving out of the way, the Arillian narrowly escaped being bitten clean in two, the dragon's teeth snapping shut just above his cloak.

Cornered and unable to fly away, the Arillian flattened himself to the ground. Rolling onto his back with the dragon's throat just above him, he grabbed the scales in both hands and sent forth a burst of freezing wind so powerful it threw Amarah backwards.

The ice that formed on the dragon's neck shone brilliant

blue-white, and it crept slowly up, encasing every scale until its chest and jaws were frozen solid. Steam billowed from its body and its thrashing slowed.

Amarah let out a sigh of relief. The threat was over.

She'd known Arillians could fly and brought storms and destruction with them. She'd never seen one use any sort of ice attack before, but she usually cleared the skies on the rare occasion she spotted them. At least this one seemed to be on her side.

For the moment.

Trees and bushes rustled on the far side of the clearing, and she looked up in time to see an enormous tiger appear from the shadows, tail lashing and fangs bared. Moroda and her sister were there, too, clambering off the tiger's back.

Amarah blinked, unsure whether she was seeing things.

'Palom!' Anahrik cried, leaping down from the airship now the danger was over. The young silversmith crossed the clearing confidently, making his way through the half-burned, half-frozen ground to Palom.

Amarah shook her head. She should have realised the other Ittallan wouldn't be far behind. And a tiger? She'd need to be more wary of Palom than she'd first thought.

She returned her attention to the end of the battle, her stomach turning at seeing the dragon so badly injured. It was on its side, barely able to move. Ice covered its entire chest, as if it were a partially carved statue. With a weak growl, it tried to whip its tail at the Arillian, who batted it away with one arm. The dragon's breathing was laboured, wings failing uselessly.

'It's over. You won,' Amarah said. She flattened her emotions until she couldn't feel pity or pain.

The Arillian didn't reply, simply looked down at the creature.

71

Again, the dragon tried to attack, tried to get away, but it did not have the strength to do more than lift its head.

'It is over,' he echoed. Raising his right hand, he summoned another wave of freezing wind, and a blade of solid ice formed in his palm, tapered to a sharp point.

Dread rose in Amarah's gut as she realised what he was about to do. 'Wait!'

With one, swift strike, he plunged the blade into the dragon's throat, silencing the weak roars.

Amarah couldn't stop the bile in her throat at the sight. She'd turned her back on her homeland, her culture. Hadn't given it a second thought in years.

But killing a sacred creature didn't sit right with her. Never had.

Her hands balled into fists as she tried to force her emotions down again. Getting angry wouldn't help her understand how the situation had escalated, nor why such unprecedented events had occurred in the first place. Anger was for fighting. Protecting yourself.

This was something else entirely.

Hooves rumbled across the forest floor, leaf litter and twigs cracking. She looked past Palom and the two Goldstones to find Morgen atop a horse, racing towards them.

Seeing the same guard from before shot her disbelief to new heights. 'Okay, that's enough. What in Rhea's name is going on tonight?'

Sapora let out a low hiss, shrinking into the shadows. 'I don't think your goddess has good plans for you, sky thief.'

'You escaped the dungeon too, snake. You ain't any better off than me with the Imperial Guard here.'

'You made a deal with me, remember? You're getting me out of this continent and across the sea.'

She grimaced but didn't reply. She *had* promised, and if it hadn't been for the damned Varkain, she'd probably have been thrown back in the dungeons while trying to escape with *Khanna*.

Morgen held on tightly as his horse reared up, its nostrils flaring no doubt at the scent of dragon, blood, and death. It circled in clear panic, throwing its head around and twisting to get away from the clearing. Stamping close to the tiger—which let out a snarl—the horse reared up again with a cry of terror. Morgen let out a shout as the reins slipped from his gauntleted hands, and he was thrown unceremoniously to the ground, landing in a heap beside the two Ittallan. With a final snort, the horse charged into the trees, heading back the way it came.

Amarah shook her head. Damned, but Morgen was too determined for her tastes.

Palom shifted back, bright white light filling the clearing. Amarah would have flinched if she hadn't already had the tension shocked out of her by that night's events. When the Ittallan had finished, Amarah took a steadying breath. She wasn't sure whether Palom was more intimidating in this form or as a tiger.

Palom grabbed two swords from his satchel and stalked into the clearing, every muscle tense.

'I didn't realise you'd followed us all the way out here! Fight's over, though,' Anahrik said, briefly glancing at the Arillian.

'You were too busy with that to notice.' Palom nodded towards the dragon, now lying still after the final blow.

It was a sombre moment for Amarah. Her skin was flushed from the chill of the wind, her heart pounding from the adrenaline and fear from the sudden attack.

And with *Khanna* down, she wouldn't be going anywhere right now. Couldn't get away.

Amarah gritted her teeth, glancing up as Moroda drifted into the clearing, towards the downed dragon. Moroda's skirt was ripped, part of the fabric around Amarah's shoulder, and guilt twinged in her gut. The Goldstone had helped her. Now, she was here.

Leaving Moroda to stare at the dragon, Amarah walked over to the Arillian.

'I guess I should thank you.' Her skin was damp with sweat, blood and ash, but she ignored the prickling discomfort. 'If you hadn't come along, my ship might well be gone. I *should* be able to fix her after that heavy landing.'

Khanna smoked gently, but was no longer aflame; the Arillian's icy winds had seen to putting out most of the fires surrounding the crash site.

He nodded to her, but didn't say anything. There was no victory in his eyes. If anything, he looked pained, and Amarah didn't think it was from any injury.

Moroda ran her hand over the dragon's scales and the ice across its chest and front legs. 'Why did you behave that way? What did Niversai ever do to you, dragon?'

They were good questions as far as Amarah was concerned. The Goldstone was more perceptive than she'd given her credit for.

Amarah had never seen a dragon act that way before, even to egg thieves. Yes, they'd chase for a short while, then return to their lair. This one, though...this one had pursued them so doggedly she had wondered whether it would ever stop. It had been utterly crazed.

'You worry too much, girl,' the Arillian said, not the least bit out of breath after the intense battle. He held his icy blade and was dusting off his long cloak with his free hand. 'Just stay away from them and you'll do fine.' Without warning, he plunged his weapon deep into the dragon's chest and dragged down to gouge a hole into the scales.

Amarah jumped back, one hand to her mouth, and

74

watched him sink his arm in. When he drew his arm back, his fist was clenched around a small, brightly glowing rock.

Childhood memories flooded her, and for a long moment, Amarah couldn't breathe.

'Is that its heart?' Sapora asked, slinking forward without making a sound.

'In a way.' The Arillian held the stone close to his face and examined it closely as the glow flickered and faded. He dropped his icy blade and ran his other hand over the edges, almost caressing it. 'It is their strength. The source of their fire. Their magic.'

'Dragon stones.' Amarah blinked furiously. 'I've seen more of 'em in Berel. Much, much bigger, though.'

'The power of Berel is from dragons?' Sapora asked, a note of awe in his voice.

'Sort of.' Amarah shrugged, thinking back to the place she'd grown up. Berel was an oasis in the desert, a city only possible because of dragon magic. 'Nothing like what's in Berel is alive anymore. Sevastos, that's what they called those dragons. Their stones are taller than Palom. Totally different to that paperweight.' She turned her focus to the Arillian, and asked the question that had been plaguing her since they'd arrived. 'Who are you?'

Looking up, the Arillian pocketed the stone and looked at them, his gaze ever shifting, like a cornered dog afraid to be struck. He spent a long moment picking at a fraying thread on the brim of his hat, then adjusted it on his head. 'My name is Kohl. I'm a dragon hunter. I was in Niversai during the attack and thought I might help. The Imperial Guard didn't seem...able.'

'Of course we weren't able! There are so few of us!' Morgen declared, stepping forward, his hair a mess and his armour in disarray. 'Your Arillian friend, Aciel, took most of our strength this morning, and there were hardly any

75

soldiers left with the airship races going on! Our priority is the safety of the people. Restoring order isn't easy, but we do what we can.' He grabbed the hilt of his sword.

'You sure you wanna be out here, Morgen?' Amarah warned. She wondered if he'd be stupid enough to try and detain her again.

Morgen seemed to notice the others gathered then, and hesitated, calculating. With a huff, he left his sword sheathed at his hip. Raising his hands defensively, he said, 'I'm outside Niversai, I've no authority here. Just watching a bizarre occurrence is all. We're all permitted to do that.'

Palom and Anahrik approached the group. 'I have heard of this power. From dragon's stone. From...Sevastos.' Palom spoke haltingly, his gaze flicking between Kohl and Amarah. 'You say there are more in Berel?'

'Much bigger,' Amarah replied, 'taller than you.'

'Really?' Moroda's eyes were wide with child-like awe.

Amarah scowled at her. 'What're you two Goldstones doing out here? Travelling on the back of an Ittallan tiger, I might add!'

All the excitement on Moroda's face died. 'Um...'

Eryn looped her arm through Moroda's. 'You stole from us.'

Amarah's laugh turned into a cackle at the absurdity of the accusation. 'Excuse me? I might be a thief but I ain't stolen from *you*. Dresses and skirts ain't my thing.'

'No, you took...my...my florins.' Moroda's face flushed.

Amarah didn't have the faintest idea what they were talking about. She raised a hand, pointing at *Khanna*. 'I've been attacked by a dragon, my ship has crashed, and you're going on about a bit of silver?'

Overhead, the darkening clouds let out a low rumble, and the first drops of rain began to fall. Amarah shivered.

Eryn pulled Moroda a few steps away. 'See? Told you this

was a bad idea!' She held out her hand, raindrops splattering on her open palm. 'We should be getting back, Ro.'

'It would take all night to get back to Niversai.' Moroda tightened the scarf around herself. 'And after what's just happened?' She looked around, eyebrows furrowing. 'We're west of Niversai, aren't we? I'm sure there's a village near here. Burian? Why don't we stay there?'

'With my last crown? We should be *saving* that!'

'You're welcome to walk back to the city in the pouring rain all night.'

Amarah rolled her eyes. She had no interest in the squabbling of spoiled rich girls, and *Khanna* needed her attention. At least the rain would keep the wood from burning.

'Sir...? Erm. Excuse me? You're an Arillian, aren't you?' Morgen faced Kohl and awkwardly held out his hand. 'On behalf of the Imperial Guard of Corhaven, and the city of Niversai, I'd like to thank you for ridding us of the dragon threat. We are grateful for your support and are indebted to you for the lives you saved.' It sounded like Morgen was forcing the words. He'd not spoken kindly about Kohl's kin, Aciel, so Amarah supposed that explained it.

Kohl's cool gaze lingered on Morgen. 'You're...welcome.'

Morgen offered a salute when Kohl didn't shake his hand. 'Allow me to take your details so that I may obtain an appropriate reward on my return to Niversai. I'll make sure my captain authorises it immediately.'

Kohl shifted his weight from foot to foot. 'I've already given my name. I know my people are less than welcome in Corhaven and—'

'Nonsense.' Morgen had procured a length of parchment and quill from his person. 'Your place of residence, Kohl?'

More awkward shuffling. 'I...I will not be staying long here. Just passing through. There's no need for any reward.'

'You saved a city. Countless people would have burned if you hadn't done what you did!'

'Actually, I think *I'm* owed a reward for helping get the dragon *away* from the city!' Anharik stepped up, all smiles and bouncing energy.

'Naturally, any who assisted Kohl will be welcome to a share,' Morgen said.

Amarah brightened at that. She hadn't wanted to linger in Morgen's presence, but now the talk had turned to rewards, she didn't want to miss out. 'And whose ship was it following, Anahrik? Last I checked, *you* weren't flying anywhere. You were clinging on and refusing to put out fires.'

Anahrik glared at her.

'Amarah...' Morgen lowered his quill. 'Don't think I haven't forgotten your crimes. Or you, Moroda. A Goldstone you may be, but you have broken the law twice now by my count. You ought to be arrested and brought back to Rosecastle.'

Amarah snorted. 'I ain't in the mood to deal with you, Morgen. And you said yourself you had no authority outside the city, so don't even try it.' The officer meant well. He'd always been more of an inconvenience than a real threat—which was more than could be said of his captains—but she didn't appreciate him trying to throw his weight around when he was clearly outmatched.

Kohl cleared his throat. 'I wouldn't mind getting out of the rain. Morgen, the young lady said there is a village near here. I would settle for a full belly, comfortable bed, and fewer questions. No need for all that paperwork.'

'I agree with the Arillian. Food and board sounds like a fine reward after what we did,' Anahrik said immediately. 'Palom too, of course. We're in this together.'

Morgen nodded. 'Of course.'

'And these two.' Palom gestured towards the Goldstones. 'Without them, I would not have been released from Niversai to help. They earn reward also.'

Morgen paused, quill in hand. His gaze swept those gathered, evidently calculating. 'I don't think...' Morgen began, but Palom's growl cut him off.

A long fang poked out from Palom's lip, his pupils constricting.

Amarah tensed. This was why Ittallan could be difficult to deal with. Get on their bad side and they turned into savages.

'I don't think,' Morgen repeated, 'that'll be a problem. Burian is a short way ahead. The Imperial Guard will pay for food and board for one night. That'll be the end of it.' Morgen ran a hand through his hair.

Palom nodded, the tension dropping from his shoulders. 'Arillian. How did you know dragon would attack?' He squared up to Kohl.

Kohl held his ground. 'I'm a dragon hunter.'

'This is...unsavoury work.'

Morgen stepped between them, hands raised. 'Please. There's been enough bloodshed tonight. Let's get out of the rain. Amarah? I will have you know that this is an exceptional circumstance and—'

'Don't bother wasting your breath, Morgen. I wouldn't normally pass up a free bed and meal, but I ain't leaving *Khanna* out here like this. Got work to do. I'll be outta your country in the morning. Damned stupid place, anyway. We can draw a line under it. Deal?'

Morgen let out a sigh, and Amarah could tell it was in relief. Clearly he'd been expecting a fight.

'And just *how* are you going to get out of the country? Your ship is half-burned.' Sapora sneered, coming out from the shadows now the threat of arrest had passed.

Amarah had forgotten about the damned Varkain.

'What do you know about flight, snake? She's recoverable. I'll sort her out, right now. You'll get your passage across the sea, stop complaining.'

Sapora scowled at her, then crept towards *Khanna*. 'Very well, I will see if there's anywhere inside your ship I can claim as mine.'

Amarah looked back to the Ittallan traders, trying not to think about a Varkain making a nest inside *her* ship. 'Palom. My scythe.'

'How dare you demand that!' Anahrik snapped.

'If it weren't for me and my ship, *you* would've been a snack for the dragon. I think saving your life is worth one scythe, no?'

Anahrik glanced at his colleague, evidently hesitant to hand over the weapon.

'Done,' Palom said, though he looked away as Anahrik reluctantly fished out her scythe.

Morgen shivered in the falling rain and brushed water from his hair. 'I will need to report to the village guard at Burian. They'll have seen the dragon's approach, and I can inform them of the attack in Niversai. They might need to prepare if this isn't a one-off. Shall we get out of the rain? A hot meal will do us good, I'm sure. Compliments of the Imperial Guard.' He offered the group a smile, folded the parchment and tucked it away, then made for the edge of the clearing and the forest path just beyond the trees.

'You're staying out here? All night? What about...bandits or, or...forest creatures?' Moroda approached Amarah, looking warily at the shadows between the trees.

Amarah smirked. Moroda's concern was touching, considering she was nothing but a spoiled Goldstone. Usually they were the most selfish of all people.

'I can defend myself, easily enough, little girl.'

Rhea's luck was with her. She'd broken out of the dungeon, reclaimed her ship and a weapon, and was out of Morgen's clutches. Tomorrow, she'd be out of Corhaven and onto better things.

She twirled her scythe, silver glinting in the darkness. 'Nighty night.'

8

Moroda lingered on the edge of the clearing, soaked through with rain, her gaze on the dragon. Kohl had taken something from it. Something of extraordinary power. And it set her imagination blazing.

Dragon crystal.

Magic.

'Ro?'

Moroda heard her sister calling her, but she'd never been so close to a dragon before, and was loathe to leave it so soon. They were apex predators, creatures that rarely came near people. In some parts of Linaria, they were worshipped as gods.

Her thoughts drifted back to Aciel. Another strange occurence.

Were they connected?

She couldn't help but think the dragon's attack held far greater relevance than she had initially thought. Of course, the timing was conveniently peculiar—Niversai was full to capacity with the airship races, and she couldn't bear to think how many people burned tonight. Coupled with the sudden appearance of Aciel and the removal of a large portion of the Imperial Guard that morning, the dragon attack became much more significant.

'Ro! Come on! Don't want Morgen to change his mind and lock us up, do you? I'm getting cold!'

Moroda blinked and shivered. She could think about it later. 'I'm coming!'

She hurried along the woodland path, several parts of which were so thick with vegetation she couldn't even see the muddy ground. In the poor light, it wasn't long before she was tripping over branches and getting her clothes snared on twigs.

By the time she left the trees, she looked like she'd taken on the dragon herself. Wrapping her arms around herself, she joined the group as they approached the tall gates of Burian—carved of wood, rather than stone and iron as in Niversai—but well-manned and lit by a dozen burning torches.

Morgen had already stepped forward to speak for the group, and a few words passed between the guards before the heavy gate was lifted by a steel crank and chains.

She had been to Burian once before, and as the gate rose and she took in the sights, it brought a comforting familiarity. If anything, it reminded her of Niversai's quieter districts —where artists painted, tea houses brewed exotic blends, and the vast libraries attracted scholars from across Corhaven.

Torches hung off the sides of buildings and lit the main cobblestone street, making the village warm and inviting even in the falling rain.

Palom checked she and Eryn were with them, and gave Moroda a nod.

Moroda needed to thank him. It had been a rash decision to trust a stranger, but the Ittallan had cared about his comrade rather than taking advantage of them, and that behaviour was continuing now. She wasn't sure she *deserved* such kindness, and wanted him to know how grateful they were for his generosity.

'Were you caught in the dragon's fire?' one of the guards asked Morgen. He stood by the gate with a flaming torch held high for the group.

'No. We were lucky Kohl was there. He's the one who brought it down.' Morgen gestured to the scarred man, who had once again covered himself with his long cloak, the fabric hiding his enormous feathered wings.

Kohl tapped the brim of his hat to the guard in acknowledgement, but said nothing.

'We were in a state of panic. Thought the thing would come down on us. We've had a good harvest, but the boys are in the middle of bringing it in. If that dragon had attacked the fields, we'd not likely survive the winter,' the guard said, his round face puffy in his too-small helmet. 'Any friend of Burian is welcome here, especially one of the Niversai Imperial Guard. Stay at the lodge on the town's east side, and none of you will go without. I'll make sure of that.' He handed Morgen a small crest, though the insignia was too small for Moroda to see.

Clapping one arm to their chests, the guards parted, and Morgen rejoined their group. 'Looks like we're guests of honour at *The Fourth Moon* for bringing down the dragon. Shall we?' He headed down the street and led them through the town.

'*Fourth Moon*? I thought there were only three moons?' Moroda muttered, glancing up, but the clouds and rain hid all moonlight from sight.

Palom frowned at her, but didn't comment as the party followed Morgen.

Eryn kept close to her sister. 'Are you sure we're doing

the right thing? With Morgen away from the city, maybe we can get back home without fear of arrest?'

'You really want to trudge back in the dark and rain through woodland and fields to a burning city? When there's a hot meal and a warm bed right here?' Moroda stifled a yawn. 'Amarah owes me my florins, too. We need that money back, now more than ever. I'll talk to her about it properly tomorrow.'

Something metal creaked loudly overhead and Moroda flinched at the sudden noise, half-expecting another dragon descending upon them.

When she looked, she reddened in embarrassment at jumping. A dark green, weathered plaque swung in the wind, a pale grey moon painted on it. Although its hinges were rusty, the building it was attached to was in far better condition. Tall, and solidly built from stone and mortar, with a heavily thatched roof, it looked more like someone's home than an inn.

Morgen opened the low wooden door and a wave of warmth washed over her. She heard the crackle of a hearth over the raucous laughter from the patrons within.

'Ah, finally. Food!' Palom roared, following Morgen inside, though he had to duck to fit through the narrow entranceway, his shoulders brushing against the doorframe.

Grateful for the warmth, Moroda and her sister followed, with Anahrik close behind and Kohl bringing up the rear.

Whatever happened, at least they were safe for now.

~

ONCE SEATED with the others at a large, circular table nestled in the warmth of the inn, Moroda could *almost* forget she'd spent her morning in a dungeon, half the day in hiding, and fleeing her city from an attacking dragon in the evening.

Though it wasn't a high class inn, the sort she had grown used to as a child, it was comfortable, and the smell of food and fire instantly put her at ease. Much of the fear and worry which had plagued her since that morning had faded, and she was eager to learn more about the dragon and the people with whom she and Eryn had found themselves.

Morgen had spoken with the innkeeper on their arrival, presenting him with the crest from the town guard who had let them through the gate, and secured food and lodgings for all six of them. Eryn had been with him for every conversation, mostly to ensure there weren't any traps.

But it had been unnecessary, as the soldiers of Burian were as good as their word.

Either that or Eryn's fiery gaze really had made them do as Morgen instructed.

Moroda relaxed in the knowledge they would be safe tonight.

It was bizarre. Only a few hours ago, she'd have fled at the sight of the Imperial Guard. Now she was being looked after by one.

The same one who'd arrested her.

Morgen had expressed remorse for her arrest and treatment that morning, and though she remained uncertain of his apology, Eryn believed it to be genuine. He was only following orders, after all.

However, Morgen was a valuable source of information, having been stationed in Rosecastle during Aciel's visit, up until the dignitary had left with many of the Imperial Guard.

Despite her misgivings about him, Moroda listened intently.

'How can someone waltz up to a capital city and leave

with hundreds of your soldiers?' Anahrik asked, slurping from a bowl of steaming vegetable broth, his bright blue eyes focussed on Morgen. 'Wouldn't happen in Taban Yul. Council'd never allow it! There'd be outrage!'

Morgen poked at the contents of his bowl with a spoon, cheek resting on his other hand. 'It was the weirdest thing. Everyone was in full prep for the start of the races, guards doubled at the city gates...But there was a strange atmosphere. Everyone seemed on edge, even the other soldiers at my level. Couldn't get a word out of any of the captains.'

Moroda listened quietly. She remembered the Imperial Guard had been behaving strangely. Short-tempered and rude, more aggressive than she'd seen before. Their unfair treatment had been what had spurred her to speak against Aciel.

Morgen took a sip of his soup and continued,

'Then, yesterday morning, when we were just about to open the races for that day, our captain said there was an important visitor coming to the castle. We thought maybe a Goldstone family, or a rich trader from Val Sharis, maybe even royalty. But then it turned out it was just some Arillian...except he had a hundred others with him. Was reported heading east after he left, but when you can fly, I guess he could have gone anywhere.'

Moroda sat up straighter, her gaze drifting to Kohl. Aciel was an Arillian, too.

'East? You think he'll cross the sea?' Anahrik asked Palom.

His comrade watched Kohl when he answered. 'I did not see Arillians in Niversai. Except Kohl.'

'Yeah, well, neither did we. We didn't even realise they were *there*. Kinda hard to pick out individual ships when you've got hundreds of them floating above the city.' Morgen reached for a hunk of warm bread to mop up the remnants in his bowl. 'They never landed. Just waited in the skies above the castle, waiting for this Arillian—Aciel—for his business to be finished.'

Palom and Anahrik glanced at each other, but did not interrupt.

Moroda's stomach tightened. She hadn't realised Aciel was an Arillian. Like Kohl, he'd kept his wings covered. She'd never forget the effect he had on the townspeople. They'd listened, enraptured. She'd been too far away to hear his words directly, but when she'd pushed through the crowds to get closer, she'd understood the gist of it.

Even when she'd been trying to speak out, her throat had closed, like there'd been an invisible force keeping her quiet. She'd just put it down to nerves—she'd never made a habit of speaking out against anyone, let alone an authority figure. She'd never done well with conflict or having attention on her.

Now she'd learned Aciel had left with hundreds of soldiers, she wondered whether they were in their right minds.

Just like she wondered if the dragon had been in its right mind.

'That was brave what you did, Moroda,' Morgen said. 'In front of the whole city. With Aciel. I wouldn't have thought a Goldstone would speak out like that!'

At the mention of her earlier actions, Moroda glanced up. Rage washed through her at the thought of Aciel. She remembered his smug grin and cold eyes, even from halfway across the town square. 'I can't remember his words or even the sound of his voice. Everyone was hooked on what he was saying. It was belittling and cruel and...and I hated the fact no one was doing anything, just listening like a pack of obedient dogs.'

'Can't blame the Arillian for trying to get into everyone's good books,' Anahrik shrugged. 'Don't see why he had to make such a show of it. Could've just taken the soldiers and left and no one would have known.'

'But that's just it—he *wanted* everyone to know,' Moroda said. 'He needed all of Niversai, the capital of Corhaven, to see him and the influence he had. Don't you see? That's why I couldn't stand it. Talking down to us like that.'

Anahrik laughed, 'He's just some crackpot Arillian. Probably a Lord or something where he comes from, thinks he's bigger than he is. It won't be long before those soldiers see that and head back to Niversai. Especially after the dragon attack. They'll have family in Niversai. You think they'll leave 'em to burn?'

'I'm not so sure,' Morgen disagreed. 'There wasn't any mention of when they'd come back.'

'So your captains just let this Arillian walk off with over half his guard?' Moroda was shocked.

'No, no, there are more soldiers in Niversai. Of course there are. The ones he took were just the...Well, I guess the best trained.'

Palom snorted. 'Amarah would find this hilarious. Whole city burned, only looked after by handful of trainee soldiers who have never fought. Niversai is easy pickings. Shame she is too busy fixing ship. Some *great capital* of Corhaven.'

'Well, we aren't allowed to question anything. Orders are orders. You get punished otherwise.' Morgen's voice shook. 'I mean, one of the other officers tried to ask the captain who he was and what one of those damned Arillians was doing here—no offence,' he hastily added, glancing at Kohl who gestured for him to continue.

Morgen wet his lips with his tongue. 'He got a real beating, so we just decided we didn't need to know. Aciel stayed in Rosecastle with a couple of his men, kept real quiet. The next morning, he gave that speech...and after Moroda's outburst, he carried on talking to the townsfolk and then took two hundred of the guard off in his ships.'

'Rubbish. I don't believe that many Arillians were there.' Anahrik scoffed, folding his arms. 'Everyone would have known! You know what Arillians are like! All storms and devastation. There was hardly a breeze in Niversai.'

'We aren't all like that,' Kohl said, his low voice quiet among the laughter and talking of the tavern around them. 'In the same way you Ittallan are not all savage beasts, or the Varkain all soulless killers, hunting down people wherever they go.'

As far as Moroda could see, the only reason they were all alive was because Kohl had been able to slay the dragon. To then belittle his race seemed in poor taste.

An uncomfortable silence dragged out across the table.

Morgen looked at Kohl for a long moment. 'Do you know this Aciel? What he's doing? Why?'

'Aciel may be an Arillian, but we are not...' Kohl shook his head, stumbling over his words. 'I am exiled.'

'Exiled?' Moroda asked.

'I would rather not speak of it.'

Anahrik snorted. 'Seems convenient. Two Arillians show up and they aren't in league with each other?'

Kohl glared at the Ittallan, his eyes flashing. 'Are *you* in league with every Ittallan we meet? Of course not. So don't jump to conclusions.'

Moroda didn't understand the hostility. 'As far as I can see, Kohl hasn't done anything wrong. He saved us back there.'

Anahrik gave a grunt of acknowledgement and didn't press the matter further.

Eryn rested her hand on Moroda's. 'Whatever happened

has passed. Things will be back to normal soon enough. We'll laugh about this in a few days, you'll see.'

Moroda wasn't sure she believed her sister. Eryn was so desperate to cling to how things used to be that she couldn't see how much everything had changed. Refused to.

But Anahrik's words made her curious. 'I've never met an Arillian other than you, Kohl. What storms?'

Morgen glanced warily at Kohl, but kept his mouth shut, focussing on getting the last morsels from his bowl with his remaining piece of bread. The others behaved similarly, taking great interest in their bowls and mugs.

'Anahrik means the war,' Kohl said at length, taking his hat off with a sigh and setting it on the table. 'I'd be interested to hear what sort of history you learned as children, Eryn, Moroda.' He laughed, mirthlessly, his scars in full view now he had removed his hat. 'I did not fight in it; we aren't *quite* as long lived as that. But many of my forefathers did. The scars left on Linaria in those battles are worse than these.' He gestured to his face and lips.

'I don't remember going into the histories in any depth,' Moroda mumbled, thinking of her education. 'Just that the war happened several hundred years ago. The Imperial Guard was formed then to fight back, and it's still around now...' She skipped over the violence, who fought whom, and over what. In truth, she didn't know much, and what she had been taught was probably biased—something she didn't want to draw attention to.

Kohl clearly felt at ease talking about the history of Linaria and the Arillians, but Moroda was relieved when he chose to step away from the conversation.

'The past has passed,' Kohl said, closing his eyes. 'Grudges are a poison better ignored and forgotten.'

'Why did you take the dragon's crystal?' Eryn asked, holding her mug of rosemary tea with both hands and changing the subject. 'Back in Niversai, you warned us about the attack *hours* before it arrived. Were you just after that crystal?'

All eyes returned to Kohl with renewed intensity, Palom's most of all, Moroda realised.

'You *knew* it was coming? Why didn't you report it to the Imperial Guard so we could've been better prepared?' Morgen asked, voice raising. 'Our defences were so small, we didn't stand a chance! A few hours' notice would have given us the time to ready weapons, get people to safety!'

'I wouldn't have had that stupid race and been singed!' Anahrik pounded his fist on the table.

'*I* needed to bring the dragon down, not any of you Imperials. And your townspeople's safety wasn't my concern.' Kohl took a sip of water from his mug. The glass frosted where his lips touched the edge. 'The dragon's stone is mine by right. When you are victorious in battle, you can take your reward.'

'What happened to the Varkain?' Anahrik asked suddenly.

'He went into Amarah's ship,' Palom replied, leaning back in his chair. 'He's not going to stay at inn. Not in Corhaven. No Varkain would do this.'

Eryn shuddered. 'He scares me. He was in the dungeon with Moroda. I would have left him there but she *insisted* on releasing him.'

'There are few who would do this for Varkain,' Palom said.

Moroda's face flushed. 'Well...I felt bad. I don't know what he'd done...he may have been wrongly accused... And...I couldn't just leave him there.'

'Moroda, honestly, I don't know what's wrong with you sometimes.' Eryn's voice was clipped. 'They're *awful* creatures. *Killers*. They terrorise people for fun! If it was the other way around, he would have left you to rot, or worse.'

'Maybe. But I did what I thought was best,' Moroda said, suddenly feeling awful. Yes, it had been brave and she hadn't wanted to leave him behind, but she was more afraid of his wrath if she left and he had later escaped.

Selfishness more than selflessness.

And now Niversai was half-burned by a rogue dragon. The city could well be in ruins.

Everything was turning into chaos, regardless of what Eryn believed.

Even listening to her companions showed how things had deteriorated. Her childhood home, the only home she'd ever known, had become dangerous even *without* the dragon. The realisation dawned on her so suddenly she felt dizzy.

'Ryn, I'm going to bed now. Will you come?' Moroda stood up and rubbed her eyes. Exhaustion and sapped adrenaline had made every limb heavy.

'Yes.' Eryn stood up beside her sister. 'Thank you again, Morgen...well, everyone. Goodnight.' Their companions nodded to them as they made their way to the back of the inn, picking through the gathered patrons, already thinning as the night wore on, and up the wooden staircase.

Moroda heard plenty of conversation about the dragon attack, people cheering their survival and celebrating their luck.

None of them mentioned they'd been saved by an Arillian.

She didn't know why she felt guilty about that.

Morgen had arranged for the sisters to share a room at the end of the hallway on the second floor, and Moroda was sure to lock the door behind them.

'Worried?' Eryn asked, as Moroda placed the key on the cabinet beside the door. The room was small, but clean, with a window opposite the door, a large bed to the right, and a cabinet with a sink to the left. Above the cabinet, a large map was secured to the wall, faded with time, but legible.

'A little. We aren't at home after all. Better to be cautious and careful.' Moroda shrugged out of her outer cloak and took her scarf off. It had dried quickly in the heat of the tavern, though her hair was damp.

Eryn climbed into the bed, pulling the blanket up to her chin.

'I really think something has started here. Maybe Aciel's the trigger,' Moroda said.

'Not this again.'

Moroda walked to the window and opened it, allowing the cool night breeze to circulate. She could hear the rain falling outside and took a moment to listen to it. 'But surely you can see how odd this is? This Arillian, Aciel, taking so many soldiers. The way people acted in his presence. Even Morgen said there was something going on with the Imperial Guard. And now the dragon attack...it's all so unusual. *Why* would the dragon attack? Kohl knows more, I'm sure of it. He's just not saying anything. Probably hoping we won't ask too many questions after he saved us. Did you see how dismissive he was of Morgen's reward?'

'Ro...'

Moroda got into the other side of the bed and lay flat on her back, staring up at the timber roof and playing with the ends of her hair as she spoke. 'I think we should find out.'

Eryn didn't bother hiding the disdain in her voice. 'Find out what?'

'What's going on. With the dragons. With Kohl. You were right to ask him about the stone, I'd been wondering too.'

Eryn sat up.

'What about home?'

'You saw the dragonfire. Even if home *hasn't* burned to the ground, Niversai is dangerous right now. Remember what Palom said about easy pickings?'

Eryn frowned. 'You're tired. It's been quite a day, and you—'

'Not to mention I could be arrested in Niversai! Please. I know it sounds ridiculous. I know it sounds dangerous—'

'Because it *is* ridiculous and it *is* dangerous! Ro, go to sleep. You'll have a clearer head in the morning. We can't just traipse around the wilderness with no food, no coin, nothing to keep us safe! You've been reading too many adventure stories. They're *dreams*, Ro. Not reality.'

'Niversai isn't our reality anymore. Say we'd listened to you and stayed there. Cowered. We'd have been roasted in that fire, just like however many hundreds of others did.' Moroda tried to keep her voice from trembling. She didn't want to think about their home being destroyed. They'd already emptied it of everything sentimental, but to see the wood torched and stone blackened would be too much. 'Eryn. I know you're trying to help. But you aren't father. You aren't mother. I can make my own decisions, you can't make every one for us!'

'I'm the only one who *can* make the hard decisions! The only one who realises they need to be made! We can't go swanning off with people because they did one nice thing for us! You're so lost in your dreams and so willing to see good in people when there isn't any! If it weren't for me, you'd be dead! Do you have any idea how close we are to *nothing*?'

'Then all the more reason not to return to Niversai, where there's nothing.' Moroda could feel her voice rising, and she hated it.

'I'm done talking about this, Ro. I'm tired. I'm cold. It's

95

been a terrible day, and we're lucky to be alive. Let's just sleep, okay?' Eryn snapped.

Moroda hated arguing, especially with her sister. Yes, she was the one with silly ideas and lofty dreams, and Eryn was the one who kept them grounded. But this was something she couldn't let go.

Something bigger than her dreams.

She drew the blankets over her as she tried to get comfortable in the unfamiliar place.

'Goodnight, Ryn.'

'Night, Ro.'

Her mind continued to whirl as Eryn's soft snores filled the room.

Despite all the uncertainty and chaos, Moroda was sure of one thing: the world had shifted around her, and she refused to be crushed under it.

9

Palom and Anahrik were the last two at the table. Kohl had retired shortly after Moroda and Eryn, and though Morgen had certainly *attempted* to drink as much ale as Palom, the young soldier had given up after his fifth and staggered upstairs to his room.

A handful of other patrons dedicated to their late night drinks were dotted at tables around the tavern, but they all left the pair of Ittallan alone, which suited Palom just fine.

'Well. That was an interesting turn of events.' Anahrik played with one of his daggers, balancing the tip on his finger, uninterested in his ale.

'*Interesting* is not word I would use.'

'What word would you use?'

'Suspicious.'

Anahrik laughed. 'When *don't* you find something suspicious? We aren't in Val Sharis. Things are different here.'

Palom raised an eyebrow. 'I do not trust this Kohl. Any who kills dragons for no reason is suspicious.'

'That dragon wasn't gonna be deterred. Don't think Kohl had much choice.'

Palom stared down at the bottom of his empty mug.

Better to stop now, before the drinking got out of hand. He'd already had more than he'd expected, but this trip hadn't exactly gone as he'd expected either. 'But what Amarah said...about Sevastos. These dragons do not exist any more, but their crystals do. In Berel, she said. We should go there.'

'Since when were you thinking about that?'

'Since dragons started attacking random airships and cities. And Arillians are skulking about stealing people.'

Anahrik shook his head.

Palom let out a sigh, his words coming out just above a whisper. 'I did not think I would find information about *Valta Forinja* outside home.'

Anahrik dropped the blade, all joking gone. 'Are the dragon stones really that potent?'

'Why else would Kohl take it? If Aciel is stealing people. Soldiers. From towns. He may go to Val Sharis, too. If I have *Valta Forinja*, that might...dissuade him from trying to steal Ittallan.'

'So...you want to go to Berel?'

'Why not? We are on right side of world. Is not so far from here.'

Anahrik shook his head more violently.

'What is matter? You said we should get out of Val Sharis. This is what we are doing.'

'I didn't mean for us to go on a wild goose chase for some mythical weapons.'

'Is not wild goose chase. Is staying outside of Val Sharis. Is what you wanted, no?'

Anahrik sighed. 'I wanted you out of trouble. That was the important thing! Away from Mateli and Lathri, before—'

'This is also important. This is legend of our people. We will go to Berel and see. If there is nothing there, I am still outside of Val Sharis.' Palom's mind drifted back to his homeland, to Lathri. He'd ended up wounding Mateli over her. Had wanted to paint the golden streets red with his blood. Anahrik had been right. Getting away from Val Sharis had been the only thing that had saved him, else he'd have ended up imprisoned.

Anahrik groaned, unable to argue. 'And what about those Goldstones? You don't plan on babysitting them much longer, do you?'

'If not for them, I would not have escaped Niversai to reach you.'

'Well, they're paid back now. Food and bed, what more could they want?'

'Morgen paid. Not me. And...' Palom stared at the remnants of his ale, discomfort growing in his gut. '...they remind me of Solvi.'

'What? Why?'

'No father. No mother. Lost.' Palom had last seen Solvi when she was a baby. He squeezed the handle of his tin mug. Another person he'd failed to protect.

'These Goldstones are weak. Deadweight. Why not dump them here and be done with it?'

'I will not.' The mug's handle crumpled in Palom's grip and he released it.

Anahrik stared flatly at the broken handle. 'I swear this stupid attitude will get you killed one day, Palom. Not like you owe them a life debt! Favour's been repaid, let it go.'

Palom took a deep breath to steady his emotions. 'They are not home. Because of me. Until they return home, I will look after them. This is no discussion.'

Anahrik rolled his eyes. 'I hope you're not expecting some coin in return for our trouble. Poorest looking Gold-stones I've ever seen.'

'Of course not. We help people in hard times. If I had not helped *you*, we would not be where we are today.'

Anahrik reddened. 'That's different! We're both Ittallan.

We had an arrangement! Mutual benefit. *And* it was life and death. What can *they* do?'

'I am not having this argument with you, Anahrik.' Palom got to his feet, wooden chair scraping on the floor. 'In morning I will tell Amarah we want to go to Berel. She can fly us.'

Anahrik rolled his eyes again. 'Great. *More* time spent with that thieving pirate.'

~

PALOM WAS up with the birds, their unfamiliar song rousing him quickly from sleep. Dawn painted a thin line of orange across the horizon as murky black gave way to navy blue. The sky was clearer here than above Niversai; fewer buildings and less smoke allowed the rich colours to be seen more clearly.

He made his way downstairs, ears telling him he wasn't the only one awake before he reached the ground floor.

A serving girl was working her way around each table, wiping away spills with a thick rag and laying down fresh tablecloths. The innkeeper stood behind the bar, thumbing through some parchment with a deep frown.

'Breakfast be served shortly,' he said without looking up.

Palom spied Kohl sitting at one of the tables beside the bar, a flask in his hand as he read notices nailed to the wall opposite. He wore his hat and thick travelling coat, which gathered at his feet, hiding his wings.

If Kohl had heard Palom's approach, he gave no indication, and Palom had no intention of greeting the Arillian warmly. Not when he distrusted the storm-bringer.

Palom kept eyes on Kohl as he headed to the main door, eager to speak with Amarah.

Although it was early, and the rain had not quite let up

from the previous night, the village was already alive with activity.

It wasn't a rich place. Most buildings had patchwork thatched roofs where they'd been repaired countless times. Aside from the main thoroughfare to the town gates, which was paved, other roads and paths were gravel or dirt. Young men and women went about their business, carrying wood, water, and freshly baked bread. If the surrounding forest had been a little thicker and wilder, and the town a little closer to the mountains, it would *almost* be like being back at home.

As the sun rose, the wind brought the scent of burnt wood from deeper within the surrounding woodland. Palom doubted that smell would be gone any time soon.

The guards at the gate nodded at him. Though they weren't the same ones who'd been there when they'd arrived, clearly news of the dragon-hunting party had spread, and they let him leave Burian without so much as a question.

His boots squelched through the mud as he retraced his steps from the night before. He quickened his pace, worried he'd missed Amarah, though he doubted she would have had time to fix her ship *and* sleep before dawn.

Once in the forest, the birdsong increased, and he spotted the occasional burst of colour as a songbird flitted from tree to tree. Palom followed the forest path, orange and red leaves littering the edges.

When he reached the clearing, he breathed a sigh of relief. The canopy had been torn open, casting early morning light on the airship where it lay.

He hadn't missed her.

Amarah had done an excellent job of clearing the space of broken branches, leaves, and other debris. The remains of a small fire smoked lightly, not far from where the hastily repaired airship rested. Though there was no sign of Amarah herself, he doubted she'd have left *Khanna* unattended. The foliage circling the clearing was blackened, smaller trees uprooted, and he winced at the carnage.

The dragon's carcass remained where Kohl had slain it, and Palom closed his eyes, whispering a brief prayer, before returning his attention to the airship. To his untrained eye, it didn't appear to be any better than when it had crashed. 'Amarah?'

'Who's there?' The muffled reply came from deep within the ship.

'I wish to speak with you.' Palom approached cautiously. There was no sign of Sapora, either, and it put him on edge. He listened for any disturbances within the trees. He knew he was unlikely to spot a Varkain who didn't want to be seen, and tried to push away the worry of the snake stalking him in the shadows.

'Amarah?' Palom called again, his voice booming, vibrating the soft wooden panels along the ship's side.

'Keep your voice down. Do you wanna bring the entire forest down on us?'

'I am glad you survived last night.'

Amarah stepped out onto the deck of the ship, cleaning grime and dirt from her hands with a grubby wash cloth. 'I ain't some frail Goldstone, you know. I can take care of myself.'

Palom laughed. 'I want to go to Berel.'

She threw the cloth over one shoulder and peered down at him. 'Okay?'

Palom squared himself. 'I want you to fly us.'

'That's nice. I got other plans, I'm afraid.'

'I am *telling* you to fly us.'

She cackled, loud enough that several startled birds in a nearby tree took flight.

'Things are moving in this world. Powerful magic.' He folded his arms. 'What plan do *you* have that is so important?'

She wiped away a tear from one eye and rested her hand on her hip. 'None of your business. But I'm packing up inside and will be gone soon. Nice of you to come say bye. Didn't think any of you lot cared that much!'

'I am not saying bye. I am telling you to fly us to Berel. There is...important matter there.'

'Well I got *important matters*, too.' She waved a hand dismissively towards him.

Palom scowled, then reached into his pocket and pulled out a small pouch. The coins within jingled, and Amarah froze in place. 'I will pay.'

Her eyes brightened. 'Ah. That changes things don't it? Two crowns'll get you to Berel. I'm guessing Anahrik'll be coming, too?'

Palom was appalled at her price. 'Two crowns would be enough to cross *ocean*! Berel is not far. I will pay four florins.'

'Have a nice walk.' Amarah leaned over the side of the ship, grinning down at him.

'Six florins.' Palom tried not to allow her to get under his skin.

Amarah shrugged.

A fang poked out from his lip. 'Fine. Ten florins. Is double what room and food would cost at inn. Is fair price. And I think *you* need money more than I need ship. I *can* walk. You have nothing but damaged ship and one of *my* scythes.'

Amarah considered it. 'Ten florins and I'll get you to Berel. But I wanna leave sharpish. And you do what I tell you. Might need you to pull your weight on *Khanna*.'

Palom didn't want to argue, so he nodded. 'I will get

Anahrik and our things. We can go then.' He turned to head back to town.

'Hold on a second!'

'Yes?'

'Half upfront.' She held out her palm, expectant.

Palom bristled at the insult. 'Excuse me? You are thinking what?'

'I think you and Anahrik get back here and force me to take less money.'

Palom turned to face her fully, rage boiling. 'I am not pirate like you. I do not break my word when I give it. How do I know *you* will not fly off with my florins?'

Amarah reddened at that. 'I might be a pirate, but I have my honour, too. Just protecting myself in these crazy times. That's all. I gave you money for the scythe before my race, didn't I?'

With a huff, Palom threw the coins up to her, silver flashing in the morning sun. 'I will be back soon.'

Although his pride had been hurt, Palom made his way to *The Fourth Moon*, content in what he had negotiated. He paused a short distance from the inn, spotting Moroda lingering just outside the entrance. Even without his superior hearing, he could tell the young woman was crying.

Although Moroda was slightly older than his niece, Solvi, her pain and confusion made her seem younger. More vulnerable.

Anahrik was right.

But he couldn't just ignore her. Not if he could help.

'Why the tears, Moroda?'

She whirled around at his voice and took a step back. After blinking, she must have recognised him, because her fear shifted into relief, and she smiled. 'Oh, it...it's nothing,' she stammered.

'Doesn't look like nothing.' He narrowed his eyes as he looked her over. 'Are you hurt?'

'No, no, nothing like that. I'm just...unsettled being away from home.'

He shifted his weight. Now he was paying Amarah, he could direct her flight. An idea struck him, and he spoke before he gave it any thought. 'Moroda. It is okay. Anahrik and I are travelling on Amarah's ship. I will tell her to drop you and your sister back. In Niversai. If you want to go home.'

'W—what?'

'I smell bread inside. Come. Food will help after crying.' Palom gestured for her to enter the inn before him.

He didn't care if Anahrik disapproved. He refused to let those weaker than himself suffer. Not when he could do something about it. Too long he'd let others fend for themselves.

'There you are!' Eryn hugged Moroda as she entered the inn. 'Are you okay? You've been crying!'

'No, no...' Moroda pushed Eryn off and sat at the table where the remainder of their party had gathered, her head bowed. Palom wondered if she was trying to hide her tears.

Morgen had his back to the others and was talking to the innkeeper by the bar.

Thick slices of walnut bread with melted cheese had been set on a wide platter in the middle of the table, and Anahrik looked up from his portion to give Palom a quizzical glance. Palom returned it with a nod, then sat down and helped himself to breakfast. 'It is arranged. Amarah will provide transport.'

'That seemed easy?' Anahrik spoke around a mouthful of bread.

'We will take Moroda and Eryn. Drop them at Niversai.' He glanced at Morgen. 'Probably the soldier, too.' He kept a wary gaze on Kohl. He'd half-hoped the Arillian would have left, but he seemed part of their peculiar group.

'Sounds good.' Anahrik shoved another slice into his mouth and chewed.

'Where...are you and Anahrik going?' Moroda asked, her voice small.

Palom saw no downside to being truthful. 'Berel.'

Her eyes widened at that. 'The city of mages! Is it...is it because of the dragon stone?' She glanced hesitantly towards Kohl, who said nothing as he sipped from a tall glass of water.

Palom hadn't expected her to be so sharp. The children of noble families and royalty rarely had wits between them. Though he was impressed, he wasn't about to talk about the *Valta Forinja*.

Anahrik coughed, though it only added to the awkwardness instead of distracting from it.

'Is...our own business.' He took a large bite of bread, more so he couldn't talk than out of hunger.

'I've always wanted to go there,' Moroda said, staring wistfully out the window.

'Ro, don't you dare start getting *more* ideas. Look how terrible your last one was! Now we're in the middle of nowhere and reliant on strangers!' Eryn snapped.

'My last idea stopped us from getting burned alive in Niversai by a rogue dragon!' Moroda's voice had risen an octave.

'We *need* to go home!' Eryn hissed.

'To what? An empty building? Probably burned? No coin to our name?'

'And Berel will have that waiting for us? Don't be so ridiculous.' Eryn tried to pull Moroda away from the table, her own voice rising.

Moroda snatched her arm away from her sister. 'Morgen

is still here!' She jerked her chin towards the bar, though she lowered her voice again. 'I don't want to go back with *him*! To be arrested!'

Eryn scowled, but didn't argue.

Palom wasn't the only one watching—Anahrik and Kohl were both staring—and Eryn's face was getting flushed.

Palom glanced at Anahrik. 'Moroda. Your sister is trying to protect you. Like I do same for Anahrik.'

Anahrik shrugged. 'We're basically brothers.'

'Yes. You are like annoying little brother I have to save all of time.' Palom shook his head, though he allowed a smile to linger on his face.

Anahrik gasped in mock affront.

Kohl chuckled and busied himself with his hat, smoothing it out before putting it on his head. He said, 'There are worse things to argue about, Moroda, Eryn. You should make peace with your kin.'

Before Palom could tell the Arillian to keep his nose out of it, Morgen returned to the table, a grin on his face. When he noticed the tension, it slid off. 'What's happened?'

'Palom was generously explaining how he's commissioned Amarah to fly us back to Niversai,' Eryn said between gritted teeth. 'We're going home.'

Moroda opened her mouth to respond, but said nothing at Eryn's glare.

'Oh. That's...useful,' Morgen said. He'd had a slice of bread in his hand, but he let it drop back to the plate.

Palom wondered what the soldier was thinking. Surely Morgen should be enthusiastic about being able to return to his post. Not wishing to put the young man on the spot, he and the others ate in silence.

Just as they were finishing, the innkeeper returned, carrying a large wicker hamper with both hands. Resting on the white linen on the lid were several bread rolls, still hot from the oven and dripping with butter.

Morgen passed them out while Palom inspected the hamper's contents—it was loaded with loaves of bread, cheese wheels, salted meat and fish, several large potatoes, a handful of green onions, two small sacks; one of rice, the other of beans, three cloves of garlic, a wedge of butter laced with red berries, and springs of scented herbs wrapped with twine. There were also several glass bottles wrapped in leather and sealed with corks—filled with water or wine, perhaps, or cold tea.

'Thank ye kindly again.' The innkeeper shook Morgen's hand. 'Safe travels. Let's hope no more towns are attacked by dragons. Would hate this to be the start of something bigger.'

Palom couldn't stop himself from interjecting. 'Dragons do *not* behave like this. It is one time thing. I am sure.'

The innkeeper shrank away from him. 'I didn't mean nothin' by that. I just hope you're right.'

Keen to get away, Palom helped Morgen carry the hamper out of the inn, and the group made their way back through town.

Morgen once again spoke for the party at the village gates, and a few moments later, they entered the woodland beyond.

Anahrik carried the pair's plethora of weaponry on his shoulders, blades clinking together inside the satchel. Moroda and her sister followed Anahrik, though they spoke with each other in low tones. Palom managed to hear the occasional sentence, but tried not to eavesdrop too much on the pair. It was clear they were both deeply uncomfortable and unsure of themselves.

'I can hardly believe Amarah stayed out here all night.

How cold it must have been.' Eryn drew her woollen cloak tightly around herself.

Moroda replied, 'She looks like she knows how to handle herself.'

Palom turned away, glancing at Kohl who brought up the rear. The Arillian had kept to himself, speaking only when spoken to. He certainly didn't trust him.

The sky pirate cared about money, that was obvious.

But Palom had no idea what Kohl cared for. Arillians rarely travelled alone. Was his presence in Niversai a coincidence? Was he in league with Aciel and the other Arillians who'd left with soldiers? Surely he'd have gone with them, if that had been the case.

And he'd killed a dragon. Taken its stone...

'This is what you've been sorting out all night? This hunka wood don't look like it'd get off the ground!' Anahrik said when they reached the clearing.

Amarah was clearing away the last of her fire. She balled up the rag in her hand and threw it at Anahrik none-too-gently. 'You can fly *yourself* the whole way there unless you keep your damned attitude in check!'

Ignoring her retort to his partner, Palom held up the hamper. 'Breakfast?'

'Sounds good. Ship's ready to fly.' Amarah took a buttered bread roll from the top of the hamper, now cool after the walk through the trees, and shoved it into her mouth. 'Skinned a rabbit last night. Of course nothing beats fresh bread first thing in the morning!' She wiped away butter and grease from her chin with the back of her hand. When she lowered her arm, she seemed to take in everyone for the first time. 'What's this? Everyone coming to say bye?'

Palom said, 'We will take Moroda, Eryn, and Morgen to Niversai.'

'Excuse me?'

He straightened his back and repeated, 'We will drop Moroda, Eryn, and Morgen at Niversai.'

'What? They ain't paid for that!'

'We are *going* to Niversai. It is on way to Berel.'

'You have my money, Amarah,' Moroda said. She stood beside Palom, chin raised in defiance. 'The florins you took from the cell.'

'Finders keepers, Goldstone. You ain't paid me anything.'

Palom let out a low growl. 'Niversai is *on way*. If necessary, I will give extra florins. But is not necessary, really. Is it?'

Amarah's scowl told him exactly what she thought of that. She looked past Palom and Moroda to the others. 'Oh, and I suppose I have to make space for the Arillian, too?'

Kohl tipped his hat to her. 'I can fly myself, but I appreciate the offer. I will accompany you.'

Palom wasn't sure whether Kohl missed Amarah's venomous tone, or simply chose to ignore it. 'You are coming too? You are not following your Arillian colleagues?'

'I seek dragon stones, not Aciel. There are many such stones in Berel, which I had not realised. And I'm sure you would prefer *not* to be burned by another dragon, Amarah?'

Amarah threw up her hands and whirled around. 'Fine. Everyone who's coming, get on.'

Palom's lip curled. The dragon stones were essential to forging the *Valta Forinja*. There was no chance he'd allow Kohl to take a single one.

Moroda, Eryn, and Morgen boarded first. With a final nod to Anahrik, Palom followed, making his way quickly up the steps carved into the airship's side, and clambering onto the deck. *Khanna* was sparsely furnished, no doubt to keep weight down and allow for greater speed and agility.

The raised deck behind the main mast—Palom thought it was called the quarterdeck—held the ship's controls. Set into a raised platform and covered by a thick, dark fabric, the quarterdeck looked the most comfortable part of the ship. Crates and boxes were littered behind the controls to suffice as seating. Moroda drifted towards the controls, fingers trailing along the large, spoked wheel.

Palom made his way towards her, wedging the hamper between two large crates that had been welded to the floor.

Anahrik, meanwhile, had raced along the deck, past the main sail, and come to a stop at the ship's pointed bow, arms on the raised wooden sides as he peered over the edge.

Parts of the exposed deck were blackened and splintered from either the dragon or the landing, and unease crept along Palom's spine. Amarah had claimed the ship was ready to fly, despite his own reservations. Then again, the sky pirate was unlikely to state her only means of travel was sky-worthy if it wasn't.

He stared out towards the forest, now light in the morning sun.

Kohl was in the air moments later, hovering a short distance above, presumably scouting the surroundings. Anahrik transformed and flew straight up to meet the Arillian. Unable to hover as Kohl could, Anahrik instead circled widely, rising and falling in altitude.

By the time the two landed back on deck, everyone was present and eager to get going.

'Sapora not joining us?' Morgen asked Amarah, glancing around.

'He's below,' Amarah replied, rubbing sleep from her right eye. 'We'll head east to Niversai, drop off you three. Then we'll follow the Flynn River south into Ranski, all the way to Berel. *Khanna will* fly, but she'll be no racer 'til I get her properly repaired. I've lost half my power, and I don't wanna push her. She runs silent as stone at least, so that's something to be said for my engines. If the weather's good, we'll be in Berel in three days.'

Palom nodded. Three days to Berel. It was a good speed. It gave him time to think things through, prepare himself for the challenges ahead.

Amarah went below deck to get the engines going.

'I hope that Varkain sleeps for the whole journey. I don't like having one on board,' Anahrik said once Amarah had disappeared, folding his arms behind his head. 'Looks clear from up there. We shouldn't have anything to worry about. After that dragon attack, I doubt anything will be in the skies for a while.'

The engines below kicked into life with a violent shake, the ship's side and main sails fanned out, and the propellers began to turn with a low thrum that even Palom could hardly hear. He steadied his gait as the airship lurched underfoot.

They were heading towards the *Valta Forinja*.

Whatever Aciel was up to, he would be ready.

He would not allow the Arillians to attack his home. Not if he had anything to say about it.

10

The bustle aboard *Khanna* reminded Moroda of market day in Niversai. Although on a much smaller scale, the efficiency and brusqueness with which Amarah moved was reminiscent of traders and merchants barging their way through the cobbled streets, half-bullying passers-by into buying their wares.

Eryn was overwhelmed, hugging her shawl close to her face and leaning away from everyone except Morgen—who probably was the closest reminder of home for her. Something familiar and stable.

Moroda, on the other hand, loved the excitement. It was new and thrilling.

'Leaving Burian forest!' Amarah shouted. One calloused hand rested on the steering wheel, the other on one of the myriad levers in the control panel. 'Kohl, you see anything?'

Moroda stared up at the Arillian, who hovered a short way above the ship. He lifted his wings and caught the wind, gaining height until he was just a speck circling in the distance.

'Guess it's all clear then,' Amarah muttered, steering her ship due east and hugging the treeline. She glanced at the gathered passengers, and Moroda struggled not to flinch under her cool gaze. 'My weapons bay was badly burned by that dragon. We'll be flying low and slow, keeping outta sight, seeing as we can't fight. Kohl and Anahrik should give us warning enough to keep out of danger. I expect you all to pitch in where and when I say, and we'll get to Berel all the sooner. Everyone got it?'

'We understand,' Morgen said, raising his hand to salute before catching himself and dropping his arm. 'How long until we reach Niversai?'

Amarah shrugged. 'At this speed, an hour? Far cry from last night at full thrust.'

Morgen nodded and sat down on one of the wooden crates near the control panel. He lifted the hamper, pulled out one of the bottles provided by the inn, and offered it to Eryn.

Eryn shook her head and shivered, wrapping her shawl tightly around her neck.

He took a deep swig instead. 'Might as well sit down, Eryn. Can't do anything until we get back to the city.'

Moroda wondered if he was leading up to talking about re-arresting her when they returned, and she wanted to keep away from him. Eryn had dark circles under her eyes, and her hair had turned ashen from the dragon smoke, despite her rinsing it several times. 'Ryn, shall we put our things in the crew quarters?'

'Good idea. Plus it'll be warmer down there!'

'We're heading below deck!' Moroda thought it best to tell Amarah rather than just wandering away.

The sky pirate grunted in reply, which suited Moroda just fine.

She tried to ignore Sapora's stare when she and Eryn crossed the deck to the hatch, and couldn't help but shiver.

It was indeed warmer below, though noisier, and far

more cramped. Eryn led the way, heading down the narrow metal steps and through the door which ran above the engines. Three cabins led off to the right and two to the left of a short hallway, and they had to duck as they cautiously tried each door.

Both doors on the left were locked.

The remaining doors were open, tiny cabins waiting behind each, and Eryn checked all three before selecting the largest one. A pair of bunk beds had been built into the wooden wall opposite the door—Moroda suspected they may have started out life as shelves—and there was a wash basin. The ceiling sloped at such an angle that there was only room for a small square crate, which served more as a seat than anything else.

A far cry from their formerly luxurious bedrooms at home, or any of the inns they'd stayed at throughout their youth.

Moroda could see it was clean enough—probably wasn't used much—though Eryn fought to keep her lip from curling.

Her sister sat on the lower bunk with a heavy sigh, pulled her satchel off and rested it by her feet. Moroda put her bag on the floor next to her sister's and sat on the crate, hunching over to avoid hitting her head on the ceiling. 'Are you okay, Ryn?'

'With the threat of attack by dragon or Arillian looming over our heads?' Eryn raised an eyebrow, some of her scathing humour back.

'All the more reason to stay with Amarah and the others. Go to Berel. This sort of thing doesn't just *happen*. The more we know, the more we can find out...well, I think the safer we'll be. I know it sounds silly.'

Moroda suppressed the urge to chew her lip in obvious unease.

Eryn signed and rubbed her eyes. 'Oh, so staying with thieves and pirates and…and…*snakes* is better? Ro, I don't want to keep arguing with you about this.'

'Nor do I! Please, Ryn. A quick trip away, like when we were children.' Moroda grasped Eryn's hands. 'I want to learn more about the dragons. Their crystals. The Arillians. If change is coming, we need to be ready. *This* is what we've been hoping for. These people have seen an opportunity. We should take it, too.'

'Hoping for change, yes, but not like this.' Eryn shook her head. 'I know things have been hard. You think I *want* to keep mothering you? Telling you we can't do this or that?'

Moroda dropped her gaze. Even before their father's death, Eryn had been the responsible one. Now they only had each other left, her sister's behaviour had intensified. 'Ryn…'

'Dragons above, I wish we could go back to how things were. To eat and ride and dance and shop and play and have no cares at all save choosing the best tea to go with our meal, or which flowers to have delivered that week.' Eryn laughed bitterly. She pulled her hands away from Moroda's, balling them into fists.

'But Palom said he'd—'

'We *don't* ask for help, Moroda. We've always had what we wanted.'

'But we need help now. Father's gone and—'

'I *know* he's gone.' Eryn took a breath and lowered her voice. 'Look at us. Relying on charity. Like peasants.'

'Eryn!'

'If I knew something in Berel would get us back to how things were. Something that would get rid of the fear. The uncertainty. If I *knew* for certain it was the right thing…'

Moroda had rarely seen Eryn so low, so vulnerable. She'd been so concerned with the dragon and their new companions that she hadn't put much thought on how her sister was taking it all. Eryn had been putting on a brave face in front of these people, and it was only now in this tiny cabin that she'd been able to let it all drop.

'We're no good at running a stall,' Eryn continued, her voice so low that Moroda had to lean forward to catch the words. 'With winter on the way, all our sales would have dried up. We were running it into the ground. *I* was running it into the ground. It kept us afloat during summer, but...' Tears gathered at the corners of her eyes.

'That's not true. It was one of your better ideas! We would have pulled through, we *would* have!' Moroda almost shook Eryn by the shoulders. Eryn was always the positive one, the hard-working, resourceful one who could think her way out of any problem.

'We were running out of jewellery. Linen. Everything. We didn't have enough saved to cover us during the winter season. Let alone buy more to keep us going. Dragons above, I was so stupid to think we'd be okay alone.'

Seeing Eryn so worried ate at her.

Eryn wiped her face, red eyes glistening with tears.

'You should get some rest, Ryn. A nap will help.' She daren't say anything about pushing for Berel. Her sister didn't need that. Not right now. 'I'll go back on deck so you have some space.'

'But what if something happens? I don't trust any of them. Well, perhaps Morgen has some honour.'

Moroda didn't want to remind Eryn that Morgen had been the one who'd arrested her, that she trusted him perhaps least of all, save Sapora. 'I'll be fine. Nothing will happen while we're in the air. Not if Palom has anything to say about it. Besides, it's better to keep them in sight, isn't it?'

Eryn frowned, but didn't argue.

'You saved me from the dungeon. Let me look after you

for a while.' She kissed Eryn on the forehead. 'We'll get through this together, Ryn. Promise.'

~

LEAVING Eryn to nap in the cramped cabin, Moroda returned to the deck. Although she *did* want to keep an eye on the others, she mostly wanted to enjoy the views above Corhaven while she could. Luxury airship cruises had been some of her favourite childhood memories. As she came up the stairs, she saw Palom, Morgen, and Sapora lingering near the front of the ship. Morgen's hand lingered near the hilt of his sword, while Palom frowned at the Varkain with folded arms and a furrowed brow.

She wondered whether Morgen would try and arrest Sapora again, or if he had more sense than that.

Wishing to avoid any part of their conflict, Moroda made her way to the ship's controls, where Amarah steered *Khanna* alone.

Despite Eryn's reservations, Moroda had no trouble approaching Amarah now they were outside of a locked cell. The sky pirate hadn't *actually* hurt her, and in fact had helped them more than anything else. Sapora claimed she was a murderer, but Moroda didn't want to judge people based on what others said. Anahrik had claimed Kohl's kind brought storms and devastation, and Moroda hadn't seen any truth in that.

Besides, it was an opportunity to talk about the florins. She cleared her throat, deciding to open the conversation with praise. 'When did you purchase this airship?'

'Seven years ago.'

'Wow, it looks so new! You must have maintained it very well.'

Amarah turned from the wheel to look at Moroda, suspicion evident in her narrowed eyes. 'You wanna buy it off me?'

'No, no, nothing like that. But I would be curious to have my own one day.' Moroda looked around, trying to pick something neutral to comment on. 'A ship of this size would be perfect, I think.'

'Hah. You Goldstones are all the same. Throw coins at whatever you wanna claim for yourself.'

'I...I didn't mean any offence.' Moroda's cheeks flushed. 'I only meant to say...you're so lucky to have all this. The freedom it grants you.'

'Ain't nothing lucky about it. Didn't wake up one morning to find this ship sitting outside, did I? Damned hard work. *That's* how I got there. You ever done a day's work in your life, Goldstone?'

Moroda lowered her gaze. Amarah's use of the slang term for nobility stung, especially because she wasn't considered one anymore, and her initial bravery began to dwindle.

'You even know how to clean anything properly? Or your servants do everything for you while you never lifted a finger?' Amarah whirled round to focus on the wheel and thrust the engines forward, jolting the ship. 'I got *Khanna* with blood, sweat, and gold. A whole double-crown I paid for it. The only one I've ever seen, and I paid a seller for this ship. I could have lived off that money for *months*.'

Moroda decided not to respond lest she received another scathing reply.

Amarah's blunt words hit home again—*the only double-crown she'd ever seen*. They were the most valuable of all Linaria's currency, yet she and Eryn had regularly seen them when their father returned from his trips away. He had once brought back a tea box from somewhere deep in Ranski— carved out of red wood, embellished with the jewels of the

Samolen, and ornately decorated in gold. It had been a gift for them, but when their money began to dwindle, Moroda had traded it for six double-crowns at one of Niversai's auction houses.

The money had lasted them four weeks.

Amarah continued, 'Learning to fly was the best thing I ever did. Could leave whenever I wanted, go wherever I wanted. Never had to rely on no one again.'

Moroda listened quietly, internalising everything the sky pirate said. Amarah's strength was her self-reliance and unwillingness to compromise. She showed no fear of anything or anyone, not even of Sapora.

For all her big dreams and lofty aspirations, Moroda was helpless in the best of situations.

All she had known was a life of ease and luxury, where every need was catered to. Her world had collapsed when her family's income disappeared, and she'd relied on Eryn's quick-thinking to keep them from starving.

It was clear she didn't know how to cope, no matter what she said to convince herself or Eryn.

She had to do *something*, so she decided to try again for those florins. 'Amarah? Do you remember, back in the cell in Niversai, there was a loose stone slab on the floor?'

'These florins *again*? Why d'you keep going on about 'em?' Amarah asked, shifting her back to Moroda as she swooped low over a hillside, a group of pigeons taking to the wing in fright.

Moroda took a steadying breath. 'I...I hid them there when I was arrested. It's all the coin I had left.'

Amarah straightened. 'Those three florins? Your *only* money?'

Moroda wasn't sure she liked the fact she now had Amarah's full attention, but she was pleased she had finally spoken about it. At least Eryn wouldn't chide her for not asking for them back. 'All I had left, yes.' Moroda confirmed with a nod.

Amarah burst into hysterical laughter and *Khanna* juddered when she lost her grip on the wheel. 'A Goldstone with *three florins*? What has Linaria come to? Maybe the world really is about to end!'

Moroda blinked and lowered her head. She was not used to being made a mockery of, and had no idea how to deal with such a vicious response. 'So, you'll give them back?'

'Don't be stupid, girl. The florins are mine. Like I told you.'

Moroda's eyes widened in shock. 'What? But—'

'You Goldstones make me laugh. You want money, you damn well better work for it. What's a few florins to you, anyway? Pocket money? No, that's ridiculous. You probably got a couple of *crowns* in pocket money, didn't you?'

'But you *have* to give them back?'

Amarah turned to face Moroda fully, one hand gripping the wheel to keep the ship under control. 'Come and make me.'

Moroda wanted to approach but was unsure what to do. She wasn't about to try and hurt the other woman.

'Well? I'm waiting.' Amarah wasn't smiling any more.

'But...But, I...But that's *not fair!*' Moroda had always hated conflict, and she actively avoided confrontations. Her mouth went dry and her heart raced, and she regretted ever mentioning the subject.

'Not fair? Then sit down and shut up about your florins. You were born never having to worry about food or clothes or money. I didn't have that luxury. How's that fair on me? It ain't! I didn't expect anyone to pick me up every time I made a mistake. If I didn't sort myself out, I didn't live to see tomorrow.'

'What about your parents?'

'Never had 'em.' She turned her attention to her ship and adjusted her sails. 'Everything I have is off my own back. Everything I've learned is from my own lessons. I don't have time to babysit entitled, lazy shits who can't take care of themselves.'

Moroda felt the heat of rage in her belly as the pirate insulted her yet again. 'I'm not lazy.'

'Really?'

'I'm *not*! And I'm not sorry I was born into a family that had more than yours. That wasn't my fault! I didn't choose it! No more than you chose yours! You don't have to be so rude all the time or act like I'm ungrateful!' Moroda's voice shook with emotions she couldn't place.

Amarah cackled again, 'All right, calm down Goldstone. I'm glad this was a wake-up call for you.'

'Losing my father was a wake-up call!' Heat rose to the back of her eyes, but Moroda didn't want tears to spill, not in front of Amarah. 'Everything I've ever known has gone! It's just Eryn left. Just Eryn and those three florins. Now there's an army being built by an Arillian? My city's half burned down? My home! Dragons are attacking people! I'm trying to adapt to this new life and I'm trying to take care of myself. You don't need to make all that even harder!'

Amarah said nothing, and while Moroda was stunned by her own outburst, her words continued, a torrent that she couldn't stop. 'What if you lost *Khanna*? What if you lost the ability to fly a ship? What if you lost everything you had and were put in a world where everything and everyone was against you all the time? I'm sorry I don't know how to deal with that as well as you want me to!'

Tears flowed down her cheeks. 'Keep my florins, then, if you don't think I deserve them. Eryn and I will find a way to make it work. I'll make sure we learn the lessons you did, and know what to do.'

When she finished, her whole body trembled. It was a wonder her explosion hadn't woken Eryn.

'All right. Glad to see you actually have some fight in you, girl.' Amarah grinned at her, sunlight catching the scar on her cheek and her unkempt hair. 'I was waiting to see what you were made of. Keep thinking like that and you might just get through life without your family's money.'

Moroda angrily wiped away the tears from her face, grateful Amarah had spared her another insult.

On the one hand, Moroda admired Amarah's confidence and ability to fly an airship with such skill, but on the other, she detested how little she cared for anyone, or their feelings.

Moroda's lip trembled as she tried to steady her breathing. She looked back to the front of the ship, but the others weren't paying her any attention, thank Rhea. She had been so determined to do the right thing, to make sure everything would be fine, to stop the bad things happening, yet all her attempts seemed futile.

Perhaps *she* should have burned that night instead.

Perhaps Linaria would have been better off without a silly girl with no idea about the real world and how it worked.

Moroda took a deep breath. If she wasn't doing the right thing, at least she was doing *something*. Eryn wanted to return to Niversai, to keep doing what they'd always done. Probably while the last of their money ran out. She could understand why her sister wanted to do that. It was familiar, even if it was doomed.

Outside Niversai was a world of unknowns.

As far as Moroda was concerned, there was no chance they'd last in Niversai another year except by some miracle.

More than likely, Arillians or dragons would destroy everything, and it'd be too late for them.

Palom and the others were going to Berel. The city of mages, who studied—if not outright worshipped—dragons. And dragons seemed to be at the heart of the change in Linaria.

Digging her fingers into her palms in a woeful attempt to prevent more tears, she walked away from Amarah and peered over the side of the ship, hoping the greenery below would soothe her frustration.

She'd always done what Eryn wanted. What her sister thought was best.

Eryn wanted to return to Niversai—whatever was left of it.

But *she* wanted to go to Berel.

Moroda had never needed to question anything she had done, her life had always been relatively set. Working hard hadn't ever factored into it, just as Amarah had accused. Yet, here she was, willing to do more, and it was being thrown in her face.

Minutes ticked past, and her emotions settled somewhat, taken away by the soft breeze on her face.

'We're coming up to Niversai now, if you wanna have a look off port side,' Amarah called, catching her attention.

Moroda crossed to the other side of the deck, where Anahrik stood, having returned from scouting. Blazing sunshine filtered through the thin clouds, lighting up Corhaven below. Niversai sat near the horizon, perhaps five leagues away. Even from such a distance, Moroda saw the smouldering rooftops from the dragon attack the night before.

The stone of the outer city wall was blackened, along with Rosecastle's turrets and surrounding roofs. Stone crumbled, wood charred, and anything less hardy was simply...gone. Even the Imperial flags, which had once flown proudly in the sun, were now black, or had completely vanished.

The charred hulls of airships that had been caught in the flames lay blackened on the ground surrounding the city, like corpses.

Her stomach tightened.

Streams of people, carts, and horses flooded out of the city gates. There were a few members of the Imperial Guard mounted on horseback, carrying flags and banners high to signal the way as they wound past farmer's fields and crops.

No doubt they were heading to nearby towns. It wouldn't be long before there was an influx of people heading to the capital to help rebuild.

Surrounded by naked, smoking trees, Niversai's natural beauty was tarnished in the wake of the attack. Moroda could not distinguish people from this distance, but it was a large crowd; hundreds, if not thousands strong.

Her mouth went dry as she watched the citizens carry their only belongings in search of safety elsewhere. Moroda knew if she hadn't perished in the blaze, she and Eryn might well be among those now trying to escape Niversai.

'Are we there?' Eryn rubbed one eye as she crossed the deck to reach Moroda.

'Did Amarah's call wake you?'

'Mmhmm.' Eryn blinked and stood beside her sister. Her mouth fell open when she stared at the city that had been home. 'That...that's Niversai?'

'We were there, Ryn.' Moroda looped her arm through her sister's. She felt her shaking. 'It was *real*. 'We could have burned there.'

Eryn nudged her sister back. 'It was...probably a once in a lifetime experience. A freak occurrence. Won't happen again.'

Eryn's voice trembled as much as her body.

'Freak occurrence? You are more stupid than you look.' Sapora appeared silently, surveying Niversai with a deep frown. 'This is the start of something great. I only hope I can understand it before the rest of Linaria is destroyed by dragon flame.'

Palom joined them, his footsteps shaking the deck as he approached.

'I agree with Varkain. Linaria is disturbed, and dragons are in middle of it. Corhaven has fallen to this, I fear. Perhaps we should go to Val Sharis instead.'

'*Khanna* wouldn't make it across the sea in this condition,' Amarah replied, her voice clipped. 'I'm going as far as Berel. Then you're on your own. Moroda. You want me to drop you here? Or you wanna be closer to that stench?'

It was at that moment that Moroda caught the scent of something foul burning on the wind, and she wrinkled her nose, eyes watering. She didn't want to think about the charred bodies that caused it.

She stared at the people fleeing Niversai, at the wreckage of the city itself. Everything that had once been home was now torn down and destroyed.

'I want to go to the city of mages.' Moroda was hardly aware of her lips moving. It didn't sound like she was speaking with her own voice.

'Ro!' Eryn gasped.

Moroda looked at Amarah, determined. 'Please. Take us with you to Berel, too. We'll chip in however you want us to. Teach me what you want. I'll listen. I'll learn.'

Amarah raised an eyebrow.

'Ro! We have to go home!'

'Look at the city, Eryn. Home's gone.' She was surprised how flat her voice sounded. How final.

Eryn spluttered, looking around. 'Morgen! You have to

return to your post in Niversai, don't you? An officer of the Imperial Guard can't just...just...*run away*?'

Morgen tore his gaze away from the city at Eryn's words, his cheeks red. 'I...I have a duty to the Imperial Guard, true. But...perhaps learning about this threat...perhaps learning how to *prevent* it happening again, would be a better use of my time. They will only be on damage control now, anyway.'

'You don't wanna check that with your captain?' Amarah goaded.

'Returning to the city as blind as my peers won't help anyone. If I come back with answers, that'll help us defend the city. Might even get a promotion out of it, too.'

'How noble,' Anahrik said.

Amarah snorted. 'You're all putting a lot of hope on Berel. What if you don't get nothing?'

'Then at least we'll have tried,' Moroda whispered.

11

P alom sat at the prow of the airship, eyes unfocussed, thoughts swirling. Everywhere he went, destruction seemed to follow.

He and Anahrik had travelled to Corhaven for trade and nothing more. Now it was as if they were being pulled back into the jaws of battle by Rhea herself.

To think they were travelling on the same airship as a Varkain and an Arillian! It would never happen if they were in Val Sharis, and he wondered what Lathri would have to say about his choice of companions. She'd probably laugh and poke fun at his—

Movement overhead.

Palom's thoughts shattered and he glanced up in time to see a falcon diving towards them in full stoop.

Anahrik.

Something was wrong.

Before he could scan their surroundings for the threat, Anahrik landed on deck in a blaze of light and feathers, hastily transforming. 'Arillians!' His breathing was ragged from panic and exertion. 'Arillian scouts ahead! We've gotta get out the sky!'

Palom immediately drew his broadsword and looked for Kohl, but the Arillian was too high or too far from the ship, and he couldn't see him. Did Kohl have something to do with the sudden appearance of the scouts?

If those damned storm-bringers were onto them...

Kohl might not have done anything wrong—yet—but Palom didn't want to drop his guard around any of them. Especially if these ones were part of Aciel's band. Given the rarity of Arillians on the continent, he'd put money on them being Aciel's scouts.

'Great.' Amarah snarled. 'Caught out in the open and with *Khanna* damaged, too.' She tried to accelerate—evidently her default response to a threat—but the ship juddered and dark smoke rose from *Khanna's* left engine. With another sickening lurch, *Khanna* dropped several feet.

'Dragons above, I can't outfly them like this!' Amarah lowered her throttles and returned the airship to a quiet, slow flight.

'Just my damned luck!'

Sapora cracked his knuckles as he stood up.

'Fantastic, I've not killed an Arillian in years.'

Palom glared at the Varkain. 'We do not want to kill anyone. If it *is* Aciel somewhere near...We do not want his attention on us. We defend ourselves if they come. That is all.'

Sapora scowled back at Palom. 'I'll do as I please, Ittallan. And I defend myself in one way only.'

Palom lifted his sword, the tip pointing at Sapora's throat. 'Not at risk of this ship.'

Trust the Varkain to want blood. The snakes were always after a fight, always looking to spill blood, even if the situation could be avoided.

'I ain't putting *Khanna* in danger again. Another fight and she won't fly at all!' Amarah yelled. 'Can we avoid them,

Anahrik? How far are they? Where's Kohl? Can't he do something?'

The young Ittallan held his thighs, doubled over as he tried to get his breath back. 'Doubt it, they're only a few fields away, all of them armed and armoured. Reckon they're up for a fight. I dunno about Kohl.'

'Perfect.' Amarah picked up her scythe. 'Looks like this might be a short trip. Knew it would be too much to ask to get to Berel before being spotted by *something*.'

Palom rounded on her. 'This negativity will not help.'

Amarah let out a short bark of laughter. 'Ain't being negative if it's true.'

He shook his head, about to retort, when a flash of movement off the ship's port side caught his attention. 'Arillian!' His warning came out half choked when he recognised who approached them.

Kohl's arrival was preceded by a burst of freezing wind that set the hairs on the back of Palom's neck on edge. Palom watched the Arillian land on deck a few moments later, arms raised in defence the moment Kohl spotted his drawn sword.

'Hold! Put your weapons down, please. I will deal with my kin. It may not have anything to do with Aciel.' He frowned, lips pursed as if calculating something. 'Amarah. Get the ship low and out of sight. Land, if possible. They haven't seen you yet.'

'What are they doing?' Palom demanded, but Kohl took to the wing and flew rapidly in the opposite direction without replying.

Palom glared at Kohl as he flew off, convinced it was some kind of Arillian trick.

More than likely they'd join forces and attack the ship. He caught Anahrik's eye and raised a quizzical eyebrow.

Without any words exchanged between them, Anahrik nodded.

'I'm gonna follow him.' Anahrik leapt into the air, transforming again in another flash of white light, and flew after Kohl.

Amarah immediately folded in her remaining sails, and brought *Khanna* down to land on the edge of a wheat field, using a line of conifers for cover. The engines whirred quietly as they stopped, and thankfully no smoke rose to give away their position. 'We'll wait here. Everyone get under cover.' She beckoned them over, crouching down between two of the crates behind her steering controls.

'You don't trust Kohl?' Morgen asked Palom, his voice hushed.

'I do not. Anahrik is not sure,' Palom said, 'but I want to find out. Morgen, come with me. Let us see what we can learn from ground if they are this close to us.'

'Wait, you ain't gonna leave my ship undefended are you!' Amarah hissed.

'You can fight. You said yourself. And you have Varkain here. We will not be long.' He didn't like leaving Sapora with the others, but if he had a chance to find out more about the Arillians, he had to take that opportunity. It wasn't as if Kohl was forthright with what he knew.

Besides, Sapora was unlikely to destroy his easiest chance at getting out of Corhaven.

He didn't wait for Amarah to object further, and hurried away.

Moroda and Eryn would be fine, he was sure.

Morgen followed on Palom's heels as they clambered down the side of the ship and ran along the edge of the field. 'Wait, Palom! You aren't...you aren't seriously going to fight these Arillians are you?'

'I do not fight unless I have to,' Palom replied. He wasn't

sure if the young soldier was cowardly or had a stronger sense of self-preservation than he'd realised. 'You chased after me. After dragon. Are you afraid of these Arillians?'

'Of course! If you aren't, you should be.'

Palom grumbled in response. He didn't think it would come to a fight. Not if he kept out of sight. But he wanted to know what Kohl was up to, and he couldn't do that without getting closer.

Wary of sudden movements from above, Palom was grateful for the tall wheat to keep them somewhat hidden as he sprinted away from *Khanna*. It took barely a minute of hard running—crossing two fields, mud tracking up his legs —before he spotted the Arillians hovering thirty or so feet in the air. Kohl was easily distinguishable with his hat and travelling cloak, set apart from the others.

Palom flattened himself to the ground, hiding in the tall stalks, eyes locked on Kohl and the group of Arillians. He was glad he'd brought his sword.

In unison, the Arillians faced Kohl, who slowly dropped to the ground.

Acutely aware *Khanna* was hidden nearby with only a line of trees for cover, Palom steadied his breathing. There was a good chance they hadn't spotted the airship, else it'd have been destroyed already, and he hoped they'd keep their focus on Kohl.

Storm-bringers.

Arillians were an exiled race that had brought destruction to the face of Linaria. No good could ever come of them being on the mainland.

He held his breath as the Arillians descended, landing in a loose circle surrounding Kohl.

'Dragons above, you're fast!' Morgen panted heavily as he caught up. He sank to the ground, keeping his head low. 'Should we get closer? I can't hear 'em.'

In response, Palom crept forward as quietly as he could, trying to get within earshot.

Six Arillians.

Palom wasn't sure they could defend against that many, even with Amarah, Sapora, Morgen and himself fighting together.

Worse, they were all in armour, just as Anahrik had warned. Evidently, only the fighting classes had chosen to visit Corhaven.

Palom came as close as he dared, close enough he could see their faces in detail. One dark-haired Arillian stood apart from the rest. He wore less armour than the others, his stance more relaxed. Palom held in a snarl at the brazenness. These Arillians were in a foreign land, where their kind were shunned at best and openly attacked at worst. How dare they saunter about as if they were royalty.

'Kohl. It's been a while. We did not expect to see you in Corhaven.'

Even from several feet away, Palom heard the underlying anger in the dark-haired Arillian's tone.

'General Fogu.' Kohl kept his eyes on the ground.

Silence stretched between them. Palom tried to keep an eye out for Anahrik, but the falcon was outside his field of view. If he couldn't see him, the Arillians wouldn't be able to, either. Anahrik could be impulsive and reckless, but he wasn't fool enough to turn the Arillians' attention on himself.

'Well? Anything to report? How many dragons have you killed?' Fogu snapped.

'One, sir,' Kohl answered, and the scouting group surrounding him snickered like children.

'You've been gone three months and all you can show for yourself is *one* dragon?' Fogu snarled, his wings ruffling. 'Are you taking your orders seriously? You are aware this might be your only way back home?'

Palom leaned forward, despite himself. So Kohl *was* working for someone.

'I've been tracking their movements, sir.' Kohl raised his gaze slightly.

Palom expected the general to reprimand him, and braced for a lightning storm, but Fogu was more interested in silencing the other Arillians. They all seemed to be young and relaxed, informal, even. They were lazy in their stance, fiddling with their armour or glancing around, uninterested in the conversation between Kohl and Fogu.

Distracted.

Careless.

Perhaps they weren't the ranks of elite fighters Palom knew to bring chaos and destruction. But he wasn't going to chance getting closer. Any enemy could switch in a heart-beat, idle one moment, a threat the next. Palom shifted his weight, glad Morgen was keeping quiet, either due to his instincts or training.

'I suppose it proves you're good for little else than exile.' Fogu shook his head.

'Where is Jato? She's not with you?'

Fogu's easy demeanour shifted to steel in an instant. 'How *dare* you speak of General Jato!' He struck Kohl across the face, thunder rippling through the air.

Kohl staggered, but kept himself standing. 'I only wish to know if she is well.'

'Better than *you*, exile.'

Palom flinched at the venom in Fogu's tone.

'Who's Jato? An ally of his?' Morgen whispered.

Palom shrugged. 'They do not seem happy to hear Kohl speak of this Jato.'

Fogu circled Kohl like a cat, easily a head taller and with

broader shoulders, but Kohl didn't cower. Above them, the clouds darkened, more thunder rolling behind the grey murk like a ravenous beast waiting to be freed.

Palom's skin crawled at the electricity that crackled in the air.

This was the precursor to Arillian destruction. He tensed, ready to flee if lightning descended.

'At any rate, General Jato is not your concern. Your orders are. Not that you've been following them very well,' Fogu said, voice edged with some bubbling, violent emotion.

'There are fewer dragons in Corhaven, sir. Younger and weaker, too.'

Fogu cracked his knuckles. 'Aciel will turn the weak ones against our enemies. They have their uses. But the world is bigger than Corhaven, and we need other dragons. We *need* their stones.'

Kohl remained silent.

After holding his gaze for a long moment, Fogu shook his head. 'We received a report of a small ship seen heading in this direction. Not of the Imperial Guard. I don't suppose while tracking your elusive dragons, you happened to see anything?'

Palom narrowed his eyes.

Kohl shook his head.

'You're very sure?'

'Absolutely, sir.'

'Too much wildlife around here,' one of the scouts commented, pulling Palom's attention away from Kohl and Fogu. She seemed younger than the others, with short brown wings and matching hair. She watched a spot in the sky, fixated by a group of birds flying tightly together. Raising her left hand, she drew her fingers into her palm then released them skywards—sending a bolt of lightning shooting up into the fray. The birds cried out and scattered, and she laughed. 'After that dragon burnt down half of Niversai, there's been hardly anything in the sky. We wanna keep it that way.' She smirked at Kohl, electricity flashing in her palm. 'It belongs to *us*. Not ships.'

Palom's rage boiled. He didn't think Anahrik would have been in that group of birds, but her callous disregard for life angered his soul.

He took a step towards the Arillians when Morgen's hand on his arm steadied him. 'Morgen?'

'Sshh. No rash moves, Palom. We're outnumbered here.'

'But—'

'It'll put everyone in more danger.' Morgen's voice dropped even lower, gaze flicking towards Fogu and the other Arillians.

Although Morgen was half Palom's size, and several years younger, the soldier held firm. Palom would have fought back, his instinct was to shake off the foolish human, but he saw the sense in Morgen's words and exhaled slowly, allowing his anger to dissipate.

None of the Arillians had heard their fervent whispers, at least.

'Looks like that's about as much excitement as we're going to have. Nothing but farming fields here. Won't be long before it's a pile of ash.' Fogu mused, turning back to Kohl. He mirrored the other woman's swift hand motion, and Kohl buckled as an invisible blow struck his chest.

'Fogu...friend...' Kohl coughed.

'You have no friends here, exile.'

Despite Palom's mistrust of the Arillian, his anger rebuilt as Kohl sank to one knee in evident pain.

It wasn't a fair fight.

Outnumbered six to one, and his kin, no less.

A growl rumbled in his chest as Kohl whimpered with the strikes that followed. Bolts of lighting and cutting wind joined the fray as the other scouts released their powers on him. Thunder accompanied their attacks, rolling around the field and shaking the ground beneath Palom's feet. Sparks of lightning burst through the air, raising every hair on his arms.

'His own people are doing that!' Morgen said, mouth hanging open in disbelief.

'I want to stop them.' Palom knew it was stupid as soon as he said it.

'We can't.'

'If he dies...'

'It isn't our fault. Who knows what this means in Arillian culture.'

'In any culture, *this* is torture.'

Even several paces away, searing heat filled the air with every strike, and Palom hunkered down to protect himself. He didn't want to know how much worse it would be for Kohl.

Before he could say anything more, the lightning and thunder abruptly stopped. He froze, afraid for several heart-pounding seconds that they'd been spotted, but the Arillians had simply tired of their game. Taking to the sky, they hovered a short distance above where Kohl hunched among the wheat.

Fogu remained standing above Kohl. 'You're lucky you're a dragon slayer. Be grateful for your exile.' He spat at the ground beside Kohl, then leapt into the air with a beat of his wings. 'I wonder whether you'll ever be allowed home when it's finished.'

Kohl collapsed as the Arillians laughed, rising higher and higher until they were gone from sight and sound.

Palom rushed forward.

'Wait! They might come back!' Morgen hissed, but Palom ignored him.

'Kohl? You alive?' Palom grabbed Kohl under his arms and lifted him to his feet as gently as he could. Just because he mistrusted Arillians didn't mean he enjoyed seeing cruelty.

Kohl's breaths came short and sharp. 'You...saw?'

'Heard whole conversation. Want to tell us who Jato is? Fogu? Your relationship to Aciel?' Although his kin clearly had treated Kohl poorly, the whole encounter threw up more questions as far as Palom was concerned. 'This sounds like war.'

'I'm touched...you came to check on me.' Kohl coughed, his breaths spluttering.

'We *felt* that thunder. Are you all right?' Morgen came forward, hesitant, gaze darting around like a nervous deer.

'What makes you think...I wouldn't be?' Kohl winced.

'Arillians...you can't be too careful,' Morgen said.

Kohl picked up his hat from the ground and dusted it off. Placing it securely back on his head, he said, 'I know my people are...not loved. No more than the Varkain are. And... even I am shunned by them.'

'Why?' The question burned Palom. 'What did you do?'

'It is of no consequence. Things are as they are. They're gone, now. Let's move on.' Kohl coughed several times before his breathing calmed.

'I do not like that you are not telling us full story.'

Kohl shrugged. 'Neither are you. None of us are. The ship is okay, correct? Let us continue.'

'What about the Arillians? Where did they go?' Morgen asked.

'Deeper into Corhaven, I imagine. They won't bother us if we make haste,' Kohl replied, brushing down his clothes and adjusting his heavy cloak.

'Sounds like dragons are the bigger threat to our towns and villages.' Morgen's gaze continued to rove the skies, and Palom wondered if the soldier believed his own words.

'*Khanna* is this way?' Kohl hobbled towards the line of trees, his limp far more pronounced following the Arillians' attacks.

'You aren't flying?' Morgen asked, watching the dragon hunter carefully.

'Saves energy by not. Besides, Anahrik keeps trying to push our pace. I'm quite tired after the first part of this morning's excursion.'

'The same reason I do not transform,' Palom added, hoping Anahrik wasn't in the same patch of sky the Arillians had flown through.

'Sorry, it sounds obvious, but I didn't know,' Morgen said, shaking his head as the trio made their way into the second wheat field. 'I'm from a tiny village in north-east Corhaven. Niversai is the biggest place I've ever been, and I've only been in the Imperial Guard about a year. Just as soon as I feel I've got the hang of something, I'm thrown back to the bottom of the pile with more to learn.'

'You will never learn until you experience new things, go to new places,' Palom said. 'Many Ittallan are travellers, you know. We rarely stay in our birth town.'

Thinking about those who would threaten the weak had always angered him, though not nearly as much as he was angry at himself for failing to protect them. Morgen was clearly inexperienced and in over his head, but he was trying his best. Palom couldn't fault him for that.

Kohl continued to fill the silence with ramblings about how wind speed and temperature would affect their flight south, though Palom ignored it. If he had to guess, he'd say the Arillian was embarrassed, or perhaps ashamed. It was a far cry from the silent, brooding dragon hunter from earlier.

There was much more to Kohl than he'd thought.

He glanced down at Morgen, whose eyebrows were furrowed, his lips pressed together tightly. 'You are very quiet, Morgen.'

'Oh. Yes. I'm just thinking about my report,' Morgen said, though Palom wasn't convinced the soldier was telling the truth. 'I need to make sure I remember everything that happens, or my captains will have my hide!'

'I think this Amarah will have your hide if we keep her waiting. We should make haste—the sooner we get to Berel, the better.'

'I'm not sure what's scarier, the thought of another dragon, or her wrath!'

'Keep your distance if you know what's good for you,' Kohl murmured. 'She's nothing more than a thief and a pirate. She'll look for any opportunity to gain the upper hand.'

'Is that not what we are all doing?' Palom questioned.

'Not in such an illegal manner,' Kohl retorted, one hand on his chest.

Morgen frowned. 'I don't know what game Aciel thinks he's playing by taking people away from cities. Especially soldiers. But if he's building an army, if he's preparing for war...preparing to take over somewhere? We have to be ready. And I don't think you can judge the sky pirate after what your kin are doing.'

Palom parted the wheat before him as the three reached the edge of the field and found *Khanna* blending into the shadows of the trees. 'We were lucky Anahrik spotted the Arillians so soon.'

Kohl crouched momentarily, before taking to the wing, gaining height and landing on deck. Cold wind whipped around in the wake of his flight, and Palom shivered. He remembered the ice Kohl had used against the dragon and wondered what the Arillian was going to do with the stone he'd taken from the creature. If he'd understood Fogu correctly, they were looking for those stones.

He wondered why Kohl had kept it from them.

Palom allowed Morgen to board first, giving their surroundings one final check before getting back on board.

'Moving on now,' Amarah said, ever-efficient. She stepped over to the wheel and unfurled her sails. 'Gotta get away before anyone else thinks to sweep the area. Be just my luck the Imperial Guard decides to patrol here.'

'No problems with your kin, I hope?' Sapora asked, slinking over to Kohl. 'I'd be most interested to hear your conversations.'

Kohl watched Sapora carefully. 'There isn't much to say. They were looking for the ship, I did not know its location, they moved on. We'll be safer in Berel.'

'That's a shame.'

Palom sat down, one eye on Kohl who slumped near *Khanna's* prow. He may have kept their presence a secret, but there was no love between himself and the other Arillians. Kohl had been exiled, and Palom didn't know if it made him more or less trustworthy. But whatever he'd done had been terrible enough for his kin to push him away permanently.

The sooner they reached Berel, the sooner Palom would have a chance to unlock the secrets of the *Valta Forinja*.

And the sooner he could truly protect himself and those he cared for.

12

M oroda's heart thundered like a horse at full gallop, and it took all her effort to keep from hyperventilating.

Arillians.

She had never given much thought to the race exiled from mainland Linaria. She had heard stories, of course, but had only recently learned more about the great war. They'd been defeated and subsequently exiled after the destruction they'd wrought to Linaria, and only existed in books or paintings.

From the way everyone had responded to Anahrik's warning, she couldn't help but feel their fear as her own. Even *Amarah* hid, and Moroda hadn't thought the sky pirate was afraid of anything.

She tried to count her heartbeats to measure the passage of time, but lost track somewhere near three hundred. She tried again, only for the numbers to slip from her mind. After losing that tiny semblance of control for the third time, anxiety spiked in her gut. But before the accompanying nausea could surface, Sapora moved.

'They're coming back,' said the Varkain, creeping forward.

'Thank Rhea for that.' Amarah stood and stretched out her arms, joints popping. 'Arillians might've ignored an empty ship, but if they'd seen us...'

Moroda thought she sounded more angry than relieved. She'd initially wanted to hide in the cabin with Eryn, but the idea of not being able to see what happened was somehow more terrifying, so she'd stayed on deck.

She'd wanted to help. Felt like she *should* help.

But she couldn't.

At least Amarah had her scythe. She and Eryn had nothing. They were as helpless as lambs, and it ate at her.

Eryn might have been ashamed of their situation, at having to rely on others. Moroda wanted to use the opportunity. She was outside Niversai, with people who were far more knowledgeable and well-travelled than she or Eryn. She needed to learn from them and make the most of the experience.

Their world had changed, and she didn't think her life could go back to how it had been before.

When Kohl landed on deck, reassuring them the Arillians had moved on, Moroda let out a sigh of relief. She'd been almost as afraid as when she'd been locked up in Rosecastle, and just the memory of that was enough to make her shudder.

By the time Amarah had the ship back in the air and trundling south above the river, Moroda had made her decision. 'I'm going to talk to Palom.'

'What for?' Eryn asked, her shawl held tight as she tried to tame her wild hair in the strong wind.

'I want to learn to fight.'

Eryn's mouth dropped open. 'Excuse me?'

'Or at least...' Moroda struggled for the right words. 'I

want to defend myself. We can't be so helpless! He's a weaponsmith. He'll have knowledge.'

Eryn was aghast, her mouth working but no sound came out.

Moroda took advantage of her sister's momentary speechlessness and hurried along the deck to Palom. Even sitting down, the man was formidable—a mass of muscle—and Moroda could almost see the tiger within him. Despite his clear strength, his eyes were gentle, and he'd not once raised his voice to her.

'Moroda?'

She almost curtseyed before catching herself. 'Palom. You've done so much for us, and I hate to ask more...but I would request a favour.'

Eryn scurried up behind her.

'*We* would ask a favour,' Moroda corrected. It was better they appeared united, even if Eryn had her reservations.

'Yes?' Palom spoke slowly, cautiously.

'You and Morgen went to find out what happened with those Arillians. Were willing to defend us. I wish to learn to defend myself, too. Would you...would you show me?'

'Teach you to fight?'

'She doesn't really mean that! Just a silly joke of hers,' Eryn interrupted, waving her hand towards Moroda's face as if to bat her away.

'Fighting is no joke.' Palom frowned at the pair of them.

Moroda pushed Eryn's hand down, irritated. 'I know. It isn't a joke. I don't want to be helpless if anything happens again.'

'Ro! Palom said *he* would help look after us. Look after the whole ship!' Eryn said.

'True. But it is always good to be able to fight back.' Palom stood up and peered down at them. 'Having right weapon is

144

important. We must find what is best for you. Sword is too heavy. You cannot get close. You will be vulnerable. You need something so you can help from distance and be in less danger.'

Eryn's expression went from shock to pure horror as Palom spoke, and Moroda tried not to smile at her sister's discomfort. Eryn was desperately trying to hold onto the past, onto how things were.

She was trying to embrace their new future.

The Ittallan dragged his heavy satchel over and began rifling through it.

As he pulled weapons out and laid them on deck, Anahrik flew close by, his feathers more ruffled than Moroda remembered. Anahrik tilted his head towards Palom and the weapons, then light engulfed him.

Before Moroda even realised he was transforming, a man leaned against the side of the ship where a bird had been just moments before. He had the same easy smile as he always did, even though his appearance was somewhat dishevelled.

'Training?' Anahrik asked.

'For Goldstones,' Palom replied, without looking up.

'Oooh. Exciting!' Anahrik bounced over to them, totally at ease with the shaking ship underfoot. 'What experience do you have?'

Moroda glanced at her sister.

'None, really,' Eryn admitted.

'What about your school?' Anahrik asked, holding up two short daggers and inspecting them.

'We weren't really taught that sort of thing,' Moroda said, embarrassed for the first time about her education. 'We learned to ride, to dance, to sew. History, geography. Writing. Numbers...'

Anahrik's eyes widened. 'You've *never* learned to fight?'

'We have the Imperial Guard for that,' Eryn retorted, arms folded in defiance.

'You may not always have someone to protect you,' Palom said.

Eryn reddened and Moroda squeezed her hand in what she hoped passed for reassurance.

Anahrik discarded the daggers and continued rooting through their satchel, shoving Palom aside in his enthusiasm. 'We didn't bring our full stock to Niversai and we don't have any shields. Maybe we can get you a bit of armour and work on evasion and defence?' He scratched the stubble on his chin. 'The last thing we want is for someone to get hurt. Kohl, Palom, and Amarah are fighters...Morgen obviously knows how to handle himself in combat too, so you shouldn't *need* to get involved.'

'We're fast learners. And we don't want to be on the sidelines or get in the way.' Moroda shivered in the wind, trying to focus on Anahrik and Palom despite the chill.

Palom folded his arms. 'Longbows and shortbows need much time to train. Won't hurt dragons anyway. Crossbow, I think.' His accent thickened the more he spoke, and Moroda watched in awe as he pulled out the metal weapon with one hand. 'Slow but strong. Use it as last resort. Leave any dragons to Kohl and I.' He offered them the weapon.

'We understand.' Moroda accepted it, trying not to stare at the wicked lines of the crossbow nor at Eryn's grimace. She held it delicately—the crossbow was far heavier than she thought it would be. Painted a sleek, dark purple with black detailing, its silver edges glinted in the sun. Moroda couldn't help but admire the craftsmanship that went into the making of such a fearsome thing. Even Eryn leaned in for a closer look.

'That's my work there,' Anahrik said, hovering over the girls like an excited child. 'See the silver? Took me six days to get it just perfect. Custom order it was for some pompous Goldstone but he decided he wanted it blue instead of black.' He put his arms behind his head, and Moroda noted it was a stance he took up frequently when he boasted. 'Worked out in the end though, we got to keep it. He paid for both no problem, so then we had this one spare to show off the silver and how it works. Had six more orders after last summer's trade back home.'

He flashed a smile, and Moroda nodded, unsure of the reaction he was hoping for.

Palom offered a handful of bolts to Eryn. 'How we have this weapon does not matter, Anahrik. We are not selling it.'

'I know, I know.' Anahrik waved his hands before putting them in his pocket and strutting over to the edge of the ship. Moroda wondered whether he was embarrassed.

As she inspected the bolts, she felt eyes on her, and glanced around to find Morgen watching. His eyebrows furrowed every time Palom paused in his explanation of how the weapons worked. Clearly, Palom understood the weapon, its strengths and weaknesses, but he was used to *selling* weapons, not training people to use them.

Especially in a second tongue to two inexperienced women.

After Palom had repeated himself for the third time on wind speed and the weights of the bolts, and Moroda thought her head was full of fog, Morgen approached.

'Don't worry about all that fancy stuff. Just point it and fire.' He gently took the crossbow from her. 'Bolts are loaded here,' he pointed, 'string is pulled back.' He gestured for Eryn to pull the crank back, 'and secured into place. You see the recess? Then just pull the trigger.'

'But...but don't we have to be sure we'll hit the target? What if there's a crosswind?' Moroda recalled Palom's words.

'If we're in a situation where you need to fire this, it'll be against a dragon. I think even someone without eyes could hit *that* big of a target.'

Moroda tried not to think about possibly fighting a dragon.

'Shall we fire it?' Morgen suggested.

'Go ahead.' Palom gestured.

'Then, let's aim into the distance.' Morgen guided the sisters to the edge of the ship, and the three of them peered out to the fields below.

Moroda took a few breaths to steady her shaking, more to do with the weight of the weapon than nerves. On her next exhale, she pulled the trigger and released the taut string with a sharp twang. The whole weapon recoiled and Moroda dropped it, pulling her hands back as a short, sharp pain tore through her fingers.

Morgen caught the crossbow before it clattered to the floor, and Anahrik leaped overboard, transforming and folding his wings back immediately into a dive. He returned a minute later, the metal bolt held tightly in his talons.

Moroda and Eryn both watched him return to the ship with wide eyes. She could hardly believe the speed of his reactions.

'You'll need to practice—learn the strength, learn how quickly you can reload and fire, learn how far you can carry it,' Morgen echoed Palom's earlier words.

'And just hope the Arillian kills any dragons we come across.' Sapora appeared behind them, his approach silent.

'Sapora!' Eryn gasped, taking a step back.

Moroda whipped her head around, suddenly realising that everyone was watching. Even Amarah peered over at them from behind the ship's wheel. They'd all seen her drop the crossbow the first time she tried to use it. Heat flushed to her cheeks and crept along her neck, along with shame at her own naivety.

'I doubt you'll need to use that before we get to Berel,' Sapora said, inspecting his nails. Moroda couldn't help but notice how sharp they were. 'I have no need of weapons to defend myself...or attack.'

'We don't all have your skills,' Morgen said, one hand lingering near the scabbard at his hip.

'I am most interested to see what we learn in the scholar's city. I've not visited Ranski before. Thought it was nothing more than a desert,' Sapora said, ignoring Morgen's jibe.

'It ain't nothing more than a desert,' Amarah agreed. She pulled a lever, adjusting the main sail, and *Khanna* rose higher. 'Anyway, Sapora. Why're you always slinking around?'

Sapora leaned on the side rail. 'My kind has learned to use stealth to our advantage. We are hated and feared by Linaria. So I embrace the talents of the Varkain. If people are too scared to approach you, then they are too scared to attack you. Self-preservation is the most important of all skills.'

Amarah snorted. 'Well don't use any of your other *skills*. Berel's a place of peace. Mages won't like you trying to start a fight.'

Palom said, 'It will be interesting. I have always wished to travel there, to learn of old legends. But there is no trade for my merchandise.'

Amarah shrugged. 'Ranski is the dullest place in Linaria. It's a whole country of nothing, and always preaching peace. But I got some contacts in Berel, and I'll be able to get *Khanna* fixed. That's all I want.' Venom laced her voice.

Moroda hadn't heard such disdain from Amarah, not even when she was talking about the Varkain. Perhaps her childhood was something else the sky pirate was defensive about. Moroda sat down on one of the crates, trying her best

149

to ignore Sapora's piercing gaze, while the pain in her arm subsided. 'I've heard their knowledge is incredible. I dreamt of being a scholar as a child.'

'There is indeed knowledge there,' Palom agreed, taking the bolt Anahrik had retrieved and checking it for damage.

Moroda watched the Ittallan. 'You two have always worked together?'

'Yes. We are like brothers. One will go where his heart leads, and the other will follow. When I arrived in Taban Yul few years back, I had no...path. Anahrik helped me find it. If not for him, I would have been lost. We were competitors, first, but he had idea to work together for more profit. But for him it was always new idea, next thing to do, always more, more, more. It was his idea to come to Niversai for the races. It is like his instinct.'

'That's just what I'm doing!' Moroda said to Eryn, allowing her emotions to fuel her excitement. 'Following my instinct, my heart. I've always wanted to go to the city of mages, and now I have my chance.' She was anxious about it too, but didn't dare mention that with Sapora nearby. He'd already seen her weakness with the crossbow, and knew Varkain preyed on those who were vulnerable.

Kohl circled far above, no more than a dark speck against the clouds.

She wondered if he was truly keeping watch, or whether he used it as an excuse to keep his distance from them. There was nothing stopping him flying away if he wished, so he must have wanted to stay with them. Quite why, she couldn't say. Perhaps it was a desire to protect, like Palom. After all, he *had* warned them about the dragon in Niversai, and defended them when it had attacked.

'We call it *meraki*,' Palom continued, drawing Moroda's attention. 'It is your...essence, your soul, your mind and heart, all together. It is deep in Ittallan culture. It is our blood, our life. *Meraki* allows us to transform.'

'How does the transforming work?' Morgen asked.

'There is not lot to say.' Palom shrugged. 'Family history tells what form you will take, but your *meraki* tells the specific. It is innate...calling. Anahrik needed speed. It was part of his essence, his soul. When he came of age, his *meraki*, his true form, was falcon. It would have been clear to everyone when he was child that's what he would be.'

'So he could have been another animal?' Moroda asked, wondering what she'd like to transform into if she had the Ittallan ability.

'If his family were not birds, yes. Maybe he would have been deer or something else for speed. You are not completely free to choose. Your *meraki* comes from your family, from your blood.'

'If Anahrik wanted speed, what did you want?' Morgen asked.

'Strength. Power. To protect and fight. I could maybe have been bear or bull. But there are many...felines in my blood. My brother was...leopard,' Palom explained, pausing every now and then while he chose the right words.

'Was?'

'He died twenty years ago.'

'I'm sorry, Palom.' Moroda apologised for Morgen, an instinctive response, her eyes dropping in embarrassment.

'Things happen. It was my fault. I was young. I did not have strength to save him. But my *meraki* gave me form of tiger when I came of age. Too late to protect my brother, but I can look after Anahrik...and now this group of travellers from what dragons and Arillians are doing.'

'Don't the Varkain transform as well? I'm sure I've heard that. What's the difference?' Eryn ventured.

'The Varkain are fucking dirty creatures,' Amarah

snapped, evidently eavesdropping on the conversation while she flew the ship. 'Only snakes. That's *all* they change into. What does that tell you about 'em?'

'Very rich coming from a thief. *I* have never stolen anything in my life,' Sapora retorted. He pushed away from the side of the ship, slinking towards Moroda and Eryn. 'We are just as different from the Ittallan as they are to anyone else. Just as ancient, with our own customs, culture, languages. We are *nothing* alike.'

Palom said, 'Some believe we were once same as each other. But oldest Varkain split away centuries ago, cursing them all to take same form over and over.' He shook his head. 'A lost, sickened *meraki*.'

'Not true,' Sapora replied, his eyes glittering in the sunlight. 'Snakes, yes, but different types. We do not fly or prowl as Ittallan can, but we have just as much diversity. And ours is of far greater significance.'

'What...type are you?' Eryn asked.

Sapora blinked slowly, but did not entertain a response.

Moroda squeezed Eryn's arm, hoping that her sister wouldn't push her luck with the Varkain.

The conversation died as they continued onwards, minutes trickling into hours. Moroda expected Amarah to tell them more of her home country, but the sky pirate had surprisingly little to say of Berel, of which none was positive.

Moroda knew hardly anything of the place. She knew of the famous university in Berel, and knew that the Samolen practised magic there.

Whenever Amarah did speak, it was usually against Sapora. Those two often showcased their distaste for one another, and Moroda hated the tension their outbursts created. Conflict had always made her uncomfortable.

She thought of Kohl and Anahrik, who could fly off if they chose and keep away from the spats, and wished she could do the same. Yet in the same breath, she looked to Palom and his calm voice of reason, and Morgen, who had a knack for defusing tension, and realised she could learn a lot from both of them.

Moroda listened to their arguments, trying to work out why they disagreed so much. Sapora seemed to loathe Amarah's vocation, and Amarah seemed simply to loathe Sapora's existence.

The arguing between Amarah and Sapora intensified as they entered Ranski, two days later. Moroda had been certain they would come to blows, but the heat increased several hours after the border crossing, and Sapora retired to his cabin.

Although Amarah had warned them Ranski was a desert, Moroda hadn't been prepared for the intensity of heat. Her thick travelling cloak didn't help either, but it protected her skin from burning under the harsh sun. Amarah hadn't been lucky—after only a few hours, her arms were red and her bare shoulders sported blisters.

Corhaven, to Moroda, was beautiful—full of hills and forests, fields and flowers, all swathed in lush green grass. Ranski had plains of brown, brittle grass which soon gave way to a barren, sandy landscape. The wind strengthened, too, and on the vast, flat land, it picked up loose dust, pushing it into huge clouds which bombarded the airship every time it flew too low or too quickly.

'Kohl, what's that?' Amarah called out sharply.

Moroda had been cleaning the crossbow of dust for what had to be the hundredth time, and stood up, grateful for the distraction. Wiping away the sweat on her forehead, she squinted in the sunlight, looking for the Arillian.

Against the yellow-brown skyline, she could not easily spot their scouts, but Kohl came back into view at Amarah's call. He held his hat low as he reached the ship, keeping it safely on his head against the rush of cool wind that accompanied his landing.

'Phoenixes, Amarah. A pair of them, half a league ahead.'

Far in the distance, there was a faint orange glow in the sky.

'Phoenixes?' Moroda repeated, trying to see the scaled birds.

Amarah adjusted their course. 'Great. There'll be dragons about then.'

'None anywhere near us. Your ship will be safe. Phoenixes are everywhere in Ranski. They don't all follow dragons here.'

'Phoenixes won't hurt you anyway, don't worry,' Morgen said.

'I'm not worried!' Amarah replied, too quickly. 'But *Khanna* ain't fireproof, whether phoenixes intend to harm me or not!'

Eryn hugged Moroda's arm. Moroda knew her sister was exhausted from the heat and their rations were swiftly dwindling. Talk of more fire and danger put her on edge, and Moroda could sense her sister's anxiety.

'Lucky for us the ship has a good pilot.' Morgen flattered Amarah.

Amarah snorted in response, but Moroda saw a grin playing on the captain's lips.

Palom and Sapora stood opposite one another on the open deck, tension thick between them. Amarah could often be appeased by a calm word or a hint of flattery, but Sapora was more unpredictable, and Palom seemed to have taken it upon himself to keep a close eye on the Varkain.

Their dislike for one another seemed to run even more deeply than Amarah's.

It was close to evening on the fourth day of their journey when Amarah announced Berel was in her sights.

'We're coming up on the old town now.' Amarah slowed the ship's approach and lowered their altitude. 'The university's down there, on the lake.'

Moroda's eyes widened. The lake was enormous, sprawling in all directions for several leagues, an oasis in the dry landscape.

Torches shimmered across the water's surface, the current visible even in low light. A huge stone building dominated an island in the lake's centre, flanked on all sides by pillars of the same material.

Moroda leaned over the side, trying to get a better look, before being jolted back as *Khanna* turned under her.

'Docks are in the new town,' Amarah explained, bypassing the university, and approaching the land on the lake's far side.

Berel's new town was larger and more advanced than the old, and much more built up. It reminded Moroda of Niversai, and it wasn't long before she could make out individual streets and buildings.

'Looks like the docks are pretty empty. See, no one visits this bastard desert.' Amarah steered *Khanna* towards a large overhang jutting out from a hillside.

The fabric canopy above the dock entrance was thick and red, richly embroidered with jewels, which shone more brightly the darker it became. Using their light as a guide, Amarah navigated *Khanna* into the hangar and docked the ship near the entrance—no doubt for a swift escape.

Moroda tried not to smile. She was beginning to understand Amarah more and more.

Killing her engines, Amarah sighed loudly. 'We're here, finally.' She yawned, stretching her arms above her and cracking her joints. 'Dragons above, I ache. This girl needs a good rest, too.' She fondly patted *Khanna's* wheel.

Eryn rubbed her eyes, flicking away dust and sand. 'Me as well. I'll be so glad to be off this ship. I think I've decided I don't like flying on airships *quite* so small and cramped.'

'Or with a touchy Varkain aboard,' Moroda whispered back, once she had checked the offending person wasn't within earshot.

'We have no planned arrivals this evening?' A male voice with a rich timbre called up to the passengers.

'Captain Amarah—this is *Khanna*, a racing ship that had a tangle with a dragon outside Niversai,' Amarah called back, clambering down the steps to disembark. 'I would have thought you'd recognise this old girl, Topeko. She ain't changed that much.'

Moroda caught Amarah wink at the approaching Samolen.

'Amarah? I can't believe it!' He wore ornately jewelled red robes, which matched the canopy above the hangar entrance. His bright eyes sparkled green against his dark brown skin, and the two thumbnail-sized jewels embedded under his left eye shone vividly in the torchlight, both purple.

'I saw the ship fly overhead and came to the hangar to see for myself who was landing at this hour. Dragons above, *Khanna* is in a state. I hardly recognise it! Or *you*, for that matter!'

Topeko embraced the dirty, burnt sky pirate, wrapping his arms completely around her and spreading warmth into the cool air. 'It has been far too long. I feared I would never see you again! We heard of the dragon attacking Niversai. It is a wonder your ship survived the flames.'

He released Amarah and took a step back to greet the others who were disembarking. 'These are your...friends?

You've always had quite eclectic tastes, haven't you? Not only do you have those from Corhaven, but Ittallan, an Arillian, *and* a Varkain, too? Who would have thought one small airship would bring Linaria's peoples together!' Topeko exclaimed, the jewels under his eyes bursting with light as he became more animated.

Drums beat somewhere beyond the hangar, accompanied by lilting flutes. The music enticed Moroda forward, along with the warmth emanating from the Samolen. Seeing a friendly face was a relief after so much animosity aboard the ship.

Topeko smiled at them as they passed, then clutched a hand to his chest and gasped. 'Goodness me! A *prince* of the Varkain, no less! My word, Amarah, whatever have you been doing these past few years?'

Sapora froze mid-step, glaring at the Samolen and refuting the warmth he gave off.

'Prince?' Amarah echoed, staring at Sapora.

'Sapora's a prince?' Moroda gasped, both hands covering her mouth. She couldn't believe Topeko's words, and thought back to all the times she had been less than courteous to Sapora, or when Amarah had outright insulted him.

She'd had no idea they had royalty on board. All she had wished for the entire journey was for him to leave them alone. She'd been so wrapped up in Amarah calling her "Goldstone" every chance she had, she didn't think anyone else would be as...important.

Her stomach churned at the realisation.

'You...you did not know?' Topeko bowed low, some of the sparkle from his jewels disappearing.

'My prince, I apologise if I have affronted you.'

Sapora turned away, poorly concealing his annoyance. 'I'm sure *someone* would have figured it out soon enough. I am too tired to be angered now. Is there somewhere we can rest?'

Topeko straightened up. 'Of course, of course. Please come to my quarters, you're welcome to stay. Amarah, all of your friends are guests just as much as you.'

'Thank you very much, sir,' Moroda said, mirroring Topeko's earlier bow and hoping not to show any disrespect. 'Are you one of the mages here?'

'Indeed, I am a scholar.' He pointed to the jewels under his left eye. 'Purple is the colour of the teacher. There are many colours to mark the specialities of the Samolen,' he explained. 'Come, come, there is plenty of time to learn.' Topeko once again became animated, his jewels dazzling as they pulsed with ever brighter light, and he left the hangar in a flourish of red and purple.

Pushing away her growing trepidation, Moroda took her sister's arm and followed him into the city of mages.

13

A prince.

A damned Varkain prince.

How in Rhea's name hadn't she *realised* that?

Amarah thought back to every hurled insult and snide comment she'd sent Sapora's way and bit the inside of her cheek to keep herself from grimacing.

No wonder he'd had that damned smug grin glued to his face the whole time.

Not only did she have to face being back *here* of all places, she had to deal with that embarrassment. He was on her ship. Part of her crew, for all intents and purposes.

She should have *known*.

Topeko was unreadable, as always. He rarely shared his emotions or thoughts, even in private. She *knew* he felt things underneath the confident, optimistic facade.

Trust him to see Sapora for what he was the moment he stepped off her ship. Kohl, too.

The scar under her left eye twinged, and she scratched it. It had been years since she'd left Berel. Despite her affection for Topeko, she'd not envisioned herself returning for at least...well...ever.

Any joy she'd felt at seeing Topeko had been dashed by the revelation about Sapora's status. She'd called him a maggot.

Several times.

Shit.

Those two Goldstones twirled around as if they were at one of their dances. Yes, it was warmer here and even she enjoyed solid ground underfoot, but did they have to act like a pair of lovestruck puppies?

Amarah allowed Topeko to lead them through the streets of the new town while she kept to the rear of the group. She'd never liked anyone walking directly behind her. Too easy for them to stab you in the back.

The flutes and drums grew louder with every step. If Amarah hadn't known better, she'd have sworn the walls themselves were alive with music. There was nothing like Berel's magic anywhere else in Linaria that she'd experienced. The music was *heat. Fire.* Flickering and dancing, rising and falling. It dragged the aches and pains of the journey away from her body, cleansing her muscles of fatigue and leaving her numb. The pain from her shoulder moved through her limbs, pulled down through her legs, her feet, and into the ground below. She shuddered, the sensation stirring up long-buried memories.

Moroda gasped.

'Eryn, can you feel that?'

'It's incredible! I hardly ache anymore!' Eryn grinned broadly. 'I've read about Samolen magic, but *feeling* it? My goodness, I never knew it could do *this*!'

Topeko laughed from somewhere ahead, 'Of course it can! We start and end every day with music. The Kaloset play in the morning to refresh and energise us, and in the evening to remove the stresses and pains of the day. There is no truer way to be at peace.'

Amarah's childhood had been full of Samolen magic. Of the huge dragon stones powering the city. Wondrous, perhaps, to those silly Goldstones.

But it wasn't wondrous at all.

Without the dragons, the Samolen would be nothing but nomadic people eking out their survival in the desert. They'd have no power, no glory, no status.

She wondered how long it would be before Topeko started with his lectures about everyone being one of Rhea's children or holding innate magic within them. Her scar ached with phantom pain at being in this place.

Amarah did her best to ignore it.

As they followed Topeko through the streets, more memories tried to force their way in, and she gritted her teeth as she pushed them back.

She didn't *want* to remember the bad times.

They passed the place that made the best flatbreads. The wall she'd fallen off when she was six and broken her arm. The tree she'd been too small to climb.

Fear, sadness, and regret enveloped her like a cloak, and she quickened her pace. Keep moving, keep running. Don't let the emotions catch up. Keep them at arm's length.

Archways and bridges crossed the wide, paved streets overhead, all made of the same sandy coloured brick. Lush, green vines covered most of the bridges, bringing natural colour to the desert city. Lanterns hung from the archways at regular intervals, burning brightly and lighting the streets below. Square, flat-roofed buildings dotted the path on either side, every door with its own lantern burning above— some with yellow flames, others with purple flames that matched Topeko's jewels, some green, some blue, some fierce red; others were silvery-white.

Each colour was a beacon of her failure. A reminder of what she could never achieve.

Amarah glared at them as she passed.

With the chill of the descending night cooling her skin, and now that her aches had largely been removed, tiredness crept in. Amarah allowed her anger to keep her awake and alert.

Before she realised where they were, Topeko halted beside a large building elaborately draped with looping sashes of thick, purple fabric. 'Here, we will stay.' Topeko looked back at the group, his eyes twinkling. 'My home is your home, Amarah. And so it is also home to your friends.' He waved his hand, gesturing for them to enter.

Amarah spotted Sapora on the edge of the group. She'd thought he might have gone off to hide, as he had done in Burian Forest, but his deep scowl showed his anger. She smirked at seeing him so riled. Topeko's reveal wasn't on Sapora's terms. He'd lost the smug control he'd held onto since Niversai, now his secret was out.

That alone was enough to lift Amarah's mood.

At least there was someone here more miserable than herself.

Dragons above, she was bitter.

Rum. That would help.

Anahrik and Palom kept close to Moroda and Eryn, and Amarah couldn't help but notice the glances they cast towards Sapora every so often, as if looking at him would answer the questions they wanted to ask but dared not.

'Andel, please,' Topeko called into a dark room once the party had entered.

Barely a moment later, a youth appeared. He couldn't have been much older than fourteen, and wore the same robes as Topeko. He had the brightest blue eyes Amarah had ever seen, with a shock of dark hair in contrast. Andel bore one small blue jewel under his right eye, and bowed low to the party. With a wave of his hands, the torches fastened to the walls burst into flame, lighting the large, circular room and providing warmth against the night chill.

The light revealed a bookshelf carved to follow the curved wall, several cushioned chairs, and the same enormous oak table Amarah had spent her childhood years sitting at. Her stomach turned, though it wasn't fear. Shame was there. And repulsion, though she couldn't say towards what.

'Andel. Amarah has returned, and she is with company. Please ensure each guest room is stocked.' Topeko instructed.

The youth bowed to the scholar, before disappearing down the hallway he had emerged from, bare feet tapping the wooden floor.

Moroda spun in a circle, her skirts skimming the floor. 'I've always wanted to come here. To learn the history of Berel, to learn about the dragons! It's more inspiring, more wonderful than I ever dreamed!'

Amarah rolled her eyes, but Topeko was delighted.

'Why thank you, my dear! Perhaps if you have no plans for tomorrow morning, I could show you the university?'

'That would be incredible!' Moroda grinned, nudging her sister, who didn't appear to share her enthusiasm.

Amarah couldn't help but sneer as Moroda's accent became more pronounced in her breathlessness. She'd seemed vulnerable when she'd admitted not having money. Had even cried. And now look at her. Typical Goldstone.

'Thanks for your hospitality.' Anahrik lowered his head in not quite a full bow—clearly an imitation of the motion he had seen Topeko and Andel perform. 'But to tell you the truth, I'm not happy with any of this. All this secrecy.' His gaze rested on Kohl and Sapora as he spoke, before flicking over to Amarah.

'About you, Kohl. And the dragons. What you're not

telling us. And you, Amarah—how in all of Linaria do *you*, a low-class sky thief, know a mage of Berel?'

Amarah bristled at his words, but the magic had sapped too much of her energy to retort.

Anahrik rounded on Sapora, not in the least bit intimidated by the Varkain. 'And how did we have a *prince* among us without realising?'

'You're too ignorant to realise, Anahrik,' Sapora responded coldly.

'*Too ignorant*? You skulk about, criticising us and throwing out your sly comments!' Anahrik's voice rose in indignation. 'I'm keeping busy, scouting ahead and making myself useful. You and your kind bring nothing but fear and misery to Linaria.'

He jabbed a finger towards him. 'Even if you *are* a prince.'

Sapora narrowed his eyes. 'I'd be very careful what you say, Anahrik.' His hands dropped to his sides.

'Hold your tongue, Sapora,' Palom interjected, drawing his sword and pointing it at the Varkain. 'You delight in causing conflict and misery. This is second time I am stopping you from doing this.'

'Ah, of course, Anahrik's backup. The *great tiger*.' Sapora lowered his voice to a cool rasp. 'Drawing your blade in a show of strength will do nothing to stop me from doing *exactly* as I wish, Palom. You won't always be around to protect everyone. One day, that young Ittallan will mouth off too much and I won't be in such a forgiving mood.'

'Please, this is a place of peace.' Topeko stepped between the Ittallan and the Varkain with raised hands. 'Do not squabble. Your rooms are prepared. You will find food and drink there, and comfortable beds. There are no airships flying out this evening, and the desert is too dangerous to travel on foot at night.'

'Thank you, sir.' Morgen bowed, more deeply than Anahrik's attempt, then turned to follow Andel.

'Make sure you lock your door, Anahrik.' Sapora grinned, flashing all his teeth in a pointed smile.

'Don't you dare.' Palom snarled.

'I have the strength of my crown behind me, yet I have no need for it against arrogant Ittallan like you,' Sapora continued. 'You rely too much on Palom's strength to get you out of trouble.'

'Sapora!' Palom lunged.

Amarah knew Topeko had been ready to stop any fighting, but Sapora had already dodged the blow and was behind Anahrik in half a heartbeat.

'Get away from me you damned snake!' Anahrik shouted, drawing a short dagger sheathed at his hip and slashing at Sapora as quickly as he could.

Amarah hadn't seen the Varkain move.

She bit back an alarmed gasp.

Anahrik trembled.

'There. *Now* you feel the fear, as you should. You are nothing but prey. Fodder. Entertainment for me.' Sapora hissed, pupils dilated.

Topeko raised his hand and a gust of cool wind filled the room. It was calming, and very nearly sent Amarah to sleep right then and there. 'I have once requested you cease. I will not do it again. Please, retire for the evening. My home is yours, as my honoured guests. Accept it and do not insult my generosity.'

Amarah rolled her eyes. 'See what I've had to put up with, Topeko? Guess I learned your patience to have not booted any of 'em off my ship.'

'Oh, Amarah, you need not be so aggressive.' Topeko turned to the others. 'Please follow Andel, he will show you to your rooms.' He gestured to the hallway, where the youth stood silently, patiently waiting and entirely unfazed by the shouting and aggression.

Amarah stayed exactly where she was, watching as Moroda and Eryn sleepily shuffled away, yawning every second step. 'Even snakes have to rest?' She looked at Sapora, who seemed altogether too pleased with himself.

'Indeed. I shall sleep safely knowing Berel is a place of peace.' Sapora yawned widely, fangs on full display, and Amarah shivered. She couldn't believe she'd let him travel with her.

She was a fool.

Only when Sapora and the others had disappeared to their rooms did she finally relax, sitting down on the large bench in what passed for Topeko's dining room. Even the Samolen music couldn't rid her mind of the chaotic thoughts and negative emotions.

'Amarah...?' Topeko ventured.

'What?' She didn't mean to snap. It was a default reaction, one she hardly thought about.

'It is good to see you, my dear.' Topeko sat down beside her, the heat emanating from his body soothing.

She almost cried at the comfort in his presence, the lack of judgement in his voice. 'Yeah. You too.' Amarah didn't dare say more lest her voice broke and he saw how emotional she was.

'You had sworn to not return, as I recall? Yet your ship is in a state of disrepair. I can of course allocate some resources to mending it.' He paused. 'Are you in some trouble?'

'Hah. Always.' That was the truth. Since she'd decided to rely only on herself, survival was usually jumping from one sort of fight to another.

'It must have been a trying journey. You should get some sleep.'

Amarah ground her teeth together. She was exhausted, but sleeping here again, in this place...

'I can brew a poultice for you? Something that'll help you sleep? Dreamless. I use it sometimes when my students give me too much to—'

'No.' Amarah stood up, annoyed at herself for her brusqueness towards the only person who'd ever shown her real kindness. Kindness *without* expecting anything in return. 'No, thank you.' She didn't look at him, kept her gaze fixed at the wood grain in the floor.

'Well, if there's anything more I can do...?'

Amarah owed him an explanation for barging in uninvited. Topeko would never complain or begrudge her for it, of course. It wasn't in his nature. She took a breath and looked at him, saw the confusion and concern in his eyes. 'Dragon attacked *Khanna*.'

'What happened?'

Again, Amarah held back the wave of emotion. Anyone else would have accused her of being in the wrong somehow. Just assumed she'd done something to deserve it.

Topeko never asked those questions. Never seemed to even think them.

'I was racing that Ittallan, Anahrik. All above board. In Niversai,' she said. 'We were outside the city and it just came down on us. No warning. Suddenly fire everywhere.'

Topeko frowned, light from his cheek jewels fading.

'Even flew back to the city, but it chased me like a dog with a bone. Couldn't shake it and you know how fast *Khanna* is!'

'How did you get away?'

'Kohl.'

'The Arillian? Hmm.'

'Says he's a dragon hunter. I believe him.' She couldn't keep the bitterness from her voice at that. No matter how much she tried to run away from her birthplace, the Samolen culture of dragon worship and reverence wasn't so easily shaken. 'He took its stone.'

Topeko's eyebrows shot up. 'What for?'

'Spoils of war.' Amarah shrugged.

'It may be nothing. But that is...concerning. Hmm.' Topeko stood up and began to pace, his robes swishing along the floor with every step. 'Amarah, dear. You really ought to get some rest. Nothing can be done tonight as you well know.'

'Topeko. I ain't a child you send to bed.'

'No. But I can offer some advice to a friend, can I not? And your room has remained here, unchanged.'

Amarah knew better than to argue with the mage. Besides, he wasn't wrong. She just wasn't sure how much sleep she'd get in this place. Already her skin itched and she could hear desert crickets outside over the music. It all brought back memories she'd rather forget.

But she couldn't hold out forever, and a safe bed was a rare indulgence. She would be an idiot to ignore it. 'Fine.'

'No need to sound so upset about it, Amarah!' Topeko laughed, his whole body shaking. 'Think of breakfast, hmm? That usually got you off to bed.'

Her stomach rumbled and she hid it with a snort. 'This ain't a long-term thing, okay. Just until *Khanna's* fixed. I... appreciate the help.'

'Anytime. You know that, Amarah. I mean it. I've always meant it.'

She nodded, not trusting herself to reply, and allowed her feet to carry her down the well-trodden hallways to her old room—and solace.

∼

AMARAH SLEPT BETTER than she had any right to, and it irked her. This was a place of bad memories, bad emotions. Somewhere she *hated*.

Why had she slept so well?

It was a rest of convenience, nothing more. Once *Khanna* was fixed, she'd be off.

And be done with the lot of them, too.

The Varkain. The Arillian. The Goldstones.

All of them.

Her job to get them here was done.

She wasn't surprised to find Topeko and Andel up and setting the table when she returned to the communal room in the centre of the house. Dawn had barely coloured the horizon, but Topeko had always been an early riser. So early, in fact, that as a child she'd wondered whether he actually slept.

'Good morning, Amarah! Please. Sit. Be comfortable.' Topeko's long sleeves draped along the table as he adjusted the bowls. 'I have already assigned several apprentices to repair your ship.'

Amarah did as she was bid, gaze drawn to the tall bottles on the table, the liquid within clear and sparkling. She considered whether she should take one for herself or pour a glass like someone more civilised. The labels on each bottle meant nothing to her, but she recognised the pale green drink inside and unstoppered the cork.

She was about to take a swig when Andel placed a glass in her free hand.

She flinched, having not noticed his approach, then poured from the bottle as Topeko finished laying everything out.

Black rice, bitter greens, and sweet, yellow tomatoes were piled high on platters in the centre. The bowl beside her empty plate held grain scattered with currants and mixed berries, alongside slices of boiled eggs. Spiced flat-breads filled with dried fruits and covered with oil sat next to every plate, and she grabbed one, shoving it into her mouth before she'd realised how hot it was.

She might have hated her childhood home. But this was one taste she missed.

After the rations on *Khanna*, a large meal was most welcome, and Amarah eagerly spooned a generous helping of everything onto her plate. She was half-way through her second serving when Sapora slipped into the room.

Topeko bowed to him. 'I apologise it's not fit for... someone of your standing, but—'

'It is adequate. Thank you.' Sapora sat down and helped himself to several eggs.

Amarah narrowed her eyes. 'Sleep well, *prince*?'

'Well enough.' He didn't rise to her bait, and that irritated her, too.

'It was good of Amarah to ferry you here. I'm glad you all arrived safely,' Topeko said as he pottered around the table, refilling jugs and adding more bowls of rice.

Amarah grinned. 'Yeah, I thought so too.' Trust Topeko to shine a good light on her.

Sapora looked at her, his pupils dilating slightly.

She fought to hold his gaze, wondering what the damned Varkain was thinking about, when Kohl swept in with a burst of freezing wind.

'Ah. I believe I owe you my gratitude, Kohl. If not for you, Amarah's ship would be in far worse condition!' Topeko bowed again. 'And I daresay so would she!'

Kohl paused like a rabbit caught in the sights of a fox, before he recovered himself with a cough. 'Oh. Yes. You are...welcome. Topeko, I noticed you have quite the collection of books. Might I...peruse them?'

Topeko nodded enthusiastically towards his shelves.

'Yes, please do! They are mostly related to my studies, but there are other books on world history, ancient languages, and dragons of course. Andel can help you find the right book if there's something specific you're looking for?'

Kohl nodded, ignoring both the breakfast spread and Topeko's offer, and turned his attention to the nearest book-shelf. He removed both his cloak and hat, wings stretching out for several seconds. They sprouted from his shoulders and reached almost to the floor, each brown feather dark-ened at the tips.

Amarah remembered wanting to fly ever since she could walk. Probably before. At least there were airships for non-Arillians. Kohl didn't know how good he had it.

With Sapora ignoring her for the most part and Kohl looking at the books, Amarah busied herself with her own food while the others arrived one by one. She was always sure to eat well whenever the opportunity presented itself. Lean times often appeared suddenly and lasted longer than she ever planned for.

It was late morning by the time Moroda appeared, rubbing sleep from her eyes, her hair a tangled mess. Amarah didn't hide her smile. Trust a Goldstone to sleep half the day away. Everyone else had finished their breakfasts.

'Finally, you're up!' Eryn shimmied over on the bench to make room for her sister. 'I thought for a moment we'd have to come and wake you! It's almost midday.'

'I slept that long?' Moroda looked around, stifling another yawn.

'None of us have been up very long, really. Something about their magic really takes it out of you.' Morgen drank deeply from his glass.

'Please, Moroda, help yourself. I would love to show your company around our city, and teach you more of Berel. It is hot and there is much walking, so you should eat,' Topeko said with his usual flourish.

Moroda sat down between Eryn and Morgen, who both seemed perfectly at home.

Amarah leaned back, belly suitably full, and stretched her arms above her head. Her shoulder wound was healing nicely, and she was sure it'd only be another day or two before she had full mobility again.

Kohl ran his hand along the front of the bookshelves, his fingers barely touching the volumes standing before him. His fingertips left a light dusting of frost where they brushed the spines, and he withdrew his hand immediately.

'Do not worry, my friend,' Topeko said, remarking on Kohl's reaction. 'Those old tomes have been around for hundreds of years, enduring heat and dust and being moved around. They can withstand the cold, too.'

Kohl

stared at him for a long moment, before stepping away, ruffling his wings slightly.

'But, I wish to ask. You carry a dragon stone. May I see it?' Topeko laced his fingers together.

Amarah watched the Arillian closely. In her periphery, she noticed the others watching him, too.

Kohl considered him for several long moments. 'You may.' He walked along the length of the table, past where Amarah sat, to where he'd folded his cloak. Reaching into the pocket, he withdrew the small jewel he had claimed from the dragon in Corhaven.

Amarah's heart pounded briefly at the sight of the blue-green crystal. She wasn't sure how she felt about Kohl claiming it. Spoils of war were fair and square as far as she was concerned, but taking from a dragon didn't sit well with her. She'd have to keep a close eye on him.

'Ah yes, it was a young one.' Topeko took the stone from

Kohl with both hands. He held it gently, brushing his fingers along the top of it. After several seconds of study, Topeko sighed. 'Yes, very young, and not, I think, in complete control of its actions.'

'I ain't never been chased by a dragon before,' Amarah said, watching Topeko and Kohl with narrowed eyes. 'And I've shared the skies with them for years.'

'No, I wouldn't have thought so. This is *that* Arillian's doing,' Topeko said, something close to anger touching his voice.

'What Arillian? Kohl didn't do anything? He was with us!'

'No, no, of course not,' Topeko replied. 'Another...a more powerful Arillian who leads a growing army. I feel the power of the dragons move across Linaria with him.'

Amarah's mouth went dry.

'Aciel...' Moroda whispered, though Amarah only just caught the word.

Topeko nodded.

Morgen scratched his nose. 'The...the Arillians we hid from. Didn't they say something about using weaker dragons to attack our villages and towns? While he hunted for other dragons?'

Topeko continued, 'He has the power of compulsion. A rare gift, not seen for many generations. Hypnotism, they used to call it. A way of...coercing others to your way of thinking without violence. Aciel has skill with it. Skill enhanced with every dragon's jewel he takes. This is a rare magic, and it is why his strength grows so quickly.'

'That's how he managed to take so many of the Imperial Guard at Niversai!' Morgen was on his feet, hands balled into fists. 'They'll all be under his compulsion, too?'

'Very likely. There are those who can fight it, of course. But when you are surrounded by warriors, I imagine you'd go along with your orders. Why risk your life otherwise? As you see, even dragons can succumb to it.' He held the jewel up to the light.

Amarah glanced at Moroda. *She'd* stood up to him.

'Kohl. You knew this? About Aciel? His compulsion? That killing dragons and stealing their power is what made him stronger?' Palom turned on the Arillian.

Kohl didn't meet Palom's gaze. 'I knew of his ability. I did not know it had such scope.'

'Now you mention it, there were several small gemstones in Rosecastle that disappeared during Aciel's visit,' Morgen said, looking skywards as he thought. 'I always thought they were just jewels, nothing special about them. They're tiny, like smaller versions of the one Kohl has. If they were dragon stones...was that how he was able to control so many people that morning? The morning you spoke against him, Moroda? Because they enhanced his power?'

Moroda's face reddened, and she cast her eyes to the floor.

Cold dread began to well in the pit of Amarah's stomach. *Compulsion*. There was nothing worse than having someone else control you. To take your freedom.

This Arillian had sauntered into the capital of Corhaven, stolen dragon jewels to boost his power, and compelled the lot of them to leave with him. She dreaded to think what he needed that army for.

Dreaded to think of the dragons he was attacking to boost his own strength.

Worse, what the dragons would do in retaliation.

Topeko faced the others, the stone clutched tightly. When he spoke, his voice was grave. 'If one dragon burned the city of Niversai to the ground in a single night, think how Linaria would fare if a hundred dragons laid siege to our world.'

Amarah wished she hadn't eaten so much food, her stomach was uncomfortably tight.

She would fly to the ends of the world to get away from a fight she couldn't win. She'd always done that. Running kept you alive.

But against the dragons? Against Aciel?

She wasn't sure even *Khanna* could keep her safe.

14

Palom would always say that Val Sharis was the most beautiful country in Linaria, and Taban Yul—the capital—was the jewel in its stunning crown.

But Berel was *staggering* during the day.

A cloudless sky shone deep blue, and the soft, sandy streets blazed under the sunlight. The same arches and bridges they'd passed underneath the night before were brought to life by rich, green vines, but the torch brackets were empty.

Now in the light of day, he also noticed clusters of glass spheres pinned atop walls like enormous blackthorn fruits. Each held a red or gold feather within, and shimmered in the sunlight.

Even Anahrik was speechless as he gazed at the decorations and architecture, and that was saying something.

'Close your mouth, Anahrik. It is rude.'

Anahrik jumped at Palom's voice, stuttering a half-formed excuse, before hurrying after Topeko.

Palom held in a laugh that was quickly squashed when he saw Kohl reaching for one of the glass spheres, though the Arillian withdrew his hand before his fingers could touch it.

He was working for his kin in some way. Even if he wasn't a direct threat to himself or the others, Kohl hadn't earned Palom's trust yet.

'You may know Berel is divided into two halves—the old and new towns.' Topeko led them through the streets, his voice grabbing Palom's attention. 'But don't be fooled. The new town has been here for generations. In fact, this shop has been selling hand-blown glassware for eight hundred years!' Topeko gestured to a tall building nestled between smaller, single storey dwellings. A long chimney protruded from its flat roof, steam drifting lazily into the sky.

Palom peered in through the open doorway—clearly visible with the fabric pulled to one side—and his mouth fell open. Rows upon rows of shelves lined the walls, every one filled with glass in countless shapes and sizes. Bottles, cups, decanters, votives, spheres, and a hundred other objects he had no name for were stacked in neat rows.

Anahrik crept in, eyes wide.

'Do not say anything. Do not touch anything.'

Anahrik whipped his hand back from a glass vase. 'Why not?'

'You will make trouble. We have enough of that without adding more.'

'*You* make the trouble. *I'm* the one who gets you out of it!'

'If you want a thing I will buy it for you when we leave. Not now.' Palom and Anahrik backed out of the glass maker's shop and continued down the wide street.

'I see why you like it. There's so much here I'd love to have in my room!' Eryn leaned past Anahrik, smiling as she stared along the many shelves. 'Maybe a spot of colour here and there? They'd make wonderful gifts, too!'

Palom appreciated her attempt to side with Anahrik, who beamed as if he'd won a personal battle.

Other Samolen going about their business ignored the group, and those who didn't were nothing but friendly. One or two inclined their heads in a shallow bow, which Palom was sure to return. They seemed used to touring visitors, and he wondered how many thousands of people had walked these same streets and learned what they could of Linaria's past.

Pungent lavender and cinnamon filled Palom's nose in every street, but no music played. He'd been looking forward to seeing and hearing more of the Samolen magic. Of course, the thought of magic turned his mind to Aciel and his compulsion. To the dragons and their powers being taken.

What did it all mean for Linaria?

Had Kohl stolen the dragon's stone for Aciel? Or was he keeping it *from* Aciel?

He needed to get the Arillian alone and force some answers from him, but it was hard to pin down someone who could fly away.

'We are in the new town.' Topeko waved his arms to showcase their surroundings. Two doves that had been nesting atop a wall flew into the air at his sudden movement, white feathers fluttering down from their wings. 'Built around six thousand years ago, it has been slowly expanding ever since we laid the first stone. Each archway signifies a new section—you'll notice the further we walk, the older the streets and buildings are, with more heavily cracked and faded brickwork.'

Palom inspected the architecture around him. He ran his hand over the wall of one archway, the stone coarse against his palm. It had been built from roughly hewn slabs of sandy brick cut from the desert.

It had a sort of elegance to it, with its uneven edges and lack of symmetry.

Nothing like the pristine, gleaming city of Taban Yul, yet it had a primitive sort of beauty. The beauty of something old and enduring. There was power in something so ancient.

Topeko continued, 'The old town is the very centre of Berel, in the middle of the lake. The two sections are connected by these narrow bridges, as you can see.'

A shiver ran up Palom's spine as he looked out across the lake and the bridges above. His *meraki* writhed at the sight. There was a deep power in that lake. Ancient magic. Every sense burned with it, and he fought the urge to step back.

'The old town also houses the university, the altar where the dragon stones sit, and our most ancient architecture... everything Berel is known for. Our job is to protect the wisdom and history of Linaria, to teach it to our children and those who wish to learn. But above all, it is the purpose of the Samolen to maintain peace.'

Finally.

The university was where he'd find out more about the *Valta Forinja*.

As a boy, he'd heard stories about the mythical weapons. Created by master blacksmiths working alongside mages, the weapons had harnessed the power of dragons. The *Valta Forinja* had helped them in the Great War against the Arillians—turned the tide and forced the Arillians away from their lands in a victory so absolute, it had left a valley of scars across Linaria.

Then, they'd been locked up, never to be used again.

A huge archway marked the bridge entrance, flanked by wide pillars on either side. Palom stared at the stone dragons carved into each, their wings half-folded, tails wrapping around the columns before coming to rest on the ground.

Atop both horned heads were more of those glass spheres, red feathers within bright as flame.

He saw Amarah peering past where they stood, trying to look at the enormous crystals embedded in the stone altar on the other side of the bridge—the island of the old town. Palom recalled what the sky pirate had said of the size of the dragon stones back in Corhaven—from dragons called Sevastos—and his heart soared with sudden excitement.

'They say in ancient times, when Rhea created Linaria, she drew the first dragons from the sands Berel was built on, then she drew the people,' Topeko said, voice low with reverence. 'They nested here, side-by-side, and the people rapidly grew in numbers while living in this beautiful, fertile place. In time, people covered all of Linaria, and spread across the land and sea, outnumbering dragons a hundred thousand to one.

'The country of Ranski was overwhelmed; we farmed and fished and hunted the land until nothing remained. We claimed dominion over this place and slaughtered those who got in our way. This angered the dragons, who had brought them life, and they turned furiously on Linaria, burning the land with their breath and reducing everything to ash, thus destroying the first people.

'Once Ranski was bereft of life, they stopped, their rage over. After generations, the surviving Samolen nomads returned to this sacred, yet violent place, and made it the centre of peace and prosperity. They settled here, by the very source of all magic, and built Berel. Legends say that the dragons will one day reduce all of Linaria to ash and sand; from dragon-flame begun, from dragon-flame undone.'

'Why would they? *We've* not done anything to hurt Linaria, have we?' Eryn asked.

'That is for the dragons to decide.' Topeko sighed.

His cheek jewels pulsed with colour as he led them across the bridge. 'Behold the lake.'

They grouped along the bridge's side, entranced by the blue depths below. Palom towered above everyone, his stomach turning at the power he sensed in those waters. There was something about it that stirred his *meraki*, unsettled his nerves. But information about the *Valta Forinja* would be on the other side, and the lake posed no threat that he could see.

He'd have to push his instincts aside and cross.

'It carries no life, no fish or plants, but it is immeasurably important to Linaria and the Samolen. It is the root of... the deepest of our magic...its very essence. I have shown many people my city over the years, but I am always overwhelmed when I reach this point. Words...cannot describe...' Topeko took a moment to gather himself. 'It is Rhea's breath, the source of all Linaria's energy and life. The very blood of our world.'

'Fascinating, Topeko.' Amarah huffed, flicking her hair out of her eyes. 'Are you gonna stand here and gawp all day?'

The scholar ignored Amarah's outburst and remained motionless, gazing down at the lake in reverie.

Moroda gestured towards his face. 'Topeko? The jewels you have, is that... are those from this water too?'

'You are most perceptive, Moroda.' Topeko gave her a knowing smile. 'Yes, we Samolen have condensed the water into jewels of power which we can call upon as we need.' Topeko raised one hand to his cheek. 'They are as much a part of every Samolen as one's hands or feet.'

'How do you do that?' Palom asked, also studying the jewels embedded in Topeko's skin.

Perhaps it would be a similar process to create the *Valta Forinja*.

'Who cares about your damned face! I wanna know about these dragons and how to avoid going up in smoke when the next one turns on my ship!' Amarah demanded, striding onto the bridge, hands on her hips.

Moroda apologised, 'I'm sorry about her.'

'I know Amarah and her ways quite well, I take no offence,' Topeko reassured them. 'It is a...sore subject for her, I think.'

'Sore subject?' Palom interjected, watching Amarah cross the lake. 'How?'

'It is not my place to speak for her—but you wished to know more of our jewels. Come. I will show you.' Topeko crossed the bridge behind Amarah.

Palom took a breath and followed, crossing quickly. He was on the other side before he'd thought about it, and his eyes lit up when he realised he was standing before the dragon stones. Five of them, each embedded on a raised altar in the centre of a large, stone courtyard. At just over eight feet tall, Palom almost reached their height, and he shielded his eyes from their intense shine.

Green. Red. Blue. Yellow. White.

Each pulsed with power, and pressure built across his arms. He could hardly believe a country of peace had so much power at their fingertips and hadn't used it.

Even the stone altar they sat upon was decorated with runes and pictures, carved by skilled stonesmiths. They depicted the dragons in their glory, wings spread, flames leaping from their jaws. People had also been carved into the stone, most on their knees in supplication, others with hands outstretched, light shooting from their fingertips. Embedded in small alcoves within the altar were five glass spheres—one beneath each Sevastos crystal.

If Val Sharis had access to such crystals, they could have used them to create an armoury of *Valta Forinja*. Every single member of their Imperial Guard would have had one, and the Ittallan would no doubt have conquered all of Linaria.

There'd be no threat from any Arillian. Nor Varkain.

No threat from anyone at all.

Moroda passed him, stepping up to the nearest stone and staring up at it in wonder. 'This is incredible. I can't...I don't have the words to...'

'Ah, Moroda! You do know the real treasure when you see it,' Topeko said.

Moroda's cheeks flushed, but she circled the other stones, looking closely at each one, before coming to a stop beside Amarah.

The sky pirate's scowl hadn't diminished.

'What are these? I've seen them everywhere in Berel?' Moroda pointed to one of the glass spheres.

Topeko's smile broadened. 'These are called ereven spheres. Well, these are ornaments, actually. The real things are as lost to us as the Sevastos dragons themselves.' He brushed his hand against one in the altar, the purple gems in his cheeks bursting with colour. 'We Samolen worship dragons. They brought life to Linaria, so why wouldn't we call them gods? The first mages created an artefact that allowed us to scry for them so that we could study them, offer gifts, service, loyalty. The spheres are an important part of our culture.'

'They are all gone?' Palom asked.

'They are ancient treasures. A few of our towns have some, but most are probably scattered throughout Linaria. Perhaps even with people unaware of what they do. Most ereven spheres that people see are these decorations.'

Kohl took to the wing as the others wandered around the courtyard, sending out a chill breeze and raising dust from the ground. He perched on the archway by the bridge and crouched down, feathers rustling.

'Scry for dragons...? Truly these spheres can do this?'

'Of course. You forget the dragons' magic was far more powerful back then. As was ours.' Topeko waved a hand at their surroundings. 'This is the university's central courtyard —in fact most of the old town is part of the university—and these crystals are from very old, very powerful dragons, willingly sacrificed.' Topeko looked up at the altar as he spoke, his own cheek jewels flashing in unison with the crystals. 'They were given to those who would not use their immeasurable power for destruction. It is why the Samolen do not partake in war and do not take sides in conflict. We are above all political involvement and we are bound to this eternal pledge.'

'*Not* to be used for destruction?' Sapora asked, speaking for the first time since they'd left Topeko's home. 'What about your ability to create fire? Seems destructive to me.'

Topeko shook his head. 'We are capable of creating fire and weapons, yes, but not for war. Though permitted, our magic is strictly regulated.' Topeko turned slowly to look at each of them. 'The last ancient dragon, the last Sevastos, died and gave its stone long before the war.'

The scholar touched the stone nearest him and looked up at it. 'Throughout Linaria's history, only five Sevastos dragons have willingly sacrificed themselves, and we hold their stones here.'

'So, these are the source of your magic?' Eryn asked, looking up at them, eyes wide.

'Not the source—that's the lake—but they do enhance it immeasurably,' Topeko replied. 'These power our city and strengthen our own magic.' With a wave of his hand, the torch mounted at the top of the archway burst into flame. A matching wave later, and a new flame appeared on the torch set to the left of the first.

'How do you do that?' Moroda asked.

'It's just energy.' Topeko smiled. 'It is the simplest of magic. Our children learn this technique. I am moving the energy from here,' he pointed, 'to here. No more. Anyone can learn to do this, not just the Samolen. Everyone has innate magic. We are all of Rhea's creation.'

Amarah snorted, shifting her weight.

'There are a few who...do not.' Topeko smoothed down his robes. 'Arillians, for example. They have another type of magic in them, a far more destructive one, giving them the power of lightning, storms, and flight. The Ittallan and Varkain have their *meraki*. But the source of *all* magic, all power and life in Linaria, is the dragons. And *that* comes from the lake.'

Anahrik circled the altar, taking in the details of the stones. 'And these...dragon stones. Crystals. They're power, too?'

Topeko nodded. 'The heart-stone, the dragon's jewel, the soul, the stone, the crystal...it has a thousand names. It is what makes them sacred to us.'

'I thought they were just beasts? Nothing sacred about them?' Anahrik questioned.

'Oh, they are beasts. In the same way *we* are. But as descendants of Rhea's children, as gods in Linaria, their stone is their heart and soul. It is the source of their fire. Here in Berel, we have no need for engines to generate power, we use our own stones.' He gestured to his cheeks, where his two small gems protruded. 'But we have to take the water from the lake and condense it into our jewels to harness this strength. The dragons are born with this power already within. This is why many people have come to revere them as gods. Rhea, the oldest and most powerful of all dragons, the strongest Sevastos to have ever lived, is known as the Goddess. Some believe she is the creator of Linaria.'

Palom's jaw tightened. The *Valta Forinja* were the greatest weapons ever forged. Topeko surely wouldn't approve Palom's desire to use them, or create his own...

Topeko closed his eyes and took several deep breaths before speaking again. 'This Arillian, Aciel, his strength grows every day. He came here, to my country, and tried to use his compulsion on us.'

Palom's attention sharpened. Morgen, too, straightened up, chin raised.

'He didn't get far. But he is willing to desecrate our laws of peace. Willing to slay the most precious of Rhea's children.' Topeko shuddered, as if speaking of this was a drain on his body. 'He must be stopped. I do not know to what end Aciel works...but it cannot be anything other than war. And a war that drags the dragons into it will spell Linaria's doom, mark my words.'

A cool breeze swirled through the courtyard, though it didn't seem to come from Kohl.

'Did...did you see him? Aciel?' Moroda had walked forward, one hand raised to rest upon Topeko's sleeve.

'No. He came to one of our other towns, further to the north. But even from so many leagues away, I felt his power. Felt his compulsion brush over my very soul...My magic protected me, I think. As it would have done for the more powerful mages across Ranski. But there are so many who will fall to his compulsion. I felt his power move through Corhaven, felt it swell just days ago. He grows stronger with every dragon he kills.'

Moroda shivered, rubbing her arms. 'I felt the same. In Niversai, when he was talking to the people. I felt a...coldness...it made me slow, sluggish. Like I was walking through a dream but trying to run. It's hard to explain.'

Topeko stared at her, then bowed his head as if in acknowledgement of what she'd experienced.

'Are...are there any real ereven spheres left?' Moroda spoke haltingly at first. 'Why would Aciel attack you? If he... if he's after dragons. Wouldn't an ereven sphere—a real one —help him find them?'

Palom suppressed a growl. Dragons were common in Val Sharis, less so in Corhaven. If Aciel had a reliable way to find dragons, it would lead him to his home country.

Near everyone.

Near Lathri.

Topeko frowned. 'It...I mean, most of the valuable treasures and artefacts are kept here, in the university. But there *are* other treasures across the country...'

'If Aciel has a method of finding dragons, that would explain a lot. Chiefly *how* his power has grown so quickly,' Kohl said. His face was a grim mask.

'If that's true...If he has the ability to scry for dragons instead of flying blind...Rhea help us...' Topeko's voice dropped as realisation dawned. 'We sent our most decorated mages to the ravished cities to aid with reconstruction. But there had been no deaths. None of our people had been taken. It...we had thought it was a show of strength. The bluster of one who feels self-righteous in his actions. Not a calculated attack. If he took a real ereven sphere...'

Anger flared within Palom at the thought of Aciel, at the thought of the power these mages had and yet refused to use. 'You are supposed to be clever. Why do you not *do* something? You have power. Knowledge. Why not share with council of Val Sharis? With Imperial Guard? You could protect many people.'

'We do not partake in war,' Topeko said simply.

His words infuriated Palom even more. If the mages would not act despite their power, *he* would.

Palom had never before considered dragons as creatures to be protected. But he would do what he could to stop Aciel from killing them.

'This is source of Aciel's strength? Slaying dragons and seizing power?'

'I believe so.' Topeko nodded.

Palom fought the urge to pace. Just *seeing* the *Valta Forinja* had been a boyhood dream. Now, he *needed* the *Valta Forinja* to defend his country from the Arillian upstart. He'd show Aciel what *real* dragon power was.

'Well that's done nothing to reassure me.' Amarah brushed her hair away from her eyes. 'You keep telling them your stories of dragons and magic. I'm gonna make sure your mages are getting *Khanna* sorted. Sooner she can fly, the sooner I can get clear of whatever Aciel's trying to do. And any other dragons he pissed off, too.'

Palom didn't blame her as she left the courtyard. He thought he smelled fear in the sky pirate, and realised she had more sense than he'd first thought.

Topeko said, 'Is there anything else you wished to see?'

Palom *had* to ask. Even if Topeko resented him for it.

He caught the scholar's gaze. 'The *Valta Forinja*. Weapons made with dragon stones. You hold the ones from war here? Or is that just stories?'

Topeko's eyes narrowed.

Palom braced himself for a rebuke.

The scholar said carefully, 'Using dragon stone as an ore in weapons is indeed real. An ancient art no longer practised, the consequences were too devastating. Several of these weapons exist, these *Valta Forinja*, as you call them. They are part of Linaria's history and so are kept here in our university.'

'They are legendary in my home. I would see them.' After a moment, Palom added, 'Please.'

Anahrik leapt up. 'It would mean a great deal to us both. Our heritage, you know. We don't have anything but stories back home, even though they were *made* by Ittallan smiths.'

Topeko considered them both, the corner of his lip pulling down in the beginning of a frown. 'You would not be permitted to take them.'

'Just looking would be an honour.' Anahrik offered the scholar one of his trademark smiles.

Several long seconds passed, then Topeko sighed and turned to the others gathered in the courtyard. 'Will you all be able to find your way back to my home if you need to rest? I will be taking Palom and Anahrik into the university.'

Moroda was the first to respond with an enthusiastic nod. 'Yes.'

'Very well. Then I shall see you back there for refreshments later. You are of course welcome to explore the rest of Berel as you wish.' Topeko swept past the dragon stones, heading for the enormous building looming beyond: the university. Sigils that Palom did not recognise had been carved above the doorway, and he wondered if it was an ancient language.

Did it offer encouragement or a warning?

'Let's go, Anahrik,' Palom said as his trading partner stepped up beside him. For once, he was sure his own excitement matched Anahrik's. This was more than a hopeful dream becoming real. This was something he could use to make a difference. To protect those he cared for, and defend his country.

University students—at least Palom presumed they were —loitered in the entrance hall in grey and blue robes, carrying books, reams of paper, and various devices he had no name for. They each had a small blue jewel embedded in their cheek, though a few of the older students had a second jewel of a different colour.

They all bowed to Topeko as he passed, several of them muttering, 'Kalos,' which Palom took to be a title or mark of respect. Most ignored himself and Anahrik as they passed.

Palom was reminded somewhat of the Imperial Palace in Taban Yul. The hallways were wide, paved in pale stone, with occasional floors of marble. Portraits, tapestries, and mirrors hung along the walls, broken up at regular intervals by large hearths. Much like in the rest of Berel, torches of different coloured flames brought light to the university interior, and he could almost smell the magic emanating from the very stones themselves.

'Makes my skin tickle,' Anahrik murmured.

'And me,' Palom assented.

Topeko strode with a hurried gait, the first time he'd appeared ruffled. Clearly he was unhappy about their request, but must have wanted to be a gracious host and not refuse them.

At any other time, Palom would have enjoyed discovering more about the university, the students, and what they learned. But today, he was on a mission. He was here for a single purpose, and he wouldn't allow himself to be distracted.

Anahrik, on the other hand, darted in and out of rooms as they passed them, peeking into those whose doors weren't closed, and touching everything he could reach.

'Anahrik!'

'What? I'm just having a look. Might get some ideas for new silver work! "Inspired by the city of mages," has a nice ring to it come the winter sales. Don't you think?'

'Hmm.' Palom didn't disagree, but he didn't want to give Anahrik the satisfaction, especially after he'd just admonished him.

'Down here. Please, mind your step.' Topeko darted down a wide staircase, the smooth bannister carved from mahogany. It had to have been shipped into the desert at great expense, and Palom wondered what other treasures the university kept deep in its vaults.

As they descended, the wall torches burned lower, and Palom half wanted to draw his sword in case some vile creature lurked in the dark, waiting to pounce. It was a ridiculous thought, and he couldn't help but keep his guard up. Even in a place of peace, he had to be careful. Before Anahrik could race down ahead of him, Palom held out his arm, blocking Anahrik's path and forcing him to slow.

Topeko waited at the foot of the staircase, a small ball of fire floating above his open palm to light the way. 'Some of the stone here is loose. It is a very old vault and repairing the stone would impact the wards, so we leave it as it is. Have care where you walk.'

Palom glanced at Anahrik, one eyebrow raised. Surely the scholar's warning was for Anahrik, not himself.

Anahrik shrugged, an apologetic grin on his face, and they followed Topeko down the tunnel. It didn't help Palom's growing sense of foreboding, but his excitement at finally seeing the *Valta Forinja* pushed most of it away. That was more important than any personal fear.

It didn't take long before they stopped at a door, similar to many others they'd passed. This one was circular, made of iron and fixed to the wall, seemingly without hinges. He couldn't see a keyhole.

Palom frowned. 'Here?'

Topeko's ball of flame shot forward, slamming into the door and creeping around the edges. It burned hot for several seconds, before something heavy within clicked, and the door rolled open, disappearing into the wall. 'I do not wish to be so close to weapons of war. You may see the items from your heritage. Should you attempt to take any, the wards in this doorway will...hurt.'

'Would we do that?' Anahrik gasped.

'It is not a matter of *if* you will do that. It is the principle. I'm sure you won't flout my hospitality.' His purple jewel flashed bright. 'I need to speak with my colleagues about the possibility one of the last true ereven spheres is with Aciel. I'm not sure anything can be done now, but the knowledge must be shared. I shall await you by the staircase. Please, take your time. I understand this means a lot to you both.' With another bow, Topeko backed away, leaving the entrance unblocked.

Anahrik was first in the room, though he didn't run. Even he was in awe at this place—at what the room held—and cautiously walked inside.

Palom was on his heels a moment later, every step measured.

He soon realised the room was empty, save a plinth at the far end, which emanated soft blue light. Several weapons had been mounted on wooden braces atop the plinth: swords, knives, axes, even a halberd.

They all glowed blue, casting a gentle light and creating long shadows.

Palom's mouth was dry by the time he reached them.

'Shame we can't take them,' Anahrik said, his voice trembling slightly.

'Of course not. They cannot let anyone take these. At least they are safe here. Away from those who might misuse *Valta Forinja's* power. Imagine if Aciel had one.'

There was no maker's mark on any of the weapons, no way to identify the original forgers. Had it been deliberate, or an accidental miracle? Palom licked his lips. Such power, and so close...

'Look! The crystal!' Anahrik pointed to one of the bigger

axes, its blade cracked and chipped from use. Buried into its hilt, its crystal flashed blue, emitting a low hum.

'From Sevastos...' Palom was drawn to it like a moth to flame. Goosebumps rose on his skin and his *meraki* thrashed. *This* was the dream. The weapons that had won the war.

How many lives had they taken?

How many lives had they *saved*?

His nails elongated into claws, and Palom struggled to hold his transformation back.

'There's more here.' Anahrik's voice sounded distant. He'd taken a few steps to the right, where shelves had been built into a recess in the wall that Palom hadn't seen before. 'Letters. Books.' Anahrik scanned through a heavy tome, dust rising into the air as he disturbed the pages. 'Attempt thirty-eight, failure. The explosion tore half my forge apart. Time to rebuild...It just trails off,' he read from the pages, squinting as he held the book close.

'Instructions?'

'Partial. Most of it is faded. And it's in the old tongue, I'm not sure it's usable.'

Palom turned away from Anahrik, drawn back to the crystal in the nearest axe. It was easily the span of his hand, nothing near the size of the stones outside. Perhaps shards of the original crystal had been split into each weapon.

Just a *sliver* of that power would make such a difference...

'I'll study this later.' Anahrik pocketed the book.

'Topeko said—'

'Not to take the weapons. And we're not. He didn't say nothing about the books though.'

Palom frowned. 'You have been spending too much time with Amarah. Talking like thief.'

'I'm borrowing it for a bit. It's for a good cause.'

193

Palom shook his head.

'Guess the weapons are powerful but not indestructible. That crack would weaken it.'

When Palom looked again, he noticed a hairline crack near the base of the crystal, which ran into the axe head itself.

An idea struck him, and he immediately dismissed the guilt that accompanied it. *For a good cause.*

Carefully, so slowly he wasn't sure he was doing it, Palom raised his finger to the weapon.

'You can't take it!'

'I'm not.'

Palom's claw hardly scratched the crystal, skittering off the edge as if repelled. He tried again, even slower, catching the tip in the crack. With one twist, several splinters broke off.

Anahrik caught them in a flash, no doubt reacting on instinct, given his astonished gasp. 'You...we...' He took a moment to gather himself, then wrapped the shards in a scrap of linen and folded them in his inside jacket pocket.

'Now, we have chance.' Palom endured the rush of guilt for stealing, then tried to push it away. It would be worth it.

It had to be.

15

Moroda wanted to spend every waking moment exploring Berel, both the old and new towns. There was something for her to discover in every building and around every corner—dozens of sights and smells she had no experience of.

Their magic, of course, held the greatest draw. Yet even the *clothes* worn by the Samolen held wonder—long robes in vibrant colours, sigils in a long-forgotten language ornamenting their sleeves.

But the oppressive desert heat put a stop to her curiosity shortly after Topeko had left with Palom and Anahrik, and she cursed herself for having slept in so long that morning.

Eryn had been keen to explore as well, and the frustration of having to go back inside ate at Moroda. It had been the first time since...well, since before their father had died that they'd seen eye to eye on something. Both wanted to do the same things, together.

She'd missed that feeling.

But if they didn't get inside soon, she was certain she'd pass out from the heat.

As incredible as Berel was, the harsh desert climate took

its toll, and she reluctantly returned to the scholar's home. She promised herself that before she left, she'd explore Berel properly. And she *definitely* wanted to see the Sevastos stones again.

Though not vast, Topeko's home was cosy without being claustrophobic, and the circular nature of all the rooms and hallways coupled with the sandy stone walls made her feel like she was underground.

Andel catered to their every need without so much as a whisper, bowing to acknowledge their requests and even grinning in enthusiasm. Neither Andel or Eryn seemed put out by his silent service, but Moroda found it uncomfortable. She had grown used to doing things for herself, and it was unnerving to have a servant cater to her again. He'd fetched them tea and a bowl of figs—cooked in honey from their sweet smell.

As much as she wanted to sit back and enjoy the hospitality, she wasn't here for leisure.

Her mind buzzed with questions—about Aciel's compulsion and what it meant for Linaria, the dragons and their stones, and how to stop more attacks. What was to stop other towns and cities falling to dragon-flame like Niversai?

The tour, though brief, had opened her eyes and mind to the wonders of Linaria, and she yearned to understand more.

It had proven how little she knew, how sheltered her life had been.

More than that, it had made her realise she wanted to make a difference.

She and Eryn could have died in dragonfire. But she'd seen an opportunity to escape the city with Palom, and she refused to squander what that had given her.

There were only a handful of people who had any knowledge of what was happening with the dragons, let alone with Aciel, and she *had* to use that information to help. Before things grew irrevocably bad. Topeko had told Amarah how incredible it was she'd managed to get people from across Linaria onto one small airship.

Perhaps she could use that rare luck, too.

Moroda considered talking to Palom and Anahrik again about the crossbow. But she'd already asked so much of them, and it wasn't as if they were there to serve her and Eryn.

She *had* to stand on her own.

Morgen had accompanied them back to Topeko's home. She'd lost sight of Kohl and Sapora in the crowds, but knew they'd be fools to start any trouble in the city of mages where peace was law, so she didn't worry about them.

'It was good to see Palom finally happy again,' Eryn said, sitting down on a cushion by the window, a mug of hibiscus tea clutched in both hands. A warm breeze wafted inside, blowing loose strands of hair around her face. 'Ever since he and Anahrik found out about Sapora being a prince, they've been so dark and angry.'

'I know what you mean. At least Sapora is back to picking on Amarah instead of Anahrik. I don't think Palom liked that at all,' Moroda replied.

She'd opted for saffron tea, though there were a handful of other spices mixed in that she didn't recognise. There was nothing magical about their drinks, but Moroda savoured every sip. Her father had often brought back exotic and rare teas from his business trips away, and though she didn't recall having this blend before, it was a reminder of her past life.

Of better times.

Morgen sat opposite them and leaned forward. 'Palom doesn't like Kohl either. Well, he certainly doesn't *trust* him.' He glanced around the room, though only Andel was present on the far side, refilling several glasses of water from a large decanter and completely ignoring the three. 'Best keep a close eye on him, too. I wonder what Topeko knows of Arillian magic and Aciel's compulsion.'

'Kohl? Why?' Moroda raised her eyebrows. Kohl had given her and Eryn a warning when they'd been in Niversai, and for that, she trusted him. He'd saved their lives from the dragon, too. If anything, they should be indebted to him, not keeping their distance.

'Well...you know...' Morgen scratched the back of his neck, something outside the window suddenly catching his interest.

'No, we don't. Why isn't he to be trusted?' Eryn asked, her voice disdainful.

'He's an Arillian, isn't he? Can't trust 'em. Don't you remember what we talked about in Burian?'

'Morgen! If it weren't for him—' Moroda began, but Morgen shook his head.

'I know, I know. Just telling you what Palom said is all. Maybe Topeko'll have the better measure of Kohl. This magic, it's all...powerful stuff.' He shivered as if a sudden chill had taken him.

Moroda chewed on her lip. Aciel was bad news, that much was clear. And Arillians weren't looked upon with much love in the rest of Linaria. If she thought about it, other than Kohl, she couldn't recall seeing an Arillian before.

Changing the topic, Moroda said, 'I've been wondering for a while, Morgen. What had Sapora been arrested for?' She forced herself to hold the soldier's gaze, though her desire to look away was intense. Even that felt too much like confrontation.

'I don't know the details. He was already in the dungeon when I started my shift.' Morgen shoved a fig into his mouth and chewed. 'There are laws and curfews in Corhaven for... the Varkain. Probably had something to do with it?'

'But he's a *prince*!' Eryn said, voice high with incredulity.

Morgen seemed to hunker into himself. 'None of us knew. It isn't like their royalty ever leave the continent, let alone come to Corhaven! One random Varkain dressed in rags, no mention at all of who he was or what he was doing in Niversai? What were we supposed to think?'

'I'll bet he'll hold a grudge against you for that.' Eryn took another sip of tea. 'Be careful around him, Morgen.'

'Don't remind me.' Morgen sounded more like a boy than a soldier of the Imperial Guard.

Although Moroda didn't like it, at least she wasn't the only one who was vulnerable. The others just seemed better at hiding it. Hiding *behind* something else. Morgen had his position in the Imperial Guard. Amarah her ship and scythe. Even Sapora made threats and skulked about, relying on fear and intimidation to get his way.

Amarah stormed in a moment later, boots clanging against the stone floor, face dark as thunder.

'What's happened?' Cold panic churned in Moroda's gut. Had Aciel done something? Come back for a second attack?

'Damned mages. They have magic at their control. Actual, *real*, magic! Can heal wounds in minutes, mend bones in hours.' Amarah sat down at the wooden table in a huff and grabbed one of the glasses of water. 'Still can't fix *Khanna* quick enough.'

Moroda took a breath. She had been silly to jump to such a conclusion. Her nerves were too fraught for her liking. 'How long until your ship can fly?'

'Two days. Dragons above, if I'd *known* I'd be trapped here for so long...'

'It...doesn't seem that bad?'

Amarah snorted. 'Easy for you to say.' She downed the

glass in one gulp and immediately grabbed another. 'Looks like you get every need catered to here. Must be like being back home, eh Goldstones?'

Moroda fought to keep from frowning. Trust Amarah to bring up her heritage again. 'I'm no better off than you, Amarah. We'd *both* be arrested if we set foot in Niversai.'

Amarah snorted again but didn't reply.

'Moroda, I...I could petition for you. Request a pardon?' Morgen's voice was small, as if his thoughts leaked out rather than were consciously spoken. 'After all, you helped with the dragon.'

'I didn't? Kohl was the one who—'

'My captain doesn't know that. And you *were* part of our group at Burian. Maybe it would be okay...'

'Why help us? *You* locked her up?' Eryn raised her voice.

Morgen's cheeks coloured. 'I was only following orders. You think I *like* doing everything I'm commanded to do? That I *want* to?'

'Why don't you quit if you don't agree with your orders?' Moroda was genuinely curious.

Morgen sighed and leaned back in his chair. 'I suppose Amarah has something right about you Goldstones. I have to work to pay for my room and board, you know. Imperial Guard is security of that, if nothing else.'

'You joined the guard so you could pay for a room?' Eryn raised an eyebrow.

Morgen laughed. 'What? No! I wanted to be a knight. You know. Famous hero. Help people. Bring justice to those who needed it. All that.' He gestured vaguely with one hand.

'Sounds like you read too many of those heroic adventure books as a child.' Eryn's voice was flat with disapproval.

'Maybe. Turns out getting coin is more pressing than rescuing lost children or taming wild horses.' Morgen shook his head, though he smiled. 'If I go back to Niversai with information that'll help defend our city, perhaps my captain will listen to me requesting a pardon for you, Moroda. Say it was a misunderstanding, or something?'

Moroda's heart pounded at the possibility.

It was quickly squashed by the realisation that even granted a pardon, her life wouldn't change. She and Eryn had hardly a coin left to their name, with no notion of how to make more—and she certainly *didn't* want to join the Imperial Guard.

Not to mention it was very probable that half the city had been destroyed by the dragon. All they had were the clothes on their backs, the handful of possessions in their bags, and each other.

'That would help,' Eryn said. 'We can get back to normal once you've spoken to your captain.'

Moroda looked at her sister. 'You really want to go back?'

'Our life is there! Our home is there!'

'It *was*. When father was alive. When we had money coming in. Now that's changed, we have to change too.'

'But-'

'I know it's scary. But we'll do it together. Think of all the things we could do now that we couldn't before?'

'Travel on a sky pirate's airship? I prefer the life of a Goldstone.' Eryn shook her head.

'That's not our life anymore. Mother's gone. Father's gone. It's just us. We have to make what we can of it. Hanging onto the past, it...it won't help.'

'Ro...' Eryn shifted in her seat, gaze flicking to Morgen.

Moroda leaned forward, squeezed her sister's hand. 'I'll be okay. You don't have to look after me all the time. It's not fair on you.'

'I *like* looking after you!'

'Except when I get arrested?'

Eryn laughed, and the tension that had built between them dissipated. 'Except when you get arrested.'

Before Moroda could respond, Topeko strolled inside, Kohl on his heels. 'I'm sorry, Kohl. Truly. If anyone else at the university has books that might help, I'll be sure to inform you immediately.'

The Arillian shook his head. 'It's fine. I appreciate the time you've already put in.' He drifted away, taking off his cloak once inside and laying it over the back of a chair, evidently comfortable enough in Topeko's home not to hide his wings.

Topeko brought a rush of warmth and light to the room, and Moroda looked up, catching his eye. She was glad for the distraction.

'How are you feeling, child?' Topeko crossed the floor towards her. She rose to meet him and he embraced her in a warm hug, enveloping her in his robes, before doing the same to Eryn and Morgen—who looked somewhat bewildered. 'The heat here can be a bit much for those used to Corhaven's cooler climate. Are you all well? Are you hungry?'

'We're fine, thank you,' Moroda said, picking up her tea and sitting down.

Although she hadn't known him for very long, Topeko's presence was calming in a way she couldn't describe. Sapora and Palom could erupt into battle and she'd hardly worry with Topeko around.

'You're a delightful host. None of us have wanted for anything while we've been here. We're indebted to you.' Eryn raised her mug to him. 'A shame you can't come home to Niversai with us!'

'Perhaps it's for the best *that* city is avoided,' Topeko replied, sadness colouring his tone.

Morgen dragged a hand through his hair. 'Maybe. But I... I'll need to go back at some point soon.'

'I thought you wanted to find out more about what was happening?' Moroda asked.

Morgen gestured around the room with both hands. 'Look at this. At what Topeko said earlier. I think I've learned enough to know that Niversai has to be prepared. The Imperial Guard *must* mount a defence before more dragons attack. Not just the capital, all of Corhaven, all of Val Sharis needs to be ready. If Aciel continues, more people will fall to his compulsion and more dragons will attack.'

Kohl sighed. 'There's no chance your Imperial Guard can defend against Aciel. I'm sorry Morgen, but he's too powerful, and getting stronger by the day. He already took hundreds of your soldiers.'

'It does feel like this is beyond the Imperial Guard...' Moroda muttered, though she didn't know *who* would be responsible for putting a stop to it if not the Imperial Guard. She'd almost been able to forget about the dragons and growing Arillian army when she had been sipping her tea and feeling the sun's warmth on her face.

Now, her stomach dropped at the realisation.

'If there was some way to break the compulsion Aciel holds on his...followers...that would help, wouldn't it?' Morgen suggested. 'Maybe there's some magic that makes those kinds of changes?'

'That'd work. His forces would drop. Might even turn on him and do the job for us,' Amarah said, tapping her toe against the stone floor.

'What? We aren't out to kill him!' Moroda was shocked. 'Can't we just help the people who are under his compulsion? They'll probably be confused, hurt, angry. It's such a cruel thing. Do they even have any memory of their actions? They're...they're losing part of themselves. He's *taking* it from them. Time. Their hopes and dreams. Memories and hearts.'

'You should be a poet.' Amarah smirked.

'I had hoped there would be a way to break his compulsion, but I'm not sure there is,' Kohl said bitterly.

'Looks like we're all doomed to be controlled by an Arillian upstart.' Sapora's drawling voice was the only noise he made as he slunk into the room, hands in his pockets, face devoid of emotion. 'Lucky for us Varkain that he decided to start his conquest on *this* side of the sea.'

Topeko replied, voice stern, 'Those few who can resist Aciel's compulsion seem to have the luck of the Goddess on their side, if not their own magic like those of us here in Ranski.'

'Wait. Moroda. You were near him, weren't you? *You* managed to resist him,' Amarah said.

Heat crept up Moroda's neck that had nothing to do with the desert climate. 'Not...not completely. Any longer and I'd have fallen to his compulsion, I'm sure.'

'We are all Rhea's children. We all have innate magic,' Topeko said, echoing his earlier words. With a glance at Amarah, he added, 'Some have more than others, of course. You, Moroda? I think yours must be strong. You have potential if you didn't succumb to him.'

'I didn't do anything special. Standing up to him got me thrown in the dungeon!' Her palms were clammy and she wiped them on her skirt, careful not to catch Morgen's gaze.

'Perhaps if you had been closer to him, or if you had been in his presence longer, you would have been affected more strongly, or his compulsion would have taken hold more quickly. But none of that occurred. And I believe things happen for a reason. Whether it is Rhea steering us towards her preferred future or some other power at work, I cannot say. But I shall aid you, if I can.' Topeko's jewels sparkled.

Amarah cackled. 'Topeko, you've been in the sun too long. Nothing happens for a reason.'

'You're here.'

'Because I needed my ship repaired!'

'Yes, but you brought everyone with you. People from across Linaria, despite the animosities and rivalries.'

'That's coincidence. Nothing to do with me.'

Topeko smirked at her, but didn't continue the argument.

'So your advice is, what, to avoid Aciel?' Morgen asked.

Topeko nodded. 'I think it would be for the best if you do.'

Morgen shared a worried look with Moroda and Eryn. 'But what if he finds us? If his Arillians attack us, how are we to defend ourselves? I don't know about you, but I don't wanna be compelled to do anything!'

A hush descended, broken only by Andel pouring more glasses of water for them, then his slippered feet as he left the room.

Topeko's shoulders sagged, 'I suppose running and avoidance can only work for so long, if Linaria has come to war.' His eyebrows were furrowed in deep thought. 'One Arillian with compulsion is bad enough. The fact he has brought dragons into it? They will destroy Linaria if pushed.'

'Amarah has agreed to fly me across the sea. When her ship is repaired, I will bring my sister into this knowledge.' Sapora withdrew his hands from his pockets and tapped his nails together. 'She is the princess in Val Sharis. I am a prince of Sereth. If this rogue Arillian really does threaten Linaria, we need to act. I can put plans in motion to bolster our defences.' He stopped by the edge of the table. 'You say your magic protects you from his compulsion. We Varkain and Ittallan have our *meraki*. Perhaps we can fight against it, too.'

'Even with that, you may not be immune,' Topeko warned.

'No. But it will slow his attack. That's an advantage I can use.'

Moroda was stunned by Sapora's words. Until now, she'd thought of him as nothing but a selfish, creepy Varkain who delighted in causing fear.

If *he* was doing something, *she* wanted to as well. 'We'll help, too.'

'Help? What are you talking about?' Eryn hissed back at her.

'I don't know. We can't go home. We have to move forward.'

Eryn sighed. 'I don't think we can do much.'

Topeko tilted his head. 'Do I understand correctly? You're willing to step forward and defend Linaria? Though you have neither the training nor ability to do so?'

Moroda nodded. It felt futile, but she refused to sit back and do nothing. Amarah would be right about her, otherwise. Even when her father had died, Eryn had been the one to step up, despite being younger. It was *her* turn to be the responsible sister.

Topeko scratched his chin thoughtfully, gems glittering. 'Perhaps...'

'Perhaps what?' Moroda dared to hope.

'Perhaps...Well. It's a ghost of an idea, really. If you're willing to band together. To stand against him...Perhaps a dragon might well be the best solution.'

'What're you talking about? You said dragons are the one causing half the problems!' Amarah snapped.

'Young ones, yes.'

'But there are no Sevastos dragons anymore either? You said so earlier?' Moroda's head was spinning.

'No. But that isn't to say there aren't old dragons. We refer to them as Archons. An honorific. A dragon of that power would be crucial to Aciel's cause. If we could get one on our side. Get one to attack Aciel before he grows too strong...'

Moroda wasn't sure she liked where he was going with this idea.

Kohl folded his arms and paced the room. 'Take the source of his power away before he can grow stronger. Aciel was never much of a threat until he started killing dragons. It could...it *could* work.'

'It is always best to disembowel the opponent before they grow too strong,' Sapora added.

Amarah stood up. 'You can't be serious? You ain't killing more dragons!'

Kohl shook his head. 'No, no. But *preventing* Aciel from amassing more strength? Allying with the dragons themselves? There might be something in that.'

'I had been thinking...Wondering...' Topeko trailed off, eyebrows furrowed.

'Whatever you're thinking, it can't be good,' Amarah said, her voice low.

Moroda couldn't understand why Amarah seemed to trust Topeko enough with her ship and to stay in his home, yet be so wary of him.

Topeko plucked a wooden box, slightly larger than the palm of his hand, from a chest of drawers opposite the bookcase. The same insignias she'd seen on the clothes of the Samolen decorated the box's lid. 'Something from the university. A gift that I think will help you, Moroda. And any who wish to protect Linaria.'

'That seems convenient.' Amarah sounded like she was speaking through gritted teeth.

'Convenient?' Topeko looked hurt.

'This is just another of your manipulations, ain't it? It's always the bloody same. That's why you had us wandering around the university listening to your damned stories. Putting ideas in our heads.' She folded her arms.

'Amarah. Rhea sent you to me. Perhaps *this* was the reason.'

Amarah's scowl darkened, all laughter gone. 'No. I came here because my ship was damaged by some rogue dragon. There's no *reason* for any of this! Shit happens. People chase power. You were just the closest bolt hole.'

Moroda didn't know what to think of Amarah and Topeko's fractured relationship. He was old enough to be her father, if not grandfather, and clearly cared for her. Amarah seemed to both desire it and be repulsed by it.

Topeko ignored Amarah and held the box out to Moroda. 'Here. Open it.'

Moroda wasn't sure she liked everyone's attention on her. Topeko, Eryn, Amarah, Kohl, Sapora, and Morgen all stared, and she didn't know where to look. She took another sip of her tea, clutching the mug tightly as if it would give her strength.

Then she turned her attention to the box.

She shivered, some unseen power caressing her mind. Whatever was in the box reminded her of Aciel's touch, though far less terrifying.

'If you have a gift, Topeko? We would be honoured.' Eryn took her sister's hand in hers, and the touch soothed her.

'What is going on? What is all this?' Palom's booming voice echoed as he and Anahrik entered the room.

They'd all formed a semi-circle around herself, Topeko,

and the box, and though Anahrik bounded in to join, Palom lingered in the doorway.

Amarah rolled her eyes. '*Apparently* we're going to find a dragon to fight Aciel.'

Palom nodded. 'Fight Aciel? Good. I am ready.'

She looked at the two Ittallan by the door, saw strength and stubbornness in equal measure, and took a deep breath.

Before she could talk herself out of it, Moroda reached forward and took the box from the mage.

16

Something pulsed within the box.

If Moroda hadn't braced, she was sure she'd have dropped the box in shock.

While there was no flash of light or spark of electricity, there was *something* inside. Something that pressed against the air.

'Open it.'

Moroda's gaze snapped to Topeko. Worry must have shown on her face because he chuckled and gestured to the box. She unfastened the clip holding the lid in place and carefully peeled it back, revealing three silver rings each studded with a blue gem.

She furrowed her eyebrows, unsure what she had expected, but three rings certainly hadn't been it. If anything, she'd thought a creature was inside. The way the air pressure had shifted, she'd have put money on there being something alive in the box.

Then it clicked.

The stones in the rings were the same as the gems embedded in the Samolens' cheeks.

'This will enable you to defend yourself against even Aciel. For a time.' Topeko offered an encouraging smile.

'I can really take one?'

'Yes. And your sister. Morgen too, if you wish.'

Moroda hesitated. Kohl, Sapora, Palom, and Anahrik all had their race's magic. As far as she was aware, Amarah didn't have access to such powers. 'What about Amarah?'

'I can fight the old-fashioned way, thank you very much,' Amarah said, almost as if she'd expected Moroda's question.

Moroda glanced from the sky pirate to the scholar.

'Amarah's strength is with the scythe. That's her preferred way of protecting herself. Besides, she'll be navigating the ship. No need for this,' Topeko said.

Despite her uncertainty, Moroda offered the box to her sister and Morgen. After they'd taken their rings, Moroda gently lifted hers out of the box and slipped it onto her index finger. Heat flared through her palm, warming every inch of her skin as if she stood in an open plain during midsummer.

'This is an honour, Topeko.' She bowed her head. It was more than an optional class of study. The point of the rings, of giving her, Eryn, and Morgen access to this power, was so she could take a stand against Aciel.

Moroda was sure not to forget that.

'Of course, non-Samolen students at the university study a minimum of two years to learn as much as we are able to teach, and those of Samolen descent study far longer as their capabilities reach greater depths. *Khanna* will be repaired in a matter of days, so I will give you books of theory to study on your way. I shall teach the practical side of things as best I can in the time we have.'

'I definitely want to learn,' Moroda replied.

'And me,' Eryn agreed, taking her sister's hand and nodding to Topeko.

'Good. Morgen?'

'I can fight already. But I'll take whatever I can from you, too,' Morgen said.

'Good.'

Moroda caressed the stone with the thumb on her other hand, excited but feeling out of place.

'I said earlier that we are Rhea's creation. We all have access to the power she has given us, the energy, the same magic of the dragons. *Ra*, it is called. Life magic,' Topeko began, intoning slowly. 'The crystals in these rings will harness your inner power, and bring it forth to protect you when you call upon it. You will not have much time to practice, so you must listen carefully, and do as I tell you, to be able to access it. The crystal is a conduit of your own abilities. Do not forget this. The stone does not hold the power. *You do*. The stone simply helps enhance it in useful ways. Do you understand?'

'Yes.' Eryn said, echoing Moroda's thoughts.

'Linaria is full of life. Of energy. Every living being is connected to it. So we can move flames, we can warm up or cool down, we can take the energy we have moved or drawn and shield ourselves from harm. It saps your own energy while you are learning, so you will find it draining. But, it will keep you safe when you have no other options.'

He waved his arms, every torch around the room igniting, save one, right in front of where they stood. 'Raise your ring hand to one of the lit torches,' he instructed. 'Feel the heat, feel the vibration on the palm of your hand. Allow your vision to blur and see yourself and the flame as one stream of energy, of light.'

Moroda did as she was told, and although she could feel the heat from the fire, she struggled to see herself and it as one.

'Relax your arm, bend your elbow. Your stone will identify your energy and the fire's energy when you do. When you have this knowledge, this connection, you can see it can be moved easily from one place to another, like tipping water from a jug into a cup.'

The three of them stood beside Topeko, arms outstretched. Moroda found her arm trembling with the effort to keep it held up, and Topeko's advice to relax was not helping.

Amarah snorted again, loudly eating fruit and watching, but giving no encouragement.

Moroda could feel Sapora's eyes on her, and her stomach quivered at the sensation. His gaze made her uneasy, and she tried to regain focus. But the cold sensation on her back was hard to ignore, and she whipped around to see whether he was actually looking at her or imagining things.

It was a mistake.

The flame from her torch burst from the bracket and followed her hand movement, whirling around the room and flying towards Sapora.

Moroda's eyes grew wide as she realised what was happening, and Sapora, reflexes on form, bolted out of the way as the chair he sat on burst into flame. 'Watch what you're doing, Moroda!'

Moroda blinked and jumped back—Sapora was right beside her, and he did not look pleased.

'I...I...I don't...'

'She is a student, Sapora. No harm was done,' Topeko said, extinguishing the flames with another wave.

'She is careless and stupid,' Sapora replied, glaring at Moroda, his nose almost touching hers. 'In my country you can be killed for attempting to harm royalty.'

'Then it's a good thing we ain't in *your* country,' Amarah said, voice almost growling.

Moroda's stomach churned as Amarah defended her.

She was already overcome with fatigue from the ring, and her hands trembled. 'Sapora, I'm so sorry, I...I didn't mean... I was trying to do as Topeko said, and I...'

'All is well,' Topeko said, earning another scowl from Sapora. 'An excellent first attempt. It's a natural ability, but it isn't easy to harness. Eat, all of you. Then try again.'

'*Without* using me as a target,' Sapora added, skulking off to the other corner of the room, as far away from where they would be practising as he could get, without leaving.

Moroda and Eryn shared a look, and Moroda grimaced at Morgen's concerned frown. The last thing she wanted to do was incite a battle, especially with Sapora, but elation filled her regardless.

She had used Samolen magic and hardly realised she had done so!

She sat down and gratefully took some of the fruit, her mind spinning with possibilities. 'Think where we could go. What we could do.'

Eryn frowned. 'You shouldn't have to learn all this. If it weren't for Aciel...'

'Why is he doing this?' Moroda asked aloud, not that she expected Eryn to have the answers. 'Is he so filled with wrath? Despair?'

Topeko sat down and chose a small, round fruit with lightly furred skin. He peeled it slowly. 'This will not be so much a war of Aciel and his followers against the people of Linaria, I fear. It will be Arillians against the dragons...and, perhaps, the dragons will cast their flames on the remaining people and burn us all, reducing Linaria to nothing. If Aciel continues, this will be Linaria's fate.' Some of the sparkle left his jewels and he stared at the pale yellow flesh of the fruit. 'Perhaps it is time Linaria was cleansed of the hate that has grown in its people.'

'The war is past. Arillians know they cannot stand

against us for second time. We will crush them again,' Palom boomed.

Kohl flinched. 'I do not agree with Aciel or his behaviour. But he *is* hurting. Our people have been mistreated for generations. Many Arillians seek to right the wrongs inflicted by the rest of the world.'

Amarah scoffed. 'Plenty of people have been mistreated —you see them building an army and trying to burn down half the world? Damn coward. I bet he'd lose in a fight by himself, that's why he's hiding behind all these people who don't even want to follow him!'

Kohl lowered his gaze.

'Nothing to say to that, Kohl?'

'I will not speak ill of my kin out of respect, no matter what they do.'

'Excuse me? They start going around compelling people to do Rhea knows what, and you ain't got nothing to say about that?'

'Amarah,' Topeko warned.

'No! I've had enough of being pushed around. I do what *I* want. Always have. Yes, I help myself to pickings, but I don't kill for fun like that snake.' She glared at Sapora. 'If anything, prince, you should get your subjects to take on this Arillian. Destroy each other. That'd do a world of good and rid Linaria of both you vermin.'

'Watch your tongue, thief.' Sapora took a step towards her.

'Ro, what are we going to do?' Eryn asked, clutching her ring.

'Well, what can we do?' Morgen got to his feet. 'We need to stop this Arillian. And avoid any dragons, too.'

Palom said,

'What Amarah says may be true. This Arillian...He may be weak alone.'

'Exactly.' The sky pirate agreed.

'You're not going to fight him alone, Palom? I thought you just wanted to get back to Val Sharis?'

Anahrik asked, a slight tremble in his voice.

'Yes, I do. But there may be no Val Sharis left if he continues his rampage. Our cities can fall as easily as Niversai.'

Moroda took a breath. 'So...we need to seek an old dragon. Reach it before Aciel does. If his power grows with every dragon he takes, we have to act quickly.' She didn't like everyone's attention on her, but she held firm.

'There are many dragons in Val Sharis. Aciel has not yet touched my homeland. I would know if he had.' Palom's voice deepened into a growl. 'If these old dragons, or even Sevastos, still live...there is where we will find them.'

'I agree,' Sapora said. 'The time of my birth approaches, and with winter, I shall ascend the throne of my own people. Returning across the Sea of Nami is the best next step.'

Topeko nodded, solemn. 'Then it is decided. Amarah, I will ensure your ship is repaired as swiftly as possible. In the meantime, you should rest and resupply before your journey across the ocean. Moroda, Eryn, Morgen, I shall teach you what I can while you're here.'

'What if I don't wanna fly you all there?' Amarah folded her arms, defiant. 'Why should I risk *Khanna* or myself again hunting for these bloody beasts? You saw what the last one did to my ship, and apparently that was a young one!'

'Where else would you go?' Topeko asked gently. 'You told me you wished to cross the ocean and find a new crew. Why not take this group with you? Surely they can be of use on the ship? Keep it clean?'

'A clean ship does not clothe, feed, or arm me.'

'Then I shall pay on arrival to Taban Yul,' Sapora hissed,

approaching her slowly. 'My sister, the princess, will have enough crowns for even your thirst, I think.'

Amarah glared at the Varkain. 'This is bigger than me. Find someone else to fly you. Why should I risk my ship for a snake?'

Topeko raised his hand. 'Amarah, you are like a daughter to me. Do not spoil your chance to help something far greater than yourself because of selfishness.'

'Selfish indeed. You won't even save your own skin unless you profit,' Sapora replied with a sneer. 'Shame you can't earn gold fairly—you could have wowed the crowds in Corhaven with a few of your Samolen magic tricks. Easier gold than airship racing. But even that was beyond you.'

'What did you say, snake?'

Sapora's grin grew wider, exposing a few of his teeth. 'Just because you were incapable of learning magic does not mean you need to insult me every time I'm in your presence. I am a prince, and do not take kindly to threats.'

'How dare you!'

'It's so very obvious. I now see where you developed that chip on your shoulder. You're a *worthless* Samolen. I did wonder how a low-class peasant knew one of the esteemed scholars in Berel.'

Amarah drew a small blade from her pocket and brandished it towards Sapora. 'One more word and I'll slit your throat!'

'Amarah, calm yourself,' Palom said, standing beside her. 'Ignore him.'

Amarah's hand shook where she held the blade, and Moroda stepped towards her sister, her heart racing as she watched.

The sky pirate's face was flushed, and she widened her stance, ready to attack.

'Looks like I've hit a nerve, thief. It explains that scar on your cheek, too. Did you cut it out yourself or were you cast out by the Samolen?' Sapora added.

Amarah lunged at the Varkain's jibe, but was held firm by Palom's swift action. 'Let me GO!'

Unable to wriggle out of Palom's grasp, Amarah hurled the blade at Sapora, who easily stepped aside as the weapon clattered to the ground.

Moroda saw tears well up in Amarah's eyes, and a swell of sympathy rose for her. 'Amarah...'

'I don't need your fucking pity. Get your hands *off* me, Palom!' Amarah yelled, attempting to wriggle out of his hold and resorting to scratching the Ittallan before he relented.

Sapora smirked. 'See. You can't do anything, can you?'

'I do whatever I choose! How *dare* you try and say I can't do something!'

'You still haven't managed to get me to Val Sharis. Don't forget that was our bargain. If it wasn't for me, you wouldn't even have *Khanna*.'

'I'll do what has to be done. You just see if I don't!' She snatched up her thrown blade and stormed out.

Moroda saw the smugness in Sapora's grin, and her stomach knotted. She was embarrassed for Amarah's inability to use magic, and hated Sapora for insulting her so very publicly.

It was shameful.

She wanted to follow Amarah to make sure she was all right—but knew the pirate's pride would probably be injured even more if she did so. That, and she wasn't even sure she would be able to comfort her.

'So easily manipulated,' Sapora sighed, as if disappointed.

Moroda risked another glance at Sapora and wondered why he felt the need to attack Amarah so much. The two had bickered constantly, but Sapora seemed to enjoy feeling superior.

Regardless of whether Sapora found it amusing to pick on Amarah, or wanted to tear them all apart, Moroda wasn't going to stand for it.

In the past, the people of Corhaven and Val Sharis banded together to form the Imperial Guard and drive out the Arillian threat. They set aside their differences to fight a common enemy, and were all the stronger for it. 'And that's what we're doing, too,' she whispered to herself.

She stood up, raised her hand, and practised.

17

Palom circled the Sevastos crystals, gaze lingering on the desert sunlight reflected in each facet. If he closed his eyes and concentrated, he could feel the deep power residing in the stones.

The power of dragons.

It had gone into the forging of the greatest weapons Linaria had ever seen, ended the great war, and become something to study.

At least they were shown proper reverence here, and hadn't been forgotten.

Soon, he'd make his own mark on Linaria. If anyone could crack the writing, it would be Anahrik. And Palom believed his weapon forging to be second-to-none in Taban Yul. Together, they'd add their own page into Linaria's history. That's how Anahrik had sold the idea to him.

Palom simply wanted to see the weapons that featured in his childhood stories. Now, he had the chance to forge his own. To use the weapon's strength to protect those he loved, and decimate any who might harm him.

Including Aciel.

He thought back to the eclectic group of people he and

Anahrik travelled with. Two Goldstones. A sky pirate. A soldier of the Imperial Guard. A dragon-hunting Arillian. A prince of the Varkain.

Together, they'd agreed to do something about Aciel before he brought his destructive forces to Taban Yul.

It might have been folly. But knowing he had a chance to recreate the *Valta Forinja*, no matter how slim, their stand against the rogue Arillian might be enough. The strength of the Arillians was well known, and for all their brave talk, he wasn't sure they'd be enough.

The weapons would give them an edge, if he and Anahrik could recreate them.

Heat emanated from the crystals before him, thrumming with power. Just a sliver of that went into the *Valta Forinja*. He wondered what the dragons looked like when they had been alive. What a force of nature they had been.

Ereven spheres—at least, the decorative ones—offered a burst of light as the morning sun shone through the glass. University students streamed past him in a line, their matching robes easily identifying them.

Music of the Kaloset echoed through the streets, rejuvenating him and lending energy to the morning. It was too early for the intense desert heat to oppress the air, and in the cool stillness, it reminded Palom of his homeland.

Amarah was busy loading up the ship and they would be in the air soon enough.

Despite knowing returning to Val Sharis was the right course of action, the idea of it filled Palom with trepidation. There were people he didn't want to face. Wasn't sure he could.

After two days in the desert, they were finally going back.

He wondered whether Moroda and Eryn would stay in Val Sharis or if they'd insist on returning to Corhaven.

Either way, he would ensure they were comfortable. If it meant flying back with them to Niversai, he'd do that.

Perhaps once they saw the beauty of Taban Yul, they'd apply for residency. Then he could keep an eye on them while he worked.

They'd probably find the capital of Val Sharis more to their tastes, especially after seeing Eryn's reaction to the glassworks. Everything in Taban Yul put the rest of Linaria to shame. Even the—

Footsteps lighter than the students' caught his attention, and he turned around in time to see Moroda approach the courtyard, her gaze drawn to the five enormous crystals on the altar. She was so focussed on them, she didn't see him as she walked past.

The blue crystal on her ring shimmered, reflecting the enormous crystals.

He'd known she was a determined woman, and brave, if a little shy. Topeko had said she'd stood up to Aciel. Held his compulsion at bay, even for a short time. There was more to her than he'd initially thought, and he was pleased with his decision to aid Moroda and her sister.

'One last look before we leave?' Palom raised an eyebrow.

Moroda blinked, forcing herself away from her apparent daydream, and stared at him. Embarrassment reddened her cheeks, and she smiled. 'If only I'd studied here. I can hardly imagine what I'd have learned. What heights I could have ascended to.' Sadness tinged her voice.

'Perhaps. But you are here now. You have that ring. Topeko tutored you.' As far as Palom could see, she had plenty to be grateful for.

Moroda reached out to touch the side of the nearest crystal. 'It's rough.' The stone in her ring pulsed, the crystal under her palm flashed, and a shard splintered off. She withdrew her hand swiftly, as if burned. 'Oh, sorry!'

Something akin to shame flooded Palom for an instant, then it was gone. After what he and Anahrik had done, there was no chance he'd be angry with her. He glanced around, but there were no scholars, and all the students had already filed away inside the university. 'I will not tell if you do not.'

Moroda chewed her lip and nodded. She delicately held up the splinter and studied it. A sliver of crystal, its colours changed in the sunlight, blue one moment, pink the next. The stone on her finger pulsed, sending out a flash of blue light. It twinkled as much as the nearest Sevastos stone. 'Perhaps...perhaps it's a sign of good luck from Rhea?'

'Perhaps. But we should get back to ship before you incur any more of...Rhea's luck.'

'Oh! Amarah will *kill* us if we're late to leave!' Moroda gasped. Sliding the crystal into her pocket, she whirled away and raced across the bridge. 'Come on, Palom!'

Palom stared at the crystals a moment longer, sure to show proper reverence, then followed.

By THE TIME Palom and Moroda reached the hangar, *Khanna* was ready to fly.

Topeko and Andel were saying their goodbyes, waving from the ground, while Amarah stared out, fingers drumming on the side rail impatiently.

'Hurry up, hurry up. I was about to fly off without you!' Amarah said the moment she caught sight of them. 'You're lucky Topeko gave us so much to load, or we'd have been long gone by now. Everyone's been waiting.'

Palom tipped his head in apology. There were several

sacks on the ground, straining with the weight of their contents. 'This is for us?'

Topeko beamed. 'Food, drink, clothes, accessories, books. All essential supplies! Moroda, I hope you and your sister will study.'

'Essential?' Palom knelt slightly to scoop up two of the bags and hoisted one over each shoulder. 'Amarah you should not leave without rest of this.' At least if he helped load *Khanna*, Amarah would be less frustrated with him. Topeko's generosity staggered him, and he wondered why Amarah was so cold towards the scholar. If Topeko had been his friend, he'd be making him free weapons every spare moment he had!

A shame the Samolen had no use for such things.

'I'll treat the books with the greatest care. Thank you so much, Topeko.' Moroda offered the scholar a full curtsy.

At the commotion, Eryn peered over the side rail and her face lit up when she saw them.

'What have I told you about wandering off and daydreaming?' Eryn reprimanded her sister, though she didn't sound angry, and helped her clamber on board.

'It's okay! I just wanted to see more of the city of mages while I had the chance.' Moroda hugged Eryn, no doubt to placate her.

'We ought to stay close, Ro. Morgen was about to head out and look for you!'

'I'm sorry! Palom was with me. Don't worry so much.'

Palom offered both Goldstones a nod, though he wondered how much protection Moroda really needed, as he placed the last of their supplies where Amarah pointed.

Just as they were settling down to take off, Andel waved frantically, grabbing their attention.

He and Moroda approached him, and the young apprentice pointed at Moroda's ring.

'This?' Moroda held up her finger.

Andel nodded enthusiastically, then withdrew a small, palm-sized parcel wrapped in linen. When she took it, he pointed down at Topeko.

'Is from Topeko?' Palom asked.

Andel nodded again, then scampered off the ship just as Amarah started *Khanna's* engines.

'Another of Topeko's gifts? I'm dying to know what it is!' Morgen hurried over, Eryn on his heels.

Palom leaned forward to get a closer look.

Moroda carefully unwrapped the linen to reveal a glass sphere that sat heavy in the palm of her hand. A curled phoenix feather lay within, shimmering in the sunlight.

'An ereven sphere!' Eryn gasped, reaching forward to take it from Moroda with both hands. 'What a treasure!'

'Treasure? What?' Amarah yelled, peering at them over her ship's wheel.

Palom tried not to laugh at the sky pirate's sudden interest now that treasure had been mentioned.

'Topeko gave us an ereven sphere,' Eryn clarified.

Amarah nodded knowingly. 'Stole a bagful of those when I left the country. The Goldstones in Corhaven love decorating their homes with 'em. Sold 'em four crowns a piece.'

Palom wondered why Andel and Topeko had chosen an ornament as a gift. It was valuable, true, but he couldn't see the point. There was so much he didn't understand about the Samolen culture. No meat in their food. Unable to fight or use weapons in their cities. Peculiar gifts.

'We could bring it back to Niversai and sell it!' Eryn pulled on Moroda's sleeve. 'Four crowns? I'll bet we could double that when we say it was from a scholar of Ranski!'

Moroda frowned. 'We aren't selling Topeko's gifts! He gave it to us for a reason!'

'Yes, because we're going through hard times. What else would we do with it?'

Moroda took the sphere back and held it close. 'We *aren't* selling it.' She ignored her sister's protests and pocketed it, then held up her ring. 'Topeko gave us another gift. That's not something to sell, either.'

'I dunno about all this Samolen magic. Bit unnatural, isn't it? Give me good steel in my hand any day.' Morgen leaned over the side of the ship.

'It's okay, Morgen. You've been training with swords and shields a while.' Moroda plucked one of Topeko's books and thumbed through it. 'A bit more practice, and you'll get the knack.'

'Goldstones. I'm warning you, any fires on my ship and I'm holding you personally responsible. Don't think I won't throw you both overboard!' Amarah snapped.

Palom watched Moroda take a seat with her book, while Eryn and Morgen stood next to each other, watching the desert landscape roll pass from *Khanna's* side rail. They spoke of Niversai, and how things used to be, and Palom wondered how he'd feel if a dragon or Arillians destroyed his home.

Kohl and Anahrik scouted in shifts—Amarah didn't want any other surprises while they crossed the sea—and Palom settled down on deck and checked his longsword.

It was time to rest.

Time to prepare for the challenges ahead, and for whatever awaited in Val Sharis.

As the hours dragged by, Moroda paid less attention to her books and listened more to Amarah, though with the wind blasting across deck, Palom only caught a handful of their words. The Goldstone seemed to want to know more about the ship—and flying it—and he watched with interest as Amarah's dark looks lessened, eventually giving way to her becoming more animated and open to discussion. He supposed a thirst for knowledge and ever-present curiosity were good traits to have. Far better than being empty-headed cowards—which many considered Goldstones to be.

When not flying ahead, Anahrik studied his own book from Berel. Much of it was in poor condition, the text illegible or missing, yet slowly but surely, Anahrik pieced together the basics of the process.

They would need to return to the forge immediately to get things underway. What wasn't apparent in any of the text was the time it would take. Was it something that would take two hours or two years? It would be useless if they couldn't make the weapons before Aciel reached them.

On the second day of travel, the Sea of Nami opened under them—an expanse of dark water that divided the two largest continents. With *Khanna* at full speed, they ate up the distance, and Palom found himself ahead, eager for a glimpse of his homeland.

He tried not to pace the deck—that was Anahrik's nervous tell—but it was hard to keep his rising emotions bottled up. Palom prided himself on keeping calm and unflinching in most situations, and he wasn't about to let emotions get the better of him.

Below the ship, seawater churned, and overhead, clouds swept in from the north, blotting out much of the sunlight. Looking up at them, trying to decide whether rain was on the way, Palom spotted several dark shapes circling high above.

His stomach tightened.

'Dragons!'

Moroda approached him, her gaze matching his gesture. She smiled when she spotted them, which confused Palom. He and the others had grimaced.

With everything Aciel had been doing, any dragons could be a potential threat.

These dragons were too far away to make out their features, but when the few shafts of sun caught their scales, he saw rusty red-orange, pale yellow-gold, and mottled brown. He broadened his gaze, trying to count them, yet more and more seemed to appear—their wings spread wide, catching thermals to keep their vast forms aloft. He'd counted twenty-seven before the wind gently pushed them away, further east, towards the darkening clouds.

'Probably going to Val Sharis,' Palom said, watching them. 'Better there than on us. This ship struggled with one dragon, what in Rhea's name would we do against whole tribe?'

'*Khanna* would be fine, stop complaining,' Amarah retorted.

He wondered whether these dragons would be safe from Aciel, or if they would be controlled, too. Whether they really stood a chance.

Moroda's smile faded, knuckles whitening as she gripped the handrail.

'You've lost your light-step,' Palom said.

His words brought her out of her daze. 'My what?'

'Not right word, I think...but...you look now like you carry pain of world in your heart. This should not be so, Moroda.'

'Don't be silly, Palom.' Moroda laughed at his jest. 'I'm tired of studying Topeko's books, that's all. It's quite draining!'

'I know. You have spent whole flight reading and practising. You should rest—even I cannot spend more than few hours in my true form, and that is most natural of all things to me.'

'You're probably right. I've been working too hard. I'll—'

A wave of something not unlike water, but not quite as tangible, hit Palom square in the chest. Goosebumps rose on his arms and legs as he faced the source, peering out into the cloudy sky and the sea which raged below.

The gathering clouds were darkening by the second, and thunder rolled out low and slow in the distance.

He rested a hand on the hilt of his sword.

'I feel something out there. A storm?' Moroda stared out towards the horizon.

'Something more than that,' Morgen said, joining the two of them. Eryn trailed behind him, hands clasped together. The soldier contemplated the horizon for a few moments. 'Look. Clouds are moving much too quickly. Aril- lians, I'll wager.'

Palom shivered as the wave of energy pulsed again, the air thick around him where it touched his skin. If it *was* Arillians, they needed to stay clear. They weren't ready to fight.

Moroda turned away. 'We'd better warn Amarah. Is it...is it him...?'

Palom sincerely hoped it was *not* Aciel.

It did not take long for the rain to fall, and when it came, it was relentless. The wind, which had been nothing more than a calm, cool breeze for most of the day, turned vicious, buffeting the deck. It caught the rain and threw it into his face like a thousand tiny needles, all the while thunder echoed off the waves in the distance.

'What the hell is going on?' Amarah angrily wiped rain- water off her face and tried to peer into the darkening sky. 'Whoever heard of rain rolling round *that* fast?'

Khanna trembled in the wind, and the low lighting in the cabin and out on deck was snuffed out in an instant, plunging the airship and her crew into murky darkness.

Moroda wrapped her thick cloak around herself. 'It's so

dark. Are Arillian storms *this* strong? Is this what Anahrik meant when he spoke of them before?'

'This ain't right. This definitely ain't right,' Amarah said, opening her sails and wings fully, her right hand hovering over *Khanna's* weapons. Her eyes darted around, looking for the hidden enemy.

Morgen drew his sword and stared at the skies. 'Palom, do you think it's Aciel?'

'It is an Arillian storm. But Aciel? I do not know,' Palom replied, on his guard. As if to give his words truth, a winged man approached the ship from overhead. He was about to spring into action, when he recognised the cloak. 'Kohl is coming in, look above.'

Sheets of rain slowed Kohl's approach, but he landed just as another peal of thunder rolled through the sky, louder than before.

'It's another airship. Seems like they have an escort of Arillians.' Kohl held his hat down in the wind. 'Amarah, if we change course, they won't see us. It's too dark and the storms they've brought with them have reduced visibility. No need to get involved.'

'But...they're crossing the sea, aren't they? What about the dragons?' Moroda's breathing quickened. 'We'll just run into them again when we reach Val Sharis...even if we get there before them, it won't be long before they start attacking the cities! And doing what they did in Niversai?'

Palom had been in favour of avoiding them, but Moroda's words changed things. If they were heading for his homeland already, he had to deter them. 'I will not let Arillians attack Val Sharis.' He strode towards Amarah. He and Anahrik didn't have any of their legendary weapons forged yet, so any sort of attack was out of the question. But perhaps a distraction? Something to delay them? 'This ship has weapons, does it not?'

'Depends how many Arillians are there? If it's one or two, maybe we can pick them off in a sneak attack,' Amarah replied, raising the altitude of *Khanna*.

'There are more than two,' Kohl confirmed.

Amarah rolled her eyes. 'I ain't risking my ship a second time. Kohl, is it a warship they're on?'

The Arillian shrugged.

'It...may be.'

'There you are. *Khanna's* ain't got a chance against that. I'd rather fly away and avoid any chance of a fight.'

Palom rounded on Kohl.

'What do you know about this?'

Kohl walked away, further out onto the deck, where the full assault of wind and water besieged him. 'Flight may be preferable to fighting in this instance. Everyone should get below deck while Amarah steers the ship away.'

Why did Kohl want to be alone on deck with Amarah? Kohl was a coward, and in league with the Arillians if his conversation with Fogu had been anything to go by.

Taking his eyes off the enemy, even when retreating, was never a good thing.

Palom shook his head.

'I am not going below. Not while these Arillians are here. I want to see what I am up against.'

Kohl didn't face him, his attention locked on the sea. 'The weather will only get worse as we get closer. Visibility, whatever we have of it, will be reduced to almost nothing.'

'Amarah cannot go below. I will be her eyes at front of deck. And I want to see what your colleagues are up to.'

'Colleagues?'

'You are all family aren't you? You know great deal about them. I need to see for myself what you are up to—you are not going to hide, are you?'

'What exactly are you accusing me of? If it weren't for

me, you'd all have been captured by those scouts back in Corhaven!'

'Palom! Kohl! Please!' Moroda cried, rushing over to them, one arm pressed against her face to keep the wind and rain out of her eyes.

Palom drew his sword and Kohl crouched, flexing the lower feathers on his wings, the temperature dropping as he called upon his own power.

'We may have a very real battle on our hands! Please don't fight one another!' Moroda pulled at Palom's arm.

A flash of lightning ripped through the dark sky, bringing with it a shockwave that shook *Khanna* and brought everyone to their knees.

More wind slammed into the airship, pushing it lower, towards the writhing sea

Amarah cursed as she adjusted the flight. 'This is getting dangerous!'

Palom staggered back and grabbed the rail to anchor himself. He looked overboard, gasping as a maelstrom formed in the churning waters off the port side. 'Amarah! Get higher! We might be pulled in!'

'Another maelstrom!' Anahrik yelled, pointing at a second vortex on the ship's other side.

'It's Jato,' Kohl spat, watching the first maelstrom grow. 'She's the only one able to create a storm like this.'

'Jato?' Palom asked.

He remembered Kohl had asked his colleagues about someone called Jato and been attacked for it.

'One of Aciel's generals. His second-in-command, in fact.' Kohl stepped away from the side. 'It probably means Aciel himself is with her on that ship.'

Palom followed Kohl's movements. One of Aciel's generals? No wonder this storm was so powerful. He thought he knew what Arillians were capable of. But he'd been wrong. This was beyond that knowledge.

He'd had no idea it could affect the sea, too. What if it created a vortex and sucked airships from the sky? They'd be dead meat. 'When this is over, you will tell us everything you know about Aciel and his followers. If we had known he had this person to create this storm and water maelstroms, we would not have come this way!' Fangs began to grow in his mouth as his fury took over, his body beginning to transform.

'Don't you dare attack me, Ittallan!' Kohl retorted, backing away from him.

'Palom! Come on, this ain't the right time!' Anahrik rested a hand on his shoulder.

He coughed and took several pained breaths. The situation reminded him of what had happened back in Taban Yul, with Mateli. Back when he'd failed to protect people. Failed Lathri.

'Kohl, do they even know we're here? Or are they just creating this weather for a damned laugh?' Amarah ignored the flared tempers.

Palom was glad she'd kept her cool, and was ashamed for letting his own fear and anger get the better of him.

'It...is possible. Jato might well be causing this for the pleasure of it. I suspect a storm as large as this would be seen from the coast of Val Sharis—it would be just like her to announce her arrival on the new continent with such a display of strength. Or perhaps there are other trading ships crossing the sea which are her intended target, and we're simply caught up in the size of her attack. It seems a lot of trouble to go to for one, lone ship, especially as small as *Khanna*.' Kohl turned away from Palom and Anahrik and made his way to where Amarah fought the wheel. 'Whether it's a direct attack on us or not, Jato's storm is *not* something to be caught in.'

Palom was about to ask Anahrik for his opinion when he noticed Sapora had crept onto the deck despite the rain. His fear intensified, and he hoped the raging storm masked it.

'I think you are missing a most valuable opportunity, my sky thief.' The Varkain casually joined the rest of the party, as if they were discussing food, not on the edge of an Arillian storm. 'An opportunity to obtain something *most* valuable and precious.'

Amarah huffed. 'I ain't in the mood to deal with you, snake.'

'I thought sky pirates were always on the lookout for treasure?'

'Sapora, what are you on about?'

'The Arillians are hunting dragons, no? To steal their power for themselves? Their power has grown quickly. They must have a way to track down the dragons. A way that *we* could use...'

'An ereven sphere! Topeko said they might have one!' Moroda reached into her pocket and took out her ornamental sphere.

'Very astute.' Sapora grinned, baring his pointed teeth.

'They will be crossing the sea, looking for more powerful dragons. We've learned their method of hunting them down. Stealing the *real* sphere from them would have two benefits—they would no longer be able to find the dragons, and *we* would have the means to.' Sapora drew out the silence until it became uncomfortable. 'Now. If *only* we knew someone who was good at stealing valuables...'

Palom bristled at the audacity of asking them to risk so much. 'That is not happening.'

'I don't steal from people who usually fight back.' Amarah laughed and waved a dismissive hand.

'Well, they won't fight back if *I* come along, too,' Sapora said.

Palom's throat tightened at the thought.

Surely Amarah would not degrade herself by working with the Varkain?

Amarah narrowed her eyes and mulled over the idea for a few, long moments. 'If they found us, they'd kill us, you know that, don't you?'

'Amarah. You cannot be thinking this?' Palom spluttered.

'Stealing the sphere *would* make Aciel lose his edge—he certainly won't be able to add to his power—but it'll turn his attention onto *Khanna*,' Amarah continued, one hand on her hip. 'But we've got the cover of darkness, of the brewing storm, and *Khanna* at full speed.'

Palom could tell Amarah was convinced already. Anything else she said was an act to save face in agreeing with Sapora. He shared an uneasy glance with Anahrik, who returned his worry.

'I'll ensure their attention is not on *Khanna*,' Sapora pressed.

Palom stepped forward. 'Amarah, this is not good idea. This is too much risk. There will be other ereven spheres in Val Sharis, I am sure. We can find one there, where it is safe. We cannot fight these Arillians, even Sapora cannot take on entire ship of their warriors!'

'I would not offer if I could not do it,' Sapora replied, though his attention was on Amarah.

Amarah said, 'Yeah, buying...that'll cost a few crowns though, a real one will. That's assuming we can even *find* one.'

'I know all the main traders. My network in Taban Yul is huge. I'll be able to track one down, easy,' Anahrik added.

Amarah scratched her nose. 'Or...there's *this one*. Right here. And it takes away the enemy's eyes.'

Sapora's grin grew until Palom was sure his face would split in two, and he turned away from the Varkain in disgust. He knew what Amarah's decision was, and he didn't know what game Sapora was playing, but his happiness made Palom uncomfortable.

Amarah probably wouldn't care what Sapora did as long as she got what she wanted.

But attempting to steal from the Arillians was beyond foolish. Their power was too great, couldn't they see that, even on the edge of the storm?

'Let me come with you.' Moroda blurted out.

Palom whirled around to face her. Was she really volunteering herself? 'You cannot be serious Moroda!'

Instead of shrinking under his gaze, she raised her chin, steeling herself. 'I just...I don't want anything to happen, *bad* to happen, and I...I want to go to make sure everything works out. I can help, too, if you need me. With the Samolen magic, I mean.'

'Ro, what are you *thinking*? You *want* to go on the Arillian ship with those two?' Eryn gasped, echoing Palom's own thoughts.

'Fine by me. Darkness is upon us, we should move, now, before their scouts see us.' Sapora walked to the ship's bow.

'Hold on a minute,' Amarah barked. 'I ain't got a plan, yet!'

'I will board their ship first, and ensure you are not met with resistance. You will locate and take the sphere, then return. We'll continue our journey, with the Arillians none-the-wiser.'

'That's not what I meant...' Amarah shook her head.

Shame flickered through Palom. The young Goldstone couldn't even fight, and yet here she was, volunteering herself.

Much like Amarah, the Goldstone was either brave or foolish. Probably both, lacking experience as she did.

'Morgen, you'll have to hold onto *Khanna* for me while I'm off ship. You do remember what I told you about flying? You and Eryn are always hanging about while I tell Moroda what's what.'

Morgen shuffled forward at the mention of his name. 'I *have* flown an airship before, you know.'

Amarah snorted. 'You can't compare those Imperial ships to my *Khanna*. Just keep her in one spot and adjust for any blasts of wind.'

'I know what I'm doing,' he muttered, face pink.

Amarah took a deep breath. 'Fine. I don't see as we got a choice. This is an opportunity, like Sapora said. It's too good to pass up. Plus it gives our snake a chance to make himself useful for once.'

Palom watched, stunned, unable to say or do anything to help, as Moroda readied herself to join Amarah's ranks of thieves.

18

'All right. My heist, my rules,' Amarah said, keeping *Khanna* low, close to the churning sea while she approached Jato's ship. 'I'll get as close as I can. Morgen will hold the wheel while Sapora gets on the rear deck. We'll use the steps on *Khanna's* side to get down. Me and Moroda wait while Sapora deals with any guards. Once the coast is clear, we join him, get the sphere, and get back onto *Khanna*. Kohl will be our eyes, and Anahrik, too, in case we have to get off sharpish. Everyone clear?'

Eryn shook her head, the only one in a crowd of agreement, but Amarah ignored her. One spoiled Goldstone's opinion didn't matter. The winds were getting stronger near the warship, and she had to get *Khanna* closer without being spotted. They hadn't seen any Arillians in the air, thank Rhea, which meant they had surprise on their side.

For now.

Eryn turned to her sister. 'Ro, I don't like this. This is far too much. This is above *anything* we were going to do.'

'Please try to understand, Ryn.' Moroda gave Eryn a hug. 'Without this sphere, we've no chance of finding a powerful dragon in Val Sharis. Without the dragon, we've no chance of stopping Aciel.'

Amarah tried not to roll her eyes. This wasn't the time for sentimentality.

As annoying as Goldstones were, at least Moroda could see the opportunity they had and was willing to act on it. Though she was a novice, she had some magic, too, thanks to the ring.

'I *do* understand! But I don't know why *you* have to go, too! I don't know why anyone here needs to get involved! Can't we just go home?' Tears formed in the corners of her eyes as she pleaded. 'You're going onto an enemy ship. Aciel himself could be on board! You'll be trapped there with a Varkain and a sky pirate, except this time, I can't come and save you!'

'Hey! Your sister ain't in any danger from me!' Amarah scowled. She was trying to get *Khanna* in position in the middle of a thunderstorm, and Eryn's whining wasn't helping.

Moroda said,

'I have the Samolen magic, don't forget. I can look after myself.'

Eryn's words choked in her throat, and she sobbed.

Khanna jerked in the air and Amarah glared at the sisters. 'Will you two be quiet? I'm trying to work here!'

Moroda lowered her voice. 'Please, Ryn, I'm scared enough as it is.'

'Then *don't* go! Stay on the ship with me!'

'Ryn, I promise I'll stay safe. I promise it'll be worth it.'

'Ro!'

Amarah huffed, finally quieting the two, and manoeuvred the ship into position. Once happy, she flattened her sails, locked her engines in place, and stepped away from the wheel. 'Hold her here, Morgen. Do *not* mess this up.'

She didn't trust anyone with her ship, but barking at the dutiful soldier who was used to taking orders was probably her best bet of keeping *Khanna* in one piece.

Morgen nodded, though he looked more nervous than Amarah would have liked.

Eryn's sniffles were muffled as she cried into Moroda's shoulder.

'Ro, I'm so scared.'

'I am too. But...I'm less scared when I *do* something. And I have the power to do something, now. You do, too. We've never had that before. It'll be all right.'

'Ryn, you're safe here.' Morgen offered some encouragement. 'For all their flaws, Amarah and Sapora can handle themselves if Moroda needs back up.'

'See? I'll be just fine.' Moroda stepped back when Eryn lifted her head. 'We won't be long.' She brought Eryn's hands to her lips and kissed them.

'Moroda. We're going. Now!' Amarah called, before walking to the ship's prow where Sapora waited. She hunkered down against the torrential rain, readying herself. Peering over the edge, she got the measure of the distance, and checked the way was clear.

When no scouts appeared, she nodded to Sapora, who slid down the steps and onto the waiting warship below without a sound. She had to admit, for a stealth mission, a Varkain was the ideal candidate.

Amarah drew her scythe and followed him down the steps carved into *Khanna's* side. Jato's warship flew below them, just a short drop beneath the edge of the steps. If she had any luck, they wouldn't encounter a single Arillian before they had their prize.

She was halfway down and readying herself to jump when Moroda finally joined her.

'You best not get in my way, Goldstone,' Amarah said.

Moroda nodded, though her breathing was already ragged.

Amarah heard the crashing waves far below, but it was too dark to see the water. The rushing wind drowned out all other noise, and her ears rang. She focussed on her footing, slipping into old, familiar habits. 'Sapora's on board. We wait here,' she shouted above the wind.

She hoped Anahrik and Kohl would do their jobs. Kohl was mostly good at keeping his word, but she didn't know how he'd react so close to the other Arillians. And Anahrik's attitude was irritating at most, though she couldn't fault his eyes or the speed of his warnings.

Amarah shifted her weight and braced herself against the gale, flexing her fingers. She needed to wait for Sapora's signal before leaping down into enemy territory. Patience was the virtue of all good thieves, but the stress of working with a new crew—including an inexperienced Goldstone— was a layer of pressure that Amarah could do without.

She couldn't even explain why she'd allowed Moroda to come along. Stupid Goldstone. Talking about *Khanna* and making her soft.

Damned Goldstone better make herself useful with Topeko's trinket.

Before Amarah could berate herself any more, Sapora stepped into view, eyes and teeth glinting in the darkness.

'He's back. Do we go?' Moroda asked, breathless.

'We go.'

Amarah grabbed Moroda's hand as they shuffled down the last few steps. Without checking whether Moroda was ready, Amarah leapt, and the pair of them dropped like stones onto the deck below.

Rolling on impact, Amarah was on her feet and across the deck before Moroda had managed to stand up again. She took a moment to get her bearings, then turned to

Moroda and grabbed her by the elbow. 'Follow me. Keep up. Keep quiet.'

Amarah darted after Sapora as he disappeared below deck, the familiar surge of adrenaline pushing her forward. Scurrying along the wide corridors, Amarah focussed on her breathing, keeping it even despite the urge to give in to excitement.

While she'd been aboard luxury cruise ships before, it was the first time she'd been on a warship. It dwarfed *Khanna*, and after a minute of darting down corridors and glancing into empty rooms, she realised the whole place was a maze.

The warship had several decks, with others towering above the rear one they had landed on, and most were well lit with oil lamps. A ship of this size could easily hold a thousand people, yet seemed eerily deserted. It put her on edge.

She and Moroda crouched low when they reached new corridors, waiting for Sapora to scout ahead and check the way ahead was clear for them.

Outside, the storm continued to rage, so even Moroda's less-than stealthy footsteps wouldn't be heard above the shrieking wind. It gave her some comfort.

'There's no one close by,' Moroda whispered as they waited at a crossroads.

'You're sure?' Amarah knew Samolen magic was real. She wasn't entirely sure of Moroda's understanding of it.

The Goldstone tapped the crystal on her ring, holding it up. 'People give off a warm buzz the closer I am to their energy. But the crystal is quiet.'

'Hmmm.'

After checking everything on the rear half of the ship's floor and finding nothing, they followed Sapora up a flight of stairs.

Just before they reached the top of the stairway, the lights on the floor above flickered.

Moroda hesitated. 'Amarah, there are people up there.'

Amarah dropped back as Sapora raced ahead. It didn't take him long to reappear. Giving them a curt nod, he continued on.

'Must be safe.' Amarah followed. When she reached the floor above, she froze.

Three members of the Imperial Guard were lying on the floor in various states of undress—no doubt due to the late hour. She spotted blood on the arm of one of the men, and as she crept closer, she shook her head.

They were dead.

Moroda shuddered and stopped where she was, gagging. 'No! I didn't want any casualties!'

Amarah forced back memories of her own experience with a Varkain attack. Moroda, it seemed, needed a lesson in their true nature.

'Hah, Sapora *chooses* to kill them, you know. His venom can paralyse as well as kill. Depends on the strength of the bite.' She crouched by the bodies and rummaged through their pockets.

Coins were always good, but they could have weapons, keys, any number of useful items.

'No. That's...that's not true? A Varkain bite *always* means death,' Moroda replied, watching as Amarah moved to the next body. 'Why would he choose to kill them if he didn't have to? I know you don't like Sapora, but...' Her lip curled.

Amarah stopped and rolled up the bottom of her breeches to expose her left calf. 'These scars? A Varkain attack.' She traced a finger along her discoloured skin, thin white scars ribboning her leg. 'I'll tell you about how I got 'em another time, if it makes you feel better.' She stood up, pocketed the florins and crowns she had stolen, and made for the door Sapora had slipped through. 'Keep up, Moroda. You wanted to come. Remember why we're here.'

Moroda's lip trembled, but she held firm.

The woman was surprising Amarah more and more every day. She'd expected her to have fallen over, vomited, or given away their position. The determination Moroda had in herself astounded Amarah.

She'd always thought of Goldstones as weak pushovers.

Amarah headed along the corridor, only to pause when it split ahead of her.

'Dammit, he's disappeared.' She glanced down the corridors to the left and right, doors on both sides. 'Which way, which way?' Frustration and impatience made the decision for her, and she picked at random, heading left. 'This way.'

Moroda yelled, 'Wait!'

But

Amarah had already opened the nearest door and entered one of the ship's cabins, finding herself face to face with an armed guard in full red and gold Imperial livery.

'Who're you?' he bellowed, drawing his sword.

Amarah raised her scythe as he lunged at her.

She managed to duck out of the way and countered with her own weapon, bringing up her blade to his throat.

The guard reacted instinctively, blocking her attack with a round, metal shield attached to his vambrace, and the clang of steel-on-steel rippled through the air.

'Amarah!' Moroda shouted, raising her hand.

Amarah didn't know what Moroda had done, but the guard's arms were pinned in place, his sword held high and unmoving. It may only have lasted a moment, but that was all she needed. Amarah brought her scythe across his face and knocked him to the ground.

Spinning the weapon in her hand, she lunged again, blade aimed at his throat.

Then her strength was sapped, the scythe falling from her grasp. The familiar tingle of Samolen magic raced through her body, and she turned on Moroda, rage fuelling her. 'What d'you think you're doing?'

'No more casualties. Sapora will kill too many. I don't want that number added to!' Moroda replied, defiant, the stone on her ring glowing vivid blue.

Suddenly, she regretted calling the woman determined. More like stupidly stubborn.

'You're far too forgiving, Moroda. It'll get you killed if you don't change!'

Moroda lowered her hands and said nothing, the hold she had on Amarah's energy disappearing as she dropped her gaze.

Amarah let out a gasp and got to her feet, picking up her scythe. The guard bled onto the carpeted cabin floor, his unconscious body shaking, but he was alive. It wasn't a fatal wound, and as loath as she was to leave him like that, she had more important issues to address.

She made her way back to the door of the cabin. 'We're getting close if there are guards here.' After checking outside, she exited.

No sign of Sapora.

Damn. She should have known better than to trust a snake.

She could get the treasure without him. If he wanted to try and strand her here—

'I think we need to carry on this way,' Moroda said, one hand on her ring. 'Heat surges every time I face a certain direction. Someone is definitely further along here. More people could mean the sphere?' Without waiting, she took the lead and made her way down the corridor and up another flight of stairs at the end.

Amarah tightened her grip on her scythe. Perhaps the

ereven sphere was on the top deck, as high as they could go. An Arillian had it, after all. They were probably more at home in higher places, where they had nothing but the sky above them.

'What did you do to me?' Amarah whispered, catching up with the Goldstone.

'Just moved your energy,' Moroda replied, as if it were the most obvious thing. She paused, checked her crystal, then continued on.

'As easy as that...' Amarah muttered.

'The crystal taps into my own intuition. Like it's intensified and enhanced a hundred-fold. I can *feel* people chatting behind closed doors. It's getting busier and louder the higher up we go.'

While Amarah couldn't pretend to understand, her theory about the treasure being higher up was accurate.

They reached another crossroad, and a crackle of electricity flashed through the air for half a heartbeat. Amarah grabbed Moroda by the shoulder and pulled her down behind a large barrel of supplies. 'Ssh, people coming.' She crouched beside her, holding her breath, waiting.

Moroda frowned, turning her ring this way and that, then ducked down at the sound of approaching footsteps.

Two Arillians wandered into view, laughing with one another as they stopped and stretched in the middle of the corridor.

Amarah watched them closely, keeping herself hidden and waiting for an opportunity to get past without being seen.

Where *was* the damned snake?

'Won't be long before the fun begins,' one Arillian said. He was taller than Kohl, more strongly built, and held himself with more confidence.

'Tell me about it. Glad we finally cleaned up the last of

those damned merchant ships,' his companion replied, rolling his shoulders and yawning. 'Took over a year to pick them all off! How many times do they need to be told? The sky belongs to *us*!'

'Aciel's got everything under control. Won't be long before the land is ours again, too,' the tall one said. 'Now the last of them Goldstones are gone.'

Moroda trembled beside Amarah, and she turned to the woman beside her. 'Hey. You okay?' She shook the Goldstone. Tears fell down Moroda's cheeks, and she leaned forward, staggering to her feet.

'Moroda!' Amarah grabbed her arm, trying to hold the woman in place.

But Moroda had already raised both hands, fingers trembling.

Flames rippled across the barrel they hid behind, raced along the walls, ceiling, floor—to the two Arillians. They cried out in shock, wings flapping as fire surrounded them.

'Moroda!' Amarah screamed. Fire burned the barrels, and she leapt back.

'Amarah...I...' Moroda stammered, blinking. Her mouth fell open as if she'd only just noticed Amarah was there.

Amarah wasn't going to waste the chance.

'Go, go, go! Up the stairs!'

She shoved Moroda in the back and pushed her forward.

The pair of them raced away as the fire kept the Arillians busy, and ascended to the next deck.

'Amarah, I don't know what came over me.' Moroda put her hand to her chest, her ring pulsing gently with blue light.

Amarah was just pleased the woman hadn't done the same trick on *Khanna*. 'Perfect diversion, Moroda. Don't be silly.' Amarah tapped the blade of her scythe against the floor as she continued. 'Could have done with a bit less fire, though. That'll spread quickly. Most of the ship is wood. Won't be long before it hits an engine or two.'

Moroda inhaled sharply. 'I just...the heat...' She blinked away more tears. 'They were talking about what they'd done. The people they killed. Merchants. Goldstones. I think...what if they'd been talking about my father? He was a merchant. He died last year.'

Amarah kept the pair of them moving, though she wasn't completely unsympathetic to the Goldstone's sorrow. As they rounded another corner, the ship lurched underneath them, and Amarah steadied herself against the wall. She glanced back.

'Let's hope that's one of the auxiliary engines.'

A moment later, the ship juddered again, and the lights went out, plunging them into darkness. 'Hope ain't on our side, then.'

'Will the ship crash?' Moroda grabbed Amarah's shoulder to steady herself. 'I'm so sorry!'

'Nah, big old lump like this'll drop a bit. Worst case it'll float on the water. Arillians are on board, don't forget. If they wanna, they'll keep something in the air.'

Amarah strode forward, trying not to stumble in the semi-darkness, the orange glow of flames partially lighting things from below. The low, flickering light made it harder to focus than if they'd been in pure darkness. 'Watch your step.'

Moroda tripped over a thick coil of rope and slammed into the wall.

'I said watch your step!'

'Sorry.' Moroda kicked the rope out of the way and clambered to her feet. 'Stupid thing.' As she shoved it away, the light caught it, and Amarah realised it was not a length of rope at all.

It was snakeskin.

'A...Amarah!'

The skin moved, and Moroda jumped back.

'It's Sapora,' Amarah said, tutting. 'Harder to see a snake in darkness.'

Trust him to turn this mission into his own private hunt.

The snakeskin was dark grey, almost black, and about three feet wide, but the light was too low for her to make out any more details. She watched him move silently down the corridor, and wondered how many he had killed that night. How many he would go on to kill.

Amarah tried not to think about it.

'Moroda. The upper deck is at the top of these stairs, I can see the clouds from here. Captain's cabin will be there, I bet. Reckon that's where our treasure is locked away. No sign of this Jato yet, either. Dragons above, we've been lucky.' Amarah clambered up the final set of stairs and stepped out onto the open deck, where rain pelted down and thunder echoed overhead. Though the cold wind buffeted her, she was grateful for the fresh air and open space.

Flames licked one end of the deck, and the ship groaned. Her feet told her the ship was slowly dropping from the sky.

They didn't have much time.

She took in her surroundings and spotted what had to be the captain's quarters.

'It's there. It's in there!' Moroda raised her hand, the blue crystal glowing.

Amarah darted across the open deck, but the door wouldn't budge. Licking her lips, she picked the lock, breaking in just as Moroda caught up. The door swung open quietly, odd, amidst the chaos outside, and as Amarah stepped into the large cabin, she immediately saw *him*.

The Arillian sat in the corner of the well-furnished, richly carpeted cabin, eyes closed, arms folded, hunched forward, a staff of ebony laid on his lap. A large jewel had been mounted atop the cane. Dazzling red, blue, gold, the colours were ever-shifting.

It had to be a dragon stone.

The ereven sphere was mounted on a stand behind the ship's wheel, completely unassuming for those who did not know what it was: a pale glass orb nestled among rich mahogany.

Amarah took a few steps, then paused, before daring another few paces, her attention fixed on Aciel all the while. Any sudden movement and she'd spring into action. She could hear nothing but her blood pumping in her ears and the wind rushing outside, and Aciel seemed completely unaware of their intrusion.

She crept closer to the sphere and reached out with her free hand. Fuck it, if he wasn't going to do anything, she'd just grab it and run.

'Amarah.'

Amarah gasped as Aciel opened his eyes and looked directly at her. She stared back at him, tightening her grip on her scythe, ready if it came to blows.

Where was Sapora when you needed him?

'What are you doing?'

His voice drowned out the wind, fear and panic. He didn't speak another word, but her mind rang with his voice, his whispers, and the intense, biting cold that came with it. She held her head in her hands, trying to drown out his words.

But she had to obey. Had to answer his question.

'The sphere,' Amarah said.

'Is not yours to take, is it?' Aciel replied, hardly any inflection in his speech.

'No.'

'Then leave it and go back where you came from.'

'Amarah!' Moroda rushed forward. 'Don't listen! We need the sphere!'

'You.' The cool voice left Amarah's head as he turned his attention to Moroda—who grabbed Amarah and shook her, trying to pull her away from the Arillian.

'Moroda.' Aciel's voice filled the cabin, echoing back and forth like they were in a cave.

'No!'

The Goldstone screamed, raising one palm to him, the gem on her ring flickering into life.

An explosion rang out, blinding Amarah for a moment, and sending her to her knees. A high pitched trill filled her ears, and she carefully squeezed one eye open.

Her mouth fell open.

The cabin was alight, though rain poured in from the gaping hole in the roof. Aciel lay on the floor, broken chunks of wood and splinters covering his shoulders, his cane thrown to the far wall.

Fuck, if that Goldstone wasn't useful to have around.

And that was her advantage.

Vision dancing, Amarah leapt forward and drove her scythe towards Aciel.

The Arillian glared, but she moved too quickly for him to speak, and all he could do was snarl in fury as he snatched up his staff to block her lunge. His ebony staff met her scythe, the weapons ringing as they clashed. She pressed down hard, pinning him in place and forcing him to focus on her.

'Moroda! Grab it and run!'

Amarah gritted her teeth as Aciel pushed up, but she had him in an awkward position, and whatever strength he had he couldn't use while she was on top of him.

His skin and hair were pale, and he wore similarly light robes with white gloves, but his wings were deep black.

Aciel's eyes, though, were silver-white, with a hint of green, and she could not see his pupils.

She snarled at him as he pushed against her, their weapons trembling as neither gave way to the other. How *dare* he touch her mind like that.

How dare he try and take control! 'Be a shame if I cut you. Get red all over those nice white clothes.' Amarah couldn't help but taunt him.

In her periphery, she saw Moroda grab the ereven sphere with both hands, but she yelped when her skin touched the glass.

If the damned Goldstone could use Samolen magic, she could use the sphere, too.

Aciel shifted under her, pushing harder and forcing Amarah back. She widened her stance and leaned into her scythe with her good shoulder, using her full weight to keep Aciel pinned. But the wooden floor was wet from the rain pouring in, and her feet were slipping.

Moroda raced from the cabin, her head low and the hood of her cloak up.

It was time to get away.

Aciel had one foot under him and was slowly getting to his feet, pushing Amarah back.

Sliding on the wet floor didn't help.

Gritting her teeth, she wrenched her scythe away and kicked out with one foot. It connected with Aciel's staff and went clattering to the floor.

Amarah bolted out onto the deck.

'I've got it! Where's *Khanna*?' Moroda called, holding the sphere close to her chest.

The few Arillians and guards that Sapora had yet to deal with were out on deck, trying to douse the flames which ripped through the wooden hull. Panic and chaos filled the air.

Another shockwave rattled the deck as a second engine took to flame, and the ship let out a mighty groan. In the smoke, wind, rain, and darkness, Amarah couldn't see *Khanna*, and she bit back another curse.

'Moroda.'

Aciel's voice somehow penetrated Amarah's mind in spite of the noise around her. He spoke to her companion, but she heard an echo of it, and it sent every hair standing on end. She wanted to get away from him, terrified of what he might make her do.

Nausea swelled in her gut as she made her way across the burning deck, avoiding people and Arillians both, staring out into the roiling grey clouds and looking for her familiar sails.

'Where are you going? Stop running. There's nowhere to run. You cannot run.'

She looked back at Moroda, who halted in place. 'Moroda!' Amarah called, but her voice paled in comparison to Aciel's. Just *hearing* him speak to Moroda made her feel violently sick.

'Turn around,' Ariel commanded.

'I don't want to,' Moroda whimpered, turning around.

'That's okay. Hold out your hand.'

Amarah watched him walking towards her, his feathered wings in contrast to his hair, his staff held in his left hand. He did not hurry. He did not seem to mind the raging fires surrounding him—he simply allowed his energy to extinguish the flames. A few gusts of strong wind pushed them away, and another reduced them to embers.

Amarah could *hear* Aciel's thoughts, too. Could just *touch* on them, as he instructed Moroda. It had to be an after-effect of his compulsion, and she wondered when it would fade. Images and sounds flashed through her mind, coupled with intense emotions. His hunt for dragons. His desire for power.

Moroda shivered where she stood, and held out her hand, the sphere held tightly.

Aciel said, 'Step forward.'

Moroda shook her head, but her body obeyed, and she stepped toward him. 'Please don't.'

'Hush. It's okay.'

Amarah couldn't get closer to them. If she did, he'd control her too, and she couldn't allow that. Refused to. 'Moroda! Fight him!'

But the woman was under his compulsion now, and her body trembled.

Topeko may have been right. Moroda may have done well to fight him before. But so close? She didn't stand a chance.

Amarah watched as he fluttered his wings, loose black feathers floating to the burnt deck underfoot. She saw each step, felt every wave of energy, and couldn't move.

Moroda backed away, then flinched as Aciel's power rooted her to the spot. Her lip curled. Amarah saw Eryn's face flash bright in her mind, and realised Moroda was thinking of her sister. Realised she could see Moroda's thoughts in the same way she'd seen Aciel's. In such close proximity, everything merged together, and emotions tore through her mind. Bile rose in Amarah's throat.

'It's not okay!'

Moroda screamed.

'Yes it is. Step forward. Give me back what you stole. You're above stealing, aren't you? Why are you travelling with thieves and criminals, Goldstone?'

What felt like ice sheeted down Amarah's back. She was lost and ignored on deck. The Arillians *had* to know what Aciel was doing. Those of the Imperial Guard, too.

Like her, they probably saw their leader's thoughts. Heard his orders.

They didn't *need* to attack her. Not when Aciel had everything under control.

Sickness and shame wrestled in her gut at her weakness.

Aciel continued, 'You cannot get away without being punished, Moroda. What would be a suitable punishment for you? Murderers are beheaded, aren't they?'

'I'm not a murderer.' Moroda's voice shook.

'You *are*. You're killing my followers. You burned my ship. These people will die in the crash, or drown in the waters below. You did that, thief.'

Tears streamed down Moroda's face.

'Give me back what you stole, murderer. And that might save them.'

Moroda trembled and flattened her hand, the sphere rocking slightly in her palm. Her hood had fallen back in the wind, and the rain soaked through her hair and clothes.

She kept her eyes shut.

Amarah tried to call out, but her throat had closed. Dragons above, she couldn't stand it.

Aciel took the sphere from Moroda's hand, and neither she nor Amarah could do anything about it.

'Murderers don't deserve to live. Turn around and walk. If the fall does not kill you, you will drown.'

Moroda turned around and a new wave of fear washed over Amarah. She forced herself to take a step closer to the Goldstone and Arillian, but the wash of coldness filled her the closer she came. Any more, and she'd be entirely in his clutches again. 'Moroda!'

Aciel smiled. 'Walk.'

Moroda's knees trembled in defiance, but Amarah knew he had complete control of her body. She took a few steps.

More images of their companions flashed in Amarah's

mind through Moroda. Eryn. Palom. Morgen. Anahrik. Kohl. Sapora. Herself.

Seeing her own face in the mind's eye of Moroda broke Amarah's sense of self-preservation. She ran towards her, scythe raised high. 'Moroda!'

Eryn's face appeared again, frowning at first, then crying desperately with grief.

'Moroda!' Amarah's voice was lost to the wind and rain. Swallowed by the Arillian's thunder and Aciel's compulsion.

Moroda stepped off the side of the warship.

19

Moroda tried to scream. The wind rushed through her hair as she fell, and the dark, angry sea rose to meet her. Salt filled the air.

Aciel had released the mental hold on her body the moment she'd stepped off the ship, leaving her mind clear enough for intense fear.

She plummeted past raging towers of swirling water.

Half a second later, cold hands snatched her by the waist and her vision filled with feathers. She stopped falling and began to rise. 'Kohl?'

Dizziness and nausea surged in her gut.

When she was dropped on solid ground, it took several more seconds before she could see—and she frantically blinked away tears.

Fires burned around her.

She wasn't safe on *Khanna*.

She coughed as she struggled to breathe and tried to get her bearings. When she glanced at the Arillian who had caught her, Moroda realised it was *not* Kohl.

But the resemblance was striking enough to disorient her again. 'You...you're Jato!'

'Pleased to meet you, my dear.' Jato flexed her wings, a cruel smile on her lips as she leered down at Moroda with grey eyes. Her hair was blonde, darker in the rain, and what little armour she wore seemed ceremonial more than practical.

'But...Aciel said...?'

Jato laughed, a hollow noise without true mirth. 'Aciel lets me play games.' She raised her hand and spread her fingers wide; blue-white light flickered from her palm. Before Moroda could respond, Jato flicked her wrist and struck her with a ball of lightning.

The force of the blow sent Moroda tumbling head over heels. Her sodden hood covered her head, and her skin smoked from the intense heat of Jato's attack. She trembled in the suddenness of the attack, and it was another moment before she felt the searing heat on her skin.

Tears streamed down her cheeks as she heard Jato's laugh. 'Why are you doing this?' Her breaths were ragged. 'I've never met you. Bear you no ill will!'

She thought of Eryn, of what Jato, Aciel, and the others might do to her.

She couldn't allow that.

Her thighs burned as she struggled to her feet. 'You must stop!'

Jato cackled. 'Who are you to tell *me* what to do?'

'My name is...' Moroda wheezed, her knees trembling. The airship lurched underfoot, threatening to send her sprawling again. 'My...name is...Moroda...'

'I don't care who you are. You and your kind have stood over us too long.'

'I haven't done anything...'

'Your Imperial Guard exiled us! Slaughtered us! Banished us for what our forefathers did!' Jato was shrieking now, lighting flickering from her hands as if matching her rage. 'You don't know the suffering we endure. But you will.' Jato hurled a ball of lightning towards Moroda.

Gritting her teeth, Moroda raised her ring and called upon the power it helped her tap into. A wall of light flickered in front of her. It held the lightning attack for a second, then burst through.

Moroda screamed as electricity rushed through her, setting every nerve on fire. She was thrown to the already burning deck with a scream.

She attempted to push herself onto her hands and knees, to get away, but was struck by the next ball of lightning before she managed it.

A third, and her body convulsed.

'Pathetic. No fight in you. Not so fun, anymore, is it? Where's your fire now? You killed my followers. Destroyed my airship! Perhaps I should have let Aciel make you kill yourself.'

Moroda coughed again, her hands burning. She couldn't even speak.

'Nothing to say for yourself?' Jato shrieked.

Moroda rolled over and lay flat on her back, body stinging, breathing quickening. She fought to keep panic at bay. Exhausted from using magic, Aciel's compulsion, and the intense fear, she couldn't gather the strength to reply to the Arillian, let alone get up or defend herself.

Jato blasted her with balls and bolts of lightning, infuriated by Moroda's lack of response.

Screaming filled her ears, though she couldn't tell if it was her own voice or Jato. The corners of her vision dimmed as pain took hold, her body spasming as electricity crackled through her, every nerve on fire.

She tried to think back to Topeko's training. How to use her stone, her innate power. How to use her own energy as a shield. But Jato's attacks were too vicious.

'I wonder whether you'll cook first? Or ignite? You *like* the fire, don't you?' Jato taunted, sending forth another strike.

Moroda shivered as she was buffeted about, her cloak singed. 'Please...'

Jato laughed, taking to the air and diving back down, striking Moroda with renewed intensity. 'Aciel has already won. You've thrown your life away by coming here. Such a silly girl.'

Another strike.

'Looks like you're almost done, now!'

Another.

And another.

Then...nothing, save the scent of burning cloth and the residual heat of electricity.

'Get up, Moroda.'

A new voice. One that wasn't full of malice.

Moroda opened her eyes, only half-conscious. Her vision blurred, made worse by the dark clouds and heavy rain, but the figure in front of her was unmistakable. 'S...Sapora...?'

'Best you stay alive.' His back was to her, his focus on Jato.

Moroda tried to respond, but she had no voice left. She shuddered, weak from the attacks.

'A Varkain? Hmph. Dirty worm. Shouldn't you be buried in the ground somewhere?' Jato said, while Moroda feebly attempted to get to her feet. 'You're a disease on Linaria. Disgusting creature. Aciel plans to get rid of your kind after the Ittallan are gone. Maybe we'll strike the holes to your underground cities and burn you in your tunnels while you sleep. Just you wait.'

Sapora didn't reply, but Moroda saw him draw two scimitars from his sleeves and widen his stance. She'd never seen him hold a weapon before. Hadn't realised he carried any.

Moroda shuffled away, trying to get her breath back, eyes locked on Sapora and Jato as they squared up to one another. She was in too much pain to register anything other than the need to get away.

After several long breaths, she managed to get to her feet, but her blackened cloak was bunched up around her boots and she went sprawling again.

She lay against the hard wooden deck, the taste of ash in her mouth and pain rippling through her limbs. The warship was chaos; fire and smoke mixed in with the heavy clouds above, torrential rain, and rolls of thunder shaking everything. She tried to work out the best way to escape, but could not see *Khanna* in the darkness.

Her body shivered, twitching involuntarily.

She'd never felt pain like it.

She heard the clang of metal against metal and blearily turned towards the noise. Sapora danced around Jato, his movements too quick for her to register at first, while the Arillian took to the wing and countered with electrical attacks.

Waves of energy pulsed through the air, intensified by her ring. She felt every blow through it.

She couldn't get to her feet. Didn't have the strength for it. So, she turned away, crawling along the deck of the warship, avoiding smoking debris, no plan in mind other than to get as far away from the fighting as she could.

'Moroda.'

She winced, closing her eyes as she heard *his* voice. Tears threatened at the pain and injustice of it all. She continued to crawl. It was painfully slow, but she couldn't get up.

How had he spotted her in the confusion?

'Stop, Moroda. You're too tired.'

She stopped where she was, unsure whether she was giving in to her own exhaustion or his compulsion again.

Her body was on fire after Jato's attacks, and she couldn't feel his chill voice numbing her like he had before.

An explosion blasted somewhere behind her, and she felt, more than heard, the crack of thunder from Jato's lightning. She opened her eyes and looked at Aciel from where she lay, waiting for the inevitable command.

He was some thirty paces away, stable and calm amidst the turmoil, a halo of light surrounding him as he fended off the rain and fires with his own energy.

Aciel was scarier than Sapora, Moroda realised.

He was evil.

Whatever his reasons for starting this war, whatever his justifications, they fell flat. He was a true horror she had never known existed.

The tears streaming down her cheeks mixed with blood, rain, and soot, stinging her skin. She shivered as he grew closer.

Twenty paces.

Ten.

Five.

A shadow passed overhead, dimming Aciel's light for a heartbeat. Moroda tried to steady her breathing and raised her hand. If she could tap into the stone's power again. Use up whatever energy she had left to set him aflame...

Her stone flashed, but her energy didn't compare to him —its heat snuffed out before a single ember appeared.

In her peripheral vision, she saw silver glint in the darkness, but didn't understand what it meant until the white of Aciel turned crimson as Amarah's scythe bit deep into his arm.

Everything happened at once.

Aciel's hold on her disappeared, her mind immediately clear. Blood gushed from the open wound on his forearm as Amarah's weapon sliced through to bone. She pulled her scythe back and yanked him to the floor. Jato screamed somewhere behind her, the noise drowning out everything else.

Amarah fell onto Aciel as he hit the deck, her knee holding him down, her blade pressed in deep. Blood pooled beneath them, mingling with the scorched wood and ash.

Moroda shivered, pushing herself up onto her hands and knees, too afraid and too shocked to do anything else. She saw the sky pirate wrestle with the Arillian leader— despite his grievous wound, he fought back, sending off waves of electrical energy, the thunder deafening at such close range, but Amarah's gaze was steely. She endured his attacks and held his good arm with one boot, her other knee in his back, pushing him down and pinning him in place. She kept one arm on her scythe, the other grasping at Aciel's neck and chest.

Jato's lightning joined the fray as she swept towards the pair like a thunderbolt.

But Sapora was faster. He slashed at her with his scimitars, ensuring she did not reach Aciel and Amarah.

Blood continued to spill and the chaos in Moroda's head shifted into panic.

She hyperventilated as terror and pain wrestled within, unable to hold back her emotions.

The waves of Aciel and Jato's attacks shoved her backwards, and she couldn't understand how Amarah and Sapora could fight them. It cemented how much she was out of her depth. How foolish and dangerous this idea had been. Eryn was right.

And she had nothing to show for it save a plethora of injuries.

Movement from above caught her eye as a falcon dived towards Aciel.

It had to be Anahrik, not that she had any voice or capacity to move or signal she needed help.

Anahrik's talons slashed at Aciel, but he and Amarah were both thrown off as the Arillian screamed and blasted lightning in all directions. The shockwave shook the ship, and they were all shunted backwards.

Moroda's head spun from the impact and another Arillian descended, though a familiar cool wind blanketed her. Even in the midst of panic, pain, and disorientation, she recognised Kohl's hat and cloak. He grabbed Amarah from the deck and flew off with her before Aciel's next strike could land.

Sapora leapt again, his scimitars flashing brightly in the darkness, as he kept Jato and Aciel's attention on him. Not that Aciel looked in condition to fight, there was so much blood pouring from his arm.

At least Amarah was safe. She'd get back to *Khanna*, get back to Eryn, and fly them away. Her sister would be safe.

Moroda struggled to her feet, though shaky, and backed away from the other Arillians. Jato rushed to Aciel's side, her screams turning into wails as a river of crimson grew under him.

Where once she would have pitied him, a dark thought appeared in her mind: perhaps he deserved it.

Jato turned to Moroda, anguish colouring her face in blotches of pink, and raised her hand.

Moroda ducked, but the lightning strike did not come; Sapora had darted to Jato's side, his claws digging into her arms. She watched, horrified, as Sapora's fangs extended from his jaw and he bit deep into her shoulder.

The Arillian struggled against him, cursing furiously, but in the seconds that passed, her movements slowed.

Within a minute, Jato was limp, and Sapora dropped her beside Aciel.

Then, the warship crashed into the raging sea, and Moroda dropped to her knees.

Overwhelmed by the smell of sea salt, blood, and burning wood, her vision blurred.

She could just make out the silhouette of a wide-brimmed hat, then her world went dark.

SOMETHING HEAVY WEIGHED down on Moroda's chest and muffled voices surrounded her. She struggled to listen, unable to make any sense of what she heard, and when she opened her eyes, she found herself wrapped up in Palom's large cloak.

Amarah stood some way in front of her, by the wheel of *Khanna*, her arms and face bloodied and darkened by soot. Beyond her, Kohl and Sapora stood side by side on deck, looking out into a grey sky.

She tilted her head to her right, and saw Palom on a crate, arms folded. To her left, Eryn and Morgen sat beside her, speaking in low voices.

Kohl walked back towards them, and Moroda took a deep breath, trying to control her shivering. 'I fear Aciel's power may have increased more than can be stopped.' He sat down beside Palom.

'More than can be stopped? You didn't look hard enough. He'll probably bleed out,' Amarah replied, voice harder than Moroda had ever heard it,

Moroda closed her eyes again, listening.

'This is a fruitless quest. Jato's power has grown since I last saw her. Aciel is also stronger, despite your attack. Unless you saw him die, his followers will be able to help him heal. It might take a while, but he won't be finished.' Kohl sighed heavily. 'We've no chance. Once we arrive in Val

Sharis, it won't be long before he decides to wipe out all non-Arillians.'

'Kohl don't be foolish,' Sapora hissed. 'When the snows start, I'll succeed my father as king in Sereth. I'm not giving up my birth-right for a rogue Arillian who wants to play war. Princess Isa will have more information for us when we reach the capital, no doubt.'

'We're in too deep now,' Amarah muttered. She winced as she pulled a lever, and Moroda felt the ship tilt underneath her. 'Give up now after everything we've been through? Don't be stupid. Besides, after that stunt, they'll be after us. Arillians seem to do revenge well. Hold grudges a long while. At least Aciel and Jato will be out of action for a bit. Buy us some time. We got the sphere though. Excellent bit of thievery if I do say so myself.'

Moroda's heart pounded at Amarah's words. She thought she'd lost the sphere in the chaos.

'If you say so,' Kohl said, his voice low.

'I am only upset I didn't kill Jato, too,' Sapora said bitterly. 'I'm out of practice, it seems.'

Kohl stared at the Varkain for a long moment. 'Sapora, if it weren't for you, they'd be after us right now. You were merciful to Jato, intentional or not. It's a good thing.'

Palom shook his head. 'Kohl you are talking rubbish. Whole lot of them deserve to burn.'

Moroda couldn't feign sleep any longer. 'No they don't! They aren't in control of their actions. It's *Aciel* who's to blame.'

'Moroda!' Eryn jumped to her feet and clutched Moroda's hands tightly.

'I'll keep watch.' Kohl tipped his hat to Moroda and walked away, his shoulders sagging.

Moroda saw the Arillian take to the sky from the relative warmth of the covered deck. The nausea she'd felt on the warship hadn't completely passed, and she regretted her decision to go. But she had learned invaluable information and Amarah had succeeded in stealing the sphere. For all his terror, Aciel's edge would be lost. She just didn't know if it would be worth it.

When Arillians had been a distant worry, or characters in a story, she hadn't given them much thought. Now, they were very real and very dangerous. 'Eryn, I'm so sorry.'

'Oh, Ro, it's okay! I'm just glad you're back with us now. We were so worried.' Eryn's eyes were red, but she smiled through it, and it lifted Moroda's heart.

'I've not...been asleep long, have I?'

'Not even an hour. Dragons above, I can't imagine what you went through down there,' Morgen said, a definite note of pride in his tone.'

'But...the ereven sphere? We have it?'

'We have it, Ro.' Eryn hugged Moroda, her cheeks wet with fresh tears. 'We nearly lost you, though. What were you *thinking*, going on that ship?'

'I'm sorry for scaring you.'

Eryn knelt beside Moroda. More tears trickled down her nose.

Moroda wriggled her hands free of the heavy cloak to wipe away her sister's tears. 'I promise I'll never do anything again without you agreeing. It was selfish of me. Much too reckless.'

'How do you feel, Moroda?' Palom asked from her other side.

Her stomach was still in turmoil and her fingers were numb. Phantom sensations of Jato's electricity rattled through her body. 'I'm okay. A bit sick, but no pain.' It was a white lie, but nothing she felt now was comparable to Jato's attacks. She'd never been stabbed before, but imagined the hot, blinding pain to be similar. 'Is Amarah okay? And you,

Sapora? Thank you for what you did on the ship. You...you saved me.'

'Both fine,' Sapora replied, curt as ever.

Moroda met his gaze and smiled, no longer feeling a chill when she looked at him. One of the Varkain, supposedly one of the cruellest creatures to walk Linaria, had stepped in to defend her against Jato. She saw him in a new light, especially after being under Aciel's control. 'I'm pleased to hear you're okay. What about Anahrik?'

'Everyone is okay, Moroda. Anahrik is scouting as always, but skies are clear to Val Sharis now. We left storm at sea,' Palom answered.

'You sure you're okay, Ro? It's okay if you aren't. I mean... Aciel...He...' Eryn trailed off.

'I don't know how *anyone* can fight that. What he does. He...his voice...it's inside you,' Moroda said, trying not to think of it, but the memories flooded her regardless. 'I don't know how Amarah managed to attack him!' She suddenly remembered the pool of blood. 'Wait! Amarah! You cut his arm off!'

The sky pirate cackled. 'Good weapons of yours, Palom. I didn't *quite* cut it off. But I made sure he knew not to mess with me. Don't think that Jato took too kindly to it, though. Imagine if I'd managed it, though. Sky pirate saves Linaria by killing Arillian Lord. The Imperial Guard would owe *me*, for once.'

Moroda's heart pounded and she wasn't sure it would ever calm. 'And...now we have the ereven sphere, his way of finding dragons...he's weaker now?'

'Damned good heist. Not had a bloody one in years. Sign me up for round two.' Despite her words, there wasn't much humour in Amarah's tone.

'Pay her no mind,' Eryn whispered, leaning close. 'She was just as worried about you as I was when Kohl brought you on board. She yelled at him for bringing her back first instead of *you*.'

'Amarah...' The sky pirate had been through Aciel's compulsion with her. Had saved her from him, *twice*. Her respect for Amarah had doubled.

Admiration and relief swelled, and Moroda almost burst into tears at the intense emotions.

Tentatively, she sat up, Eryn and Morgen steadying her on either side. After several deep breaths, her nausea began to fade. She exhaled slowly, trying to soothe her stomach and ignore the fresh, painful memories of her experience on the ship and the burns on her skin. It was no easy task. Flashes of violence tore through her mind, and she winced every time they did.

'I should have gone,' Palom said, catching her attention.

'Palom?'

'I said I would look after you. If I was there then maybe you would not...' He shook his head, a low grumble echoing in his chest. 'You should not have been hurt, Moroda.'

'It's okay. I shouldn't have gone.' She glanced at Eryn.

'No. You were doing what you had to do. This, I understand. But to see you hurting...'

'Thank you, Palom. I'm okay.' She rested a hand on his arm in the hope of reassuring him. 'If one of the Arillians had spotted *Khanna* and attacked, you'd have been here to protect Eryn.'

Palom gave her a pained look, but nodded.

'Amarah keeps saying how she's the best pirate in the skies,' Eryn said, keeping her voice low. 'Stole the most valuable treasure from the most dangerous ship, and walked away unscathed.'

'Well, almost unscathed. She *is* good, though,' Moroda said.

'What?' Eryn's eyebrows shot up.

'She defended herself *and* me against the guards we found, took Aciel one-on-one, and I have to say *she* came out better. I couldn't even stand against him. I had a few extra seconds to brace, but ultimately, he had me.' Moroda shivered at the memory. She'd stood up to him in Niversai, where there'd been a massive crowd between himself and her. But so close? There was nothing she could do.

It was no wonder he'd taken soldiers, had turned dragons against Linaria.

'Pull yourself together, Moroda. You are not as weak as you think,' Sapora said. Moroda and Eryn both glanced up. 'You do not need Palom's protection, nor anyone's. You spoke out against Aciel in Niversai. You freed a Varkain from prison. You willingly entered the enemy's warship, and did not give up against that freak Arillian. Perhaps if you stopped whinging, you'd see that.'

Her cheeks flushed. She couldn't deny Sapora's words, even if the bite in his voice embarrassed her.

Everything he said had been technically correct, though not all of her intentions were noble. She *had* given in to Aciel's compulsion, but it was true she had not given up, if there was a difference.

She had tried to fight, tried to get away, however futile a fight it was.

'Gotta agree with him,' Morgen said. 'For someone with no battle experience, who never even held a weapon until a few days ago, you're not bad off.'

'I must be dreaming.' Moroda laughed, though it seemed more like delirium.

'You know I want to look for a ship home as soon as we get to Taban Yul, though?' Eryn said, bringing Moroda back to reality.

Her heart sank.

Yes, it was dangerous. But they'd stolen a victory from

Aciel. They couldn't throw it away now, could they? They'd come too far for that, as Amarah suggested.

'As soon as you get the smallest taste of the real world, you wanna scurry back home?' Amarah laughed at them. 'Didn't you hear a word the Varkain said, Eryn?'

'Maybe...Eryn's right...' Moroda didn't believe it, but she'd made a foolish decision before. She didn't want to again. 'Everyone under Aciel's compulsion...They don't want to be there. Don't want to do what he's making them do. If only we could save them.'

'You're too soft for this world, Goldstone. You're gonna end up dead,' Amarah said.

More anger roiled in her chest. After everything she'd done, everything she'd been through, how could Amarah say that? Her hands balled into fists. 'Really? Too soft? I have no parents, no family left, yet I'm still here. I'm inexperienced, yes. Perhaps even naive to your standards. But I'm *still here*.'

'Ro...' Eryn whispered.

'I got us away from Niversai as it burned under dragonfire. I challenged an Arillian Lord and lived. And my wanting to see the good in people? What's wrong with that? If you've been through what I have, you turn into someone cold. Stone on the outside.' Her voice trembled with the sudden effort and explosion of emotion, but Moroda continued. 'I stay committed to my beliefs. My worldview. If people can be saved, they should be. It's kept me alive this far, I don't see why I would change it now.'

Silence echoed loudly.

Only the burst of wind and the distant roar of ocean waves filled the gap.

Sapora looked at her, but said nothing. Even Amarah kept her attention on the flight.

Moroda lowered her head, subdued, and pressed her

face into her sister's arm. All her confidence built from the Samolen magic had faded.

She had been in Aciel's mind. Seen what he'd seen. Thought what he'd thought. He'd killed older dragons and stolen their power for himself—shoved it all into the crystal atop his staff. He'd turned younger dragons on villages and towns to sow chaos and dissent.

And he was going to do the same once he'd crossed the ocean.

It would be worse on the new continent, now his power had grown. The Ittallan and the Varkain would be in danger. Even Sapora knew that. His deceitful manner had shifted. He no longer traded barbs with Amarah—he was serious, now. Behaving like she'd expected a prince to behave.

Moroda idly ran her hand over the crystal in her ring. She understood it could not be relied upon to get her out of all scrapes. And it certainly couldn't keep her invulnerable.

Topeko had said it was a last resort, something to use in defence if fighting could not be avoided. It had been her overconfidence that had led her to the ludicrous decision to accompany Amarah and Sapora on the heist. A hastily made decision, one she felt had been necessary at the time.

What a mistake that had been.

If not for her companions, she'd be dead.

Running head first into the heart of the Arillian war had been foolish, and now she couldn't back out. Not now Aciel and Jato had seen her, would be after her.

Sapora was a prince. Morgen was in the Imperial Guard. Amarah, Kohl, Palom, and Anahrik could fight. This was a battle they were actually equipped to fight.

As much as she wanted to keep going, to not stand aside, helpless, as others fought, she knew it was what she had to do. She hated herself for it. For the fear it would instil in her sister.

But having come so close to losing everything, having pushed Eryn's desires away so she could have her adventure, Moroda was going to take the warning for what it was. 'Ryn, I promise I'll work with you more instead of being stubborn. Next time, I might not be so lucky. I don't want to put you through that again.'

'Ro...'

She thought about telling her sister what she'd learned on the ship. That Arillians had been attacking airships for months. That they were probably responsible for her father's death.

Just the memory of that made her blood boil.

'You best get some rest,' Morgen chimed in. 'There's a short way to go until we reach Taban Yul. You, too, Eryn. You look exhausted.'

'I'm fine, thanks Morgen.' Eryn didn't look away from Moroda.

'Sure, Ryn?' Moroda asked, her body itching to rest.

'I'm sure. You rest. We're all here. You're safe.'

Moroda let herself drift into sleep, desperately hoping she would not endure nightmares of Aciel and Jato.

20

Violet and red streaked across the sky above a setting sun. Bursts of gold interlaced the clouds, burning like distant fires. It reminded Sapora of his childhood.

Unlike most Varkain, born in darkness, he always knew the sun on his skin. Saw the lands he was to rule when he came of age, mixed with the Ittallan people. That difference was his strength, not a weakness, regardless of what other Varkain and Ittallan thought.

He was about to prove that.

When his father had first sent him on errantry, he'd seen it as a slight. Worse, an insult. How *dare* he send away the crown prince? Sapora had expected to be tutored by one of the Cerastes. Perhaps even by one of the Old Guard. Taken into the depths of Sereth where he would learn more about his kin.

Instead, he'd been shunned. Again.

Now, he saw it had perhaps been to his advantage. He had more knowledge of Linaria than any other Varkain, and probably most Ittallan, too. More even than his father. Most of them rarely left the place they were born, let alone their country. He had traversed the breadth of the continents, observing, listening, and learning.

It was only fitting that he stood out in more ways than simply his mixed heritage.

Most Varkain considered themselves above the rest of Linaria. Refused to stoop lower than their perceived stations.

He didn't care about flying in a sky pirate's airship as long as it got him what he wanted.

That was all that mattered.

And it wasn't as if he had a lot of options. He was almost out of time.

Taban Yul, capital of the Ittallan homeland, Val Sharis, was said to be the richest city in all of Linaria, with streets paved in gold. It was certainly the most ostentatious. The majority of Linaria's coins—crowns, florins, pennies, and all their variants—were minted deep within the city's financial district, and the Imperial Guard had been formed within the palace walls several hundred years ago in direct response to the Arillian threat.

Funny how that same palace would be the first to mount a defence against the storm-bringer's resurgence. If he hadn't had so much fun on Jato's ship with the people guarding it, he probably could have killed her and stopped Aciel in his tracks. But he'd dealt them a severe blow.

And he'd seen first-hand what Aciel's compulsion had done to the brash Amarah and timid, yet determined, Moroda.

Aciel was an enemy who had to be removed. Unequivocally.

Before any steps could be taken towards that, there would be a celebration. His return to Taban Yul would begin the process of his coronation. The Ittallan would have their chance to show their fealty to him, not just as a travelling dignitary, but as their ruler. No doubt there'd be a feast of some kind. Music. The sort of pompous showing off that those peacocks adored.

He glanced at the pair of Goldstones. Moroda remained huddled within Palom's cloak, but her face had more colour to it, so she seemed over the worst of the pain from the attack. Her sister was afraid, and rightly so. After a brief doze, both of them were awake, gazes alert, and they reminded him of a pair of frightened mice.

Moroda didn't seem to have much common sense.

'If it's getting too much for you, we can always take a ship back to Niversai the moment we arrive.' Eryn spoke quietly, but she might as well have been shouting for how easily he heard their conversations. Even when buried in the bowels of *Khanna*, his sensitive hearing meant he heard the majority of what was said.

'No, no.' Moroda pulled Palom's cloak more tightly around her shoulders. 'We can rest properly when we arrive, and decide what to do after. How long until we reach Taban Yul?'

'We're already across the Sea of Nami,' Morgen said, brightly. 'Amarah reckons we'll be there before dark.'

'There'll be quite a party when we land,' Sapora said, drawing their gazes.

'A party?' Anahrik sneered, his tone biting. It was rare for him to be on the ship instead of in the sky, and he had no qualms in openly showcasing his dislike for the Varkain. Sapora couldn't wait to correct that.

Moroda's eyes widened. 'Not for us?'

Sapora said, 'For me. In the palace.'

Anahrik shook his head. 'Of *course* it's for our royal snake. Looks like we timed this just perfectly.' He suddenly brightened and turned to Palom. 'Hold on. This could be a great boon to business, couldn't it? New rates due to the prince of the Varkain in the city?'

Palom laughed at his colleague's words. The dark anger he'd harboured since encountering Jato had long since passed, and he was back to his good-natured, calm temperament. Sapora was glad of that. Even *he* had to be wary of a tiger.

Palom extended his arms. 'I would like to formally welcome you to Val Sharis. Birthplace of my people. Taban Yul is most beautiful city in all Linaria, no question. But, yes, business is business and we must get back to our workshop. There is not much time before trade finishes for the season.'

Moroda raised her eyebrows.

Sapora found it curious. Palom had been desperate to stop Aciel from reaching Val Sharis, yet was going to dive back into his workshop. It was strange, but he'd never understood the Ittallan particularly well, despite his own mother being one.

'Is it true the city's streets are lined with gold?' Eryn asked.

'Some are. Around palace.' Palom grinned broadly. 'But city is large. There are other sights to see, too.'

'The palace is great to see from the sky,' Anahrik added, his movements quick as he gesticulated, then began counting off districts on his fingers. 'Trader's Alley is where we're based, and you've also got the Food Quarter, The Three Bells, The Upper Rails—finance and money there— Maitload Corner, Little Yomal—that's where I stay if I'm not at the workshop—then, what else...East Cross, you can get anything you need there, it's great for tourists! And as for views on foot, all of South Galeo is worth the trip. So much great architecture there, and some of the city's oldest buildings. The mausoleum alone is beyond spectacular.'

'Sounds incredible! More exciting than Niversai!' Moroda nudged Eryn.

'Lived in the city all my life. Was born there.' Anahrik grinned, on his feet again and pacing, as though itching to be airborne. 'Taught Palom what was what and where things were when he arrived. Can't wait to be home! Before Aciel and the others get there. At least the city'll be better prepared than Niversai was.' He smirked at Morgen.

Sapora turned away from the excitable Ittallan. Once he started talking, there was no shutting up Anahrik.

'At least there have been no more sightings of Arillians. This is good thing,' Palom said.

Although Palom sounded confident, Sapora could sense his tension and swirling anxiety. There was no outright fear, and they *had* stolen Aciel's eyes, which had to count for something. It would certainly give Val Sharis some breathing space.

Aciel wouldn't be able to increase his power unless he was lucky enough to find a powerful dragon or two. That wasn't to say he'd not already amassed enough followers to attack the capital, but as they hadn't come charging after them following their escape—especially after what he and Amarah had done to Aciel and Jato—Sapora believed them to be weakened.

'I'm really looking forward to it. Father always told us wonderful stories of Taban Yul, of the people and of the wealth of the city. I want to see the jewelled fountains,' Eryn said.

'Not everywhere the city is like that.' Anahrik pulled a short dagger from the holder on his thigh and inspected the silver in the handle. 'Me an' Palom need to get back to our workshop. Got some things to repair, some things to make. When the snows really hit, tourists disappear and work slows. Dunno if we'll have time to go to the palace for this *celebration*.' He threw Sapora a look somewhere between smugness and derision.

Sapora ignored him.

'I am sure we will see you again if you stay in city for while. But our work is our life and it has been too long,' Palom said.

Moroda nodded, her eyes downcast. She played with the ereven sphere they'd stolen from Aciel and Jato, apparently without thinking.

Inside the glass sphere was a phoenix feather—a real one—suspended in clear liquid. Sapora presumed it was from the lake in Berel. *Rhea's breath,* Topeko had called it. Whenever Moroda moved it, the feather shifted, its barbs focussing on one direction, like a compass always pointing north.

'This is how we find a dragon.' Moroda turned it over in her palm, her free hand caressing the glass. 'A stronger response for a stronger dragon?'

'That thing's worth a lot of money, Moroda. Even if it don't work, I can sell it,' Amarah said.

Moroda shook her head. 'It works. Don't worry.'

'I ain't worried.'

That was a lie. Sapora could taste her anxiety thick in the air. Strangely, Moroda was calm and confident. Near death experiences tended to break people. He'd rarely seen it *strengthen* someone. Especially a Goldstone.

Moroda placed the sphere on her lap and looked up at Amarah. 'Weren't you going to tell me about the scars on your leg?'

Sapora's attention sharpened.

Amarah chewed the inside of her cheek for a moment, then adjusted her sails, slowing *Khanna's* speed as they approached Taban Yul. 'Went to Niversai as a kid. After I left home. Wandered out of a tourist spot one night and ran into a pack of Varkain.'

He remained silent at the mention of his kin, but approached them. Moroda caught his movement but said nothing, her focus on the sky pirate.

Amarah continued, 'Guess they thought I'd make good sport. Managed to get in a few blows but they outnumbered me, and they're so damned fast. Most of the scars from their blades healed, but my leg never got better. They wanted to keep me from fighting back so they could enjoy themselves. One of 'em bit me as I kicked out. It's awful when you can feel everything but your body can't move to fight. You're completely locked up. Can't scream. Even your chest can't rise when you breathe, so you take short breaths. It's crushing. It's cold.' Her knuckles whitened on the wheel.

Morgen gasped.

'Dragon's above, Amarah. How did you get away? Wouldn't they have killed you or left you for dead?'

'Fellow sky pirate drove 'em off. We became allies after. Since then, I never go anywhere unarmed. Well, not if I can help it.'

'A lucky fate. They'd have taken you back to Sereth, no doubt,' Sapora said. Fighting pits and keeping thralls was part of the lifestyle his father enjoyed. Filling their ranks with fresh blood had been part of Sereth's way of life for generations. 'Children are most prized, but anyone who gets into a scrap will do.'

'Why...?' Moroda asked, hesitant.

He didn't want to spoil Moroda's mood, so he didn't answer.

'If you were in Niversai when it happened, why didn't you report it to the Imperial Guard? They'd have helped you! They'd have *arrested* those who hurt you!' Morgen said, aghast.

'Well *I* weren't exactly meant to be there, either.'

Morgen balled his fists. 'Even so. We can overlook that if it meant capturing those who tried to murder people on the streets!'

Amarah shrugged. 'It's a thing they do. Kidnapping. Murder. Not a lot you can do about it if it's their culture.'

'I know what acceptable behaviour is and what isn't!' Morgen's passionate disdain grew louder.

'In Corhaven, perhaps.'

'What do you mean?'

'Plenty of Varkain live in Val Sharis and Sereth. They're pretty damned different to us. Behaviours change and cultures change. What's illegal here is legal there. I learned what the Varkain really were that night.' Amarah's nose wrinkled as she looked at him.

Sapora couldn't argue. His kin were known for their secrecy, their violence. There wasn't anything he could do or say that would change what had already happened.

Cold wind washed over the ship as Kohl landed on deck. The Arillian had seemed—somehow—even more subdued since leaving Aciel's ship. But he had an air of excitement in him now. His grey eyes were bright. 'Moroda. You remember the inn we went to in Burian?'

'The Fourth Moon.'

'Yes. I told you about the scars the war left on Linaria?'

She nodded, the ereven sphere held close.

'You might want to have a look below the ship.'

Moroda got to her feet and limped to the side of the deck, her movements stiff and pained.

Sapora resisted the urge to touch the rash across his ribs from when lightning had struck him during the attack. At least he hadn't lost any mobility or been seriously injured.

Curious, he peered over the side of *Khanna*. The sea was a thin, blue line, already some distance behind them.

Ahead, a wide valley splayed out. Jagged cliffs jutted out from unnatural places, breaking up the sweeping plains—the land carved up and split over several, grassy steppes.

Further inland, as the mountains grew and the steppes turned into forests, villages and towns dotted the landscape. Far ahead, just barely in sight, a city emerged from the horizon, its glistening towers spiralling up towards a sky full of airships.

Eryn shifted beside Moroda. 'Quite the view, isn't it? I'm afraid Niversai looks rather drab in comparison.'

'Built in a different time. Different purpose.' Morgen fiddled with his vambraces. Evidently, he'd thought it best to turn up in the Val Sharis capital in his full livery. 'Val Sharis is a land of gold, if ever there was one.'

'You know a lot about these cities?' Moroda asked.

Morgen shrugged. 'All part of our training. You need to understand the basic geography of the world. I don't know everything about every town. Just the important ones.'

As the sun dipped below the horizon, the cloudless sky darkened.

Sapora exhaled, his breath misting the air in front of him.

It was going to be a cold night.

'Palace is ahead. Straight east.' Amarah called.

Morgen clutched the side of the ship, his eyes distant. Eryn whispered in his ear, while Moroda peered over the edge. Palom and Anahrik paced, while Kohl's anxiety filled the air.

Emotions fluttered between the group, and Sapora blocked them out as best he could. He needed to focus.

Taban Yul stood tall, a mighty city surrounded by two

high walls of marble. They shone bright in the low sunlight, and as they drew nearer, Sapora saw ribbons of pale grey and blue running through the creamy-white marble. The inner wall stood six feet taller than the outer, with a thirty foot gap between them.

Other airships lingered in the air; most were more than twice the size of *Khanna*, and far more heavily armed. Sapora sensed Amarah's sudden fear when she spotted them, though she didn't say anything.

The skies were full of trading ships, too. Most were large, triple decked vessels, with wide sails of many bright colours and large cargo holds bursting with supplies.

Khanna flew over the outer walls at a moderate speed, and Sapora saw white marble streets below. He'd spent so much of his childhood in this city, yet he'd never really called it home, so he was unsurprised there was nothing but flat acceptance when he looked down.

'Well, Palom, seeing as this is your town, where am I docking?' Amarah asked the Ittallan.

Sapora bristled at being ignored and stepped up to Amarah. 'The palace.'

'You can't be serious.'

'I am perfectly serious. You are all travelling with me and will be permitted. I will speak with Princess Isa on the situation, and seek wisdom from the Council of Val Sharis.'

'Can't believe I'm actually flying right into the Guards' hands.' Amarah altered her course. 'They best leave *Khanna* alone!'

'Don't be so pessimistic, Amarah.' Sapora's patience was slipping away now he was a hair's breadth from his destination. 'You've benefited the travel of a royal. I'm sure you'll be well rewarded for your *inconveniences*.'

The palace became clearer as they approached, and it never failed to draw awe. Set atop a hill, the highest point in the city, and entirely clad in gleaming marble, with dark blue, almost purple veins snaking across walls and pillars for visual contrast. At least four times the size of Rosecastle and twice as high, with tall, slender turrets that rose up around it, connected by equally tall bridges. Sapora had always thought of the palace like something that floated among the clouds.

Gold statues of animals adorned with cut gemstones topped the many pillars surrounding the palace, spaced at regular intervals.

There were tigers and lions, elephants and bears, bulls, a stork, and several birds of prey he couldn't identify.

Beyond the palace, Taban Yul was set before the incredible backdrop of the distant Feor Mountains; the border of Val Sharis and Sereth.

Where he would undergo his final challenge and supersede his father as king.

'The palace docks are to the east.' Sapora directed Amarah. Sereth had waited a long time already. A few more days wouldn't be an issue.

When it was clear they were heading for the palace, one of the airships that had been floating, dormant, near one of the turrets, moved towards *Khanna*.

'Can't just fly up to the palace unannounced, eh?' Amarah asked. Though her words were light, the nerves were clear in her tone, and fear wreathed her like mist.

'Here's the envoy.' Anahrik pointed up as a white-tailed eagle flew the short distance from the airship to *Khanna*, where it circled above.

Before Amarah could open her mouth and ruin things, Sapora strode onto the open deck. '*Tismat*. I am Prince Sapora, returning to Taban Yul for the winter ceremony. I shall see Princess Isa and the Council at once.'

The eagle circled twice more, before flying back to the

airship. Two more Ittallan, both huge golden eagles, formed an escort, their sharp orange eyes glinting.

'Great welcoming committee. They better keep away from *Khanna*. Don't want any scratches down the side from those damned talons!' Amarah glared at the birds as she followed them.

'For someone who makes their living thriving on opportunities, you have an incredibly pessimistic view of the world,' Sapora said. He was glad the Ittallan had responded promptly to his command. He'd half-expected the same treatment he'd received in Niversai. 'Your precious ship will not be damaged. Stop worrying about it.'

'Money just so happens to be a worry of mine. I know you don't have the same concerns, *prince*.'

Sapora was bored of her insults and refused to rise to her bait.

'Do stop arguing, Amarah. You will be paid once we arrive, Princess Isa will see to it. I've given you my word, so try to relax and enjoy being in the palace. It's likely the only chance you'll see it outside bars, anyway.'

They followed the escort into the palace docks while there was still light outside. As *Khanna* gently flew along lines of already docked ships, their escorts slowed the pace, eventually hovering in mid-air.

'Looks like this is where we'll be docking today.' Amarah grabbed the wheel and pulled levers to bring in her sails. 'Ordered about like I'm one of them...' She continued to mutter under her breath, manoeuvering

Khanna into position, wings tucked in and sails folded down. The hull of the ship touched the wooden plinth extending from the marble palace wall with a light thump. Lines of ships were docked beneath them, and one or two above them, but the extensive hangar was, in fact, mostly empty.

Sapora wondered whether they were already acting before Aciel arrived in their country.

'After you, Varkain.' Amarah waved her hand for him to lead.

He stepped off the ship without glancing at her.

'Prince Sapora.' A guard dropped to one knee to greet the group as they disembarked. She bowed her head at his approach. 'Apologies for the brusque security. Things have been in uproar for the past few days with that damned Arillian charging about in Corhaven.'

'Rise.' Sapora looked at the pair of eagle Ittallan, who had landed and transformed back, joining the guard on her knee.

A balding man with a deeply wrinkled face and ill-fitting robes shuffled into the hangar, escorted by another member of the Imperial Guard. His sleeves were bundled up about his wrists and he hastily straightened them before sinking to one knee. 'Prince Sapora! We were not expecting you! Please, would you follow me? I'm sure Isa will be glad to see you. I'll get—'

'Princess Isa,' Sapora corrected, his eyes narrowed. He hadn't seen the steward for several years, and it seemed he had forgotten his place in the intervening time. Ravens were supposed to be clever. This one knew only how to fawn.

'Yes of course, *Princess* Isa will be most pleased to see you.' The raven echoed, bowing his head low.

'I will inform the council of your arrival.'

'Good.'

He glanced past Sapora, brows furrowing.

'What of...the rest of your party, my prince?'

Sapora turned to them and calculated his response for several long moments, his gaze lingering on Amarah, Palom, and Anahrik. He could have them imprisoned or executed for how they'd treated him. Spoken to him.

He heard Moroda's sudden intake of breath.

Fear pooled around the group like a noxious bog.

Good.

Sapora returned his attention to the steward. He'd never much liked Koraki. Even less after he'd spoken so disrespectfully about his sister.

'I expect they will have free reign of the city and palace alike. Have rooms prepared for them, and invitations extended to tonight, should they wish to attend. Everything will be at the expense of the crown.'

'Your father's crown, Prince Sapora? Are you sure—'

'I would not presume to correct me again, raven,' Sapora interjected, pupils contracting into slits, the only outward expression of his rage. 'Once more and you'll regret it.'

'Please follow me, my prince.' One of the other guards stepped forward, his arm in front of Koraki, saving the raven from the edge of Sapora's tongue. 'We will have refreshments prepared immediately for you and your guests, and preparations will shortly be underway for the banquet this evening. Please, do follow me. I shall show your honoured guests to their quarters.' He turned to lead the party into the palace.

Sapora raised his chin and followed the eagle into the palace, ears keen for any whispers that followed his arrival.

Taban Yul was about to have a rude awakening.

21

Despite living in Taban Yul for several years, Palom had never been inside the palace. He'd had his suspicions about the interior decor, though. Had visited the public gardens several times with Lathri, even delivered a special order of knives to the kitchens. So he wasn't a complete stranger to the home of the council and Ittallan royalty.

But now he was here, swept up in the excitement of Prince Sapora's return, he realised it was unlike anything he could envisage in his wildest dreams.

Taban Yul was vibrant where Berel was drab, busy where Berel was peaceful, and covered in glittering gemstones while Berel was built from sandy bricks. Tapestries adorned every wall, plush rugs carpeted every corridor, and chandeliers hung from ceilings. Elaborately carved doors were not immune from the abundance of detail, their handles coated in gold.

Palom and Anahrik kept to the rear of their group, following Sapora's lead, Amarah just behind, with the Goldstones and Morgen trailing them. Kohl's pace slowed with each step, his limp more pronounced than usual.

Although Palom held no love for Arillians, he had to admit that Kohl had been responsible for saving Moroda and the others. Been there, where Palom had failed.

For that, Kohl had earned Palom's respect. Grudgingly.

They walked past three pairs of Imperial Guard standing at attention against the walls, their white breastplates polished to a mirror sheen. They wore the same gold and red livery as the Corhaven Imperial Guard, but their helms boasted a long spike, two more on each pauldron, and a small toe spike protruding from their boots.

The Ittallan trademark fabric sash crossed their backs and breasts, secured with a triple bow at their hips, adding more extravagance and detail to their appearance. Unlike the Corhaven Guard, who had no adornments to their armour, here the material's colour denoted rank: blue for junior officers, green for senior officers, and red sashes were for captains.

It was a small difference in detail, but reminded Palom he was home.

Morgen glanced down at his own armour as they passed, and Palom saw him pick at his vambrace in disdain. Palom wondered whether the officer had been across the sea and seen his Ittallan counterparts before. It must have been a shock for him to see the Imperial Guard stationed in the palace, all gleaming and saluting as they passed.

Their raven escort wore no armour, only soft robes in dark blue and black, bejewelled slippers, and a black sash. From his manner and the way he spoke to Sapora, Palom assumed the raven to be some sort of high-ranking palace steward or butler.

The Imperial Guard bustled down the corridors in twos and threes—a far cry from the thinly stretched guard in Niversai—and every other word from their mouths was, 'prince.'

It was peculiar to be part of Sapora's entourage.

'Just look at them all!' Morgen eyed another trio as they jogged past, their armour clinking together in harmony. 'They even run together...'

'Is different place. Different regimes,' Palom said, trying to boost the soldier's esteem. 'There are other things to look at instead of them.'

He caught Anahrik's eye, but his colleague was quiet and withdrawn, his gaze unfocussed. Thankfully, Anahrik had escaped the battle unscathed, but they knew they couldn't afford to wait much longer.

They had to act soon.

Once across the bridge and in a wide foyer, corridors leading off in multiple directions, they were greeted by a retinue of palace staff. They wore similar robes to the raven, though less ornate.

There was also a captain of the Imperial Guard among them, his helm boasting three long spikes to set him apart from the other soldiers. Palom wasn't sure of the man's *meraki*, but he held himself with the confident grace of a keen hunter.

Morgen flicked away whatever dirt he'd found on his armour, and approached the captain, crossing one arm across his breastplate in salute. 'Sir.'

The captain's gaze flicked down Morgen. 'You're a long way from home, officer.'

Morgen lowered his head. 'I'm currently stationed in Niversai, Corhaven. I've been gathering intelligence on Aciel and the Arillian threat following the dragon attack on my city. Is there somewhere private I can report?'

After deliberating for a moment, the captain turned to Sapora, who offered a dismissive wave. 'Yes, of course. Follow me.'

Both men saluted each other. Morgen looked back at Palom and the others. 'Duty calls. I won't be long.'

The captain led Morgen away before anyone could retort, then one of the gathered stewards bowed deeply, his balding head reflecting light from the chandelier above. 'Refreshments for Prince Sapora and his honoured guests.' Several stewards stepped past him and proffered a large silver platter loaded with small plates and bowls, all filled with fish, meat, eggs, and rice.

Palom was too busy marvelling at how many guards were everywhere to be interested in the palace food. And he was too anxious to get back to his workshop and attempt the forging to have much of an appetite for anything else.

Moroda held up a hand. 'Oh, no thank you.'

'Would something else be more to your taste?' asked the steward.

'I'm fine, thank you.' Moroda shifted where she stood, glancing at her sister.

The steward inclined his head. 'Please. It would be our pleasure to obtain whatever food you prefer. You are our guest here.'

Palom was about to say something to reassure her, when she shrugged.

'Perhaps some...roasted peanuts?' Moroda asked.

The steward bowed and retreated down the corridor, his robe skimming the floor as he scurried away.

Moroda let out a low groan and rubbed her temple.

'You okay, Ro?'

Eryn asked.

'All okay, Ryn.' Moroda looped her arm through her sisters' and rested her chin on Eryn's shoulder.

Palom's guilt eased at the sight of them. He and Anahrik would be leaving them shortly, and he was glad the two were no longer fighting. They'd look after each other.

They'd be fine.

A door swung open to their left and the same steward reappeared, a large bowl cupped in both hands, the scent of peanuts wafting from it with each step.

Somewhat flustered, Moroda curtseyed and took the bowl from him. 'Thank you so much!'

'I bet it's like you're a Goldstone again.' Amarah sneered, taking a handful of the sweet and salty snack.

'Getting what you want just 'cause you ask for it.'

'It is. It's lovely,' Eryn said.

Palom had not missed the accusation, but chose to remain silent, his attention grabbed by one of the magnificent tapestries adorning the walls along the length of the corridor. They were meticulously woven artworks of former kings and queens, battle scenes, landmarks, and all were laced with gemstones sewn into the fabric itself.

The top half of the tapestries bore resemblance to a king or queen of old, and the bottom half flipped the image, like a playing card, depicting their true form. There was a great black bear, a swan, a stallion, two lions, an eagle, and the one furthest along the hall was a huge brown cobra.

Palom's gut twisted at the sight of the Varkain portrait inside the Ittallan palace.

'My father,' Sapora said, some unknown emotion making his voice tremble.

'I thought...but...aren't the Varkain snakes?' Moroda asked, pausing before the tapestry.

'Yes.'

'Then why on the Ittallan tapestry? In the Ittallan palace?' Moroda asked, keeping her eyes on the cobra and not on Sapora.

Palom wondered whether Sapora would deign to answer, but the prince took a breath as he stared at the portrait.

'Vasil, my father, is King in Sereth—the Varkain home-land—which borders Val Sharis to the east. He has been re-forging the bond between Ittallan and Varkain for many years.' Sapora narrowed his eyes. 'He...conquered Val Sharis and married an Ittallan woman of high rank shortly after. As his wife, she became a queen in Sereth, though she could never enter the country. I am their child. This tapestry was made shortly after Vasil's ascension—it's Ittallan tradition to have a tapestry of every Val Sharis ruler.'

Palom grunted at *conquered*. The Varkain had stormed Taban Yul and annihilated the Ittallan defences. Yes, it brought eventual peace between their two nations. But the cost had been high on the Ittallan side.

'And your sister?' Moroda asked, looking down the hall at the other tapestries.

'Princess Isa is my father's daughter, by another Ittallan noblewoman. You would call her a Goldstone.' He returned his gaze to Moroda. 'I was born here, in the palace. Vasil brought me to Sereth when I was old enough to transform. He left governing Val Sharis to the Council and Ittallan nobility, though he exerts power over them. It's the reason for all...this.' Sapora gestured towards the bowl of peanuts she held.

Eryn leaned in closer to listen.

Palom scoffed.

'Among the Varkain, it is common to take several wives or husbands. The woman who gave my father his daughter remained here, in Val Sharis, until her death. An unfortu-nate accident, I believe. My sister...when she came of age, her *meraki* allowed her to take her true form. But she was not a snake, thus could not come to Sereth under the law of our ancestors and so has remained here. Vasil took a third wife on his return to Sereth. They have a son, Tacio.

'Varkain strength and customs are a fading shadow in

Linaria, and our influence dwindles even in Val Sharis. We'll need all the strength and resources we can get if we are to face Aciel. You know firsthand how formidable he is.'

There was admiration in Sapora's tone, though his words cut deep.

Palom had to admit the snake was right. Their strength *was* waning. And if left unchecked, the Ittallan would end up submitting to a second conqueror—this one an Arillian. No one liked being ruled by the Varkain, but it was an evil they *knew*. An evil they had an agreement with. And they were of course allowed to govern matters in their own land.

Aciel would destroy everything in his path, like the Arillians in the great war.

Palom *had* to create the *Valta Forinja*. It was no longer a boyhood dream.

It was a necessary defence.

Moroda said, 'I feel for your sister. No mother and not being able to see your father.'

'Ancestral laws ought to be changed.' Sapora glared at the tapestry.

'Ancestral laws should indeed be changed,' Kohl said, speaking up for the first time since they'd arrived in the city. His breaths came heavier than before, though he held himself with dignity.

Sapora assessed the Arillian, then gave him a rare smile —an authentic one, not another smug grin. 'You'd make a fine Varkain, Kohl.'

'I'm sure you'd make a fine Arillian also,' Kohl replied, tipping his hat to Sapora. 'I hear there is to be a ball tonight —the palace stewards are asking your orders?'

Palom glanced behind Kohl to see the raven wringing his hands and pacing the floor.

The smile fell from Sapora's face. 'Koraki.' He waved the group away. 'Go. Enjoy the palace and city. Rest while you can. The ball will be tonight. I will have more information regarding our problem Arillian by morning.' He swept past Palom and Kohl and approached Koraki, speaking in hushed tones.

'I can't believe we didn't realise he was a prince for so long,' Moroda said, watching Sapora order the raven about.

'He fits the role as well as he does skulking around in the shadows scaring people,' Amarah said, twirling her scythe.

'Let's get some rest. I'm quite looking forward to a proper meal and the ball,' Moroda said, stifling a yawn. Her movements were stiff, and she clearly needed more time to recover from Jato and Aciel.

'Palom, should we...?' Anahrik whispered. He'd been uncharacteristically quiet.

Palom nodded. He didn't share Anahrik's anxiety, but he wanted to get started sooner rather than later. He turned to Moroda. 'Moroda. Eryn. We part here. My forge is in city. Anahrik and I will work there now.'

Anahrik rolled his shoulders. 'We'll be smack in the centre of Trader's Alley. Enjoy your party tonight. With everyone rushing around so much, looks like it's gonna be a busy one.'

'The city will be quiet, I think. Many people will go to the palace tonight.'

'Taban Yul? Quiet?' Anahrik laughed.

Everyone's attention was on them, and Palom cleared his throat. 'Thank you for allowing Anahrik and I on your ship.' Palom pulled out his drawstring purse and took out the coins he'd promised Amarah all the way back in Burian Forest. 'See? I am man of my word.'

Amarah counted out the coins and gave him a decisive nod. 'Appreciated, Palom. Ain't many like that these days.'

'We will meet again soon, Amarah, to give you proper parting gift. It may help in battles to come.'

If they were successful in forging the *Valta Forinja*, everyone here needed access to one. It might be their only chance against Aciel.

'Parting gift? How kind. I'd prefer another bag of coin, though!' Amarah laughed.

'Is money *all* you care about?' Sapora asked, having returned from giving Koraki orders. 'Fine. Come along and I will see you have your reward.' Sapora and Amarah turned away, their footsteps muffled by the thick rugs.

Sadness echoed in Palom's chest at the sight of their group now so small. Moroda, Eryn, and Kohl were the only ones left in the foyer. Morgen would return to them soon, he was sure. Until then, he'd have to trust the three of them to look after one another.

At least they were safe in the palace, whatever Aciel and Jato had planned.

'Enjoy your first taste of Ittallan culture tonight,' Anahrik said. 'If you fancy a tour of Taban Yul, I'm sure I can sneak away from Palom for a couple of hours tomorrow. I know all the best spots!' He tilted his head to the group and headed away.

'Farewell...' Moroda said, her lip quivering.

'We will see you soon, I am sure.'

Palom waved and followed his partner, the weight of the Sevastos crystal heavy in his pocket.

'Look, Anahrik. Exactly as we left it.' Palom grinned as he entered their workshop, hauling in their large satchel of weaponry and placing it down heavily on one of the oak benches. The palace might have been familiar, but the workshop was *home*. Two seasons since he'd last been here, and his joy was palpable. Even the scent of wood, metal, and ashes soothed his soul like no ale ever could.

And now, it would serve its greatest purpose.

A thick layer of dust had accumulated in the time they'd been away, but he preferred it like that. It meant no trespassers or thieves had broken in and disturbed their work.

'I still think you should have paid a cleaner to keep this place in order.' Anahrik cringed at the dust and grime which gathered on the tables. 'This is disgusting!' He shoved his hands in his pockets and leaned away from the benches and work surfaces, his nose crinkled. 'Five florins a week, that's all it would have been!'

'Dust will not hurt you.' Palom made his way to the back of the workshop, where his coal-fired forge sat, cold and dormant. The hearth was solid stone, blackened from years of use, with a heavy-duty cast iron fire pot bolted to the centre.

All around him, half-finished weapons leaned against walls and benches—swords and shields, spears and axes, all dull under the layer of dust. 'I am too excited about this project to worry about little bit of dirt on floor.' Palom pulled his thick, leather apron from the racking behind the forge and threw it on.

'A *little* dirt?' Anahrik gasped. 'Are you blind? It's on *every* surface, it's in the air it's, ugh...' He covered his mouth and shook his head violently to emphasise his point.

'Do not cry, you are not child. Open back door for fresh air.'

'First thing in the morning, I'm going down to East Cross to get someone to sort this mess out.'

Palom tutted, but did not reply. He had already lit his forge and was powering the bellows to feed the flames. He had dreamed of attempting what he was about to do, but never thought he'd actually be able to try.

It would take some time for the forge to get to temperature, but he had enough patience to work through the entire night if he had to. 'This is more important than cleaning, Anahrik. This is future. This is *Valta Forinja*. You are one who read text in Topeko's book. The Samolen did not think it was possible. You saw it might be.'

Anahrik dusted down a chair, then perched on it and flicked through the book for what had to be the hundredth time. Now they were in their workshop, doubts began to show. He frowned. 'There's no guarantee it'll work here as it did for the Samolen back then. Not like we have any mages showing us what to do.'

'No guarantee...but there is chance. And chance is all I need.' Even Anahrik's discomfort did nothing to quell Palom's excitement and anticipation at finally forging a new weapon—the one he had been dreaming of since he was a boy.

He'd be able to return home a hero, if they were successful.

Be able to look his father in the eye again.

Waves of heat rolled around the workshop as the flames built in intensity, but with the back door open, it did not become a furnace. Palom continued to press the bellows, watching as the flames roared and took shape. They were short on details, with no temperatures or times given. He just had to trust in the crystal, his forging instincts, and hope.

Moroda had trusted in herself, too.

Strange, how the young Goldstone had affected him. 'Brave one, this Moroda. She should not have gone on Arillian's airship.'

'No, but she did well, surviving all that.'

'Barely. Kohl had to save her.'

'And Amarah and Sapora, too. Heh. Prince Sapora. He's

no prince of mine. Damned snake.' Anahrik snorted.

'No. But he will be your king in few days' time.'

Anahrik went silent for a while, and Palom continued to work the fires, wiping his brow as sweat dripped down his face. Ever since they'd arrived in Berel, Anahrik had been on edge. Far quieter than usual. He was only ever like that when something was bothering him. 'You want to leave Taban Yul?'

'Was it that obvious?' Anahrik chuckled. 'Maybe I do. Maybe we should head up north for a while. I've got a few cousins that'd have room for us, if we needed.'

'And our weapons?' Palom looked up from the forge, his face darkened by soot.

'Bring 'em with us. Wait out until next season. At least we can defend ourselves if it comes to it. The idea of another Arillian war...Just *hearing* the thunder from Jato's ship made me wanna get out the sky.'

'Anahrik...'

'I know, I know.' He bit his lip. 'This Aciel? There's nothing like him. I don't trust Sapora to keep the Ittallan safe, even in Taban Yul. *And* he's a half-breed. He doesn't make many of us confident.'

'What about tour you have promised Moroda and others?' Palom laughed, one foot pumping the bellows, sending up wave after wave of air and heat, allowing the flame to burn hotter with each press.

It was almost white. The Sevastos crystal was a catalyst like no other. He wanted the flames to match that intensity.

Anahrik shrugged. 'Ask them to leave with us? There's nothing in Corhaven, but Val Sharis is bigger, safer. We keep on the move. Stick to the ground, away from the Arillians.'

Palom thought about leaving, then dismissed it. The idea was ridiculous. They had only just returned to the city, and now they had to leave? 'What about Lathri?'

'She can come too. Probably has contacts as well, right? Why don't you see her tomorrow, and I'll talk to the others. We get everything packed up and head off before night with whoever wants to come.'

'And this plan of Topeko's? To find dragon? To fight Aciel?' Palom burned to attack the Arillian. He wanted to defend his people, not run from a threat.

'It was a nice idea. But you really think a couple of Goldstones could do anything against him? Even with Kohl, Sapora, *and* Amarah, they didn't stand a chance. Jato's too strong. Aciel's compulsion is...you can't fight it.'

Palom cleared a space on his workbench as he considered. 'This is why we are trying to make *Valta Forinja*. You agreed to Topeko's idea.'

'Yeah. *Before* I bumped into Aciel. Gotta adapt, Palom. Gotta run when it makes sense.'

It was tempting. And if they were able to turn some of their weapons into *Valta Forinja*, they'd be able to defend themselves if trouble found them. Palom sighed. 'You led me down right path when I first came to city. I would be dead if not for you. Maybe you are right again about this, too.'

'Moroda faced Jato because she was naive. She didn't know any better, and none of us stopped her. But we *know* better, now. Sapora can stay and try and do what he can, if he wants. He's the only one with real authority, anyway. I trust my own eyes and talons first. And if we make these weapons? We keep hold of them. Make for somewhere safe, where no one can attack. Not even Aciel.' Anahrik was back on his feet, a mass of excited energy.

'The fire is ready. Give me a shard,' Palom said., keeping his attention on his task.

Anahrik reached into their bags and pulled out several small shards of crystal, barely the length of his thumb, stolen from Berel.

They'd been wrapped in a combination of linen and thick leaves to keep them from damage and moisture, though sand from the desert country spilled from his fingers as he unwrapped them. 'If this works...'

Palom rubbed the sweat from his palms onto his apron sides, readying himself to handle such a delicate and potent substance. 'You have learned way to do this, Anahrik. You have learned how to harness the dragon's power in weapon. We are forging new legends, you and I.' He took one shard and held it carefully in one hand. '*Valta Forinja.*'

'Potentially.' Anahrik licked his lips.

'My greatsword.'

Anahrik turned to the oak bench behind them, where Palom had slung the weapons they arrived with. Unhooking the satchel lid, he pulled out the enormous sword with both hands. Cast in dark steel, it had barely been used during their time out of Val Sharis, but the blade would be the first thing to test their technique.

Hands trembling, Anahrik carried it to the forge, and held it out to Palom, hilt first.

'Get ready to retreat. We do not know what may happen...' Palom clasped the weapon with his other hand and held it above the flame.

Anahrik nodded, rapt with awe.

He took a breath, not daring to look at Anahrik, and dropped the shard into the heart of the forge.

The resulting explosion was so sudden and violent that it knocked the breath out of him. Palom widened his stance and withstood the blast, but the explosion was so bright that he couldn't see for several seconds.

When his vision returned, he gasped—the fire burned purple. It was furious—thrashing in the forge like a caged beast. 'Looks like we have our chance. Let us try and make history.'

22

Amarah strolled down the halls as if she owned the palace. Most of the stewards and servants gave her a curious glance, but in Sapora's presence, they quickly scuttled off, giving both of them a wide berth.

Although it had been a long flight, she wasn't particularly tired, nor did she want to be cooped up in some room in the palace, as opulent as it was.

She was no Goldstone.

There was opportunity here.

Sapora had promised her money, and she wasn't about to let him weasel out of that. Prince or no prince.

Amarah half-considered plucking a few of the smaller gemstones from the wall tapestries, but decided against it. He owed her more than a few trinkets, and she knew when a theft wasn't worth the risk.

Sapora exited the palace through a grand set of double-doors at the end of the hall, stepping out into a small court-yard ringed by flowering plants. Spots of red and yellow petals complemented the white and gold exterior that swamped the palace.

Amarah didn't hide her scowl. Goldstones were too

ostentatious. It stood to reason that royalty would be even more so. But all this gold and red made her feel sick.

How could anyone stomach *living* here?

She looked at Sapora, who had barely given the opulence a second glance. He was probably used to it. Didn't see all the money locked in these walls. Amarah wondered what a childhood would have been like here, surrounded by gold and marble and servants running to carry out your every order—

No.

She didn't wonder.

She *didn't* care to be like those damned Goldstones. They didn't have the first idea of what the world was really like.

Heavy clouds had rolled in since they'd landed, and though they didn't carry the lurking thunder of an Arillian storm, they were dark enough to threaten rain. Probably snow, judging by the bitter wind blowing over her skin.

Amarah watched Sapora pause at the courtyard's far end, flanked by a pair of silver wolf statues, their open mouths snarling. He lingered at the top of an enormous flight of white stone and marble stairs, which led down to wide, golden gates, and the city of Taban Yul beyond. Stationary guards were posted halfway up the stairs, and six more stood at attention by the gates, blocking anyone from approaching the palace by this entrance.

The city beyond expanded as a mirage of colour, sound, and movement. In comparison to the monotony of the palace, the city seemed alive. Amarah had visited Taban Yul before, on occasion, though she'd only seen it from airship height or street level, and she marvelled at the view from the palace.

After allowing herself a moment to enjoy the view, she turned to business. 'Well? Sapora?' She folded her arms, scythe in its holder on her back. She'd half-expected the guards to take her weapons the moment they'd docked, but being in Sapora's presence clearly afforded her special treatment.

He opened his mouth to reply, but before he said anything, a low hiss from above drew their attention.

A large, red-gold cat crouched on the broad marble wall which framed the top of the palace doors. Bright amber eyes glinted, and it bared sharp, white fangs at them. The fur of the cat was short and wiry, with dark brown, almost black markings dotted about its ears, back, tail, and hindquarters. Crouching, it hissed again, then leapt vertically into the air and descended with claws drawn.

Amarah instinctively leaped back to avoid a collision with the cat, but Sapora held his ground, knees slightly bent.

Cursing her luck, Amarah drew her scythe, but before she could act, a flash of light burst from the cat as it transformed.

'Isa, I have missed you,' Sapora said, his lips turned slightly upwards as he embraced a young woman. Her bright amber eyes were the same as in her cat form, and she wore her brunette hair tied high in four thick braids. Jewelled drop earrings shimmered from her ears, and bracelets and anklets chimed as she moved.

Aside from a similar, predatory stare, they looked nothing alike.

'Sapora! I'm so glad you're here! I *knew* you'd come back before your coronation!' Isa clutched him in a tight hug.

'You have grown much since I saw you last.' Sapora took a step back, assessing her. 'I apologise for not keeping in contact. My errantry has kept me away far longer than I'd planned. There were some...complications.'

Isa nodded. 'I understand. Well travelled, I hope?' She

turned her gaze onto Amarah, and her pupils constricted into slits. 'Who is this?'

'Ah yes,' Sapora said, voice dropping to a hiss. 'Sister, this is Amarah. She is captain of the airship I have been travelling on. We owe her some coin for the trip.'

Isa blinked, suspicion gone at her brother's words, her pupils dilating again. 'Thank you, Amarah. I'll see to it you're paid well for helping my brother. Will you be joining us at the ball tonight?'

'Not my kind of thing.' Amarah leant on her scythe. She'd never thought a Varkain *capable* of showing affection, and seeing Sapora's behaviour unnerved her. All she wanted was her coin, then she could get going.

A dark rum would go down well right about now. Might even be a few of the old crews here. Taban Yul was a meeting hub for all sorts of miscreants, sky pirates included.

'Oh, please. Do come along, you can be my special guest!' Isa stepped forward and grabbed Amarah's hands, shaking her out of her thoughts. 'If you've not packed for the occasion, you're welcome to anything from my wardrobe— or I can send a servant into the city for you.' Isa released Amarah's hands and paced around, never still for a moment.

Amarah considered. The princess didn't harbour the same animosity towards her that Sapora clearly did, and she was no Varkain, even if her blood said otherwise. She wondered what Isa had to gain by inviting her along. There was always some trick to people's invitations. Especially those of higher status. Which, for Amarah, was pretty much everyone.

Surely Isa had everything she needed here?

Certainly, Amarah was *curious* about the event. It might not have been to her personal taste, but she couldn't deny it was an opportunity to stay inside the palace for an extended period of time.

Plenty of fat pockets to empty, too.

She looked into the princess's bright amber eyes, fought a brief sensation of fear, and saw a genuine offer.

Fuck it. Why not?

Amarah scratched her nose. 'Well, if you put it like that, I don't see why I shouldn't. Think I'm a bit taller than you, though. Might need to get myself something...fitting. How many people will be there?'

Sapora narrowed his eyes, but didn't say anything.

'The ballroom will be full. The whole Council will be there, and half the Ittallan nobility, I should think.' Isa paced the small courtyard, appraising the flowers as she passed them. 'Please, take this.' She reached into her pocket and withdrew a small, round onyx stone. A family crest had been etched into the surface, and she handed it to Amarah. 'Use this, and everything you buy will be paid for by the crown. You'll have no problems in the city getting whatever you need for tonight. There isn't much time.'

'Amarah, are you certain? This wouldn't be your...*usual* crowd.'

'Course I'm sure, Sapora. Ain't gonna be rude and reject such a generous invitation, am I?'

Isa cocked an eyebrow, no doubt at Amarah's brash tone. Or was it because she'd addressed the prince by his first name?

Either way, Amarah ignored Isa's expression and said as sweetly as possible, 'You're too kind, princess.' She licked her lips and smirked at the Varkain. 'Sapora, Isa, I'll see you this evening.' She bowed her head, reminiscent of the Samolen, before sauntering down the stairs and into Val Sharis.

◆

AMARAH HADN'T KNOWN prosperity like it.

Vendors and street merchants might have watched her warily—she probably didn't look particularly respectable after what she'd been through over the past few days—but one glance at Princess Isa's crest, and they treated her like any Goldstone.

It was laughable.

She'd first settled her stomach, treating herself to her favourite delicacies, including three slices of venison pie, a bowl of grilled potatoes in a seasoning blend she couldn't determine, and grabbing a large wheel of crumbly cheese made in the far south of Val Sharis, ignoring the fact she'd been uncomfortably full. But it was a favourite of Goldstones and something she'd never been able to enjoy before now. Not to mention she wasn't paying a penny for it. That wasn't something to pass up.

After biting into the expensive cheese, she decided it hadn't been worth it, and gave the rest freely to a street urchin who looked like his last meal had been some time ago.

Amarah also made sure to grab some sticky honey cakes to take with her. Might as well restock *Khanna* while she had the chance, despite having plenty of supplies from Topeko's generosity.

She then bought clothes—more practical garb than anything suitable for a fancy ball attended by Goldstones and royalty—a new pair of breeches, three new shirts to replace her own burned and ripped one, a thicker belt, and sturdy boots lined with fur for the incoming snow. Even better, she'd had all her supplies sent to her ship. One look at the crest, and people were falling over themselves to help or offer more services, and the merchant's apprentice had practically run towards the palace, her purchases neatly wrapped and bundled up.

She'd paid for a bath, too, and enjoyed it in a private room with heated water.

Dragons above, the *warmth*!

It was something she'd only enjoyed in Berel.

If anything, that hot soak had been the highlight of the whole experience.

Night had fallen by the time she returned to the palace, along with a light snowfall. Overconfident after being fussed over like royalty, she felt ready to take on the world. With a full belly, full pockets, and her ship docked safely, there was nothing she couldn't do.

Not to mention the Imperial Guard couldn't touch her as long as she had Princess Isa's crest.

She could do *whatever* she wanted.

As Amarah sauntered through the palace, imagining this must be what it was like to be a real Goldstone, she spied the raven muttering to himself under his breath as he shuffled along, away from the more crowded halls and corridors.

Narrowing her eyes, she followed him, keeping a safe distance in case he turned around.

It soon became apparent she did not need to practice any form of stealth, as he was too engrossed in his mutterings to pay any attention to anything bar where he was going. His black sash, too long for him, dragged along the floor, picking up dust and dirt where he walked, and Amarah followed as he entered an empty drawing room.

'...that damned filthy snake. Bastards! The both of them! How *dare* they stroll in here? Ordering us about like servants. And the ball tonight. Damned Varkain has no right to be doing this to us. I won't stand for it! I *won't*! I'll get together with—'

'I hope you ain't speaking about Sapora.' Amarah slammed the bottom of her weapon on his sash, pinning it to the ground.

The raven whirled around, eyes wide.

'He's a very dear friend of mine, I'll have you know.' She grasped the handle of her scythe and pushed the blade close to his chin. 'Considering I ain't seen any other Varkain in the city since turning up, I'll have to assume you were talking about your prince? Badly of him, too? Tut, tut, tut.'

'Y—you!'

'Something going on that I should know about?' She twisted the blade so the edge poked at the loose skin on his jaw.

'If...if you're a friend of Prince Sapora then there's no problem!' He raised his hands defensively, cowering at her blade.

'I'm not so sure about that. Sounded like you were plotting something.'

'You've no right to order me about!'

Amarah pushed the edge of the scythe into his skin, drawing blood. 'I think you'll find I have *every* right to know. Tell me what's going on, and I'll let you leave with your head.'

He stammered, waving his hands at her. 'Please!'

She lessened the pressure slightly and he coughed. She fought to roll her eyes at his dramatic response, but waited while he gathered himself.

'There'll be a change of power.'

Amarah frowned. 'Sapora's gonna be king in a few days, sure. Surely you all know that.'

He shook his head. 'Tonight. There'll be...Well. Don't go to the ball unless the prince is a friend of yours. And you're one of *his*.'

Damned raven was talking in riddles. No wonder Sapora was irritated by him earlier. 'You ain't making no sense! What's gonna happen at the ball?' She raised her voice

309

louder than she wanted to, and he flinched at her tone. 'Oh for Rhea's sake, get up!'

Behind her, the door opened and the clunk of metal boots preceded a soldier of the Imperial Guard. 'Koraki! What's going on here?'

Amarah looked at him as he took in the scene, his eyes lingering on her scythe and the trickle of blood dribbling down the raven's neck. Despite Isa's crest, a lifetime of running from authority turned her insides to ice. 'This is Prince Sapora's business. Turn around and go back to your patrol!'

It wasn't strictly speaking a lie, but she didn't want any damned soldier to poke his nose into what she was doing.

Koraki whimpered.

The man's hand went to the sword at his hip, though he hesitated.

Amarah grabbed Isa'a crest and held it high so he could see. 'You not hear me? Get *out*!' Aggression and confidence would be her way out of this. It usually was.

'Erm...I need to get my captain...'

'Go get him then, just get out of here!' Amarah waved her scythe towards him, which sent him scuttling away.

'And as for you,' she whirled back to Koraki, 'stop speaking in riddles and tell me *exactly* what's gonna happen.'

'You can't threaten me! The Imperial Guard will be here!'

She raised her blade again. 'Did you forget already? He'll be back with his captain, sure. Do you want 'em to find you in one piece or your beheaded body?' She was fairly sure the princess wouldn't want Amarah to kill anyone, least not a member of the palace staff. But if Isa was unhappy with what she'd done, Amarah could simply fly away.

Koraki trembled. 'The Council will be in attendance,

and those who oppose the prince will have their power relinquished. We *true* followers have nothing to fear.'

'Fear? Why would they fear giving up—' Amarah caught herself.

After swanning around on Sapora's goodwill, she'd forgotten the core of him. He was a *Varkain*.

And the Varkain killed.

Especially those they believed weaker than themselves.

Koraki stumbled away from her, tripping over his sash and landing hard on his rear end.

'Appreciate your help.' Amarah spun her weapon and smacked him across the head with the handle, knocking him out in one hit. She didn't want him blathering about being *assaulted* by her. People like him were always exaggerating, and she didn't want to have any loose ends until she was away from the palace.

There was blood on the carpet, after all.

Sapora had been kind to her, but the debt had been repaid. There was no certainty that she would be safe from his wrath. And there was no chance she was going to stick around to find out.

She had everything she needed. Money from Palom. Fresh clothes and supplies from Isa's money. A ship in good repair, all her resources restocked.

Plus, once Aciel and Jato recovered enough, they'd be on the move. She didn't doubt they'd be looking for her ship.

Instinct kicked in. She had to survive. She had to get away from the city.

Heart in her throat, and fuelled by the familiar chill of adrenaline, Amarah left the drawing room and raced down the corridors. She had to get to the hangar. Her ship would get her away from the chaos, like it always did. She could lie low in Estoria, perhaps. Or the southernmost tip of Berel. There were always options on where to hide.

Her full belly and the baths made her sluggish as reality sunk in.

Damned Varkain always found a way to ruin everything.

Even if Isa was a cat, she'd grown up among snakes. She was related to Sapora.

She was one of *them*.

Nothing was safe.

It was just like that damned dragon looming over Niversai, except this time she had warning enough to flee before it was too late.

She skidded around a corner, trying to figure out where the hangar was. A staircase led up to the upper floor, and she recognised the tapestry hanging above it. That was where she'd left Moroda and the others. They were probably up there, trying on dresses and jewellery, getting ready for the ball.

Damn it! She ought to warn them. If Sapora was going to force people out of power, people who opposed him, it was going to get ugly. Those Goldstones wouldn't stand a chance.

She hesitated at the bottom of the stairway, one hand on the smooth bannister, debating with herself whether she could risk the few minutes it would take to find them. They might not even listen. Might think they were safe with Sapora.

Amarah chewed her lip. They *might* be. Sapora had saved Moroda, too.

And they had plans. Find the dragon. Stand against Aciel. All that brave, heroic nonsense that Topeko had filled their heads with.

Here, she could cut clean. Leave on her stocked ship and continue with her life.

They wouldn't need her.

Amarah debated several more seconds, then stepped

back from the stairs and headed towards the hangar. She didn't have time, and it was already dark. Damn, she'd spent too long at the baths.

They'd be safe. She was sure.

Hurrying down a long passageway, flanked by portraits of former Ittallan royalty and leaders, she grinned. Definitely heading the way she'd come now. The hangar was just ahead.

Something akin to guilt gnawed at her for leaving Moroda and the others. For not taking part against Aciel. It had sounded good, back in Berel—a group of misfits taking a stand. Topeko was always good at putting ideas in people's heads.

He'd be disappointed, sure. But that wasn't unusual. She'd disappointed him before.

Amarah angrily dismissed the thoughts. She fancied living a bit longer. That was all that mattered.

'You! Halt in the name of the Council!' A huge Ittallan in full armour appeared at the end of the hall, three spikes on his helm marking him of higher rank. Two other members of the Imperial Guard stood either side of him, spears held aloft.

Amarah skidded to a halt. 'Get out of the way! I'm with—'

'Prince Sapora, apparently,' the guard said. He sneered at her.

Amarah was about to whirl around, see if there was another way to the hangar, when four more armoured guards marched towards her, cutting off her escape. 'Dragons above, you are stupid! You wanna feel your prince's fury?'

'You assaulted the head steward of the palace. *You're* the one who ought to be worried about the prince's fury.' The

313

captain stepped towards her, closing the distance in several heartbeats.

Amarah showed him the crest. 'See? Now what you gotta say for yourself.'

He struck out, knocking the crest from her hand and sending it flying down the carpeted hall.

Amarah was too stunned to react. Damn, she'd forgotten the speed and strength of the Ittallan. This was why she never meddled with them. She had no idea what this one's true form was—probably an eagle if their escort on arrival was anything to go by—and she knew she couldn't stand up to him as outnumbered as she was.

'We'll see what Prince Sapora has to say. I'm afraid he's getting ready for tonight, and isn't to be disturbed.' He nodded to the four behind her, who rushed in to bind her arms behind her back.

She fought half-heartedly, but there was little point in risking injury with so many of them. If only she hadn't thought about Moroda and the others. She'd have been on her ship by now if only she'd been faster. 'This how you treat your royalty's guests? He'll have your heads for this!'

'I'm sure heads will be had. But it won't be ours.' The captain chuckled. 'Take her away. Show her the palace's finest.'

His words sent another stab of fear through Amarah as she was dragged away. Moroda and the others would be okay.

Sapora might be a brutal Varkain, ruthless to those who opposed him.

But he wouldn't hurt them...

Would he?

23

M oroda was ushered up an enormous staircase and through the palace hallways by the most irate person she'd ever seen in her life.

He'd introduced himself as Elafion, blustered about the useless stewards, and all but dragged her, Eryn, and Kohl to a designated guest suite. She had to jog to keep up with his large strides, every step sending splinters of pain up her legs, but she tried to marvel at their beautiful surroundings while she had the chance. Oak and marble interlaced, and the floor was covered by thick, red carpet, jewels lining the edges.

The opulence reminded her of her youth. Galleries she and Eryn had visited with their father, auction houses where they'd discovered trinkets and treasures. Even her own childhood home had been furnished in a similar style, with much of the same wood.

She noticed Eryn's smile widening, but Moroda wasn't sure she missed the luxuries herself.

'I trust you're attending tonight's entertainment?' Elafion huffed as they passed through a large foyer. 'The ballroom is here, if you are. Don't be late.' He hurried up the wide steps, giving none of them time to even glance through the door.

Moroda glanced to her left and right; Eryn hurried along as quickly as she could, but Kohl lagged behind. Kohl *could* move quickly, but he had been exhausted on the flight after Jato's ship, and Moroda wondered whether he'd been injured in the chaos and had kept it to himself.

Elafion stopped abruptly at another wide corridor. 'Well, I don't know what rooms you've been given but the guest suites are along here, right up to the far balcony at the end.' He waved his hand vaguely. 'Use the bells if you need anything and the stewards will help. I'm sure they're already attempting to find a new wardrobe for you. Now, if you'll excuse me, I've a meeting to attend. Dragons forbid I'm late for *that*.' He snorted again and whirled around, gold chains jingling as he stomped back down the stairs and out of sight.

Moroda ran a hand self-consciously down her skirt. Several holes had been blasted through it by Jato's electricity, and in addition to the general dirt of travel, its edges were blackened.

'Why was he so irritated?' Eryn panted, one arm on the wall as she tried to catch her breath. 'We might as well have run the whole way!'

'From the looks of things, I don't think anyone expected Sapora's return,' Kohl said, cool and calm as ever. 'The reactions seem either to be fear or irritation.'

Moroda saw how stiffly he held himself, and wondered why he was so concerned with hiding the extent of his injuries.

'I'm not surprised. Sapora likes to throw his weight around. He always has! Look at how he is with Amarah, or Anahrik. Especially when he's insulted!' Eryn replied. 'But enough of him, let's go and sit down. We wanted to rest?'

'I cannot say I blame him,' Kohl said, as they chose one of the suites and entered cautiously.

Gold once again lined the ceiling and windows, and the dark wood furniture was ornately gilded with the precious metal. A small silver bell sat on a circular table beside the door, as Elafion had said, and a lit fireplace dominated the wall to their left.

Moroda was about to approach the fireplace, when hurried footsteps caught her attention. Peering down the corridor, she brightened when she saw Morgen hurrying after them.

'Glad I caught you! I'd get lost so quickly in this place.' Morgen entered the suite and ran a hand through his hair. 'Report done. Looks like Val Sharis has been dealing with rampaging dragons, too.'

At the mention of dragons, Moroda's breath caught. 'Like...Niversai?'

'Yes. A few smaller villages have burned down, but their cities have been better defended. Outside the walls might not be safe for long.' Morgen went over to the large arched window and peered out, while Moroda and Eryn sat by the fire and warmed themselves. 'Reconstruction of Niversai has begun, but it'll take a while. I'll need to go back there soon to help.'

'I'm sure Sapora will have things under control,' Moroda muttered, already worried about the possible devastation that awaited Taban Yul if dragons were causing chaos. She'd not soon forget the intense heat and thick smoke when Niversai had burned.

Kohl said, 'He is of mixed blood, and the Ittallan are a proud race, almost as proud as the Varkain. I imagine he has a lot to prove. His knowledge. His strength. His competence. The best way he knows how is with poorly veiled threats and actual attacks.'

'I'd never thought about that before,' Moroda said.

She'd seen another side to Sapora on that airship. Evil, yes, in the mindless killing of those aboard that ship. But compassion towards her, too. And what he'd said once she was back on *Khanna*. She struggled to figure him out.

'But he's their *prince*? Why would his lineage matter?' Eryn asked.

'It shouldn't, but it does. Sapora will have a tough rule ahead of him. In the middle of an Arillian war, with his own people distrusting him. I do feel for the prince.'

'Orders are orders. Doesn't matter if you agree with them or not, or even if you *like* who gave them,' Morgen said in a low voice. He peered out of the window, hands resting on the sill.

'You should question them, though. If you blindly follow what you're told, you're no different to those under Aciel's compulsion,' Moroda said.

Morgen scoffed. 'If only it was that simple. There are consequences if you don't obey.'

The last traces of sunlight disappeared, blanketing the city in darkness.

Kohl shook his head. 'Perhaps in Corhaven. The Ittallan, and especially the Varkain, do things differently. They are two races connected by ancient history, and the Ittallan try to distance themselves more with each season. Sapora will continue his father's work of trying to undo that distance to strengthen himself.'

'How can you be so sure?' Eryn asked.

'Sapora keeps talking about taking his throne. And now, instead of being respectful of the Ittallan, he's immediately putting his mark down. Although he helped you when we crossed the sea, Moroda, you should be wary of him. There's a reason non-Varkain do not travel to Sereth.'

Kohl approached the window and stood beside Morgen.

Ice cold wind whirled around the large room for an instant, the flames flickering before he regained himself. 'I do not think we should stay in the palace long. We ought to look for the dragon now, while we have a head start over Aciel. While he's injured and slow. We should sleep now and leave before first light.'

An uncomfortable silence filled the air.

'Especially after what you said about more dragons attacking, Morgen,' Kohl added.

Moroda admired his dedication to the task, but she was exhausted. The thought of travelling again so soon, especially if there were dragons to be wary of, was too much.

'What about the ball?' Eryn stepped forward.

'What about it?' Kohl turned to her, one eyebrow raised.

Eryn glanced at Moroda. 'I...I would have liked to attend the ball. It's been so long.'

Morgen said, 'I think it's impolite not to attend. Especially after a royal invitation.'

Kohl frowned, his eyebrows creasing.

Moroda chewed her lip, torn. Kohl's thoughts on finding a dragon sooner rather than later held true. The only reason they were here, after all, was to do what they could against Aciel.

But one night couldn't hurt? If they weren't leaving until dawn, would it make a difference whether they slept for most of the night, or spent a few hours enjoying a respite?

Kohl had been more distant than usual, speaking in more vague terms, with blasts of frigid air expelled from his fists every so often. Bottling up emotions was rarely good, but she assumed he had his reasons.

Perhaps he'd been so shaken by what he'd seen of Aciel and Jato that he didn't want to risk waiting. Not if the wrath of the dragons on this continent was already stirring.

But Moroda remembered her promise to her sister, and

that made it an easy decision. 'I need to read more about the sphere. How it works. And I need rest, too. We know Taban Yul is safe for the moment. We'll stay one night, and there's nothing wrong with attending the ball while we're honoured guests. Right, Ryn?'

Eryn's smile told her she was happy with her decision. 'The ball will be a welcome relief from flying and eating rations! I can't remember the last time we were able to relax and have a proper meal.'

'Best keep watch, then. Just in case.' Kohl frowned.

'You both deserve a break and to enjoy yourselves. I can get some new armour while I'm here, too,' Morgen said.

'Thank you, Morgen.' Eryn gave them both a smile.

Moroda yawned. 'For now, let's try to enjoy the evening. Dragon's above, it's been a long time since we enjoyed anything.'

IT HAD BEEN TOO long since Moroda had felt silk against her skin.

She stared at herself in one of the dressing room mirrors, admiring how clean and soft her hair was, and how much the new dress reminded her of her previous life. Servants and stewards had brought them a selection of outfits, and Eryn had delighted in trying on several selections.

Eryn had opted for green, while Moroda had been drawn to the richly embroidered dress, midnight blue to complement her ring.

Wrinkling her nose, she wondered what Amarah would think to see her dressed this way, and whether the sky pirate would join them for the ball. She could hardly imagine what Amarah might look like, perfumed up and dressed in silks.

Trying to keep the smile from her face, Moroda left the

room and made her way downstairs where the others waited in the foyer.

Eryn was deep in conversation with Morgen—dressed for the occasion in a red and gold doublet, sword at his hip —with Kohl standing off to the side, more pensive than usual. 'Kohl?'

'Moroda. You're looking lovely.' Kohl glanced over her outfit. 'You have the sphere safe?'

She reached into the pocket of her outer skirts and withdrew it to show him. 'I'll keep it with me the whole night.'

After everything she'd been through to get it, she wasn't going to let the sphere out of her sight.

Kohl glanced up, tapping his hat to the pair of Imperial Guards who approached at Moroda's arrival. 'Ladies, Sirs. You are esteemed guests in Taban Yul. The prince and princess await.'

Moroda inclined her head. 'Are you sure you don't want to join, Kohl?'

'I'm sure. No doubt you will have plenty of fun for me. I would prefer to keep watch. And my leg isn't what it used to be. I'm afraid I'm not much of a dancer.'

Morgen gestured to the swelling crowd. 'Look how many of the Imperial Guard are here! Nothing will happen. Aciel is probably still at sea, licking his wounds after what Amarah and Sapora did.'

'All the same. Enjoy the evening.' Kohl tapped his hat to them and limped away, his gait stiffer with each step.

Her heart went out to him. She was sure if he'd been well enough, they'd have parted ways here. He was desperate to keep one step ahead of Aciel, to begin the search for the dragon and follow Topeko's advice. But with the ereven sphere in her possession, he'd be flying just as blind as Aciel.

Eryn rested a hand on Moroda's shoulder. 'Don't worry,

Ro. As he said, let's enjoy the night. Don't you think we deserve some fun?'

'Ryn? Ro? Shall we?' Morgen stepped up, holding out his arms. The sisters smiled at each other, looped their arms through his, and followed the two members of the Imperial Guard into the ballroom.

The grand doors were opened for them, and Moroda's breath caught.

It seemed the ballroom was the jewel in the palace's crown of opulence.

With a solid marble floor reflecting golden light, and ten pillars lining the room on each side, each carved in the likeness of a different animal, the ballroom had been built to impress. Gemstones draped down the walls along with lashings of gold, from the door handles to the furniture. The ceiling was over thirty feet high, and three six-tier crystal chandeliers hung from it, filling the vast room in shimmering, silver-gold light.

Despite how glorious the setting was, Moroda's heart was taken by the clothes everyone wore. Gowns and suits of silk and cashmere, pearls and obsidian decorating gloved hands, heeled boots, and even combed through hair.

At least half the attendees wore bejewelled masks that covered either the upper or lower half of their faces, each a more vivid colour than the next. Many depicted animals: golden lions with rubies in their mouths, blue peacocks with green feathers blossoming from the sides, white swans, silver twisting down the handles.

She'd attended a number of balls in her youth, but none in Corhaven matched this one.

It put her capital to shame.

Tables were laid at the sides and top of the room, leaving a wide, empty square in the middle. Musicians stood on a small, raised stage to the edge of the hall; strings and wind instruments gently accompanied the murmur of conversation as the seated guests spoke among themselves.

Moroda tried to count the tables as they followed the soldiers across the room, but her head spun. The room must have held three or four hundred people at her best estimate.

Eryn's face matched her own child-like wonder as she marvelled at what she saw, eyes locked on the chandeliers above.

'Happy, Ryn?'

'You have no idea, Ro. This is *amazing*!'

They hesitated as they approached a wide table at the head of the room: the royal table.

She recognised Elafion hunkered into himself as he drank heavily from a goblet of wine, evidently uncomfortable from the way his gaze shifted around. Other Ittallan sat beside him, Council members, Moroda assumed, though she did not know their faces.

Sapora sat at the centre of the table. Out of his scruffy travelling clothes and dressed in dark blue coat and tails, he looked a completely different person. Even his ashen grey skin seemed less threatening, his posture more regal. From what Moroda could tell, he was the only one in the room without any gold or jewels attached to his attire. He was listening to a Council member speak to him, but from his distant stare, it was apparent that his focus was elsewhere. She shivered involuntarily as their escort announced their arrival.

Sapora lifted his gaze to meet Moroda's, and he blinked slowly. 'Sister, this is Morgen, of the Imperial Guard in Niversai, and Eryn and Moroda—Goldstones from the Corhaven capital.' He did not wait for a response, and instead resumed conversation with the woman beside him.

Moroda and Eryn curtseyed to Princess Isa, who

appraised them with a flick of her amber eyes. Though a blood relation to Sapora, they didn't look much alike. Her skin was paler, more white than grey, with a rosy warmth to her cheeks, but they shared high cheekbones. Pearls had been laced through her hair, and she'd opted for silver rings on her fingers, rather than gold.

When she spoke, Moroda noted sharp fangs, not unlike Palom's. 'Thank you for helping my brother. I hope you have been well looked after.'

'Yes! It has been absolutely—' Moroda's response was cut off as the pair of soldiers ushered them away. She was about to protest at the rudeness, when she realised others were waiting behind them to pay their respects to the prince and princess.

They were directed to four empty spaces several seats to Sapora's right, and the three of them sat down together. Wine was poured into their waiting goblets, then they were left alone to enjoy the hubbub of noise and activity.

'Not much of an introduction from the prince!' Morgen huffed as he sniffed at the wine cautiously. 'After all we've been through together!'

'You *did* arrest him, Morgen,' Eryn said with a giggle. 'It's a wonder you weren't thrown in the dungeon here.' She picked up her goblet and inhaled the scent with relish.

'He is playing the part well. Princess Isa seemed more open, at least,' Moroda said.

Guilt ate at her. Kohl was injured, stressing about Aciel and Jato. Palom and Anahrik had left to return to work. And Rhea only knew where Amarah was.

With all the excess around her, when her own city had burned and turned its people homeless, did she have any right to enjoy this?

She didn't know.

Eryn laughed at something Morgen said, and Moroda sighed. Seeing her sister happy and carefree for the first time in as long as she could remember had to count for something.

She leaned back in her chair, enjoying the warmth and comfort, and trying to ignore the guilt that came with it. Ittallan guests and servants bustled between tables, drinking wine and water, and speaking freely.

'You'd think they were all trying to impress him.' Eryn giggled, as the fifth pair of Ittallan approached the royal table to greet Sapora. These ones wore vivid red, feathers pluming from their masks, which resembled birds of some sort.

'Can't think *why* they'd want to be in his good books.' Morgen tutted.

As the music changed, the food was served. It was exquisite, as befitting a royal banquet, and the hall came alive with the piano and strings, drums and singers. Although nothing like the magical essence of the Berel music, it was pleasant to the ears and went well with the food.

'Ro, this is amazing,' Eryn said, resting her silver fork on the side of her dish. They had eaten well in their youth, but the richness of the meats, variety of vegetables, and depth of flavour in the sauces was beyond anything either of them had tasted.

Moroda and Eryn both cleared their plates, though Morgen picked at his food, claiming an upset stomach and frowning at a cream sauce filled with garlic and herbs.

'Morgen, it's okay to say if you don't like it,' Eryn said, leaning towards him.

'Huh?'

'Really. You're not here to prove anything to anyone.'

Morgen reached forward for a slice of bread with a thick crust and chewed on it.

'Sorry, I bet you're used to all this fancy stuff. I never had anything like this growing up.'

'Where did you grow up?' Moroda asked, curious.

'Oh, a tiny village in north Corhaven. I don't know if you'd have heard of it.' He spoke between mouthfuls.

'Try us,' Eryn said, offering him an encouraging smile.

'A place called Kebbe. Mostly farms. All my brothers were farmers.' Morgen's voice dropped.

'Sisters too?' Eryn asked.

Morgen shook his head. 'No, I think my ma would've loved one though. I'm the seventh son.'

'Seven!'

He laughed. 'Well, two of the middle ones died young. It's not an easy life. That's the main reason I left for the capital. Better myself, you know?'

'Do you ever visit?' Eryn asked.

Moroda winced. It wasn't as if she wanted to revisit Niversai after what had happened with the dragon. Seeing the city burned from the airship was hard enough. The idea of walking the streets made her shudder.

'I try to, once or twice a year. Not much going on there. Most folk can't read, they just know how to survive. How to grow food. Look after themselves.'

'What about school?' Eryn accepted a fresh goblet of wine and took a deep sip.

'Parents are your school! Or older siblings, or cousins, if you don't have them.'

'No school? Morgen, with the number of books we have, we should visit! Teach them!' Eryn was excited now, her gestures animated.

Moroda wondered how much of it was the wine talking. 'Ryn...'

'What? You *love* learning! And how many books do you have now Topeko's given you so many?'

Morgen's face had lit up. 'I don't know if you'll think much of it. Being a Goldstone and all...But any interest in my village is always appreciated. It's sweet of you to think of the community there. The kids don't have much.'

The second, third, and fourth courses passed by, and it was only at dessert—a soft sponge filled with sweet cream and winter berries—that Morgen's enthusiasm returned, wolfing down his own plate and finishing Eryn and Moroda's too.

Moroda allowed her sister her dream. Moroda was always the one dreaming, so it was nice for Eryn to have some fun for once. And it kept Eryn's attention away from trying to go back to how things had been back in Niversai.

Eryn was resourceful, quick-witted, and confident.

But she wasn't adaptable.

She'd been trying to bury her head. Get them back to how things had been before their father had...

Moroda shook her head.

That life wasn't possible anymore.

Whatever semblance of survival they'd had after the news, it wasn't going to last much longer.

Even if they'd managed to stay ahead of the debtors and carve out whatever life they could, Aciel was here now. The Arillian was changing everything.

She clutched the ereven sphere in her pocket, ring warming her hand as the two powers connected.

Moroda let Eryn and Morgen talk about a potential idea, a potential future, while she kept half an eye on Sapora for most of the night. When she spied the raven entering the ballroom shortly after dessert, she tugged on her sister's sleeve.

'What is—' Eryn cut herself off.

Koraki spoke with Sapora and Isa in a voice too low for Moroda to catch any words, then he shuffled back across the floor to the orchestra on the other side of the ballroom.

Isa stood, her chair scraping on the floor, and walked around the table's front. She stepped out onto the marble floor—so well-cleaned it held an almost mirror-like quality —her dress skimming the ground with each step. A thin length of silk draped from each wrist and connected to the back of her dress, the fabric billowing out behind her.

Conversation quietened around the room as she crossed the expanse of the floor, her shoes making the quietest of taps as she took each step.

When Moroda glanced back to Sapora, her heart skipped a beat. He'd moved, and she hadn't seen it. Turning back to the floor, she spotted him on the far edge, standing perfectly still with his chin raised. Moroda swallowed the last of her wine and placed the empty goblet on the table.

When Isa reached her position, Sapora stepped into the open space, paused, then took another few steps. He was silent as he slowly and pointedly made his way across, every eye in the hall watching as he moved.

Moroda shivered, some of her fear returning. Though this was an evening of entertainment, she couldn't help but notice Sapora looked like he was stalking his prey as he approached Isa.

The princess raised a gloved hand as he drew close, watching him with an unblinking, almost determined stare. She ignored the many Ittallan looking up at her from the surrounding tables, her attention only on him.

Sapora placed one hand on the small of her back and the other in her left hand, and they held their position for a long moment.

The pianist began to play, and the two began to dance.

Moroda watched, fascinated, as they hardly touched one

another, Isa's skirts wheeling with her motion as though she had a pair of wings. The strings joined the piano, and Sapora and Isa waltzed across the marble floor in exaggerated movements, slightly facing away from one another. Their steps were quick and light, almost completely silent.

Practised and precise.

Two hunters dancing *around* one another rather than *with* one another.

To her left and right, Ittallan rose from their tables and stepped onto the ballroom floor, joining the dance. Silks and tails spun as the dancers moved, jewels sparkled as the light of the chandeliers dimmed and the music rose.

'Shall we dance, too?' Eryn asked.

'Dance?' Morgen spluttered. 'I...I don't know...'

'Why not? We're dressed for it. We're invited guests. Sitting at the royal table, I might add.'

Tables emptied around them as half the hall joined the waltz. People changed partners as the music shifted, men danced with men and women with women, and the music rose in pitch.

Moroda longed to join them.

It had been years since she had last danced, and she very much doubted the opportunity would come up again. It was another taste of her old life, another reminder of how things were, how they could have been, if it weren't for Aciel.

'Ro?'

Moroda pursed her lips.

Eryn wanted to.

She had denied what Eryn wanted for the entire trip, so far. Now they were here, why not make the most of it and dance?

It certainly wasn't as reckless as sneaking aboard Jato's airship.

'Ryn.' Moroda stood up and held out a hand for her sister.

The two joined the other Ittallan, fitting into step smoothly.

Moroda watched as Eryn's smile broadened, then her sister giggled, the wine allowing them both to relax.

They twirled with the music, and partners changed.

Her new partner was an Ittallan man, taller than she by almost two feet, but his steps were incredibly light. He carried her with an easy strength, and Moroda felt she was hardly dancing at all.

Out of the corner of her eye, she saw Eryn partnered with a woman in purple, feathers billowing from her dress and shoes. Eryn continued to smile.

Moroda was hardly aware of the change in music and partners again, and again, and again. Eryn laughed and smiled whenever she caught glimpses of her, and she found herself smiling, too. She was hardly aware of the time, either —had she been dancing for two minutes or twenty?

She watched as Morgen finally stepped in, grinning as he timed his joining to partner with Eryn. His face was red in the heat of the room—or in embarrassment, perhaps—as he held Eryn's arm and back stiffly, trying to keep up with the music while she whirled around him, a flash of emerald green.

Partners changed again, and she found herself with Princess Isa.

Her breath caught as she realised who held her arms. They span and stepped together, then away, and Moroda was very aware of how heavy her steps were in comparison to the princess's.

Isa leaned forward as they span, almost kissing her ear. 'I'd leave now if I were you, little Ro.'

Moroda's eyes widened.

Despite the glass of wine, she knew her senses had not dulled enough to have misheard Isa's warning.

Partners changed again, and she found herself back with Eryn. 'The princess says we should leave.'

'What? Why?' Eryn leaned in, then twirled away from her as the strings grew louder. 'It's not finished yet!'

'I don't know.' Moroda's pulse increased, and she suddenly became aware of the sweat at her temples. 'Something's going to happen. Something bad.'

She stared around the ballroom, and saw Sapora and Isa were again dancing together, turning faster and faster as they moved towards the centre of the floor.

She looked for Morgen, but in the crowd of colours and fabrics, shining light and burning gold, she couldn't see him. The music continued to rise, and she froze, holding Eryn close. 'Ryn...'

Her heart thudded.

As the song reached a crescendo, light engulfed Sapora and Isa as they both transformed.

Moroda's jaw dropped as she saw the Varkain transform for the first time, and a ripple of similar shock and fear cascaded through the guests gathered in the hall as the music and dancers halted.

A grey cobra, more than thirty feet in length with fangs as long as a sword, sat coiled on the floor, hood fanned out and green eyes gleaming. Flicking out his black forked tongue, Sapora raised himself from his coil to look about the room, his pupils slitted in the bright light.

Isa, a huge cat with bristling red-gold fur, joined Sapora's hiss with her own, and bared her teeth, tail lashing.

Moroda spotted the raven hurrying away, cowering low on the far side of the musicians' stage.

She held Eryn's hand tightly, but her voice had left her.

Murmurs echoed from the seated guests.

'None can call him anything other than a true Varkain.'

'For a half-breed, he's certainly formidable.'

'What's this damned Varkain doing back in our court? Why not rule those filthy tunnels and leave Val Sharis to the Ittallan? Showing up here unannounced and trying to throw his weight around.'

Moroda gulped as she recognised the voice. Elafion. She knew the irritable man did not think highly of Sapora, but the wine had clearly loosened his tongue. In the silent hall, his voice sounded like a bell.

Sapora turned his head, gaze locked onto Elafion, and flicked out his tongue.

Moroda took a step back, pulling Eryn with her. 'Ryn...'

In the next moment, Sapora struck, his fangs so large they pierced through the Ittallan's chest.

Blood cascaded as if it were a fountain.

The crowd screamed and scattered.

'Ro...' Eryn whimpered.

'Don't look, don't look!' Moroda pulled Eryn closer, trying to protect her sister from the savagery.

'We need to get out of here!' Eryn's voice shook as she backed away from the glistening ballroom floor. 'Morgen? Where...where is he?'

'Let's move!' Moroda picked a direction she hoped was towards the door—with so many bodies and colourful dresses, it was hard to keep track of her location.

'Ryn! Ro!' Morgen called from the far side of the hall, his wave catching Moroda's attention.

She darted forward, pulling Eryn along as they tried to navigate through and around the frightened Ittallan. In her peripheral vision, she saw the enormous snake strike again. Then a third time. Every attack aimed at a different target.

By the time the three of them reached the doors, she'd counted seven strikes.

The two members of the Imperial Guard standing outside didn't move at the cacophony of noise from within the ballroom. Didn't even glance in.

They'd *known* it was going to happen.

Moroda fought back tears as she looked up at them and their stoic expressions. The guards were complicit, and the horror of what had happened hit her at that moment.

She remembered every warning she'd heard as a child, every whispered story of Varkain violence.

It didn't sit right with her. For all his threats and intimidation, for all his skill in battle, Sapora hadn't harmed her.

Still hadn't harmed her.

And yet he'd slaughtered people while they feasted and drank.

Everything had been *planned*.

Her fingers trembled and her ring grew hot as her emotions rose and flared.

'We have to get away from here.' Moroda's voice sounded distant, as if her voice came from outside her body.

'Too right. Where's Amarah?' Morgen said, one arm draped around Eryn's shoulders.

Her sister was hiccuping, tears streaming down her cheeks, her breathing coming in short, sharp gasps.

'I don't know.' Moroda couldn't remember the last time she'd seen the sky pirate. 'But we can't stay here. We have to go.'

Morgen led the pair away from the room and towards the foyer as other guests fled the carnage. 'Where? Without the ship—'

'Anywhere! *Anywhere* but here! I need to get out! I can't stand the killing!'

Eryn's voice broke.

Moroda clasped her sister's hands and tried to hold back her own tears.

Morgen winced, then nodded. 'All right, follow me. Let's find Kohl and get out of here.'

24

Moroda comforted Eryn on the palace steps as snow fell around them. Morgen had been trying to get one of the ships in the hangar to take them away from the city. Even tried to pull rank as an officer in the Imperial Guard, but they'd refused. There weren't any chartered flights and no one wanted to fly in the heavy snow.

Amarah wasn't in any of the palace suites, nor was she aboard *Khanna*.

Moroda was reasonably certain she could figure out how to get *Khanna* off the ground, but she didn't want to end up terrified of *two* former friends if she ended up making a mess of things.

The moment they'd stepped out of the palace, her ereven sphere had whirred with power and light—the phoenix feather within spinning furiously. 'Must be a dragon close by. A powerful one.'

'Oh great, that's all we need. Another attack.' Morgen glared upwards.

But other than heavy clouds and constant snowfall, nothing was in the sky.

'Distance is relative. I do not think the city is threatened yet.' Kohl adjusted his hat. 'Are we going to leave or stand here in the snow all night?'

Eryn shivered and pulled her cloak tighter around herself. They'd quickly grabbed their bags—including the crossbow—and met Morgen on the front steps. Moroda had tried to keep her sister calm, while fending off her own panic.

She'd expected doors to be barred, for the Imperial Guard to block their escape.

When she thought about it, she realised they knew Sapora would have already killed those he wanted dead. Anyone else was free to leave. They weren't a threat.

But Eryn desperately wanted to get away. She was the one who planned things, and she was a mess.

Moroda struggled to take on the role of responsible sister, but the ereven sphere was a clear sign of what to do. They needed to get to the mountains to find the dragon.

They couldn't find Amarah, and couldn't spare the time to keep looking, not with Eryn in the state she was in. Palom and Anahrik were in town somewhere, and hiding with them would have been an option, but Eryn wanted to get out of Taban Yul. Put as many leagues between it and themselves as was possible.

With airships off-limits, Morgen had returned with three horses. It was the best that could be done under the circumstances, and Eryn had settled at the sight of them. 'Come on. Let's get out of here,' Morgen said, once they were all seated. 'Moroda, you can lead the way with that sphere.'

Moroda had always enjoyed acting spontaneously. But this had a level of danger to it that she didn't like. She didn't want to abandon Amarah, Palom, and Anahrik. Didn't want to leave without saying goodbye, telling them where they were going.

But Eryn was terrified, and that was more important than her own discomfort.

Her sister's panic spurred her on, so with a heavy heart, Moroda led the four away from Taban Yul.

THE AIR WAS crisp and snow silently fell as Moroda, Eryn, and Morgen hurried through the wilds of Val Sharis on horseback. Kohl flew just above the ground, trying to keep his movements small so he didn't scare their horses.

Moroda's discomfort grew as they hastened away. Aches and bruises reawakened on her body as the horse trudged through the snow. But she didn't blame Eryn for her terror at Sapora's sudden savagery. Seeing so much violence, so much death, made her sick.

She thought back to Princess Isa's words. The nickname she called her by seemed taunting, but the warning had been real enough.

Had Isa wanted to spare them from Sapora's wrath?

If Sapora had chosen to attack them, they wouldn't have stood a chance. Or was Isa trying to protect them from the gruesome sight, perhaps?

Moroda couldn't be sure.

Kohl kept ahead, staying on the wing. The Arillian's emotions seemed mixed, and he was quieter than he had ever been, but Moroda's priority was Eryn's safety and security. She could deal with whatever mood he was in later.

All

Eryn wanted was to get as far away from the palace as possible. Evening gowns were not the most practical of clothes to wear in the snow on the back of a horse in the middle of the night, but they'd had no time to change. They'd only barely had time to grab their bags.

Thankfully the Imperial Guard had offered them some thick blankets to wrap around themselves as they rode—they were still honoured guests of the palace, after all—but Moroda grew increasingly uncomfortable after half an hour of forced pace.

Though Moroda was leading them, following the ereven sphere,

Eryn pushed the horses to canter as often as possible. Moroda had asked her to slow down several times—especially where the path narrowed as they travelled into the forest east of Taban Yul.

It was only when a small brook crossed their path that Eryn finally stopped.

'Ryn,' Moroda called, reining up and sliding off her horse so it could drink. She hurried over to her sister. 'It's okay. We're far enough away, now. You can't even see the city for the trees.'

'Ro...'

Moroda took Eryn's hand, helping her down from her horse and embracing her in a hug, blanket and all. 'It's okay,' she repeated. 'Don't worry. I know you wanted to get away. Sapora isn't here.'

The cold around them intensified with Kohl's presence.

Every step or turn he made sent a breath of cold air in every direction, and Moroda shivered.

They were on a well-used path which followed the natural hollow of the trees. The brook was only three or four paces wide, shallow and fast flowing. She clutched the ereven sphere, bringing it out from her pocket to warm her hands.

The blue gem on her ring flashed as if in reaction to the sphere's proximity.

'You okay, Ryn?' Morgen asked, clambering off his own horse. 'I know it was horrible for you back there. Goes to

338

show you can't trust a Varkain! Don't know what he was thinking. The Imperial Guard kept quiet and didn't do a thing! A *planned* massacre! There should be *consequences*!'

Eryn sniffled and buried her face in her blanket for a moment.

Moroda rubbed Eryn's shoulders, wondering how to lift her sister's spirits. She thought back to the dancing. Eryn had been happy, then.

Happier than she'd been in ages.

Moroda could hardly remember the last time she'd laughed so much. Why had that happiness ended in a blood bath?

She didn't understand Sapora—what he wanted or why he behaved as he did.

Kohl had gone some way to explaining his actions, but his killing sickened her beyond words. Did he have to show his strength over the Ittallan so violently?

Moroda touched the ring on her finger, a habit she had developed, and frowned at how cool it was. She needed to control her emotions, keep a clear head. Panicking wouldn't help her use it.

'I'm so sorry, Ro.' Eryn sniffed, lifting the blanket from her face. Her eyes were red and cheeks puffy.

'Don't be sorry, Ryn! You've done nothing wrong. I wanted to get away, too.'

Eryn let out a groan. 'Dragons above, why am I like this?'

'Like what?'

'So...so...damned emotional!'

Moroda wasn't sure she'd ever heard her sister swear before.

'I wish I could go back. Give Sapora a piece of my mind!'

'Ryn...'

'You don't think I want revenge? To get back at those who

hurt us? To show them that we're not just good, that we're thriving on our own?'

Moroda looked at the ground, unsure what to say at Eryn's outburst.

Eryn sniffed again and bundled her hands up in the blanket around her. She wiped her nose and shuddered. 'Where...are we going?'

Moroda sighed. Eryn had been in such a state, she hadn't paid any attention to what they'd been walking. All they'd wanted to do was get away.

'East of Taban Yul,' Kohl said. 'If we remain on this course, we'll be heading for the Feor Mountains. I don't know the lie of the land here.'

'We should keep going, then.' Moroda held up the ereven sphere for everyone to see, the phoenix feather within vivid red and bright in the darkness. It flickered and twisted as though alive, and when Moroda moved the sphere, the feather continued to point towards the mountains looming ahead.

Morgen grimaced. 'But it's the middle of the night. It's snowing! Sure you don't want to go back to Taban Yul now you've cooled off?'

Eryn shivered and shook her head.

'We have the ereven sphere. We might as well keep going. We'll find a village on the way and can rest. Then, we'll be close to the Feor Mountains. Best place to start looking for this dragon, anyway,' Moroda said, proud of herself. It made sense. Kept them moving forward, and kept Eryn away from the city. 'The sphere has definitely picked up on a dragon. A powerful one. It's been spinning constantly since we took it from Aciel. Now, it has a focus.'

'Smart girl.' Kohl tipped his hat to her once again. 'I can fly further and faster than any horse can run. I could be in the mountains before morning. You should find shelter and

340

stay there for the time being. I'm sure Palom and Anahrik at least will want to track you down and find out what's going on.'

'Trying to get rid of us that quickly, are you?' Moroda brushed down the mane of the mare she had ridden with her fingers. 'We're in this together, remember? Finding a dragon means as much to the three of us as it does to you. If it takes an extra day, it takes an extra day. Remember what Topeko said?'

Kohl ruffled his wings. 'Time is of the essence, or did you misunderstand that?'

'There's no need to be rude,' Eryn said, some of her strength returning to her voice. 'You wanted to look after us and make sure we were all okay. Now we're here, there's no need to race off and leave us behind.'

Kohl sighed. 'I don't *want* to leave you behind. But I know the true danger of Aciel and his generals. Not to mention the danger of the dragons we seek. It makes more sense if I continue alone. The pace I wish to set would not be fair on any of you. Go back to Taban Yul. Find an inn, if not the palace, and get some rest.'

'You aren't going to change our minds, Kohl. We left for a reason. I have the sphere, too, and these mountains are vast,' Moroda said, getting irritated at being dismissed. 'We may not be able to fly as you can, but we started this together and that's how we should finish it. Eryn doesn't want to go back to the city, and if I'm honest, neither do I. I've spent the whole trip ignoring what she wanted, and look what happened!'

Morgen sighed. 'Amarah said she'd only ever take us as far as here. Palom and Anahrik will carry on their business now they're home. Our party has broken up, so all the more reason for us to stick together, considering the dangers.'

Kohl scratched at his scarred lip and stared at the falling

341

snow for a long moment. He shook his head. 'I suppose you are on horseback. It's not as if you're as slow as on foot. But the snow is getting heavier by the minute.'

'We'll keep going until we can find some shelter to wait out the worst of the snow. Then we'll get some rest.' Morgen took the lead, looking at the path ahead. 'We can use the time to work out how to approach a powerful dragon without getting burnt to a crisp.'

Moroda clambered back up onto her horse, her brow furrowed. She had been so preoccupied with how to find a dragon, she'd not stopped to think *what* to do once they did. An old dragon would be more powerful than the drake that attacked Niversai. How would it be approached, let alone interacted with? Perhaps it could be distracted, or, if it came to it, subdued?

She held the sphere in one hand, struggling with her blanket to keep covered from the snow. Once settled, she checked it again. As before, it pointed towards the mountains. 'Come on.'

'Maybe we should look for something to feed it,' Eryn suggested, slipping into her usual, practical mindset, though her voice was quieter than normal. 'You know, how sometimes you approach an angry dog with a bit of meat? Makes it more likely to trust you?'

Moroda knew her sister hated everything about their situation, but plotting out details was her way of dealing with it.

Or perhaps repressing it.

'That's not a bad idea.' Morgen said, one hand loosely holding onto his horse's reins. 'But I don't think it'll be too impressed if you compare it to a dog!'

'That isn't what I meant.'

'Topeko and his books speak of dragons and their intelligence. A Sevastos, and a dragon of the age we seek, will likely understand our tongue.' Moroda thought back, wishing she had some of those books with her now. 'We'll talk to it, be polite and respectful.'

'I never heard of a dragon that could talk,' Morgen said as his horse crossed the brook.

'Val Sharis seems to be the home of the older dragons. I'm sure Palom said something about that, too.'

'I don't care how old it is. What's to stop it from eating us?'

'Do not concern yourself with that, Morgen,' Kohl said, irritation sharpening his tone. 'The dragons are not your gods for nothing.'

'Your gods? Don't you mean "our" gods?' Eryn asked, turning her head to look back at Kohl.

'No, I don't. Arillians don't hold with such nonsense.'

'Nonsense?' Moroda stopped her horse in its tracks. 'Arillians...?'

'We follow quite a different mythos. Rhea and her dragons *are* stories we speak of, but nothing more.' He ruffled his wings and half leapt, half flew across a stretch of forest floor. With his leg so stiff, he seemed to prefer staying on the wing, and his movement sent a blast of freezing wind all around.

Moroda's teeth chattered as the icy breeze kissed her exposed skin.

'Sorry, Moroda.' Kohl landed a short distance from them. 'Hardly realise I'm doing that, sometimes.'

'But everyone in Linaria...even the *Varkain*—' Morgen began.

'Everyone here seems to be repulsed by the Varkain, but they are just as much a part of Linaria as you, or the Samolen, or the Ittallan. We Arillians don't even live *on* Linaria, we are *above* it. Our islands float, and we are shielded by our powers. And all of the world has exiled us to the farthest reaches that we might never be seen.'

'Kohl...' Moroda bit down on her instinct to apologise.

The Arillian sighed.

'I don't agree with Aciel or his actions, but I do understand them. He is doing what he thinks is right. Why should an entire race be wiped out because of what our forefathers did? The world is against us. So he has decided to take the world back. He and Sapora have that much in common.'

Moroda saw Eryn flinch at Sapora's name, and her lip quivered. Eryn had been so strong.

Always so strong.

Quick-witted and clever, incredibly optimistic.

To see her so anxious tore at Moroda's heart.

Moroda knew she was responsible for the change in her sister. So far, she *had* kept her promise of doing as she asked, but she needed a long-term plan. What were they to do after they found the dragon?

Even if Aciel could be stopped, how could she find peace when Linaria was so ravaged?

She thought about Morgen's suggestion of going to his village. Setting up a school.

Was that a real possibility for them?

'What did you mean when you said your islands float?' Eryn asked, breaking Moroda's thoughts.

Kohl sighed. 'Arillians live on scattered islands far to the north. Those of us who are left, that is. The islands are suspended, held aloft by our storms.'

'Goodness. I would love to see that one day.'

'Ryn...' Moroda said.

'Perhaps, if peace ever comes to Linaria, you will. As it stands, no one visits our homeland. The same way non-Varkain do not enter Sereth.'

Moroda heard the sadness in his voice. She could sense

344

frustration, too, but he did not become angry. Thank Rhea for that. She didn't think she could cope with being close to more wrath again.

She tightened the blanket around her as the trees surrounding their path fell away a few leagues short of the base of the mountains. In the cold, crisp night, perfectly untouched snowy fields lay before them. Light from the three moons reflected on the white ground, tiny particles sparkling. Perfectly silent.

'So beautiful,' Moroda said, taking in the view. 'Look Eryn, we'd never see anything like this if we had stayed back in Niversai.' She tried to think of more positives to counter what they'd experienced.

Eryn nodded. 'I know. It...it hasn't been easy, Ro. But I *am* glad I came.'

Moroda smiled. Her sister wasn't herself yet, but doing her best to show confidence. It would probably take a few days before she would be able to speak about Sapora without shaking. Perhaps longer.

Another cloud rolled overhead, blocking light from one of the moons, and bringing another wave of thick snowfall.

'The sooner we find our dragon, the sooner we can bring an end to Aciel's terror,' Morgen said, taking point as he spurred his horse to the front of the group. 'There's got to be a village nearby where we can sleep for the night, before the snow gets too bad. We'll leave first thing tomorrow.'

Eryn followed him onwards, and Moroda took in the view for another moment before nudging her horse forward with a sigh.

Kohl, horseless, drifted above the group, crossing the snowy fields with gentle flaps of his enormous, feathered wings.

'Do you want to fly ahead, Kohl? See if you can find anywhere we might rest?' Morgen asked.

A bolt of lightning ripped through the black night and crashed into the centre of the field, shattering the quiet. Morgen's horse reared in fright, and he was thrown off, landing with a soft thud in the freshly fallen snow.

Moroda and Eryn's horses were also spooked, but were further back and had not reared. Moroda fought to hold onto hers, which whinnied and tried to run.

'Morgen!' Eryn called, clambering off her horse and running over to where he lay. 'Are you all right?' She crouched and pulled him to his knees.

'Y—yeah. Just dazed. Snow cushioned the fall, I think.' He sat up, one hand on his head. 'What happened?'

Kohl landed in front of them, his eyes locked on the Arillian hovering in the night sky.

'Well, well, well, what do we have here?' Jato sneered, her dark wings almost invisible in the night. 'What a find, what a *find*!' She descended to the snowy field and landed softly; several other Arillians landed at her side, all in full battle armour, gleaming in the moonlight.

Kohl stepped back and helped Morgen get to his feet, his feathers bristling.

'Oh no!' Moroda ran to Eryn and grabbed her arm, ready to pull her away.

Jato's armour was lined with gold, delicately etched in winding patterns across the silver-grey surface. Like the other Arillians, she carried no weapon, and she folded her arms as she took in the sight before her.

'Killing you three will be an *excellent* way to start the night,' Jato said, her eyes glinting. 'I'm sure Aciel would be pleased.'

Panic surged through Moroda. She hadn't yet recovered from their last encounter. Her joints were stiff, her skin bruised and burned.

'General, why kill them? They've done nothing to you.' Kohl stepped forward to confront her.

'Orders are orders, Kohl. Or have you been away so long you've forgotten how things work?'

Moroda gulped, holding onto her sister and pulling her back. Her horse stood nearby, whickering and pawing at the snow nervously. 'Eryn...we should run...' She tried not to move her lips. She was grateful Jato's attention was on Kohl.

'We'd never outrun them,' Morgen whispered back. 'A whole scouting party...we'd never make it back to Taban Yul before they caught us.'

Moroda's breathing quickened.

Morgen's hand went to the hilt of his sword. 'But they won't be expecting us to stand and fight.'

'Fight?' Moroda whispered through gritted teeth, incredulous.

'Of course I haven't forgotten,' Kohl said, looking at the other Arillians, six in all.

Jato grinned. 'Good. Your first order is to eliminate those three.'

Kohl froze.

'Where is that woman with the scythe? She near sliced Aciel's arm off! She'll pay for that. You'll soon learn that Aciel is not to be crossed. We're to kill anyone we come up against. Those three should be easy for you, shouldn't they, great dragon slayer?'

'Jato...Aciel is mistaken. You cannot—'

'Don't question your superiors! Or shall I add *you* to my list of people to eliminate?' Jato snapped, electricity crackling down her arms in her fury. 'My loyalty is to Aciel, as it *always* has been. Kill them now, or I will—and *you* after.'

'You wouldn't...don't...don't do this. Please.'

'Kohl?' Moroda took another step back, dragging Eryn with her. Her heart thundered and her ring burned. She

347

watched as Kohl turned to face her, his hands shaking as he raised them. Moroda caught his eye, and looked away.

He spread his wings and slowly drifted into the air. 'I am...sorry...' His voice wavered. Kohl called upon his own powers and unleashed a wave of frost in all directions. The few surrounding trees collapsed under the sudden freeze, and sent up thick, dusty white smoke as they crashed into the snow.

Moroda screamed, pulling Eryn down into the snow with her to brace against his attack.

She couldn't believe he'd hurt them! Was he so afraid of Jato? Of Aciel?

But there was no pain.

Both hands firmly holding onto her sister, Moroda cautiously opened her eyes. The icy dust was settling, but Kohl had vanished.

Jato and the other Arillians soared higher as the freezing air surrounded them. 'Traitor!' She turned to one of her colleagues. 'Follow him. Bring him back to me alive. He'll pay for that. I don't care *who* he is!'

'Yes, Jato.' He took off in a flurry of wind and feathers, charging after Kohl.

'As for those three...' Jato glared down at them. 'I need to report to Aciel. Finish them off, quickly. We'll regroup after. There are dragons here we can take before we strike.' She flew higher as soon as her order was given, heading off in the opposite direction to Kohl, back towards Taban Yul.

Moroda tried to control her panicked breathing. Morgen was right. There was no escaping this confrontation.

They were left with five Arillians, all of whom had been ordered to kill them.

There was no time to think or plan, no time to size up the situation.

She gripped Eryn's hand as Morgen rushed forward, sword drawn, and swung it at the closest Arillian.

He avoided Morgen's strike by leaping out of range, and replied with a short bolt of electricity. It connected with Morgen's wrist and sent his sword careening from his grasp.

Morgen dived for his weapon and grabbed it as two of the other Arillians swooped low, their attention on the sisters. The remaining horses had fled—they didn't have much bottle in them at the best of time, and their frightened whinnies carried well through the cold night air.

Moroda clenched her hands into fists, and felt the ring on her finger.

To be used when a fight couldn't be avoided.

She fumbled with the crossbow and gave it to Eryn, then stepped in front of her sister and raised her hand. Breathing deeply, funnelling her fear, Moroda summoned all the strength she could muster to form a shield in front of her and her sister. She had nothing to draw energy from except her own body, her own heightened emotions, and she was already tired from the events of the night and the ride outside the city.

But the shield worked, repelling the Arillian's vicious wind and electrical attacks, which singed away the snow to leave the scorched earth barren and blackened underneath.

Eryn unleashed bolts, the twang of the crossbow snapping through the air as one by one, she fired at their aggressors. Most were too wide off their marks, and the others that came closer were avoided by the Arillian's agility in the air.

Two hit true—one taking an Arillian in the thigh, the other shooting clean through a wing—but again and again they came, flying at the sisters. They shot balls and bolts of lightning, their wind attacks blasting Moroda and Eryn where they stood, but the shield held through pure desperation.

Morgen slashed at the enemy as best he could, but the Arillian's flight advantage stopped most of his attacks from connecting, and he was battered by their energy as thunder rolled around them, churning up the snow and foliage.

Sweat ran down Moroda's forehead, her arm straining to keep her shield of energy up. 'They'll leave, won't they? They'll...they'll realise they can't...do this...'

'No more bolts, Ro!' Eryn hurled the crossbow at an oncoming attacker, who easily avoided the metal, only to bounce off their shield of energy.

'It's okay. You did so well, Ryn!' Moroda replied, sinking down to one knee. Her sister was trying, but it wasn't enough. She winced, trying to think. 'Eryn, hold onto my arm! Maybe you can strengthen *me*?'

'Ro...' Eryn clasped Moroda's arm with her own, feeding Moroda's shield with her own energy. The blue-white field of light crackled and burst as Eryn added to it, repelling another wave of lightning.

'Kohl will...he'll see what's happening...he'll...he'll come back!' Moroda dared not look for him. She couldn't afford to lose focus, lose concentration. Her blue gemstone flared white and her hand burned with the effort of holding the shield. Her body was numbing slowly. She wouldn't be able to hold it much longer.

Morgen raced towards them, part of his cloak burning. 'Eryn! Moroda!'

'Keep pushing, Ryn! We can...hold them off!' Moroda had practised the magic taught to her by Topeko and his books, but the strength of the Arillian's attacks and her fear threatened to overwhelm her.

Three Arillians spiralled down from above, knocked back by Morgen when they came too close, but he was outnumbered, and lacked their speed.

Moroda tried to strengthen the shield, lifting her other hand to move more energy to it.

Eryn trembled beside her, and Moroda leaned into her sister, the contact always a source of comfort.

Moroda felt the breath of the Arillian's wind attacks and the sting of their electricity rippling through the shield. Knew what would happen if it dropped.

But she had nothing left. Her body was exhausted.

Their shield flickered.

Disappeared.

Then, snow crashed around her, filling the air with a white, whirling storm.

The Arillians showed no mercy, attacking without hesitation. The snow underfoot was swept away by the fury of their assault; bare trees ripped up by their roots and cast about as vicious winds whipped around in a hurricane.

Thunder roared through the air and the ground trembled. Moroda was knocked off her feet more than once by flailing branches, and it did not take long before blood and bruises littered her skin.

She had barely enough time to take in what was approaching her, much less keep on her feet or mount any sort of defence. She realised with a start that she was alone. Somewhere in that furious storm, she and her sister had become separated.

'Eryn?' Moroda cried, white snow and blue electricity filling her vision.

She had no idea where anyone else was—Eryn, Morgen, or the Arillians—they were grey shadows lost in the swirling winds, flickering in and out of focus.

Every so often, a jolt of intense heat tore through her as she was struck by an electrical blast. Whether they were direct hits or offshoots, she did not know, but the pain was cripplingly intense, and left her more stunned than when she was struck by one of the trees.

It was like being trapped with Jato all over again, but a hundred times worse now that Eryn suffered, too. Suffered, and she couldn't see her! Couldn't be with her!

Tears streamed from her eyes as her breath hitched.

Doubled over, Moroda sank to her knees, exhaustion taking hold. The biting cold from the snow left her legs and hands numb, and the pain in her head and stomach from multiple attacks drowned out everything else.

She tried, feebly, to produce another shield of magic, but the gem on her ring was as cold as she was. Nothing she attempted worked.

Something groaned to her left as another tree was uprooted, the pine needles scattered in the raging wind and digging into her skin.

The wind was deafening, and she covered her ears, trying to keep low to the ground, hoping simply to survive the onslaught.

A sudden splash of orange appeared among the swirling greys and whites.

She wasn't alone.

Forcing herself to move, Moroda stumbled back, her skirts snagging on an uprooted tree root. She wrenched the cloth free, sending tiny jewels flying, and fell onto her side.

When she looked up, she realised the roar was *not* from the whirling wind, but from the fangs of an enormous tiger that had joined the fray.

'Moroda! Run!' Morgen screamed, clutching his bloody arm as he limped over to her. Despite the cold, his hair was stuck to his forehead, sweat dripping down his cheeks.

'Morgen!' Moroda called, getting back to her feet, her eyes wide as she saw the extent of his injuries. 'You're hurt!'

'Get away! Get back to the city! Anywhere but here!

Don't worry about me!' He spun around to dive out of the way of another bolt of lightning, the heat stinging Moroda's cheeks as it passed. Feathers brushed her face from the Arillian's wings, and she saw Morgen's sword cut into them.

Blood spurted, staining the white snow with splashes of red, and Moroda backed away, unable to stop the flow of tears now. 'Eryn!' She wasn't leaving without her sister.

The Arillian landed and whirled around with a snarl, his eyes black with rage. He raised his hands and electricity flickered in his palms.

Moroda screamed.

Anahrik raced past in a blur, leapt to Morgen's defence, and blocked the Arillian's electricity with a short sword—it was hardly longer than a dagger. Moroda watched in amazement as the blade glowed bright blue, reflecting light from the snow around them.

Anahrik took in a breath before *pushing* the Arillian back, his blade glowing brighter than anything she'd seen before. The Arillian intensified his attacks, slivers of electricity bouncing off Anahrik's blade, but nothing connected with the Ittallan.

Anahrik forced himself closer, deflecting the electricity, taking slow, determined steps until he was close enough to attack—in one quick movement, he drew a second blade from the holder on his thigh and sliced clean *through* the Arillian's hands.

The Arillian's shriek was deafening. Blood gushed from his wrists, staining the ground a deep crimson. He staggered away, but Anahrik did not relent—forcing him further and further back as he slashed with the two blades. The Arillian could not call upon his magic and could not defend against Anahrik's flurry of attacks.

Moroda had never seen a glowing weapon like it.

Its destructive force *terrified* her.

She ran as Anahrik ended the scuffle, and rushed over to where Morgen tried to catch his breath.

'Ro? I told you to run!' Morgen clutched his left arm.

'I won't leave anyone!' Moroda said, shaking her head. 'Where's Eryn? Thank the dragons Palom and Anahrik came when they did!' She could hardly believe she hadn't realised the burst of orange was Palom's tiger form.

Morgen shook his head. 'Can't see her. Can't see nothing in this chaos. Damn that Kohl! *Bastard*!'

The wind buffeted them, picking up snow and debris, and flinging it around as the field turned into a blizzard. The white masked visibility, and Moroda couldn't see anything aside from occasional bursts of orange, or if an Arillian flew close to her.

She needed to find her sister and get back to the city. Get to shelter. Anywhere but here.

How could the Arillians have been so close to Taban Yul?

'Incoming!' Anahrik yelled, racing up to where the pair huddled, his attention on the sky as another two Arillians dive bombed them.

Before Moroda or Morgen could react to his warning, the sheer force of the Arillian's wind attacks slammed into them.

Squeezing her eyes shut against the violent storm, Moroda *felt* a crack of thunder as Anahrik leapt into the air to meet the tag-team attack and defend against it.

Though his left arm was weak, Morgen clutched his sword. Blood dripped down his fingers. 'Please run, Moroda. You don't want to see this!' He rushed into the midst of battle.

The tiger's roar drowned out all else, and Moroda could see the thick of the fighting was now in one location—on the ground, thankfully. If Palom, Anahrik, and Morgen kept them out of the sky, the Arillians would lose their advantage.

She wanted to run away; with every fibre of her being, she wanted to cry, to get away, to hide and never face any fighting again.

But she couldn't leave without Eryn.

Seconds passed, or minutes. She couldn't tell.

More trees collapsed, littering the once pristine snow fields with splinters of wood. Time stopped while the world spun around her. The pain from her wounds slowly made themselves known; an itch, at first, then a dull throb, then hot, searing ache as she realised her dress had been shredded around her torso.

Blood trickled down her arms and face.

Hers? Eryn's? Morgen's?

Her head throbbed. The snow and sky were too bright to discern shapes.

Where was Eryn?

Everything was too much.

She was exhausted, her limbs numbing save intense bursts of pain snaking along her body. Snow rushed up to meet her, the cold somehow burning her skin.

Grey and white shapes filled her vision, though she couldn't discern what—or who—they were.

Another ball of electricity slammed into her, fiery light crackling over every nerve.

She screamed, but heard no sound.

Her sight went black.

25

_____

Sereth was much as Sapora recalled. Smooth walled tunnels so deep underground that nothing from above could be heard. So far removed from the noise and bustle of cities above ground, Sereth seemed peaceful by comparison, even in the most densely populated areas.

Thankfully the Varkain working in its capital, Timin Rah, had not grown quite as lax here as the Ittallan had towards Isa in Taban Yul.

Still having an iron-fisted ruler in residence probably had something to do with it.

Timin Rah was a city in the loosest sense of the term; a cluster of caves and tunnels deep below the surface of Linaria, unmarked on the land and hidden from the world above. Much of it had been built around a natural underground lake, and had expanded over generations as more Varkain flocked to the area.

It kept the temperature on the cooler side of pleasant, though they never had to deal with snowstorms even in the depths of winter.

Some areas of Timin Rah were more elevated—close enough that natural light filtered down through gaps in the tunnel ceilings—though they were rare. Most Varkain followed the natural curves of caves and tunnels, and simply expanded where they made sense. It turned much of Sereth into a labyrinth, often with tunnels leading to dead ends, enormous stalactites narrowing the passageways.

Sapora had not been born in the bowels of Linaria like his Varkain brethren. He'd been born in the luxury of the palace in Taban Yul, surrounded by Ittallan, like his mother. The two races did not always see eye to eye, and mixed bloods were not unheard of, but it had always been seen as a weakness in him.

Centuries of war tended to have that effect.

His actions in Taban Yul wouldn't help relations between Sereth and Val Sharis.

But it needed to be done.

The Ittallan had grown so carefree that they'd openly disrespected his sister. *Himself.*

They'd spoken against the Varkain, and he wouldn't stand for it.

Better to cull the dissenters now, before they grew too vocal.

Bloodshed wasn't something he particularly tried to avoid, if anything he relished the fear blossoming in the room at his actions. As far as he was concerned, they deserved everything they got.

But above all, he adored proving his doubters wrong. Whatever happened, the Ittallan would not soon forget he had fangs. Crossing him was not in anyone's best interests.

If that's what was necessary to maintain order, maintain *authority*, then that's what he would do.

Isa had two small class five airships—personal crafts that she used to visit different areas of Val Sharis from time to time. He'd borrowed one, along with one of the royal pilots, to fly the short distance to the Feor Mountains. Just as they'd landed, he'd felt the air ripple with electricity, and he recognised Jato's power in that moment.

So, he'd hastened into the underground labyrinth of Sereth, and travelled to Timin Rah, the capital, as quickly as he could.

He didn't have much time if he was to fight for his crown —the Varkain liked their traditions. If he missed his opportunity, it was tough luck. Tacio would be the next one to try.

Sapora strode through the tunnels, forcing several Varkain to shuffle out of his way. A few stalked several paces behind him, their curiosity driving their behaviour. Many openly wore their weapons. He was relatively sure they would not harm him, not *immediately*, but he would have to prove his worth before too long.

Varkain did not fear him as the Ittallan did.

Every interaction was a delicate negotiation of dominance, and simply being the king's son did not guarantee respect.

It was why every shred of courtesy had to be fought for. And why Sapora often reverted to fear as the most common tactic to get his way.

Day and night merged into one in the depths of Sereth. While many of the main tunnels were wide and well ventilated, it did not detract from the loss of time or claustrophobia that set in after several hours.

Most of Sereth was underground, a labyrinth of tunnels stretching many leagues into the depths of Linaria. They clustered together near places of interest—a forest, a river, or near natural ore that could be used in making tools and weapons. Torches were fixed to brackets in the wider tunnel walls, but many remained in murky darkness. However, they were all fastidiously clean.

The cities of Sereth themselves were simply extensions of the maze of intertwining tunnels connecting one town to the next. Shielded from the worst of war and weather, the Varkain thrived underground—though it took some getting used to.

Sapora had never felt completely at home in the tunnels of Timin Rah, but he tolerated them well enough. Though his preference was to live above ground, there was always guilt for being away from his people for too long.

Timin Rah was the largest settlement in Sereth, and had adopted the moniker of capital city. Although there were no *buildings* as such, gateways and passageways had been built into the rock walls to distinguish permitted areas and separate districts from one another. There were also plenty of sections at different elevations. Various caves and dens had been dug into the rock, distinguishing residences, places of work, trade, and play, and all manner of other regions.

As Sapora clambered up a particularly steep incline, he remembered struggling underground when he'd first come here as a boy.

It had taken him almost a full year before he had learned his way around. Being confident enough to wander through the tunnels unescorted was something he'd wanted to learn as quickly as possible, though it meant getting lost for hours, sometimes days, at a time.

Sapora shook the memories away as he reached the crest of the slope and halted, looking at the expansive district before him. For the first time since his errantry, he was among people who looked like him.

Perhaps two dozen Varkain milled around, some carrying cloth bags full of food or weapons, Cerastes— guards—standing watch by the edge of the caves. One spotted Sapora as he appeared, and immediately headed for him, the metal on her shoulders gleaming in the torchlight.

'My liege,' the Cerastes dropped to one knee in front of Sapora. 'We have long awaited your return.'

Most of the Cerastes armour was ceremonial, denoting status and experience at a glance. If they needed to fight, they would transform.

This Cerastes was marked by a single yellow tassel attached to her spear. It signified one year of experience. In many of the darker tunnels, colour wasn't always distinguishable. More tassels meant more experience.

In this case, the amount of experience was irrelevant. Sapora appreciated her deference and gestured for her to rise. 'Take me to Vasil. I have urgent matters to discuss.'

'Of course,' the Cerastes replied, standing tall. 'Clear a path at once, prepare food and drink. Prince Sapora returns immediately.'

Sapora followed the Cerastes along the winding tunnel, pleased with the quickened pace.

He hadn't sent advance word of his return, nor had he before arriving in Taban Yul.

It had been so long since he had been among his own kind, and he studied the Cerastes carefully. They were second only to the Naja in strength, and served as the guards for not only the ruling family, but all Varkain. They rarely left Sereth, and ensured no enemy ever reached the people of his country.

He glanced at the spear the Cerastes carried and smirked. They were all armed, but a bite from any Cerastes would lead to death faster than his own venom.

Here, his kind were accepted. It was their home.

On the surface, they were looked upon with disdain, disgust, and even fear. Sapora had come to relish that fear— the terror he held over most people of Linaria. What other way was he to react to being excluded and shunned?

Of having to fight for his place among his people?

Unfortunately, like many on the Ittallan Council, there were many Varkain who thought his mixed blood would weaken his senses or physical prowess, and his errantry had been set to prove himself to all doubters.

Once he reached twenty-one, he would be eligible to take the crown from his father.

If he passed the trials.

With the day of his birth imminent now the winter snows had begun, this was his one and only chance to take real power. Then he could make the changes he wanted in Linaria.

The Varkain would no longer be shunned.

They would be lifted into glory.

Sapora had been disgusted at his errantry, at first. He was the blood of the Varkain and could transform into a cobra—a true Naja. Why should he have to prove himself further?

However, as he'd traversed Linaria, he'd realised there was power to be learned from others, and the journey *had* strengthened him.

Yes, it was a great pressure, and many believed he would be an unfit ruler if he returned early or even thought he'd be killed on his travels, but his eyes and mind had been opened. Having experienced Aciel's wrath, he knew he had to act to ensure the survival of the Varkain.

'How is Vasil?' Sapora asked as they pushed deeper into the city.

'Your father is well. With things as they were, they were considering having Tacio crowned!'

Sapora snorted in response. 'I'd have killed him the moment I returned, had he done so.'

'Well, you are your father's son.'

Sapora didn't respond to that—he wasn't sure whether it was a compliment or an insult—and remained quiet until they reached his father's keep.

Vasil's home was located atop of a large cliff that jutted

out from the side of the cavern, resting above a deep lake. The water was motionless and cloudy, suitable for bathing and not much else, but it was the most spacious part of Timin Rah, and Vasil had claimed it as his residence many years ago.

To the side of the cliff, several paces from the water's edge, the ground fell away sharply, careening into a wide pit. Sapora didn't need to look at the pit to know what was at the bottom. The scent of blood and sweat distinguished it from any other part of Timin Rah.

It confirmed what he had to face.

The Varkain had long ago done away with formalities. Your standing was based on merit, which meant strength more than anything else. It had always been more important than blood or birthright.

Anyone could approach their king for an audience. There were none of the regulations and restrictions here as in Val Sharis or Corhaven. Vasil held power, but he was an equal like any other Varkain.

The Cerastes left Sapora near the edge of the pit while she informed Vasil of his son's arrival.

Sapora shifted his weight and folded his arms, trying to dispel any nervous energy. He had no idea if his father would be pleased to see him, though the Varkain loitering nearby were palpably excited. A crowd grew slowly, individuals slinking into view without preamble. His senses tingled as he became the centre of attention of dozens of eyes.

He had been trailed since he first arrived, and now he was in full view before their king's residence, it wouldn't be long before the entire underground country would be aware of his return.

Seconds ticked by, drawing into minutes.

Sapora slowed his breathing, settling in to wait as long as Vasil would make him. He had waited so long already, what was a few more hours? At least it would give a larger crowd time to grow.

Might as well give them all a show.

Yes. The more witnesses the better.

'Sapora, Sapora, Sapora. Where, oh where, have you been?'

Sapora's gaze snapped up at the drawling voice, and he narrowed his eyes at the speaker.

'Come to take the Jade Crown, have you? It was *so close* to being mine!' A tall Varkain sauntered down the sloped cliff, hands casually in his pockets. He wore a black, perfectly tailored overcoat embellished with silver buttons, as well as an assortment of silver necklaces draped long and loose around his neck, which clinked together with every step.

Tacio.

Sapora's brother grinned, his golden eyes squinting at the breadth of his smile. His skin was grey, the same as any Varkain, but it was smooth, free of scars and blemishes, his ivory fangs on display every time he spoke or smiled, contrasting his dark auburn hair.

Tacio had the eyes of a true Varkain. Gold. The same as Isa. The same as their father.

Sapora's dark green eyes had always marked his blood as mixed, despite the rest of his physical appearance matching any other Varkain.

Seeing his brother was another bitter reminder of everything he was up against. Every failing he had to overcome. Although Tacio's demeanour was friendly, almost welcoming, Sapora made no move to greet him. His relationship with Tacio had always been...fraught.

When Tacio was within a handful of paces, Sapora lifted his chin. 'My timing was impeccable then. Where is Vasil?'

'Here.'

Sapora and Tacio automatically dropped to their knees

363

at their father's voice. Sapora held his position for several long seconds, before looking up.

The Cerastes who had brought him to the keep now led his father down the slope. Vasil was not old by any means, only in his late forties, but his thinning black hair had receded, giving way to grey. He wore a circlet of gold, adorned with jade stones carved from their deepest mines—the only outward sign of his wealth.

That, at least, Sapora had in common with his father.

A singularly formidable man, Vasil carried himself with the menacing, predatory grace Sapora had always known and feared.

A king. A conqueror. Someone who prized power and confidence.

Behind him, his wife Savra strode along gracefully. She was tall, younger than his father, with the same red hair and exquisite, yet arrogant walk as Tacio. Also like Tacio, she adorned herself in jewellery—silver and rubies to contrast her grey skin—and watched Sapora with a cold, calculating gaze.

'Isn't this a wonderful family reunion?' Tacio smirked, flicking at one tooth with his tongue. 'Snows started here a few days ago. We were only going to give you one more night.'

'You doubted me?' Sapora asked, not surprised in the least. If he hadn't returned on time, he gave up his right to try and win the crown, and Tacio would be able to try his luck.

It was no secret that Tacio preferred dominating wherever he could, and the Jade Crown would allow him to do just that.

Tacio scratched the side of his neck with a clawed finger.

'Heard you were captured in Rosecastle a while back.

Thought you might have been killed when the mad dragon burned Niversai.'

Sapora blinked.

'Is this true? You were captured?' Vasil asked, bearing down on Sapora with his larger frame.

Sapora couldn't hear much concern in those words. 'What of it?'

'Rather foolish, don't you think? They are quick to execute our kind in Corhaven.' Savra sneered at her step-son.

'Insulting, too. You didn't tell them who you were?' Tacio asked, incredulous.

Sapora ignored their taunts. 'It wasn't necessary.'

'We can't get involved while you're on errantry,' Tacio said, something akin to sorrow in his tone. 'We wouldn't have been able to come and help if they'd done anything to you.'

'I don't need your help. Never have.' Sapora narrowed his eyes and took a step back, increasingly aware of the crowd of Varkain that gathered by the waterfront. He couldn't show any sign of weakness. 'What do you know of Aciel?'

'Arillians have been seen patrolling our borders, no doubt looking to pick off those travelling alone,' Vasil replied. Though his voice was outwardly cool, Sapora heard a faint tremor that belied the anger bubbling below the surface.

'I had considered banning travel into Val Sharis until the birds are gone.'

'But no direct attacks on the city?'

'Correct. They are unable to breach Timin Rah.'

Sapora exhaled slowly. 'Good. I have news of what fuels Aciel's power, and how we can respond to his show of strength. The Varkain will take advantage of this and we *will* emerge triumphant. I'll not have us cower in our tunnels like rats cornered.'

'Is that so?' Vasil's voice dropped lower. A warning.

'I have already cleansed the Ittallan Council. There were several who have been speaking ill of you. Of the Varkain. I have corrected that.'

'You act like you are a king already.' Tacio laughed, mirthless. 'The pits have been waiting for you for a season now. You've not forgotten what you must do first?'

Sapora glared at his half-brother. 'It will give me the greatest pleasure to slaughter them to keep *you* from power.'

'Sapora. Mind yourself. Tacio has been in charge of the Cerastes for over a year. He is more than ready to step in should you fail,' Savra said, ever defensive of her son.

'You ought to have more confidence in me by now.' Sapora approached the pit beside the water, his nose wrinkling at the stench of death and blood. 'You were prepared to cast me aside as your ruler for Tacio, and here I am, spoiling all your fun. The least I can do is put on a show for you.'

'Prince Sapora, a moment.' The Cerastes stepped out from Vasil's keep, holding a large stone mug, and hurried down the cliff to where they waited. 'You are to be dry for your trials.'

'Dry?'

'We thought it'd be a better test of all you have learned whilst traipsing across Linaria.' Tacio grinned, one hand grasping Sapora's shoulder. He squeezed.

Sapora took a low breath to calm his rising annoyance, his pride stung again. Losing face was one thing he could never permit. He shoved Tacio off. 'Very well.'

The Cerastes handed him the mug, and Sapora faced Vasil, Savra, and Tacio. None of them offered words of encouragement or support.

He was alone in this uphill struggle.

Like always.

Sapora extended his front four fangs and raised the mug to their tips. Pressing down, he filled it with his venom, hiding a wince at the discomfort. He despised being dry, but he needed to fight by their rules, else his crown would be meaningless, and the Varkain would never accept him.

When finished, he handed the mug back to the waiting Cerastes. 'Not a warm welcome, but I did not expect anything else. Have any other rules changed in my absence?'

Annoyance was about all he could show without losing face.

'We've had a lot of Ittallan sign up, you know.' Tacio wandered to the lip of the pit and peered down. 'You have four ready and waiting. The rest depends on what they have left. It's been busy these last few weeks.'

'All at once, I suppose?'

'Of course not. We aren't savages!' Tacio grinned, his pointed teeth glistening in the torchlight.

'It is your time to show them,' Vasil said.

It was the closest to approval Sapora was going to get, and a sudden wave of nausea built in his stomach. He drew his scimitars—that had once belonged to Vasil—and approached Tacio.

He'd fought Aciel and Jato aboard their ship. He could handle whatever opponents the trials threw at him. 'You'll be bowing to me before the night is over.'

Tacio tilted his head and smiled.

Taking a deep breath, Sapora stepped off the edge of the pit and dropped the twenty or so feet to the bottom.

The ground had recently been churned up; it was sticky and damp with congealed blood. The stench threatened to overwhelm his senses, but he remained focussed on the pit's far wall, where his opponents would appear.

'The first of six rounds. Prince Sapora fights for his right to the Jade Crown.'

Tacio's voice echoed from somewhere above him, and Sapora moved across the floor of the pit to drier, firmer ground.

One final test.

He saw Ittallan creatures waiting for him on the other side.

A gila.

An eagle.

A monitor lizard.

He searched for the fourth, but saw nothing. Had Tacio lied?

Then, something low and deep snarled from the darkness, and Sapora locked in on the noise. Whatever made it waited just out of sight, in the cave on the far side where fighters and thralls waited in between rounds.

Sapora took a step towards the noise, raising one of his scimitars as he approached.

This was just another obstacle to overcome. Then he'd obtain the greatness he desired.

When the huge bear lumbered into view, Sapora tightened his grip on both blades.

One final test to take his crown and demand the respect he *deserved*.

26

P alom stepped out into the street, his sword held in both hands. It steamed gently in the cool night air, snow sizzling when it melted on contact. Half his workshop had been blackened by the violent explosions the Sevastos crystals had caused, but that could be cleaned up another time.

'This is it!' Anahrik bounded out after him, casually juggling his two long daggers. They'd packed away the short sword and the scythe—gifts for Morgen and Amarah. It was all they had managed to make with the sliver of crystal.

Palom was more surprised at the time. He'd thought they'd been working through the night, but there were a few hours before dawn. 'We should test them.'

'Test?' Anahrik looked around, arms open wide. 'You wanna start a brawl in the streets? Raid some buildings?'

Palom rolled his eyes. 'Of course not. We go to forest. See what they can do there, where no one can be hurt.'

Anahrik laughed, bouncing on the balls of his feet. 'Yeah. Well. Yeah, that makes more sense.'

Palom strolled down Trader's Alley, his heart considerably lighter than it had been in years. Perhaps he and

Anahrik *would* be better off leaving the city for a while. Just taking Moroda, Eryn, and whoever else wanted to come, and leaving Taban Yul.

Glancing down to the sword at his hip, feeling the thrum of power within, he knew it was possible. With these weapons, they'd be able to defend themselves. Stay on the move, stay safe.

He was still thinking about it as they exited the city by its eastern gate and headed south into the deep forest. Snow blanketed the land, and continued to fall in thick drifts, but he hardly felt the cold. Sounds of the night rose to meet him, owls hooting—which immediately reminded him of Lathri. He'd find her in the morning. Tell her about the Arillian danger. Make her see that leaving Taban Yul would be better for everyone. Show her that he could protect her. That he had control of his emotions.

'Look at this!' Anahrik gasped, holding up his dagger. He flinched, as if he was in pain, then blue light burst from the blade like fire.

Palom could hardly believe it. 'Is Sevastos power. Is *Valta Forinja*!' He gave his own sword a tentative slash in the air, and blue energy careened from its edge, slicing into a tree. Pinecones littered the floor from the impact and the trunk groaned as bark was severed.

Anahrik cheered, leaping high with both hands punching the air. 'We did it, Palom! We *did* it!'

Goosebumps rose on Palom's arms as power surged and prickled the air. This changed *everything*. He inhaled deeply, savouring the moment, then realised he could smell something else on the wind. The tang of electricity, somewhere in the distance. He froze, all senses on alert. 'Anahrik...Do you...?'

'Arillians.' Anahrik's joy had gone.

Above them, several dark forms flew through the air, descending into the forest somewhere ahead.

How *dare* they come to Val Sharis!

Neither of them spoke. Both instinctively reacted the same way—their humour disappeared and attention sharpened, slipping into the practised motions of a hunt. This time, they were stalking Arillians.

Palom and Anahrik hurried through the forest, trees whipping past them as they ran. They reached a well-worn path between the trees where the snow was thinner. Horses had been through here. Recently.

He skidded to a halt as another scent reached him.

He knew that scent, too.

'Kohl?' Anahrik rested a hand against the bark of one tree, where a thin layer of ice had formed on one side.

Kohl's telltale freezing, electrical scent was unmistakable. And under that... 'Moroda. Eryn. Morgen.' Palom couldn't believe it. They were supposed to be guests in the palace enjoying the ball. What were they doing out of the city alone in the middle of the night?

Above the thick treeline, the sky lit up as a bolt of lightning seared through the cloud.

'Go ahead. I'll bring the weapons,' Anahrik said.

Palom appreciated that. Anahrik knew what they planned, they'd been working together so long they didn't need to verbalise every thought.

Without hesitating, Palom allowed his *meraki* to wash over him. As a tiger, he could cover ground faster. And if Moroda and the others were near those Arillians...

If Kohl had anything to do with it...

Palom's fury drove him towards the fray. Anahrik was faster in his true form—even *he* couldn't outrun a falcon's wings—but Palom could do more damage. He raced through the trees on four legs, his senses heightened. Blood salted the air, too.

The scent of panicked horses grew stronger as he changed course slightly, following his nose.

What was going on?

He charged through the snow in powerful strides, green pine needles littering the snowy path and sticking to his fur.

Finally, when the trees fell away, an Arillian storm bombarded him. Vicious winds whipped up the snow, turning the clearing into a blizzard. Ripples of electricity passed through the air, setting everything on edge. Several of them swooped down and attacked a trio of people hunched in the snow.

Palom launched upwards with a roar and barrelled into an Arillian, knocking them clean out of the sky. He braced for retaliation, and as they careened to the ground, heat and electricity surged through him.

Enduring the searing pain, he bit down on whatever he could reach—which happened to be the Arillian's wings. Wrenching his head to the side, Palom tore off a chunk of the wing, feathers exploding outwards. The Arillian screamed, and Palom released his grip. Morgen was under fire, and he darted towards him.

Morgen hunkered down, using a fallen tree for cover. Balls of electricity exploded against the tree trunk, sending splinters in all directions. He waved his sword, doing his best to fend off more Arillians, but his arm was already a mess of blood, and they avoided his strikes.

Palom pounced again, slamming his shoulder into another Arillian and knocking them off course.

When he landed, Morgen flinched, then regained himself. 'Palom?' Morgen staggered to his feet, wiping away blood on his arm, but more leaked out of his wound. His armour had been split open, exposing skin—red raw and bleeding from the electrical burns. 'Thank Rhea. Great timing. Kohl *abandoned* us!'

Palom was sure he'd misheard. Kohl had left them? He looked around as he caught his breath, but there was too much wind and electricity in the air to pick out Kohl's scent. Moroda and Eryn were crouched on the far edge of the clearing, blue-white light flickering around them in a sphere of protection.

Must have been her ring.

Thank goodness for Topeko's teachings.

He was a fool to have trusted Kohl. Even Morgen couldn't stand up to these Arillians.

Palom snarled as another aggressor swooped down, lightning shooting from both palms. It sliced the ground underfoot as it came towards him, and Palom leapt backwards to avoid the strike. There were more screams behind him, and he tried to keep his attention on the immediate threat. Huge chunks of snow hurtled across the clearing, picked up by the storm, obscuring much of his vision.

Something heavy slammed into his legs, knocking him off balance. Palom staggered, bringing his jaws around to bite into whatever had hit him, only to find empty space. The Arillian wheeled past in a flurry of feathers, another crack of lightning sent towards him. Unsteady and with no time to dodge, Palom braced as the bolt hit him square in the ribs, shoving him several feet into the thick snow drifts.

He roared in response and staggered to regain his footing, but the Arillian was too fast. Another bolt of lightning tore through his shoulder, tearing into his fur and deep into flesh—numbing his leg. Swiping at the passing Arillian with his other leg fully unbalanced him, and he crumpled to the snow as flashes of pain laced through his body.

Palom's true form had power, but it was useless against enemies that could fly.

With a grunt of effort, light engulfed him as he transformed back.

It was time to try out his new weapon.

Blinking away dizziness and acutely aware his shoulder was bleeding, Palom gathered his bearings. 'Morgen, you are okay?'

The young officer grunted, slashing at another Arillian.

Leaving him to hold his ground, Palom made his way to the other side of the clearing, covering his face with his arms to protect it from the vicious winds. He staggered several times, but stayed upright.

Anahrik was by Moroda, his daggers making short work of a grounded Arillian. Flashes of blue light punctuated every strike, and Palom's heart soared. He tore across the clearing, heart pounding with every step.

Anahrik had dropped their satchel by a tree on the edge of the clearing. Palom skidded to it, snow melting to slush, and snatched up his greatsword. Dual-bladed and easily five feet long, it was a stalwart companion that had kept him out of danger on more than one occasion.

When he clutched the hilt, power thrummed through it.

Through *him*.

It took no thought at all for the Sevastos crystal powering it to spark to life, lighting up the blade with shifting blue light. With one flick, light and power careened from the blade, splitting both the wind and the nearest Arillian. It cut them from the sky, slicing through flesh and bone like a knife through butter.

Morgen's words echoed in his mind. *Kohl had abandoned them.*

Of *course* the Arillian had betrayed them. It wouldn't surprise him to see Kohl *leading* the attack.

Palom's rage swelled and he raised the sword with both

hands, light pulsing from the blade as if it had its own heartbeat.

With the *Valta Forinja*, he attacked.

And everything turned into chaos.

Arillian storms against the power of the *Valta Forinja* shattered the clearing. Snow burned away in the heat, and the ground blackened—scorched by their powers colliding.

Screams and blood filled the air as Palom and Anahrik rent wings from bodies, bone from flesh.

Morgen, though he had no *Valta Forinja*, fought fiercely to defend himself and drive their aggressors back. Light from their weapons filled the sky, pushing the darkness away and creating an eerie, blue dawn.

Power surged from his *Valta Forinja* in a torrent.

Palom had unleashed a waterfall of energy that flooded the battlefield, blasting everything from the sky and shredding what was left of the surrounding trees. His grip held firm on the sword's hilt, though blue fire lapped at his wrist as it vented from the blade.

He and the sword's power were *one*.

It rooted his feet to the ground, pulled up something from deep inside him, akin to his *meraki*, but more potent.

Another Arillian dived at him, and Palom sent another wave of energy crackling up to meet their lightning attacks.

They were storm-bringers. A destructive force that even Palom was loath to meet in combat.

But they were *nothing* compared to the Sevastos's power.

And this was only a *sliver* of it.

He tore across the fields, taking life from the Arillians as easily as he could crush ants. Smoke filled the sky, thick and dark from the fires started by wayward lightning strikes and waves of energy from the *Valta Forinja*. It was chaotic. Messy. Completely unrefined.

Palom wasn't sure how long he fought. Time had no meaning with the *Valta Forinja* in hand.

When the dust finally began to settle, when the roars of battle died, and there were no opponents left standing, the *Valta Forinja* remained victorious.

Elation coursed through him.

He had done it.

Not only had he and Anahrik successfully forged these weapons, he'd used them to their fullest effect.

Aciel wouldn't stand a chance.

The Ittallan *would* stand firm against him. Palom had the means to *ensure* that.

He lowered the blade, blue flames fading, and looked for Anahrik. This celebration called for ale. Perhaps even *wine*. He smiled, wondering what Lathri would think of him now. His body ached, limbs bruised and cut, muscles worn and stretched, but it was a *good* pain.

Morgen lay in a heap, clutching his blood soaked arm, his entire body shaking.

Palom walked to him, every step confident. 'You did well against Arillians.'

Morgen didn't reply.

It was only when Palom was a handful of paces away that he realised the officer was...crying?

'Morgen?'

Morgen didn't reply, head clutched between his hands. Much of his armour was in pieces, scattered on the ground around him, most of it dented and bloodied.

There was so much fear, blood, and death in the air, that Palom couldn't scent anything else. No other threat. No reinforcements. He checked the clouds above, in case a second wave of Arillians approached, but there was nothing.

Palom frowned and scanned what was left of the clearing. 'Morgen? What—'

Anahrik lay under an Arillian, their wings sliced off and feather tufts blowing in the wind. The twin daggers he'd fought with were buried in the Arillian's back, still glowing faintly, slowly congealing blood oozing from the wounds.

Anahrik wasn't moving.

Palom wasn't aware of his legs carrying him to his comrade. But in the time it took to reach Anahrik, Palom hadn't seen him breathe once. Hadn't seen him blink.

Anahrik stared into the middle distance, but there was no light in his eyes. Flecks of ice had frozen on his eyelashes and lips. His mouth was slightly parted, but no breath clouded the air in front of his face.

Palom had no voice. He lost his footing.

Morgen's sobs wrecked the air. Dumbly, Palom looked back to the officer, and his breath caught. Morgen had crawled forward through the melting slush and was cradling Eryn. She wore an emerald green ball gown. Blood soaked it. Matted her hair, strands stuck to her pale cheeks.

She wasn't breathing either.

Palom lost his grip on his sword, and it sank into the ground with a dull thud. He turned his gaze away, unable to look upon his colleague—his brother—and saw Moroda sprawled out under a tree. There was the slightest warmth in the wind and the breath from her lungs reached him.

Instinct took over. He couldn't speak, but he forced himself towards her, saw her chest rise and fall, though her exposed skin was bruised and bloody.

Sinking to his knees, Palom let out a roar of rage and sorrow. He did not care who heard, how far it carried. Emotions were too raw for that.

They had won the fight, but lost everything.

～

PALOM WASN'T PAYING attention to their trek back to Taban Yul. The only thing he'd been aware of was a weak dawn sunlight trying to warm his back as they were admitted into the palace by a concerned member of the Imperial Guard.

Morgen had helped him.

In truth, if Morgen hadn't been there, Palom wasn't sure he'd have been able to get up again after that battle.

Palom had carried Anahrik and Moroda. Morgen had carried Eryn.

They'd left the Arillians for the crows.

There'd been movement in the palace after they'd entered. Sheets had been brought forward to cover their companions. Blankets had been given to them. Stewards had been replaced by soldiers, and they'd been ushered down a narrow flight of stairs and into a windowless room down. What anyone had said to him, he didn't know.

He couldn't think.

Couldn't focus.

Moroda had been taken from him, and that had sparked enough sense to rouse the only emotion he had left: anger. 'You cannot!'

'She needs aid. If we don't get a healer to her soon, we will need to bury *three* people.'

The soldier had probably meant well, but fury, guilt, and sorrow had risen, and Palom had almost transformed in response.

It had taken six members of the Imperial Guard to restrain him.

By the time he and Morgen—who'd sat in silence, lost in his own grief—were summoned out of the room, Palom had barely overcome the shock.

Kohl was to blame for what had happened.

He'd *betrayed* them. Left Morgen, Moroda, and Eryn to

their fate—knowing full well what that fate was going to be. Anahrik and Eryn had suffered it.

'I understand this is a difficult time for you, but I need to know what happened.'

Palom looked up at the firm voice. He was half-surprised to see Princess Isa addressing him directly, her amber eyes narrowed and expectant. 'You...you want...me...talk?' Palom could hardly string a sentence together.

Isa cocked her head, then spoke again. This time, she'd switched to a variant of the old tongue—his mother tongue, and the dialect spoken in the more rural areas of Val Sharis. 'How many Arillians were there? And where exactly did they attack? Could you point out their location on the map?'

Palom slumped forwards, knowing what she asked but unable to turn his mind to that. 'I...I could not. We killed five. There may have been more who flew away. Including Jato. And they will be back.'

'What makes you so sure they'll return? It seemed you won a decisive victory.'

'Arillians hold grudges.' Palom snarled it in the common tongue.

Had the attack been revenge for what they'd done to Aciel and Jato? Or had they simply been in the wrong place at the wrong time?

Princess Isa frowned, her golden gaze darting to the floor as she thought.

Her attention off him, Palom took a moment to look at his surroundings. Daylight streamed in from several large windows that spanned the far wall of the large, white room. Several beds lay against the windows, bottles and bowls reeking of medicinal plants and tonics atop tables between them.

Moroda lay bundled up in the nearest bed, thick bandages wrapped around her torso. She was unconscious.

'She is...okay?'

Isa glanced at Moroda, as if remembering she was there, then shrugged. 'Nothing life-threatening.'

'Anahrik?' Palom knew his partner was dead. Knew it on a deep, primal level. But he had to ask.

Isa met his gaze and held it. 'I'm sorry Palom. He and Eryn were less lucky.'

He chewed his lip and balled his fists, trying to fight tears. But he wasn't strong enough, and they spilled anyway. Anahrik was the second brother he'd lost.

The second time *he* had been responsible for death.

No. 'It was Kohl.' The words came out as a growl.

'Kohl?' Isa raised an eyebrow.

'The Arillian with us. He betrayed them. Left them!' Anger was bubbling over again, the only emotion he could reliably turn to while in so much pain. The only thing he knew. 'He will pay. He *will*.'

'I *trusted* him.' Morgen's voice was small, but colder than Palom had ever heard before. Even in his rage, it sent a chill down Palom's spine. 'After everything we'd been through. We stood up for him!'

Before he or Isa could reply, a captain of the Imperial Guard appeared at the doorway in shining armour and saluted. 'Princess Isa. There is the matter of—'

'Not *again*, captain. I told you I was *not* to be disturbed under any circumstances!' Isa snapped, eyes blazing.

'I understand, but it relates to...' he jerked his chin towards Palom.

'How?' Isa's tone implied a complete lack of belief.

Palom took several deep breaths, trying to regain some composure. With Kohl, Eryn, and Anahrik gone, he realised their group was short two members. 'Where is Sapora? And Amarah?'

The guard nodded fervently. 'Exactly. Amarah. The... other *friend* of Prince Sapora?'

'Was she attacked too?' Isa asked.

At that, the guard took a step back. 'We've had her in confinement. She was seen with Koraki, and—'

'What?' Isa's shout made Palom flinch. 'She is our honoured guest. Dragons above, what do you think you're doing *locking* her up?'

'Well, she attacked Koraki! We'd run checks on her ship. *Khanna* is wanted in Corhaven for multiple thefts and piracy. Even Koraki said she was—'

'Disregard everything he told you. Release her at once and bring her to me!'

He was gone before she'd finished speaking, racing down the hallway until he was out of earshot.

Isa turned back to Palom with a sigh. 'As to your other question, my brother has returned to Sereth. I have every faith he will be crowned before the day is up. Then we might finally be able to mount a real defence against Aciel.'

Palom nodded, though he struggled to focus on her words.

He and Anahrik had reforged weapons of legend. The *Valta Forinja*.

A greatsword.

Twin daggers.

A scythe.

A short sword.

Four weapons. That was all they had to contribute to the fight against Aciel.

All they had been able to with the catalyst they had. If he'd had access to more of the Sevastos crystal, he could make enough weapons to outfit every member of the Imperial Guard in Val Sharis and Corhaven.

Topeko's voice rang in his mind. *Peace and prosperity.*

How morally and ethically corrupt weapons were, and the *Valta Forinja* most of all.

Was Anahrik's death the price he'd had to pay for such a weapon? Eryn's, too?

Even Moroda hadn't made it through unscathed, if the blood leaking through her bandages was any indication.

Palom sat down heavily on the edge of an unoccupied bed and clamped down on the tremors running through his body. After everything that had happened, nothing mattered anymore.

He would chase Kohl to the ends of Linaria if he had to.

And he'd make that Arillian pay for what he'd done.

27

Amarah paced the room she'd been shoved into.

Thank Rhea she'd eaten so well in town, because the Imperial Guard hadn't bothered checking on her once they'd locked the door. It had been getting dark when she'd returned to the palace, and now dawn light crept in through the narrow window near the room's ceiling.

Whatever Sapora had planned—that Koraki had been so upset by—had to have taken effect by now.

Was that why she'd been left? The Imperial Guard had been too busy with whatever was happening at the ball?

No one had said anything to her when they'd thrown her inside.

She folded and unfolded her arms, full of nervous energy but nothing to do with it. She'd tried the door multiple times, but she had no lockpicks on her. Nor had she any luck with the window. They'd taken her scythe and boots, and left her to rot.

'Koraki!' Amarah yelled, her voice hoarse from all the shouting she'd done through the night. 'Sapora!' Damn that she didn't know the name of the captain who'd brought her here. Another Ittallan. Someone she had no chance of over-powering, or outrunning.

She needed to relieve herself.

She needed to get as far away from this damned palace as was possible.

She needed proper sleep.

Amarah had managed to doze in the small hours of the night, but every tiny noise outside brought her to full wake-fulness in a heartbeat. She was too on edge to rest.

'Isa!' Amarah screamed, her voice breaking, her throat raw. She hammered on the door again, her fists sore and bruising from a night of hitting the heavy wood over and over.

'I'm gonna end up pissing in the corner if you don't let me out now! Don't want your fancy floor ruined, do you?' It wasn't a complete lie.

There could well have been a guard stationed outside the door all night, who was particularly good at ignoring her.

Or they'd forgotten her.

'No one here gives two shits about me, hey?' Amarah continued shouting. It hurt to keep using her voice, but she'd often made a nuisance of herself to get people to react when she was in a difficult situation. Trapped as she was, there wasn't much else she could do.

She took several moments to catch her breath and listen for a response. Ear pressed to the door, she waited for any sign of movement outside, counting her heartbeats to keep track of time.

Just as she took a breath to yell again, the faintest clink of armour echoed on the other side.

Amarah stepped away from the door as the footsteps grew louder, closer. Then, the clank of metal in the keyhole. The door unlocked and swung open with a low creak.

If she'd been anywhere else, she would have charged through the opening the moment it was there.

But she was in the palace in the middle of Taban Yul, surrounded by Ittallan. She had to play her cards right, and bursting out would probably land her in more hot water.

'Amarah. Princess Isa will see you, now,' the captain said gruffly. He didn't look her in the eye.

'About damned time! You left me in there all night!'

He backed out of the room and marched away. 'Follow me.'

'What, no apology?' Amarah followed him, sure to look around in case there were other members of the Imperial Guard waiting to throw her in irons. Her boots were beside the door, and she quickly slipped her feet into them. At least she could run, now. 'Where's my scythe?'

But he didn't reply, didn't turn back to her, and simply continued down the corridor.

Amarah squinted as daylight flooded her senses. She hadn't realised how dark the room was, and it put her off-balance. Following at a jog, she hurried after the sound of his armoured boots while her eyes adjusted to the bright light.

'Where's Sapora? I wanna see him.' Amarah had never thought she'd *want* to speak to the Varkain, but he might be her only real ally here. At least, the only one with any power.

Again, the captain ignored her request.

It was *infuriating*.

They turned a corner and headed up a short flight of stairs. Amarah kept her eyes open for any signs of treachery, or warning she was about to be attacked. There were a few palace stewards moving down the halls, but all averted their gazes the moment they spotted her.

She shivered.

Something was *wrong*.

The atmosphere within the palace had shifted. It wasn't exactly violence—or the tension that thickened the air just before violence—it was more sombre. There was fear, too. She'd bet her ship on that.

Something had happened, she didn't know what, and the captain wasn't telling her anything. Unsettled, Amarah kept her mouth closed.

Eventually, the captain led her to a large room with numerous windows and beds on the far side. It was about the only place in the palace she'd encountered that wasn't draped in gold and jewels. Sunlight streamed in, bright and harsh.

A healing room of sorts.

Moroda lay in one of the beds, bandages wrapped around her. Bloodied ones filled a wicker basket beside her bed. Palom and Morgen sat in chairs nearby, though Morgen dozed.

Palom looked up as she walked through the doorway, gave a nod, then turned his gaze back to Moroda.

Princess Isa stood off to the side, staring out the window, the light making her eyes seem to glow. Her hair had some slightly loose from her braids, a few strands frizzy. It didn't look like she'd slept, either.

'Princess Isa.' The captain saluted once, stiffly, then exited the room without another word.

Three members of the Imperial Guard waited near the door, but none spoke or moved.

Amarah took in everything, her mind racing, dread growing in her gut. Where was Eryn? Anahrik? Kohl? Sapora? Why was there *so much blood*?

When she looked at Palom and Morgen again, she noticed they too, had been injured. Wounds had been stitched up, and dried blood lined Palom's tunic.

386

Morgen's shoulder had been padded and bound, his arm splinted.

Isa nodded at Amarah, too, but stayed by the window.

Amarah's throat went dry. 'What the fuck happened?'

PRINCESS ISA SPOKE QUICKLY, clearly, and logically. Aside from a hint of annoyance, there was no emotion as she recounted events of the previous evening. Everything was straight and to the point.

Amarah had always appreciated people who got to the issue at hand quickly, and she appreciated Isa's brief summary. The princess wasn't one to wallow.

It appeared that Sapora had taken it upon himself to remove those on the council opposed to a Varkain—or a half-breed—in power. They'd become too comfortable with Vasil living in Sereth, and no longer appreciated the Varkain, including Sapora's presence in Val Sharis.

He'd done it at the ball.

She grimaced. Moroda and Eryn were going to the ball. Sapora hadn't hurt them, either, had he? They were Gold-stones, sure, but they didn't hold any influence. They couldn't threaten him.

Even if he *hadn't* attacked them, those two would have been terrified. Panicking like chickens.

Something about that imagery stirred her. They didn't know better, but they were trying.

And they deserved better.

Isa had backed up Sapora. Although the Imperial Guard and palace stewards followed her orders for the most part, her position was ceremonial. She didn't have real authority here. Once Sapora put down the dissenters and became king, things would change.

Amarah could understand that.

She'd been born to a Samolen woman, but held none of the innate magic Topeko and the other Kalos preached. She couldn't even *read*. Letters always seemed to jump about on the page, or shift as she tried to understand them. Receiving judgemental looks, harsh criticism, and being told she was being lazy when she simply *couldn't* do it had contributed to her leaving that damned desert.

If she'd had the same power as a Varkain, she'd probably have slaughtered a plethora of mages, too.

But she'd been weak. Stupid. Vulnerable. And she'd run away.

Come to think of it, she hadn't stopped running.

She didn't agree with what Sapora had done—and now Koraki's fear and indignation made sense—but she could understand why.

Damn it. She was *not* supposed to empathise with the snakes.

At least she hadn't been part of Sapora's target, as she'd feared. Being locked up had been the Imperial Guard's simple, old-fashioned prejudice. So at least for now, running away was on hold.

Palom briefly explained that he and Anahrik had been forging weapons in their workshop and had gone into the surrounding woodland to test them out.

Then, Jato had claimed her promised revenge, and Kohl had fled.

Palom had always been wary of him. She was used to experiencing a general lack of trust. Caution was essential to survival, after all. But the fact he'd left them stirred unease in her gut.

The Goldstones had been caught in the thick of it.

Palom had seen the Arillians descend and joined the fray.

Had the captain not decided to arrest her, *she'd* potentially be in that healer's bed too. Or worse.

Losing Eryn and Anahrik had been tough blows. Eryn was far more realistic than Moroda, and practical, too. Anahrik, though he'd been an irritating, arrogant thorn in her side, was useful. His scouting and quick reactions had saved *Khanna* on more than one occasion.

Of course Moroda, Palom, and even Morgen were devastated by those losses.

Whatever people said about her, she had a heart. She *cared*.

The fact that Jato had struck back wasn't unexpected, but Amarah took it as a personal affront. These people were her crew.

Had she not been in such a panic to get away from the palace, if she'd found Moroda and the others to warn them, perhaps they might all have left Taban Yul aboard *Khanna* and none of this would have happened

That was on *her*.

Amarah scowled. Sapora hadn't helped issues. If he hadn't gone on a damned killing spree, they'd never have left the palace in the first place.

She didn't like being caught between two desires. She could stay and fight. She owed them that much. Or get out of here while she had the chance.

Isa said, 'Our defences are growing. Taban Yul's remaining fleet consists of twenty-seven warships and sixty-three class threes and fours that can be modified to assist. I was hoping you would add *Khanna* to that list. We need every gun we can get.'

'That all?' Amarah asked.

'We sent a significant part of our fleet across the Sea of Nami to assist Niversai with rebuilding. Other ships are already patrolling the borders, offering protection to other cities and towns in case the Arillians strike.'

Amarah snorted, but she saw an opportunity. Isa was asking for her help. Well, *telling* her, but the fact remained they needed everyone they could get to fight Aciel. Helping out royalty could well mean a favour for her in future. And she had to admit, fighting Aciel on their terms was better than waiting for the Arillians to pick them off—or take more of their soldiers away like he had done in Corhaven. '*Khanna's* better for fleeing battle, not taking part. But give me a warship and I'll pilot it for you.'

Credit to the princess, she held in her shock well. She leant back slightly, but there were no giveaways on her face that she'd been taken aback by Amarah's boldness.

Amarah would have to keep an eye on Isa in future. She'd be an excellent liar.

'I'm sure that could be arranged,' Isa said after thinking about it for a moment. 'I must say, I thought you'd rather leave than fight.'

'I don't hold much love for Aciel. And after what Jato did...Revenge sounds good right now.'

'Revenge is best choice.' Palom stood up and approached her. 'I will kill Kohl for what he did.'

'Saving his own skin?' Amarah raised an eyebrow. If she fought Jato a hundred times, the Arillian would probably win every time. She couldn't blame Kohl for keeping himself alive. But abandoning the Goldstones to Jato's wrath?

She had a slight problem with that.

'It was not saving skin. He betrayed Moroda. Eryn. Anahrik. Why not flee with them? Why not distract Jato so they could escape? No. He left them to her. I should never have trusted him.' Palom's voice trembled with barely contained sorrow. 'I have brought gift for you, Amarah. And you, Morgen. Fight with me. We will correct this.'

Curious, Amarah didn't say anything as the Ittallan dragged his weatherbeaten satchel across the floor to them. Unbuckling it, Palom pulled a short sword from within. A scythe followed the sword, and then two daggers, dried blood on the blades.

'Palom!' Morgen gasped, stepping forward. 'What...what is this?'

'*Valta Forinja.*'

It meant nothing to Amarah, but she knew she'd heard that term before, *somewhere*. She couldn't put her finger on it.

Palom sighed. 'Dragon-forged weapon.'

'D—Dragon-forged?' Morgen leaned forward, slightly unsteady with one arm bound.

Amarah just about held in her gasp. These were the weapons that ended the great war. The ones created using the power of a Sevastos.

She had no idea Palom had been working on them. The idea had never occurred to her.

'Anahrik learned how to do this from book in Berel. We needed to guess at few bits. My workshop is half burnt from attempts and many weapons did not work. But these are done.' Palom rested his broad hands on his hips.

'You bastards, you did it!' Amarah picked up her new scythe and gave it a careful inspection. It was strange to see one of Palom and Anahrik's weapons without their sigil. 'No silver?'

Palom dropped his eyes. 'There was...no time.'

'What makes them so special?' Morgen asked, frowning at the weapons.

'Do you want your enemy dead?'

'Yes...?'

'Absolutely dead. Beyond certain?'

'Yes...?'

'Then use this.'

Morgen took the *Valta Forinja* from Palom. A spark of light burst from his skin where he held it, disappearing instantly. His eyes went wide.

'Is power. Of dragons.' Palom shook his head. 'Is unlike anything you have seen before. We cut Arillians down with these. Nothing can stand before *Valta Forinja*.'

'Incredible!' Morgen gasped.

Amarah could hardly believe the weapons of legend were here in this room. Functioning. 'This is my gift then?' She twirled the scythe. 'You're too kind.'

Palom straightened up and looked at her. 'Is gift for you *all*. Aciel is taking over. We *must* fight, we must protect ourselves. With these weapons, you can do this.'

Isa strode forward and picked up one of the bloody daggers. She held the blade up to the light, marvelling at the colours emitted from the metal. 'How did you do it?'

'Dragon ore did most of work. Unlike any weapons I have crafted before.'

'The ore?'

'Sevastos crystal. From Berel. I do not think Topeko would be pleased to learn what I have done.' He glanced at Amarah, almost sheepish. 'But with these, we have good chance to survive coming battles. No more losses.'

'Damned good idea. Why not use whatever weapons we have? Who knows what tricks Aciel and his generals will have up their sleeves!' Amarah laughed. She passed the scythe from one hand to another, marvelling at her new weapon. At the power inside it. 'You'll be a hero if these work, Palom.'

He dropped his gaze. 'They work.' Palom sat on the edge of Moroda's bed, the Goldstone's eyelids fluttering, though she did not wake. 'I promised to protect you. If I fail again, these weapons will not.'

AMARAH SPENT most of the afternoon in the hangar. She'd checked her purchases from Taban Yul had arrived, and was pleased to find a neat pile of supplies waiting for her on deck.

After squirrelling everything away, she'd checked over *Khanna* for more damage. She hadn't had a chance to look over her ship since arriving in Taban Yul, but thankfully no wayward Arillian lightning bolts had harmed *Khanna* when they'd fled from Jato.

That would probably change if she were to take *Khanna* into battle against the Arillians.

But a warship? That could take a lot of assault. If it was big enough, it could probably carry *Khanna* in its hold, too.

Isa had said something about wanting to see her air licence and paperwork, but Amarah had waved her off. She'd seen her fly. What was a document going to do?

Once Amarah was happy with *Khanna*, she'd taken a long nap on her ship, her new *Valta Forinja* clutched across her lap.

It was dark again when she awoke, and she made her way to the palace guest suites in search of another bath and something to eat. There'd been some activity in the palace—cleanup of the ballroom, she supposed from the stewards darting back and forth—which she was happy to stay out of. It didn't concern her.

She didn't want to risk bumping into Koraki again, either.

When she spotted Morgen on the far end of the guest suites, *Valta Forinja* in hand, she headed his way. She was curious what the officer's thoughts were on these weapons Palom had made, and the situation with Kohl and Sapora.

He opened a pair of double doors and wandered out onto the balcony.

Amarah hesitated before following him.

His movements had been stiff, which she'd put down to the injuries he'd sustained by Jato and her Arillians, but the angry muttering under his breath made her pause.

She loitered on the edge of the doorway, bright moonlight spilling onto the floor beside her.

Taban Yul was certainly not asleep, and even at five or six floors up, she could hear the laughter and chatter of the townsfolk as they enjoyed the night.

Shouts rang out, footsteps clattered on the stone paths, and carriages charged through the winding streets.

She longed to be down there, without a care in the world, instead of having a personal stake against the damned warlord and his stolen fighters.

Amarah watched Morgen, who loosely held his dragon-forged sword and stared at the blade. After a few moments, it glowed blue in the same way her scythe did, shimmering in the moonlight.

'With this, I can avenge her.' He lunged at an invisible target, swung round and brought it down as though to cleave through a skull. 'Anahrik, too.' The blade flashed in response, a light in the darkness.

Deciding to leave Morgen to his alone time, Amarah turned to exit the room.

'Aciel doesn't stand a chance—'

'I'm sure the Arillians will cower in fear.'

Morgen dropped the sword with a clatter and looked up at the sudden voice.

Even Amarah flinched, frozen in place.

'P—Princess Isa! How long have you been there?' Morgen gasped.

'Since you started muttering to yourself.'

Now Amarah *had* to stay. What would Isa have to say to Morgen?

Isa dropped down from above—Amarah guessed she'd been on the roof—and circled Morgen on the balcony.

If her senses were anything like Sapora's, then Amarah knew she wouldn't stay hidden for long. She just had to hope Isa was too focussed on Morgen to notice her eavesdropping from the adjacent room.

'That's some blade you have there. I've never seen one glow like that before. Who'd have thought the *Valta Forinja* are real,' Isa said, sounding mildly enthusiastic.

Morgen bent down to pick it up, and sheathed it to dim its light. 'Why did Sapora do that?'

'Do what?' She bit her thumbnail and glanced at the city.

'At the ball?'

'Bit of spring cleaning. Well, *winter* cleaning, I suppose.'

'But *why*? Why the violence? Eryn...She...She...'

'She and Moroda should have left when I warned them. They didn't seem the type to enjoy a cleansing.'

Morgen balled his hands and looked over the balcony's edge. 'I don't know what's wrong with you. Why you kill so willingly...'

'Fodder are weak. If they won't listen, they must be *made* to. I tried to make them listen but they're too stubborn. Sapora simply showed his fangs to set them in line.'

'Set them in line? Sounds like Aciel.'

Isa laughed, her voice bell-like. 'If anyone does anything you don't like, you always compare them to your worst enemy. Sapora has the *right* to rule. Aciel does not. Sapora wishes for peace in Linaria. Aciel does not. Sapora shows mercy, and kills those who continue to defy him. Aciel steals lives for his own gain.'

Morgen lowered his gaze as she approached.

'Relax, Morgen.' She darted to his other side. 'If you don't like it, it's not too late for you to leave. Go back where you came from. Leave dragons and monsters to the real kings and queens. Some of us have grown up beside the nests of vipers. We've learned what we need to do to survive. To thrive. You don't belong here—your world is cosy and peaceful—you've no idea what it feels like to be robbed of your birthright, and hated by your own kind.

'So, I have learned the art of silence. Of stealth. It's quite remarkable what you hear when people don't know you're watching from the shadows. Some of the things the councillors got up to…I fed the information back to Sereth, but Vasil didn't care. He refused to do anything about their behaviour. When Sapora takes his throne, I'll finally have the respect I deserve.'

Amarah swallowed hard at her words. Did Isa know she was there? Hiding and watching?

Isa continued, 'These dances are written in blood. Go home, Morgen, if you don't want to be part of it.'

'No! I need to avenge her!' His voice trembled.

Isa giggled and jumped onto the edge of the balcony, balancing on the narrow rail. 'So sweet. I suppose you want to keep little Ro safe, too?'

'Little Ro...?'

Isa paced along the balcony, turned, and paced back. The fall would kill her, no question, but she stepped as confidently as if she were on the ground.

'If you're staying with us, you must give it your all. Here. In case you need anything.' She pulled out her hand from her pocket and tossed him something small and dark.

'Princess, what is this?'

Amarah wondered if it was the same onyx stone she'd given her.

'Remember whose side you're on, Morgen.' Isa transformed into her cat form in a burst of light, and leapt back onto the roof, her paws silent.

Amarah took a deep breath. She needed to make her own choice, too.

Stay, or run.

28

S unlight bathed Moroda when she awoke. She
blinked several times, her mind very much alert, her
eyes struggling to adjust to the brightness.

Where was she?

Her mind raced, though her body was sluggish. She was
lying down, could feel the weight of her body absorbed by
something soft.

A mattress. Cotton sheets.

A small voice in the far reaches of her mind begged for a
few more minutes' rest, but Moroda shook it off.

She had to *concentrate*.

How did she get here? What happened in the battle?
Dragons above, she couldn't remember much past all the
snow, wind, and pain...

Twitching her fingers, she tapped each one against the
soft fabric. All digits were accounted for, and her ring was
still on her finger, though it was cold and silent.

Her body began to respond, slowly, but when she finally
managed to sit up, the strain of moving left her exhausted.

As she caught her breath, she took in her surroundings.
Empty beds lined against the wall on either side of her own,

and bright sunlight streamed in from windows behind each bed.

It was daytime. How long had she been asleep?

A large tapestry hung above the closed door on the wall opposite, surrounded by intricate gold detailing. Must be the palace. Perhaps its infirmary? The other beds were empty, which was unsettling.

Why was she alone?

Glad she still had her mind, even if her body was slow to wake up, she glanced down at herself, and found she wore a plain, white gown.

Bandages covered her arms and torso. Her skin itched underneath, but there was no pain. Only a dull throb, like she'd fallen off a horse.

Moroda swung her legs off the bed, eager to get up.

Memories of the battle came to her in a sudden, intense burst.

The chill of the snow. The biting wind.

Blood. There'd been a lot of blood. It had tinged the snow pink.

Morgen! He'd been injured. She remembered...

She hadn't been able to find Eryn. She remembered looking around, panic taking hold. Falling into the thick snow, her ring cold, the crossbow abandoned.

But the beds beside her were empty.

Eryn and Morgen must be fine, then.

As her bare feet pressed against the wooden floor, the door swung open.

Never had she been so grateful to see Palom. The huge Ittallan filled the door frame, as powerful and confident as she'd ever seen him, but his eyes were red. He had a few scratches across his face and hands, but they seemed minor in comparison to her own bandages.

He stepped through the door and closed it behind him. 'Moroda. You are...okay?'

'Palom!' Moroda was grateful her voice worked, even though it was weaker than usual.

She took an unsteady step towards him, pins and needles racing through her feet. She wobbled, grasping onto the bed rail to stay standing.

'Morgen...is bringing others, now.' He glanced back at the door, voice breaking. His whole body shook, and Moroda realised he was fighting to keep from transforming.

Was it sadness? Rage?

A flicker of terror stirred in her gut. She remembered the weapons Anarik had used. The destructive blue light, the searing heat of fire.

'Palom...?'

'I swear...by all dragons...by my blood...I will kill Kohl for what he has done.'

Moroda struggled to think, closing her eyes and casting her mind back. Kohl...

A twinge of pain raced through her as she thought of Jato and her elite fighters, and of the snowstorm that caused chaos and confusion.

Kohl had abandoned them before Jato's Arillians had attacked.

'I...I think...' Moroda struggled to form words, but she didn't want the silence to linger. 'It'll be okay. Where's Eryn? How long have I been asleep?' She wiggled her toes, but the stinging sensation hadn't left.

'Anahrik is...gone.' Palom closed his eyes, tears welling at the corners of his eyes. 'Eryn is gone.'

Moroda didn't understand. She furrowed her brow. 'What?'

'Both killed...by those storm bringers!' He wavered where he stood, threatening to topple over. 'Kohl is traitor and coward. I will chase him to ends of Linaria and make him *pay*!'

Moroda's legs buckled and she fell back onto the bed. 'Eryn...? But...I can't...but she...I didn't see her...I didn't say...'

Emotions rushed through her. Shock and confusion kept most at bay, but Palom's devastation was clear as the sun behind her.

Eryn was...gone?

She'd...she'd *died*?

Her breathing quickened and her fingers tingled. No. That couldn't be right. *Couldn't* be.

The door behind Palom flew open as Amarah charged in, trailed by Morgen and Isa.

'You're awake!' Morgen offered a weak smile. It didn't reach his eyes. He looked at her for a long moment, seemed unsure what to say or do. His left arm hung in a sling, padding and bandages supporting his shoulder. 'I...I'm sorry for...'

Moroda didn't want him to finish that sentence. She was struggling to make sense of it all. She looked at Palom, who had been a source of stability and strength from the moment she'd met him.

But his eyes were dark with sorrow. Heavy circles hung under them. He hadn't slept much.

She remembered Kohl had been with them, outside the city. No...Kohl had flown away.

She'd been focussed on the energy shield, trying her hardest to hold on. To wait for him to see sense and come back.

She'd hoped he would. Moroda swallowed. 'Kohl? He didn't come back? I thought...'

'Kohl left you to die.' Palom's voice had taken on an edge Moroda had never heard before.

Her fear intensified.

'That's right. Soon as the Arillians turned up, he took off,' Morgen confirmed. 'Palom was the one who came to help us, Ro. He and...' Morgen cut himself off, glancing at Palom. 'They didn't get there until it was almost finished.'

'Everything happened so quickly...' Tears spilled down Moroda's face. She trembled as the truth of Palom's words dawned on her. She now understood Eryn's desire to get away from the palace. Far away, wherever that was. Understood Eryn's desperation to go home. Home had been *safe*.

Something hit her, then. Something so cold she couldn't breathe. The room spun when she realised she'd never speak to her sister again.

Eryn was gone. There was no going back.

'Eryn...I didn't...I didn't speak to her. I couldn't see her. I didn't...I didn't get to say goodbye...'

Amarah stepped forward. 'I know it's tough when you can't say goodbye to people you lose. But you gotta push through.'

Moroda looked at her, vision blurry. 'But there's nothing...nothing left?'

'Right. You've hit the bottom. Only way is up.'

Moroda shook her head.

'Or you stay there and get left. Don't wallow.'

Moroda chewed on her lip. Dragons above, what was she supposed to do? Wasn't she allowed to be upset? To grieve? To come to terms with what had happened?

'Linaria is officially at war,' Isa said, speaking for the first time. 'This attack is one of many Aciel carried out simultaneously. We received word at dawn that Arillians attacked Niversai in the night. In its weakened state after the dragon attack, Rosecastle fell quickly. It's a ruin, and the city is under siege. Aciel is beginning his decimation of Corhaven, beginning with the capital. If we don't act quickly, Val Sharis will follow soon. We are mobilising the Imperial Fleet to defend Taban Yul from his inevitable strike. All we can do is gather our defences.'

Moroda blinked. She hadn't been paying attention to Princess Isa. She was done with Aciel, airships, dragons. *Everything*.

But something Isa said stood out.

Niversai had been attacked.

While weakened and recovering from the dragon, the Arillians had taken advantage and swooped in.

She had no home without the city. Whatever chance she'd had to rebuild a life there was over. It had been taken from her. 'Niversai, too...?'

'I'm afraid so,' Isa said, her voice low. 'We are the nearest city that would be able to send reinforcements across the sea. Trade, too. With no fresh supplies or troops, Niversai is unlikely to recover any time soon. All of Corhaven is going to be in turmoil. We must prepare to defend ourselves.'

Moroda's mind was a cacophony of confusing thoughts and raw emotions. The thought of going through another battle terrified her, but with Niversai under siege, would it even be possible to return home? Would it even *be* home without Eryn?

Moroda clutched the bedsheets. All the world was crumbling around her, again, and she was lost in it—unable to do anything.

First her father.

Then Eryn.

Now, Niversai.

This was more than a dragon burning down buildings and damaging the castle. This was a warlord with the power of compulsion. Someone who'd taken the power of dragons to fuel his conquest. She'd felt that power, had been frozen by it, ordered by it.

For all their good intentions, none of them stood a chance.

Morgen limped over to Moroda and sat beside her, leaning against her shoulder with his good arm as her emotions flooded out. His eyes watered, but he held back tears.

Amarah continued to talk with Isa and Palom, but Moroda didn't hear their words, nor did she care to. The war Topeko had warned them of was no longer nipping at their heels; it had overtaken them.

She'd been lucky on Jato's warship. So very lucky.

Her mind flickered to Kohl. If he had stayed and fought with them...Eryn and Anahrik would probably still be here.

But he hadn't.

He'd fled with his tail between his legs and left them all to die.

He *knew* she and Eryn wouldn't be able to fight, not properly. *Knew* they were outnumbered by the Arillians.

And his departure had sealed their fate.

Loss flooded her like an immense weight. She sat on the edge of the bed, crying until she felt her eyes would bleed. She realised she hadn't grieved her father's loss before, not truly. She hadn't been allowed to—she'd had to carry on for Eryn's sake, and for her own.

But now she'd lost Eryn, her quick-witted, sharp-tongued, resourceful, rational, remarkable sister...Now there was no Eryn, she could weep.

Anger, white hot and fluttering, coursed through her veins in her moments of respite, sapping her of what little energy remained, pushing her once again into fits of sobbing.

'Palom. You once said I looked...like I was carrying the pain of the world in my heart. I am now...I can hardly

404

breathe because of it. It's burning me, my lungs, my heart, my eyes...my skin *crawls* with it. It's my fault she's gone.'

Palom shook his head. 'No. Do not say this.'

'We can't sit here waiting for Aciel to attack!' Amarah snapped. 'I ain't waiting to be picked off! Moroda. That dragon you were going to look for in the mountains. That'll be our only chance.'

'I'm not going to mountains. I'm going after Kohl,' Palom said, voice flat.

'Kohl can wait. War won't. Didn't you hear your princess? Niversai's been taken. Taban Yul will be far behind,' Amarah said. 'I don't have time for you to go charging off. We need to do whatever we can to survive what's coming. If that means fighting, I sure as hell want a dragon on my side.'

'Sapora has already returned to Sereth to ready the Varkain,' Isa said. 'I can prepare a warship for you, Amarah. The Imperial Guard has been doubled here, and while I'm loath to order conscriptions, we need everyone we can to fight or fly ships.'

Moroda felt Morgen wince at her words. He was part of the Imperial Guard. There was no way he would get out of this battle.

'Amarah, if you want to attempt to find a dragon, you are welcome to fly into the Feor Mountains to search. If you don't return, you forfeit your warship and me as your ally.' The warning in Isa's voice was clear. 'But take care. I hope you're ready if you encounter any more Arillians out there.'

'Good. Finally we're getting somewhere.' Amarah grinned and wandered to one of the windows. 'Don't worry about me, Isa. My blade'll hit its mark, like always. Palom, Morgen, I want you both with me. If I'm coming up against a dragon, I'll need people who can fight.'

Moroda listened to the others debate and plan. Heard their determination in spite of everything that had happened. Amarah was leading the fray, speaking as if she believed in Topeko's idea from Berel.

Moroda shook her head. She'd lost Eryn, but everything else was continuing forwards.

Life was continuing.

The threat was growing.

Aciel hadn't gone anywhere. Wouldn't stop because she'd lost her sister.

Nothing stopped because one person was grieving.

It was just like she'd always told Eryn. They had to move forward.

She had to.

'I will go with you too, Amarah,' Moroda said. She was hardly aware of making the decision before she spoke. 'There may be nothing for me in Niversai...but I wish to do whatever I can to protect those who are left. I still...I still believe what Topeko suggested. There's...there's hope.'

Amarah acknowledged her with a curt nod. 'Better than sitting around moping. Let's get on with it and find this damned dragon.'

'Let us pray Taban Yul is still standing when we return,' Palom said.

'Praying is for the weak. Our actions will ensure the city stays safe,' Amarah countered. 'On your feet, Moroda. It's tough but we gotta be stronger than them. You stood up to Aciel before. You can do this now.'

Moroda heaved herself off the bed. Thoughts of her sister swirled around her mind, pain and sadness inter-twined. She smiled weakly, straining against her inner turmoil. Her tears had ceased, and now her body was numb.

'You don't have to come, Moroda. You could stay in the palace and rest,' Morgen said.

'I want to do *something*.'

'Still? After all that's happened?'

'Still,' she repeated. 'I'll be a wreck if I stay here with my own thoughts.'

'What about...seeing Eryn?'

'She and Anahrik are being kept one one of the lower levels. I can take you to her, if you'd like?' Isa asked.

Moroda wavered. She wasn't sure she wanted to see her sister like that.

Morgen put a hand on her shoulder, steadying her. 'It's okay.'

'I'll...I'll see her when we get back. I'll tell her the good news.' Moroda wasn't sure if she was trying to fool herself.

Morgen followed her out the door.

'Little Ro,' Isa called, stopping Moroda in her tracks. 'Might want to change your clothes before you leave. It's cold out there.'

'Yes, thank you.' Moroda interlaced her fingers, trying to comfort herself in some small way. There was no Eryn to lean on for support or reassurance. No Anahrik to add a quip to make them all laugh. No Kohl with sage advice.

More than anything, it was as if she was being swept away again. A familiar, unwanted feeling.

As though she were floating down a river whose current was too much for her to fight against.

She barely registered changing, or walking down the palace hallways, or into the airship hangar, or even getting onto *Khanna*. She was dimly aware of her companions, so few of them left. Amarah, Palom, and Morgen. She couldn't focus on anything they said or did.

She was in a daze, her grief drowning her.

～

IT WAS several minutes into the flight when Moroda became aware of the cold wind rushing across her face and she snapped to attention.

She was on *Khanna's* deck, her cloak wrapped around her shoulders, the dark mountain range in the distance growing larger every moment.

She blinked, tried to focus.

'Princess Isa was right. We were not only ones attacked last night,' Palom said.

Moroda glanced over the edge of the deck at his words. Smoke rose from fires yet to be extinguished. Farms and holdfasts burned.

Corpses littered the snow beneath them, and the predominant colour was now a dirty red.

It was like seeing the burned Niversai all over again.

'Arillian scum,' Amarah said, her voice barely more than a growl.

Even in her state of shock, Moroda was more than aware of the tension on the airship. The mood was low, and the storms they saw writhing in the distance did not help the sense of foreboding.

She felt sick at the prospect of more conflict, of more war, of more pain, death, and destruction.

'I should never have joined the Imperial Guard.' Morgen shuddered, shaking his head and rocking slowly where he sat.

'Should've stayed home. Farmed. Aciel wouldn't care about a tiny village of farmers.'

Moroda watched as he berated himself, mumbling aloud. His left arm remained heavily bandaged, and pity and guilt ran through her at the sight. 'Morgen.' She got up to sit closer to him, an echo of his earlier actions. 'You cannot blame yourself, how were you to know this war was coming? No one knew.'

'I couldn't stop them,' he continued, seemingly oblivious to Moroda's reassurances. 'I couldn't protect her. Eryn, I couldn't...'

'Morgen, stop it, please.' Moroda held back a fresh wave of tears at the mention of her sister. '*Aciel* is the one responsible, not you. You couldn't have done any more than you did. *You* didn't flee.'

That, of course, made her think of Kohl.

The Arillian had first warned Eryn and her about the dragon attack in Niversai. How long ago that seemed. She had always trusted him because of that first action, always given him the benefit of the doubt. It made the betrayal especially bitter.

Morgen stopped mumbling at her words and lifted his head from his hands. 'I thought he was with us.'

His eyes were red raw.

'So did I. But he didn't attack us...that must count for something, right?'

'You always have to see the best in people, don't you? He *abandoned* us, and you can only think that's better than being attacked?'

Moroda said nothing, hurt by his accusation. She knew he was right, and had always thought it was a nice trait to have—to see the best in people.

Aciel was changing her mind about that, and now perhaps Kohl was, too.

She knew Palom was keen to lump blame on Kohl, but she wanted an explanation more than anything else. 'Is that so bad? We don't know anything about him, really. He always helped us, *always*.'

At Morgen's dark look, she continued, 'I'm not excusing it. Dragons above, look what happened to Eryn! I don't know if I *can* forgive that. But if he were to explain it...? I'm hurting so much...losing... losing Ryn...and Anahrik...I don't want to think badly of anyone else, anymore. I don't want to wallow.'

Amarah said,

'I know you don't want to wallow. If you did, you'd have stayed in Taban Yul. For someone who ain't a fighter, you have strength. You just need help seeing it every now and then.'

Moroda didn't trust herself to reply, and neither Morgen nor Palom were interested in conversation.

They grew quiet, listening to the low hum of *Khanna's* engines as they drifted further away from Taban Yul, and snow began to fall more heavily than before.

'Can hardly believe Sapora'll be a king soon. Maybe even already,' Amarah said as the mountains loomed.

Moroda glanced up. She had been so wrapped up in the loss of Eryn and Anahrik, she had forgotten Sapora had also left their group. After what Sapora had done, she wasn't sure if she could trust him, either. Would he really help against the Arillians?

'Did you...did you see what happened in the ballroom?' Moroda asked tentatively.

'Afraid not. Some Imperial Guard mistook me for a thief and had me locked up all night. Sapora and Isa are shaking things up, that's for sure.'

'I'm sorry.'

'What for? You didn't lock me up.' Amarah adjusted her sails as the wind intensified. 'I'm used to it.'

Moroda didn't think that made it any better.

'I want to find dragon and end this nightmare.' Palom hunched forward, eyes dark and brooding.

Moroda's ring flashed briefly. Palom—all Ittallan—had their own *meraki* that the mages of Berel couldn't affect. But his rage and sorrow must have been strong enough that even the stone on her ring picked up on it.

Her gaze fell to the large sword by his feet. It looked like any other sword, but she knew what power it contained. She didn't need her ring to sense that.

Palom wanted to use it, and Moroda wasn't sure if that was the best idea. 'You want to avenge Anahrik?'

Palom nodded.

'Eryn, too. I want to track down Kohl.'

'I understand how you feel. That you think Kohl is responsible, but please don't let it cloud your judgement.'

'We're all in this together, we're all on the same side,' Morgen added.

Palom smiled bitterly. 'Yes. We will act with clear heads.'

Moroda could see nothing on the surface which showed Amarah had been affected by anything—that woman was a closed book—but with emotions taking their toll on Palom and Morgen, she vowed to be of more use.

She pulled out the ereven sphere and guided Amarah's flight path according to the phoenix's feather within now they were within the mountain range. Strange. Berel was a land of peace, and this item was part of their culture. It was ironic that such an item would lead them to a dragon—who would take part in war.

Yes, Aciel had to be stopped. That was irrefutable.

But did that have to end in so much violence?

Did the *Valta Forinja* have to take more life?

Perhaps she was just a silly Goldstone. An idealist, not fit for truths of the real world.

'You okay, Ro?' Morgen asked.

Moroda kept her focus on the ereven sphere, even as he used Eryn's familiar nickname for her. He'd been doing that recently, with both of them. She'd thought it meant friendship. But she'd thought Kohl had been a friend, too. 'We were unprepared to fight. *I* was unprepared. I couldn't do anything.'

'You aren't a fighter. You've been thrown into a situation where coming out alive is a huge success. I can't imagine how frightening it must have been for you.'

'I don't want it to happen again.'

'The way things are going, it *will* happen again.' Morgen rested a hand on her shoulder.

'I don't want to fight. I just want everyone to be safe. I've lost my father, my sister, and now my home. I don't want it to carry on. I just want peace.'

'Aciel lost all that and more, too. Look how he reacted.'

'It's so wrong!'

Amarah shrugged, the action rocking the airship in the harsh winds. 'Aciel is an arse, but I can't say I blame him. Arillians have been treated like shit for centuries. Not saying it ain't warranted, but there's only so much abuse you can take before you fight back. He ain't got nothing to lose and wants to destroy those who hurt Arillians.'

'But for what reason? To be left with those who adore him? I don't see that as fulfilling.'

'Maybe not. But there are thousands who would.'

'Live and let live is a kind notion, but it's not always possible,' Morgen said gently.

Moroda tried to think. 'What about the Samolen? They've practised peace since...since the beginning! They dedicate their lives to study, to love, to kindness, and compassion.'

Palom stood up, sword clutched in one hand, though he held it low. 'You speak like fighting is wrong. Defending yourself is not wrong. Revenge is not wrong. Moroda, you wanted to learn fighting, did you not?'

'How is killing another "right"?'

Moroda asked. Already, her voice had hitched as emotions rose. Her ring flared with a pulse of light.

'People must pay for actions.' Palom's sword lit with a matching blue light, as if the blade were on fire.

'And Aciel's followers? Those under his compulsion? Will you kill them, too?' Moroda asked.

Amarah shuddered. 'Moroda. I'll always run if I can. Avoid getting hurt, you know. But sometimes, when you're in a corner? Fighting is all you have. And if that means someone else dies instead of you? Well, I dunno about you, but *I'd* rather live.'

Moroda went quiet, her hands trembling. Nothing made sense. Before, everything had been simple. Clear. Now it was all muddled, and she didn't know what she was supposed to do. 'I don't want to bicker. Please. Not when we're all hurting so much.'

'There's darkness in everyone, Moroda. In Sapora, in all the Varkain. Even you. People ain't clear cut. You just gotta learn when to spot danger, and how to stay away from it.' Amarah pulled one of her levers, and her side sails flattened. 'Wind's picking up. Hold on. It'll get bumpy.'

Moroda reflected on Amarah's words. The snowfall thickened around them as the ship climbed higher, buffeted by strong gusts.

She wondered whether the dragon would see them as a threat. Or food. Or just incinerate them. Kohl, the only one with any experience dealing with dragons, was no longer there. Then again, she supposed *not* having a dragon slayer in the presence of a dragon was no bad thing.

She thought of her remaining companions: Amarah, as she carefully navigated the terrain in the poor weather, stubborn, confident, and proud as always, and fearless to boot; Palom, sombre and quiet in his grief, waves of anger pulsing from him; and Morgen, a trained soldier, but with more emotion than any of them, it seemed.

Then, of course, there was herself. A former Goldstone

of Niversai, able to clean and cook and dance, a thirst for knowledge, but lacking in wit, confidence and decisiveness, a hunger for peace, but alone in the world.

What would it matter if they were killed by the dragon, she wondered.

Would Linaria even mourn their passing?

29

Falling snow masked the way ahead. The wind picked up as their altitude increased, buffeting *Khanna* with strong surges. Palom squared his stance and braced as the airship rocked underfoot. Sword held in one hand, he clutched the railing with another.

If Kohl or Anahrik had been with them, they'd have scouted ahead and helped navigate a safe route into the mountains.

That thought brought on another wave of anger that Palom fought to master.

He couldn't let his rage consume him.

'The storm is getting too much! How far away is this damned dragon, Moroda?' Amarah yelled, holding her engine throttles as steady as she could.

Moroda walked around the deck, attention on the ereven sphere. 'It isn't exactly...clear. It's flashing more, though. It can't be too much further?'

Amarah snorted. 'I'm going to have to land soon or risk damaging *Khanna*! Not to mention I can't see a damned thing in this blizzard!'

Palom peered over the side of the ship, where snowdrifts

had built against the rocky mountainside. A flat plateau protruded from the rocks, and he pointed at it. 'Land there.' Part of the mountainside rose above it, providing some shelter. It wasn't perfect, but it would be better than trying to stay airborne in these winds.

He had to hope that Moroda's navigation with the mage's sphere was accurate.

Palom gripped the side rail more tightly as Amarah navigated *Khanna* into the hollow, wind and snow buffeting them every moment of the landing. There was a faint crackle of electricity in the air. One blast, then it was gone. 'Could be Arillians near,' he warned.

'Oh, please, no!' Moroda trembled.

Palom growled. 'If there is one, I will tear them apart.' He sheathed his sword, the power thrumming within a comfort in his grief, and disembarked. 'Moroda. Stay with me. I will pick out path up mountain. My senses are keener than yours.'

'Weapons ready. Eyes up. Any sudden movement could be an attack.' Amarah held her scythe and nodded to him.

At least the sky pirate was taking this seriously.

Moroda pulled her hood up, the fur framing her face, but there was a cold, deep fear that Palom smelled with every breath. 'I'm ready,' she said.

Palom didn't believe her, but dragons wouldn't wait, so he led them through the snow.

It was hard going. The ground was frozen solid and covered in a thick layer of snow, so he moved carefully, trying to remember the three following him were not Ittallan and could not see what he could. The sooner they found a dragon, the sooner he could hunt down Kohl. It was a deep-set rage that kept moving despite the unyielding sorrow.

Aciel had to be stopped, that much was true. But

between Princess Isa, Sapora, and their Imperial Guard, he was sure Taban Yul would be defended.

He needed revenge.

Anahrik's death. Eryn's death. They were on him. He should have been stronger, faster. Should have protected them against Kohl's treachery.

Around them, the blizzard raged, mirroring his emotions.

Perhaps he should wander out in the thick of a hurricane until he couldn't walk anymore...

'You doing alright, Ro?' Morgen asked, catching Palom's attention.

'Yes, thank you.' Her voice was quiet, but determined.

'Do you want to take a break? We can rest for a minute if you need—'

'I'm fine, Morgen. Really. It's easier to keep moving.'

'All right, just wanted to make sure...' Morgen stopped where he was, the steep path widening slightly, and waited for Amarah to catch up. 'Hopefully not long to go now. Dragons above, this is a hard walk!'

Palom was grateful Morgen was trying to lighten the mood, but he couldn't humour him with laughter. Not when his *meraki* felt so dark.

Snow fell thick and heavy, and strong winds threatened to push them over at any moment. Palom's feet grew colder with each step until they were numb.

Moroda trudged onwards, head down, following the sphere.

'Any shelter would be great about now.' Morgen limped behind, now bringing up the rear. His sword hung heavy at his hip, slowing his progress up the trail. The wounds he'd sustained in the battle against Jato's Arillians had yet to heal properly, and he struggled to stay balanced in the deep snow with one arm in a sling.

Palom halted, chin raised as he scoured the mountainous landscape. Wind brought freezing snow down in heavy waves, but there was a small gap a short way ahead, where the sheer rock face remained free of ice.

'There is break in storm,' Palom called back.

It was strange how the wind had died down enough for their visibility to clear, a small bubble protecting part of the mountain from the worst of the weather.

'There!' Moroda gasped. She clutched the ereven sphere in gloved hands. 'I think the dragon is there!'

Palom charged forwards, traversing up the steep slope in seconds. As he gained height and reached the break in the wind, he spotted a cave opening half-hidden on the side of the mountain.

'Palom! Wait! Might be dangerous!' Morgen shouted, but Palom ignored him.

If there was danger, better he face it first. Before anyone else got hurt.

Slipping on the icy slush outside the cave mouth, Palom gathered himself and hurried in—only to be accosted by a wall of intense heat. He blinked back the tears which suddenly formed and brought one arm up to protect his face from anything that might leap out at him.

Immediately following the wash of heat was the stench of blood.

And cold electricity.

There was no mistaking it. 'Kohl?'

Ahead, a battered and bloodied Arillian slumped against the cave wall, his feathers in disarray. His hat lay across his lap, sagging at the edges.

Palom roared, fangs lengthening as his *meraki* washed over him from nose to tail. The light of his transformation filled the cave, and he pounced the instant he could.

'Palom!' Moroda screamed from somewhere behind him.

He snarled, aiming for Kohl's throat. He'd tear it out. Ensure the Arillian had no chance of survival.

Before he'd crossed the distance across the cave, something enormous knocked him off his feet.

The blow forced breath from his lungs and sent him skidding back to the cave's entrance. He dug his claws into the dark rock, but there was too much ice. He fell, slamming his head on the ground. Dazed, it took him several seconds to get back to his feet. By that point, the other three had joined him inside.

He roared again, but couldn't see his aggressor. Kohl hadn't moved. Who was defending him?

Amarah raised her scythe to attack. 'Keep back!'

'No. *You* keep back. I will fight to my last breath.' A voice echoed around them, low and deep, like boulders grinding against each other

Palom's hackles raised as he readied to lunge again.

'Palom, look! It's the *dragon*!' Moroda gasped.

He cut his snarl short, but kept his muscles tense, ready to dart out of the way if he needed to. It took longer than he would have liked for his vision to adjust in the darkness, but when it did, he could hardly believe what he saw.

Moroda was right. An enormous dragon lay huddled in the darkness, tail looping around the cave's interior. The cave roof was too high to see, and he couldn't tell exactly how large the creature was, but it dwarfed the one that had attacked Niversai.

Moroda lowered her hood and dropped to her knees, the blue jewel on her ring twinkling.

'Archon, I am honoured and humbled to be in your presence.' She bowed.

Morgen sank to his knees beside her, and Amarah lowered her scythe slightly.

Palom let out a low growl, then transformed back. His *meraki* left him momentarily weakened, and he panted after all the exertion.

'Dragon! Why are you protecting traitor?' He was unable to comprehend the dragon's behaviour. 'I swore to kill him!' How dare someone—or something—stop that! He respected dragons, of course. They were powerful enough to demand it. And now one was keeping him from fulfilling his oath.

She could devour him whole, if she wished.

Or burn them alive where they stood.

The dragon moved, and he felt the shifting strength and heat, more than seeing its dark grey body move in the shadows. 'Ittallan, you do not harm this one.'

'I've been...trying to heal her...to *help* her,' Kohl whispered from the other side of the cave. 'Trying to keep her safe...with the blizzard outside.' He stumbled to the dragon's side, his own wounds fresh and bleeding. 'I made it to the cave...after the Arillian attacked me. I hid here. This dragon, she...she...has had her power taken by Aciel. I've done what I can...but I have nothing left.'

Palom shook. Kohl was *right there*. Weak and vulnerable. He'd have his revenge *now*. Anahrik and Eryn's deaths wouldn't be in vain.

'Her stone is gone. Aciel carries it...' Kohl coughed, his breathing ragged.

Palom held back his rage and took a closer look at the dragon. Her scales had to be grey or green—dark enough that she seemed a part of the shadows. Blood filled the air and had pooled on the cave floor. It took him another moment to realise the blood wasn't Kohl's.

It was the dragon's.

420

A gaping wound on her chest was the source of it, her scales bent back or torn out.

This was what had triggered the war in Linaria. Tipped the balance of power. Aciel had been stealing the power of dragons, and this one was one of his victims.

'That cannot be, she would be dead!' Moroda said, getting to her feet. 'If her stone is gone—'

'My power was stolen from me!' Steam vented from the dragon's nostrils and heated the air. 'I was tricked by an Arillian...'

'Aciel's compulsion?' Amarah gasped.

'Like the young dragon that attacked Niversai!' Morgen added.

Moroda tentatively approached the dragon, heedless of the danger.

'But...how can you be alive?'

'I was stronger than he thought. I am now...very weak. I have prolonged my death for countless days.' She breathed, a hissing growl filling the air at the motion. 'Hibernation has helped, but I cannot heal from this wound. It kills me slowly. But...I do not wish to die. So I hold on.'

The cave walls and floor rumbled, and Palom was suddenly very aware of the enormous strength the dragon possessed. She must have been ancient, to speak the common tongue. She could think and reason, and held intelligence far beyond the younger beasts.

'Aciel took your stone and left you to die, yet you live?' Moroda said, a hand to her mouth.

'Yes.' Slowly, the dragon shifted. Many of her scales were black with dried blood. 'I have no fire. I cannot fly. My residual power will move to the despicable, thieving Arillian when I die. I refuse to give him that...'

Anahrik meant too much to Palom for him to let Kohl get away with his betrayal. Anahrik had been the first one to

421

treat him as an equal when Palom had arrived in Taban Yul, instead of a tiger to be feared. They'd been rivals, at first, but Anahrik had seen an opportunity. Had thrown himself into the business idea, dragging Palom along with him.

They'd stuck together, like brothers, since those early days.

Always looking out for each other. Anahrik was responsible for figuring out the *Valta Forinja*!

Palom picked up the sword he'd dropped when he'd transformed, the power within burning as bright as Moroda's ring. He stepped closer to the Arillian and ignored the dragon, his attention focussed on the traitor in their midst. 'Kohl. You left them! *Left* them!'

Kohl shuddered, leaning against the dragon as the strength went in his legs. 'I do not deserve to live.'

'Then I shall kill you!'

'Do not touch this one.' Again, the dragon warned him with a snarl, heat rising from her nostrils.

Even in her weakened state, she was formidable.

'I have done such terrible things...' Kohl stammered. 'I should have...stayed and fought with you. But I could not fight her. I *could* not...'

'Because you fight for Aciel!' Palom roared, blue light licking up his blade as the *Valta Forinja* activated. It filled the cave with ethereal colour. 'Traitor!'

'No. No! I'd *never* fight for him.' Kohl shook his head, his wings fluttering from underneath his long cloak, loose feathers falling onto the cave floor. 'I am in exile...*because* of him.'

Palom shifted his stance.

'I do not believe you. If you do not fight for Aciel there is no reason for you to leave Anahrik and Eryn to *die*!'

Kohl's mouth hung open. Pain, shame, and anger warring on his face. 'They...?'

'You could have stopped this. You are responsible!'

'I...I did not know...' Kohl heaved, blood trickling from gashes on his arms. 'Killing one's own kin...is a shameful, abhorrent act. We Arillians are so few. But Aciel has permitted such deplorable behaviour. Those who disagreed, he has controlled. But it is against our laws, against...our beliefs.'

The dragon's ragged breathing filled the cave. Palom didn't care for Kohl's excuses, but he would let him speak his last words.

If anything, Moroda deserved an explanation.

Kohl continued,

'His compulsion has...changed our kind. For better or worse. Most are under his control. I am immune to his sorcery. But some, like Jato...believe in him and his words. *Truly* believe. I had hoped...I had prayed...that she was under his compulsion, too. But...But...'

'Kohl...?' Moroda asked, holding her ring tightly.

'For all...the terrible things...she has done. I cannot harm her. I *cannot* defend myself against her. If she had been...under his spell, perhaps I could have...I could have done something. Found some way to break his compulsion. To *free* her. But she is...she is...' He sobbed.

'Why couldn't you?' Moroda's voice was quieter than before, hardly above a whisper.

Kohl shook his head. 'She...she is my daughter.'

Shock ran through Palom at those words. His *daughter*?

That's why he'd been so reluctant when they'd found Jato's warship over the sea. That's why he'd left them.

Kohl was a broken soul.

Were the scars on his face from Aciel, too? Or his generals?

Palom tightened his grip on the *Valta Forinja*. There was

no excuse he would accept. Not when Anahrik had been killed due to Kohl's treachery.

Moroda put a hand on Palom's arm. Tears welled in her eyes. 'Please, Palom. Try to forgive Kohl...What would you have done if you were told to kill Anahrik?'

Palom growled, but said nothing. She couldn't honestly believe his words? Care for his struggles when her own sister had died?

But he considered her words.

Would Anahrik attack Kohl if Palom had been the one to die? Anahrik had stopped him from a rampage in Taban Yul. That was part of why they'd crossed the sea to Niversai.

He looked at Moroda, saw the pleading in her gaze. Dragons above, what was he supposed to do?

'I escaped the battle...barely,' Kohl continued. 'I sheltered here and found this dragon. I...I used my strength to create the blizzard...So Aciel and the others wouldn't find her...I do not think he...realises she lives. I knew you were looking for a dragon nearby. *This* is that dragon. I knew that if you found her, you could help her...It matters not what... happens to me. But you have a chance...you can...take back...Aciel's stolen power.'

Moroda squeezed his arm. 'Please, Palom.'

Palom thought of Lathri, his former lover. He thought of his niece, too. And his brother—long dead. People he'd wanted to help, to support and protect. People he'd had to leave.

How would he feel if they were on different sides?

Palom wanted to wrench away from her grasp and sever Kohl's head.

But with her pleading and the dragon a threat, he had to step back. He'd always told Anahrik off for acting rashly. For not thinking through his actions. He didn't want to do the same thing.

He turned away from Kohl and sheathed his sword. Fine. He'd spare Kohl for now. 'I do not forgive you for what you have done. You do *not* turn on friends. No matter the enemy. You are coward. Betrayer.'

'Palom,' Moroda whispered again.

'I will let you live for now. But when I next see you? When Aciel is no longer threat? When you do not have dragon here protecting you...?' Palom let the threat hang in the air.

It was all he could do to keep his grief at bay.

Morgen said, 'We need to carry on with our task. We *need* the dragon's help, don't we?'

Amarah twirled her scythe, allowing the blade to clatter loudly on the cold stone floor. 'Enough babble. This dragon is alive, but you say Aciel has her power. What do we do about that? If we could somehow return the dragon's power, wouldn't that weaken Aciel?'

Palom hated that they were dismissing everything Kohl had done.

But Amarah was right. Their priority was Aciel.

Moroda cautiously approached the dragon, gazing upon her scales and the deep wound she bore. 'Remember Aciel's cane, Amarah? The jewel on top? That must be *this* dragon's stone, where her power is held...' She slid her ring off her finger and held it up. It flashed blue in the darkness. 'What if...? No...'

'What are you thinking, Moroda?' Morgen asked.

'Her power is energy, isn't it...? That's what Topeko said in Berel? What if...what if we just *moved* her energy back? The way the mages move candles and flames?'

Amarah exhaled through her nose. 'That's a heck of a long way, Moroda. You're good with that magic, but...I dunno.'

'But it *is* the same thing as the candle, isn't it? Just

moving energy? From Aciel's stone back to this dragon here?'

Morgen shrugged. 'I didn't pay as much attention to Topeko as you did, but it sounds like what he said. What you gonna do? Move the energy into that ring of yours?'

Moroda smiled. 'Kohl, do you still have the stone from the drake? The one who attacked Niversai?'

Kohl put his hand in his cloak pocket and retrieved the small crystal.

The dragon hissed. 'Fallen brother.'

'There! I think...I think we could move the dragon's power into *this* stone. It would weaken Aciel, save the dragon's life, restore her strength...?' Moroda's voice wavered.

Amarah took the stone from Kohl none-too-gently. 'Up to you, Moroda. You're the one who understands all this Samolen stuff.'

The dragon spoke again, 'Rhea herself has kept me alive. Given me the strength to live on through pain and anguish. Perhaps this is the reason.'

Palom could hear desperation in the dragon's voice. If they saved her life, perhaps she could be persuaded to fight alongside them.

'What's to stop Aciel finding and killing more dragons, though?' Morgen asked.

'Us.' Amarah folded her arms. 'We already have his ereven sphere. We've taken his eyes, and now we take the heart of his power. When we fight, odds'll be in *our* favour.'

'There is chance to take main source of his power. Take the risk,' Palom said. Whatever his thoughts on Kohl, Moroda had the right of it. The mages in Berel had given him the knowledge to re-forge the *Valta Forinja*. Perhaps they'd given Moroda the knowledge for this.

'Moroda. What do you need us to do?' Amarah asked,

426

laying her scythe against the cave wall and rolling up her sleeves.

'Start a fire, provide light and warmth. This...may take some time.' Moroda shrugged out of her cloak and sat cross legged on the ground.

She took a deep breath, raised her hands, and began to work.

30

———

Moroda worked long into the night. While the fire crackled and the blizzard howled outside, the dragon seemed to sleep, closing her eyes and resting her jaw on her chest, motionless save for the steam rising from her nostrils.

Moroda had spent some time studying the dragon, amazed at how close she was to one of this age and power. The dragon's scales were dull green, but the bulk of her body lay hidden in shadow, her wings drooped lifelessly at her side.

Morgen had bound up the worst of Kohl's injuries, while Amarah and Palom kept watch at the cave's mouth. Moroda had never seen Palom so angry before, and the Ittallan kept his distance from Kohl. She hated conflict, but hoped he could forgive the Arillian for his betrayal.

Most of Kohl's strength was focussed on keeping the blizzard going—Aciel's scouts were unlikely to be found so high up, but no one wished to risk being discovered at such a critical time—which meant he did not respond to Palom's glares.

Moroda found the howling wind strangely comforting,

as though no one could pierce their bubble. She closed her eyes and focussed on her breathing. Her ring flashed several times, reacting to the dragon's presence, perhaps, as she tried to move energy from wherever Aciel was to the stone Kohl had given her.

It was just a matter of patience, she was sure.

While Palom and Morgen's thoughts on Kohl were clear —they were disgusted with the man—Moroda's feelings were more mixed. Sorrow and grief ruled, but she wasn't angry with Kohl. Not after finding out Jato was his daughter.

That explained so much about his nature. Why he'd been keen to avoid Jato's airship when they'd crossed the Sea of Nami. Why the other Arillians were against him. And why he'd refused to fight when Jato had ambushed them.

She was conflicted. But being angry at Kohl wouldn't bring Eryn back.

Neither would hurting him—or killing him—as Palom wished.

If anything, it would only make matters worse.

Seeing him trapped here, injured and in pain, using the last of his strength to defend the dragon, she couldn't help but feel for him. He'd been backed into a corner and done what he could to avoid hurting his family.

She could understand that, though she wished Eryn and Anahrik hadn't had to pay. 'Kohl?'

He looked up at the sound of his name, his pale grey eyes bright in the firelight.

Moroda said, 'I know you didn't want to...behave as you did. I know you didn't intend for anyone to be hurt.' She swallowed, thinking about her words and trying to hold back tears. 'Jato didn't stay. She went to report, and her other Arillians were the ones who attacked. You could have stayed, you know. I don't think she wanted to fight. She seemed more interested in getting back to Aciel.'

Kohl grimaced. 'She didn't attack you?'

'Not then, no. I guess we *will* see more of her, or Aciel, or the other Arillians before this war is finished. Maybe...you should stay close. We really need you with us.'

Palom let out a low growl, but she ignored it, her attention on Kohl.

They needed allies, and Kohl was an ally. She wasn't sure she could forgive him immediately, but she could accept he hadn't hurt her out of malice.

That was more than could be said for how Sapora had acted.

Kohl coughed again before answering. 'Surely you wish for me to die, Moroda? What I did was deplorable.'

She was shocked. 'No, of course I don't wish that. You dying would not...bring...Eryn back. Or Anahrik. If anything, I'd feel worse.'

'Moroda?' Morgen asked.

'I know you were fearful. We all were. If I had a pair of wings, I'd have flown away, too! But it was an awful situation you were in, one you tried to avoid,' Moroda said.

She wasn't sure what she was trying to say. Reassuring Kohl she didn't hate him? Telling herself that it had been a mistake?

Kohl took his hat off and held it over his chest, his scars clear in the firelight. 'You honour me, Moroda. I do not deserve your kindness.'

'Everyone deserves kindness.'

Morgen shook his head with a grunt.

Amarah said, 'Moroda. I've met a lot of people in my time but I can't say I've met anyone like you. I told you before and I'll tell you again: your nature will get you killed. Linaria ain't built for such soft hearts.'

'I don't know how to be any other way, Amarah. I'm doing the best I can. And I'm not afraid.'

Amarah laughed. 'You should be.'

Moroda cleared her throat. 'Well, I *am* afraid. But...but I feel more strongly about doing what's right, than what scares me.'

Being powerless was a level of discomfort she hated. And she was trying to do everything to avoid that feeling again.

Palom returned to his silent watch, and Moroda was happy to give him as much space as he needed to. He was more intimidating than ever before, even though his rage was directed at Kohl.

Moroda wanted to speak more with Kohl, to find out about Jato and what happened with Aciel to cause his exile, but she had no energy left for a deep conversation, not if the Samolen magic was to work.

She returned her attention to the stone, focussing on it. Feeling the energy and moving it like a cup of water. Like Topeko had said. Strange how a fun experience in Berel had turned into something so important.

Her mind wandered as she worked. Her companions were all doing what they thought would be best. Whether that was right or wrong.

Even Sapora, with his brutal violence, and Aciel, in his justification of his takeover.

She shuddered at the memory of the ball.

Shuddered at the memory of Aciel's compulsion taking over her. That was true powerlessness.

She thought of Eryn, and wished her sister could be with her now to offer comfort, conversation, and company. She thought back to her former home in Niversai, half a world away, and wondered what was left of the great city now that Rosecastle had fallen.

~

MORODA WOKE WITH A START, her cloak bundled up around her, and it took several moments before she remembered where she was.

Licking her lips, she yawned, piecing together what was real and what was a remnant from her dreams. A wave of sadness passed over her as she remembered Eryn's death, and she whimpered quietly.

Annoyed with herself at having fallen asleep, she sat upright, wincing as her muscles objected to the sudden movement. Sweat had matted her hair, sticking several strands to her forehead and cheeks. She ran her fingers through it, trying to clear her face, though her fingers were numb.

Tapping into her ring's power, she tried to sense the energy she'd been working on moving.

She'd found it easily enough. Aciel had certainly amassed the most amount of energy anywhere in Val Sharis, and she'd been slowly syphoning it off, a bit at a time, dragging it across to the stone in front of her.

She hadn't realised how long it would take to move so much power, nor how draining it would be.

Kohl and Morgen were asleep, their quiet snores filling the cave, and Amarah and Palom's backs were to her, so she couldn't tell whether they were awake.

Moroda returned her attention to the small crystal sitting in front of the fire.

Shuffling over to it, she stared down at the stone and reached forward with one hand. Again, her ring flashed bright blue, the light filling the cave.

Her vision blurred.

It wasn't done. She'd been working all night, and it still wasn't done!

Was she doing it correctly?

The energy was *there*, she could feel that. But had she

messed it up? Dragons above, what if she lost hold of it? And the energy dissipated? Was that possible? She'd have ruined the one chance to save the dragon's life!

She closed her eyes and cast her mind back to Berel. Imagined she was warm in the desert again, the sun beating down on the mage city. She'd loved that place. Wanted to visit the university, learn more from Topeko and the other mages. Had wanted to stay there, if she was honest with herself.

If only she'd had more time to learn!

A stiff breeze filled the room, gently pushing away the last of Kohl's frigid air. It was warm. Soft. Like a candle's flame.

Was this it? The last of the energy?

She exhaled slowly, trying to keep everything steady. In control.

She just needed to believe in the process. Believe in *herself*.

'Come on, Ro. You can do this...' Moroda whispered aloud, imagining Eryn was there, giving her support. Reassurance.

More heat. It tickled her skin, like someone drew a goose feather down her arm.

Then it *pinched* and flooded through her ring.

Tentatively, Moroda opened her eyes and stared down at the crystal—just as it began to glow. It was a bright, pinkish-purple, rich in hue, and shimmered in the firelight. She had not dared to hope it could truly be done, but the result was clear.

She stared at it for several long seconds, almost daring her hallucination to fade.

But it was there. Real. She'd moved the energy!

'Amarah! Palom!' Moroda gestured wildly.

'What's wrong?' Amarah was on her feet in an instant, scythe drawn.

'I've done it!' Moroda picked up the stone gingerly. 'It's warm!'

'You have?' Morgen got to his feet with a yawn and hurried over.

At her touch, the stone ignited and burned a bright, violent purple, flickering for a few seconds, before extinguishing itself.

'Reminds me of forging *Valta Forinja*,' Palom said, admiration evident in his tone. 'This is impressive, Moroda.'

With a low rumble, the dragon stirred, her eyes opening. 'You have done it. The Samolen taught you well, child.'

Moroda smiled at the stone. At her success.

She'd *taken* Aciel's power from him, and hadn't hurt anyone in the process.

'Kohl, you took this stone from my blood brother. You will now give it to me.' The dragon moved, shaking the cave with each step, her bulk dragging along the rocky walls.

Moroda stood up, excited and nervous, eager to see what would happen.

'We've saved a life!'

Kohl struggled to his feet, his movements stiff but determined. He took the stone from Moroda and made his way to the dragon's side. The cave rumbled with her breath and growl, a dormant power that set everyone on edge.

Moroda shivered.

This was myth and gods, magic beyond her understanding. After seeing the damage the young dragon had caused to her city, saving this one's life didn't seem like the best thing to do.

But she was sure it was the *right* thing to do.

And it would help put a stop to Aciel. Help peace come to Linaria.

434

Beside her, Amarah, Palom, and Morgen watched intently. Amarah's grip on her scythe tightened, and a tiny blue flame licked the edge of her blade.

Another rumble from the dragon. 'Do not think I have not noticed those weapons. They carry the spirit of a Sevastos. You paid no price for access to that power.' Her voice came out as a hiss, and Palom's gaze darkened. 'Actions are never without consequence.'

Moroda wasn't sure what the dragon meant, but Kohl was by her side, the gleaming stone clutched in both hands.

'Quickly, Arillian,' the dragon demanded.

Moroda didn't know if the energy would stream out of the stone, whether or not they needed to act quickly. 'Kohl?'

Everyone was tense, every breath held. Only the remains of their small fire made any noise, crackling and spitting.

Kohl plunged the stone into the dragon's chest.

The dragon's roar shook the cave, her primal bellow a fearsome sound, made more terrifying by the sudden flames she released from her gaping jaws—straight through the cave mouth and into the blizzard outside.

Immediately, the dull scales on her back shifted to bright, coppery-green, her horns thickened and darkened —rich black instead of the dirty grey they had been. And her eyes—before a pale yellow—were now vivid gold, flecked with red and chips of silver, burning brightest of all.

The scar on her chest was pronounced, bright red and sore, but it was clear that her strength had been restored. She was no longer a shadow of a dragon, but a godlike creature and apex predator of flame and claw. Muscles shifted under her scales as she tested her limbs, claws digging deep gouges in the cave floor.

'Moroda. You have restored the balance that Aciel took.' She let out another hiss once the intensity of the fire had passed. Her voice had taken on a new tone, the timbre stronger.

Finding herself under the weight of that gaze set Moroda's nerves prickling. She trembled under it, but held the dragon's stare. 'No matter how many dragons he has killed, it would never compare to that of an elder such as you.'

The dragon growled, a low rumble she felt in her bones. Moroda dropped to her knees again and lowered her head.

'I thank you.' The dragon returned Moroda's bow. 'Arillian. Lower your blizzard. I wish to fly.'

'Wait a second. The battle ain't over yet.' Amarah helped Moroda back to her feet. 'Aciel's gonna be furious when he realises his power's mostly gone. Wouldn't surprise me if this speeds up his attack on Taban Yul. You gonna help us with that?'

Moroda's breaths were shaky. She couldn't fault Amarah for getting directly to the point, though it wasn't how *she'd* have asked a dragon for a favour.

'Meddle in your affairs?' More steam vented from the dragon's nostrils.

'Aciel meddled in yours! This would help...get revenge?' Morgen added.

'I care not. My power is back. Nothing else is important.'

'Please, Archon.' Moroda used the honorific. 'Returning your power was the first step. Won't you help us save Linaria from Aciel? We have crossed the *world* looking for you.'

Smoke continued to pour from the elder's nostrils as she considered Moroda's words. 'You do not bargain with your gods, Moroda. All dragons are linked. We know when hatchlings emerge from their eggs and when others die. We feel nothing but pain from the deaths of dragons slaughtered in pursuit of power. Many of our number have turned on your towns and cities in revenge. I am more likely to join them than you.'

'This destruction isn't needed! It's *Aciel* who needs to be stopped! Then peace can return!' Moroda cried, heart thudding.

The elder ruffled her folded wings in irritation. 'That, I cannot help you with.'

'If you're afraid Aciel will injure you again, don't be! We'll be on your side. We'll have an entire airship fleet! Warships to fill the skies!' Morgen stepped forward.

'I am *not* afraid.' When the dragon spoke, fire blazed between her teeth.

'We saved your life and you ain't gonna help us?' Amarah said.

The dragon snorted once more, then barged past the group. 'My power is returned, and I must see to clearing the skies of Aciel's filth.' Saying no more, she exited the cave in one swift leap, extended her wings and was lost to the sky.

'Archon! Wait!' Moroda called, her voice hoarse, but her words fell on deaf ears. She walked out of the cave and stood by the entrance. The snow was deep all around them from Kohl's blizzard, but the skies were clear and the morning was bright. 'All that work...everything...for...for *nothing*?'

'Always agree the terms of the deal *before* you do the work.' Amarah ran a hand through her hair. 'Of course I've never done a deal with a dragon. Guess if they don't like you they can just bite your head off.'

'What...do we do now?' Morgen sank to his knees, the snow crunching under him.

'We cannot rely on others. We fight alone in this.' Palom stalked ahead, dark as thunder.

'Nothing we can do. We can run, but I don't see that happening. Aciel's been weakened. Might be closer to a fair fight now, so we go back to Taban Yul and prepare,' Amarah said.

'The dragon...She...' Moroda whimpered. She couldn't

believe how callous the dragon had been. Kohl had helped protect her. *She* had restored her power.

And the dragon didn't care.

Kohl joined them by the mouth of the cave.

'She is starved. Wounded, pride and body. Beaten to an inch of her life and left to rot in a cave on a mountainside for weeks if not months. I am not surprised she left.'

Moroda sat down on a small rock that protruded from the snow. 'I miss you so much, Ryn. If only you were here with us, you'd come up with a plan.' She didn't care what the others thought of her. She missed her sister. She wasn't going to hide that.

She drew her knees up to her chest and rested her chin on them. Without Kohl's blizzard, she could see down into the valley where Taban Yul lay ahead. She sniffed and wiped her nose on her sleeve.

Then, movement caught her eye. Far to the south, a dark smudge moved slowly over the land like a group of ants. 'What's that?'

'Oh shit.' Amarah walked over to her, gaze locked on the horizon. 'That's not good. Shit, that's *not* good!'

Moroda stood up quickly, her legs and knees protesting. 'What is it?'

'Army,' Palom said. He lifted his chin. 'Airships in sky, too.'

'You can see that from here?' Amarah asked.

He nodded, frowning. 'I do not think is reinforcements for Princess Isa.'

'Aciel?' Moroda asked.

Their silence was answer enough.

'But, what about the dragon? Shouldn't we wait for her to return?' Morgen suggested.

Kohl stood beside them, his wings spread to keep him

438

standing straight. 'You can wait. But she may not be back for days.'

'There is no time. We must return to palace. Now,' Palom said.

Moroda sighed. She was mentally and physically exhausted, and wasn't sure how much longer she'd have to endure the crushing sense of defeat and dismissal.

They gathered up their supplies and made their way down the clear mountain path as quickly as they could. Dread rising in her gut, Moroda looked up into the bright morning sky.

Overhead, lesser dragons circled.

31

B lood trickled down Sapora's arm, but it was not his own.

When he won these fights, he'd not only be able to claim the crown of his people, he'd also prove himself worthy in the eyes of his father.

He just needed to survive. *Endure.*

The bear that had once stood tall and formidable now lay gasping on the edge of the pit, its throat slashed open. As it died, it transformed back in a burst of light, throwing the rest of the pit into harsh focus. Sapora paid the Ittallan no mind—the Gila was already lumbering towards him.

At six feet long, it left deep trenches in the muddy ground with every step. His opponent weighed a fair amount, and what it lacked in speed, it no doubt made up for in power.

He widened his stance, bracing himself, when from the pit's other side, the giant monitor lizard trundled forward, too. The lizard was more than twice the size of the Gila, its bulk shaking the pit as it moved.

Both flicked out their long forked tongues.

Sapora gripped his scimitars, planned his next move.

The thick hide of the lizards would render his weapons ineffective, and if he was caught by one, he'd be finished off before he could fight back.

He had to be cautious here, try to—

The monitor lizard charged at him.

Sapora darted back reflexively, using his speed to get him out of trouble before the monitor's attack could connect. He heard jeers above him as the onlookers voiced their excitement and annoyance, but drowned it out.

The Gila lunged—its flat, wide head suddenly at his torso.

Sapora slashed down with one blade, deterring it more than harming it, and leapt back again. His feet were slow on the soft, damp earth, and he cursed Tacio for making him fight in the smaller pit.

Behind him, the monitor hissed, and he whirled round and stabbed at its nose.

Another glancing blow.

But he overreached, and the great lizard opened its jaws and clamped down on his exposed wrist.

Sapora dropped his blade at once and brought his other hand round, plunging the scimitar deep in the soft flesh of the monitor's ear, just behind its face. The great lizard roared and released his wrist, toppling over with a furious crash.

Sapora darted forward to pick up his dropped blade, and lost his footing on the sticky ground.

He landed face-first in the dirt.

The Gila was on him in moments, pinning him with its weight, jaws open as it bit down.

Sapora lifted a knee, digging it into the Gila's softer belly, while he held its throat away with his good hand. He grimaced as drool spilled from the creature's open mouth, laden with venom, but he was unable to push it off or attack with his wrist bleeding.

The stench of the creature made it hard to focus, but he would not let the Gila—no, *Tacio*—beat him.

He had first claim to the Jade Crown and he would *not* give his brother the delight of seeing him ripped apart by an Ittallan. It would prove Sapora had been too weak to rule.

And he wouldn't let that happen.

Sniggering rippled through the crowd, fuelling his anger. With a hiss, Sapora transformed.

'He is a true *Naja*, father,' Tacio said. 'Even has your markings, see? On the front of the hood?'

Sapora's senses heightened in this form, and his brother's voice carried easily enough. He tried to ignore it and coiled his body around his opponent, shutting down any counterattack.

'Taking him a while, though.'

'Hush, Tacio. This is his chance. Your time will come in due course.' Vasil's admonishment was immediate.

The crowd grew in size and noise as more and more Varkain approached the edge of the pit, all calling down insults or praise. It was a distraction more than anything else, and Sapora let out a hiss of frustration. His

coils covered the Gila's mouth, forcing it shut. He smothered the Ittallan and squeezed, cutting off the air to the Gila, and suffocating it.

'He is doing well. I know you cannot bear to admit that,' Vasil said.

'We'll see. Three more rounds to go. Great numbers always break them.'

Sapora couldn't help but smirk at Vasil's words. Whatever his father had thought of him before was rapidly changing. Sapora hoped the same would be true of his people. The other Varkain had always looked down upon him with a mixture of disdain and pity.

These trials would change that for good.

He risked a glance up, saw Tacio staring down, glum acceptance on his face.

Or was his brother simply waiting for him to fail?

Sapora turned away quickly, biting down on the emotions that threatened to rise. He couldn't afford to be distracted. He'd show his brother he was good enough. Just as he'd show his father.

He'd show them all.

Sapora waited until the strength of the flailing Gila weakened. When it went limp, he released it.

Before its body hit the floor, a gate opened from the pit's far side. Men and women poured out—a mixture of ages and in various forms of dress. Some had armour, some had weapons, some had shields.

Most were dressed in rags.

Thralls.

Sapora narrowed his eyes and faced the new threat.

CORPSES LITTERED the pit and the ground swam with blood.

Sapora had lost one scimitar, buried too deep in the skull of a thrall to remove in the intensity of battle, but his other was strong enough to see him through the last two rounds of his final test.

There was no food or water between bouts, no resting or chances to re-arm himself.

This was a brutal fight to survive, a fight to claim his crown.

Sapora's wrist throbbed from the earlier monitor's bite,

and he bore wounds of the fighting he had endured, but he remained on his feet, determined.

Another Ittallan stepped forward, an older man with white hair and a crooked back. Chains dangled from metal cuffs around his wrists, and his robe was caked in years of grime and dirt.

Sapora narrowed his eyes, wondering how a thrall had lived to such an age in the bowels of Sereth.

He did not wish to transform any more than was necessary, and readjusted his grip on his scimitar.

Opposite, the Ittallan picked his way past dead bodies and pools of blood. He was engulfed in light as he transformed, and Sapora snorted as an eagle, almost seven feet tall, stood before him. His wings were ripped, feathers torn from the bone, but the talons on his feet were easily as long as Sapora's own weapon. In contrast to his white feathers, the eagle's beak and eyes were coal black and piercing.

Sapora raised his scimitar as the eagle lashed out with talons extended; four huge blades on each foot. He danced around the eagle as much as he could, but with the pit getting full, the ground soft underfoot, and the injuries he had sustained, he could not move with the speed of the earlier battles. Fatigue was taking hold.

The eagle's beak was also deadly—it was hooked to pierce and tear through flesh, and it nicked Sapora several times as he continued to move around his enemy.

He jabbed at the eagle with his blade, but was deflected and thrown away by the strength of its beak, and it forced him into a corner of the pit.

The crowd's chanting and cheering was louder here than in the centre of the battlefield, and Sapora heard their disdain for him.

'How could he, a mixed-blood bastard, ever hope to survive the trials?'

'It should be Tacio down there.'

'Vasil should rule another two years.'

'Send the half-blood back to Val Sharis!'

The eagle struck, the force of its attack shoving Sapora into the wall with a crunch. Its talons tore through his coat, but missed his flesh, and Sapora pressed himself flat to avoid another strike.

The jeers grew louder.

He switched his hold on his scimitar into a reverse-grip for more power. He kept control of his breathing and watched the eagle's every move. All he needed was an opening and—

Sapora pounced, reaching past the bird's neck and drawing his blade down the length of it. There was a brief moment of resistance, then feathers and flesh gave way.

When he came to a stop a moment later, time stilled around him. He used his incredible speed for strikes more than anything, but he could also use those same muscles to move faster than most could blink.

And he was faster than the eagle could strike.

The Ittallan fell to the ground in a heap, its head severed.

The booing above turned to cheers, and Sapora straightened, panting heavily.

One round to go.

He stared at his brother. 'Tacio. Prepare my crown. I'm ready for it.'

'Don't be so sure of yourself, Sapora. The best is yet to come!' Tacio called back in his lazy tone.

But Sapora was certain Tacio's voice had wavered. Perhaps in fear or disbelief.

Either was good.

At his brother's words, his final opponent fell into the pit

445

from above, shaking the ground and dislodging loose rocks and chunks of dirt from the pit's walls.

Sapora stepped back, getting the measure of his new target, and grimaced.

It was a Varkain, one of the old guard—a constrictor with dark coils thicker than tree trunks, almost double the length of Sapora's transformed state.

Another faceless, nameless opponent.

Another life to be taken.

Sapora was expected to transform, too. To face his opponent as true Varkain to true Varkain. Sereth had little need of the old guard these days, but they were brutal fighters, the strongest of all Varkain castes.

Defeating one was always the final challenge for any new ruler wishing to take the Jade Crown.

At least this was the last thing he had to overcome.

Sapora stepped to the side, moving constantly so he'd be harder to hit. Without his venom, he'd be crushed if he transformed. So he had to show them what he was truly capable of.

It was the only way to silence his doubters.

Fuelled by adrenaline, Sapora darted forward and slashed at the huge snake. His scimitar was well-made and sharp, even after so much heavy use, but against the enormous snake's hardened scales, he might as well have used a butter knife.

Thankfully the constrictor, while enormous, did not have the speed of a Cerastes or Naja, and Sapora managed to evade the few strikes it attempted. It battered him with its body, blocking off an attack or forcing him away.

Sapora heard the whispers above him, tried to ignore their words, but failed. They expected him to wear down his opponent, getting in an attack here or there, turning it into a battle of stamina more than skill.

But Sapora wanted to shock them, to prove that he was a worthy ruler. That he was not just his father's son, but *greater*.

With one hand limp from the bite, Sapora inhaled sharply.

The snake took up most of the pit, its bulky form pushing away bodies to create the space it needed to move freely. It hissed, golden eyes burning like embers.

It was now or never.

Sapora shot forward, expending all his remaining energy in a final burst of speed.

The huge snake shifted, moving its coils and slamming its body towards him.

Sapora leapt over the first coil and landed heavily on another. Using his clawed hands to grip scales, he clambered up the snake's body, darting higher and higher as his enemy writhed and shook, trying to fling him to the ground like a wild auroch.

He slipped once, digging the tip of his scimitar in between two scales to maintain his grip, then darted forward in another burst of striking speed, until he crouched on the top of the constrictor's enormous head.

Sapora plunged his scimitar through its skull, right to the hilt.

Blood erupted like a fountain, dark and sticky, and the snake howled in pain. The shriek burned his ears, and he toppled to the ground as it collapsed, body violently spasming.

Something roared around him, and Sapora staggered to his feet, wondering what he had to face *now*. It took him several seconds to realise it was the crowd cheering.

They were *chanting* his name.

Emotions he'd never quite felt before rushed into him, giving him renewed strength. Pride was there, the most familiar. But there was a sense of gratitude he hadn't experienced in a long time. And shock that he'd *actually succeeded*.

Sapora scanned the crowd, spotted Tacio, Vasil, and Savra, their expressions unreadable.

'Well fought, brother.' Tacio clapped slowly. 'Well fought.'

Sapora gritted his teeth against the pain from exerting so much energy, and made his way across the pit. He couldn't put his full weight on one leg, but tried to hide the limp as best he could. He retrieved both scimitars from his fallen foes, wiped them clean, then pulled himself up the side of the pit and into the open cavern.

Blood dripped down both arms and part of his torso where his tunic had been ripped open, but the smile he wore was nothing short of triumphant.

He'd done it. Survived the trials. Defeated every opponent. Killed one of the old guard without transforming.

In Val Sharis, he'd needed to attack those who opposed him. Fear was the only way to get through to those pompous Ittallan.

But in Sereth, he'd needed to prove his strength before they would allow him to rule.

And he had.

Tacio dropped to one knee, as did Savra and the Cerastes beside them. The other Varkain gathered also followed suit, a ripple of motion across the gathered bodies.

Sapora blinked slowly and took several deep breaths to steady his emotions.

No one would begrudge his rapidly beating heart, not after what he'd just done, but the urge to hide himself from so much predatory attention was hard to ignore. Especially in front of his father.

Vasil stared hard at him, and Sapora did not flinch from his father's gaze.

After several long seconds, Vasil turned away and raised his hands to address those gathered. 'My subjects in Timin Rah! Varkain gathered here from all reaches of Sereth. You have witnessed the trials. You have seen the strength my son holds.'

Sapora's mouth went dry. His father was really saying the words.

He was about to be crowned.

He'd envisioned this day for so long, the reality felt like a dream.

There was no pomp and ceremony like in Val Sharis. No formal dresses, no feasts. There were no peacocks trying to gain favour with the new leader.

It was simple. Primal. One ruler acceding to the next. Blood and death. That was all.

There wasn't even a Valendrin present.

Vasil removed the circlet of gold from his head. In the low light of the tunnels, the jade jewels glistened, and Sapora's breath hitched.

'You are in witness of the passing of sovereignty to my son. Sapora, Crown Prince of Sereth and Val Sharis, will be the ruler of these lands and protector of the Varkain now his errantry is complete. His worth has been proven in our trials. By blood, he will honour his crown.'

Vasil stepped closer to Sapora, the circlet held delicately between his claws.

Sapora dropped to one knee before his father. The last time he would ever have to bow to him.

To anyone.

Their eyes met as Vasil placed the crown on Sapora's head, and his father nodded.

Vasil didn't smile.

Sapora knew the words. Had memorised them years ago. He exhaled slowly, ensuring his voice did not waver. 'I receive the Jade Crown, symbol of my people, and all the powers and holdings that come with it. My father Vasil shall remain an advisor to me, as will my brother Tacio, and sister Isa, as our world is in the midst of war. This shall remain so, until such time as I have no need for counsel. You are all witnesses.'

Sapora stood up to an eruption of hissing, applause, and cheering. He rose as the new king.

And he had work to do.

'To the keep. I wish to dine.'

He brushed past Vasil and Savra as they kneeled, and stopped by Tacio, who remained mid-bow. He assessed his brother for a moment. 'Put your hatred of me to one side and we Varkain *will* come out of this better off.'

Sapora continued up the overhanging cliff and into his new home.

32

Two days passed in a blur of stress and sorrow. Palom and Morgen had both spent time with Moroda individually, offering condolences and kind words. Even Amarah had invited her aboard *Khanna* on another tour, and explained the finer points of how *Khanna* functioned. Moroda appreciated it all. Amarah had known Moroda had expressed interest in flying, and showed her compassion in her own way.

Palom and Morgen, too, had offered whatever kindness and generosity they could.

She was alone without Eryn, but she didn't feel it as much with her friends there.

On the third day, Moroda awakened to the sound of armoured feet charging up and down the corridor outside her room. Thunder roared outside, shaking the walls and making the palace tremble.

She raced to the window and peered out. It was light outside, but thunderclouds gathered ominously above the city. Ripples of sheet lightning streamed across the sky, and as they lit up the clouds, warships descended.

Her heart pounded.

This was it.

Aciel was here, with all his strength.

The Council had sent Ittallan scouts to Corhaven in the hopes of bringing back reinforcements, but with the recent fall of Niversai, Isa did not have high hopes they'd be back in time.

There were few cities large enough in Corhaven to have enough soldiers to aid Val Sharis, and many of those would be focussed on restoring the country's capital.

It was simply too little too late.

One thing was to be said for the Arillians—once they sacked a city, they immediately moved on to the next one. No hostages were taken, but they left few alive.

Only those who went deep into hiding survived; everyone who fought back had been killed or compelled to join Aciel's growing infantry. Latest reports stated it was over 30,000 strong.

Moroda had toyed multiple times with the idea of returning to Niversai. It would have been easy to get there on one of the Ittallan scouting ships—Isa would have facilitated it, she was sure—but the thought of returning to a blackened city under siege scared her more than she realised. She did not know, after losing her sister, whether she would be able to stomach returning to a home that may not even be there.

All this time, she'd fought her sister tooth and nail about returning. Now, Eryn was gone.

Even if she *did* return to Niversai, her guilt would be great. If she'd listened to Eryn and they'd returned, perhaps her sister would still be alive.

Too many lives had been lost in this war, and she did not wish to see more. In Niversai, there would be people she knew.

It was all too much to face alone.

She wished Topeko was there to guide her in the short time they had before the battle. His knowledge would have been invaluable, but all she could do was pore over the tomes she carried and practice with her magic.

The weapons Palom had created and gifted them were incredible. Even Amarah was stunned into silence by their abilities. Not only could the weapons slice through almost anything, but they were able to send out a wave of power, causing significant damage.

Moroda didn't like them.

Aside from preferring to prevent damage than cause it, the distinctive blue flames they emitted reminded her of the last time she'd seen Eryn. It was chaos and destruction and death, and it made her nauseous. Even the dragon in the mountain had warned Palom against using them.

She quickly dressed, then pulled on her thick travelling cloak and hurried down the corridor, following the Imperial Guard as they raced along.

'Get outta the way, you cowards!'

As Moroda rounded a corner leading to one of the large reception halls, Amarah's savage words reached her. Of everyone she had come across in Taban Yul, none rivalled the sky pirate for uncouth language and behaviour.

'I wanna get on my warship to defend *your* damned city! Stand aside!'

Moroda saw Morgen beneath an archway, watching Amarah battle against a small crowd of Imperial Guards who blocked access to the passageway leading to the hangar.

'Lady Amarah, the warship belongs to the princess. We cannot just *let* you on board,' one pleaded, his brow covered with sweat as he battled with the sky pirate.

'I don't care what you think! It's *my* ship! Now *move!*' Amarah bellowed, drawing her scythe along the marble floor and sending sparks up the blade.

Morgen approached the group, his helm under one arm, Palom and Kohl several paces behind. He wore a full suit of armour, polished and gleaming under the chandeliers. 'I have orders from Princess Isa.'

Hearing his words, the Imperial Guards lowered their weapons. 'Sir, are you certain?'

'I heard it from the princess herself. Moroda, Palom, Kohl, and I are accompanying Amarah on board.' He held up an onyx stone, and the guards backed away.

'Yes sir. Apologies Lady Amarah.' The guard moved out of the way and nodded curtly to the group.

Amarah scoffed at the niceties and brushed past them.

Morgen waited until they'd marched off, then followed Amarah. 'You're really going to fight?'

'What a question.' She tapped her blade on the floor every few steps, the sound echoing off the marble. 'I'm not about to let these Arillians destroy my best chances of riches.'

Moroda wondered whether the riches Amarah hoped she would earn was worth the risk. But she knew the sky pirate would not fight unless she was confident of victory. That was reassuring.

'I will be fighting too.' Kohl glided down from a stairway to their left, sending out a cool breeze as he landed.

'I thought you didn't fight your kin?' Amarah asked, balancing her scythe on her shoulder.

'Aciel is different.'

'How do we know you will not turn tail and run like you did before?' Palom asked. 'Or attack *us*? If Jato appears? Once a liar, always a liar.'

'I've never lied to you...'

'Please, Palom,' Moroda said. 'Aciel is at our doorstep! If Kohl said he'll help, let him.'

In truth, she was also worried about the relationship

between Kohl and Jato. But despite the odds, she trusted him. She *had* to trust him.

If she didn't, she'd be no better than Palom's outrage.

'You don't have to fight, Moroda,' Morgen said, as the group entered the hangar. Airships of all sizes floated either side of them, the hangar a flurry of activity as pilots, crews, and soldiers scrambled aboard their designated vessels. Palace stewards attempted to direct events amidst the chaos.

Moroda pressed a finger to her ring. 'I don't want to stand by and do nothing. I'll fight with you all.'

She hurried along, the intensity of the storm outside rattling the entire hangar. Orders were barked, engines were started, propellers turned, and the wind picked up as half a dozen ships took to their air. They were large and ungainly, heavy with ammunition.

The ships were barely out of the hangar before cannon fire could be heard, with smoke billowing back inside from immediate impact.

Coupled with the heat and steam rising from the many engines, Moroda found herself sweating before she was even on board Amarah's new warship.

'I won't lie, I'm more used to running from a fight than charging into it. But this ship has enough power to hold its own, and I've no plans on going down.' Amarah announced, striding along the wide upper deck. '*Khanna* is below deck, nice and safe in the cargo bay.'

Moroda thought back to Amarah's words on fleeing from battle and wondered why *Khanna* had to come along, too.

Would she run, if everything seemed lost?

Amarah cracked her knuckles, forced the ship's engines into life, and raised the sails as they took off. 'Palom, Morgen, get the cannons ready—pull every hatch open, load every gun, and get them into position! Moroda, come up here with me.' She turned the wheel sharply to starboard as she manoeuvred around other docked ships towards the wide hangar entrance, and the dark sky beyond.

Moroda made her way into the large cabin where Amarah steered. It was surrounded on all sides by thick glass housed in wooden frames. The ship was definitely built to last.

'Fighting is coming, you know that,' Amarah said, keeping her eyes focussed on the sky as it opened out in front of them.

'I know.'

'I'm a better fighter than you. Years more experience. I need you to keep this ship out of harm's way while the rest of us fight. Cannons are at your control. You remember what I told you about flying *Khanna*, right?'

Moroda's eyes widened as she realised what was being asked of her. 'I...remember...but I should, shouldn't I...The Samolen magic—'

'You're no Topeko. Dragons above, we could do with his help now. *If* he could even be convinced to fight. We've more chance of pulling through if you stay outta the way and keep us near the action. Not too close. Weapons panels are here.' Amarah lifted a flap to the right of the large, spoked wheel, 'And here.'

There were eight small levers in each.

'We have to load them manually, but all control on shooting them is in this cabin.'

'But...I...'

'We don't have time!' Amarah pushed the engine to full thrust, avoiding a surge of lightning—an attack from one of the hundreds of Arillians who filled the sky above Taban Yul.

Flipping another lever to pull back the nose, Amarah turned the ship again and opened fire with the main cannon, just as a cloud of black smoke rose from the hull.

'Amarah they're swarming the deck!' Morgen cried.

'Dammit! Moroda keep this thing in the sky!' Amarah charged, swinging her scythe to fend off their aggressors. It glowed at Amarah's touch, sending out dazzling blue fire with every movement.

Moroda had no choice but to lurch forward and grab hold of the wheel, her palms slick with sweat. Her heart pounded as fear threatened to take hold once again, and she cast her gaze above her, peering through the thick glass which ceilinged the cabin.

Perhaps two hundred Arillians swarmed overhead, the wind of their attacks tearing into every warship in the air, the clouds thick with electricity, which whipped up Moroda's hair.

There were fifty or so warships in the air already, and countless smaller airships unsuited for battle. It was a formidable sight, though Moroda worried it would not be enough against Aciel's entire army.

They would be overrun.

Claps of thunder rolled through the sky, crushing smaller airships as they were overwhelmed by Arillians.

Spinning the wheel and pushing forward, Moroda tried to position the ship away from the thick of the fighting, as Amarah had told her. Though very much on the side of the Ittallan, Amarah's warship was not garbed in Imperial colours, which, she supposed, made it less of a target.

When she heard the clash of steel quieten, she ran to the edge of the cabin and out on deck.

'Well fought.' Morgen panted, lowering his sword as the last of the Arillians flew off, leaving the deck scalded, but intact. His sword glowed soft blue, almost green, and smoked slightly now the fighting had stopped.

'Where's Kohl?' Palom growled, staring at the clouds. 'Can't tell him apart from Arillians up there.'

Amarah raced back into the cabin. 'Good move! Keep us out of danger. We'll pick off whichever stragglers we can. Looks like the fighting is moving to the valley outside Taban Yul. Least the city itself shouldn't be too badly damaged.' She patted Moroda on the shoulder and took stock of the battle as it unfolded around them.

Moroda and Amarah spotted a small cluster of Arillians at the same time. They were diving towards another warship some distance across from them. Amarah grinned, manic. 'I don't think so! I'm gonna blast you outta the sky!' She flattened one sail and pulled at another, swinging the ship around to face the group with its broadside.

It groaned under its own weight, but she held firm and pushed the throttles up. When they were in her sights, she flicked two switches and fired twin cannons.

The warship jolted with their launch, and Moroda struggled to keep her footing. She watched the two, long grey shapes shoot out of the side of the ship somewhere below deck, a thick plume of brown-grey smoke following in their wake as they careened towards the Arillians.

The resulting explosion sent a shockwave in all directions, fire and smoke billowing to join the fracas.

'Keep us moving, Ro!' Amarah said, as the attack drew the eyes of surrounding Arillians to them. She raced back out, scythe in hand, to aid Palom and Morgen with the incoming attacks.

Moroda couldn't bring herself to fire on the Arillians—they were just following orders, likely under Aciel's compulsion—and busied herself with moving the ship out of harm's way each time they were assaulted by another wave of attacks.

Guilt wracked her at the suffering and death. She didn't want to do *nothing*, but fighting went against her nature.

How many people out there had brothers and sisters? Wives and husbands? Friends and relatives?

Arillians fell like flies, and three airships had already gone down in smoke. On the ground, troops charged forward, clashing with Aciel's followers, staining the valley with blood. Overhead, lightning crackled across the sky, and below, fires raged, sending up black smoke.

Moroda lost all sense of time.

In the chaos, she saw Palom transform into the stronger, fiercer version of himself; taking out those Arillians who had been foolish enough to land on deck with devastating swipes of his huge paws.

Morgen and Amarah were also able to fend off their attackers with their *Valta Forinja*. In the thick smoke, the weapons glowed, and her own ring flashed brightly.

They fought viciously, and it didn't take long for them to clear the skies around the ship. Arillians quickly learned to keep their distance—out of range of the *Valta Forinja* strikes.

Moroda continued to move the ship around the sky, keeping to the edges of the battlefield, trying to stay away from the thick of the fighting. Visibility dropped as minutes flew by. Cannons were fired so often from so many ships, and claps of thunder rattled so intensely that Moroda could no longer distinguish between one blast and the next.

The only thing which seemed unchanging was the glow of her friends fighting on deck with their dragon-forged weapons.

Although they had taken back much of Aciel's power, and had the *Valta Forinja* at their fingertips, they were outnumbered ten to one.

She trembled, watching as one by one, warriors fell from the skies to their deaths.

It had to stop.

It *had* to, else they would all destroy each other.

Unless the tide of battle was turned, everything would perish.

As strong and skilled as Amarah, Palom, Morgen, and Kohl were, they could not fight on indefinitely.

More tears formed as she realised they were all who remained from the original group in Corhaven, barring Sapora.

She had lost her sister.

Palom had lost a brother.

They had all lost friends.

Aciel had amassed too much power, too many followers, and his goal was the eradication of all non-Arillians. How were you supposed to fight something like that?

Talking wouldn't help; none of them would listen. None of them would stop.

There *had* to be another way. There had to be a way to protect those who remained from perishing.

'If I don't do anything, we'll all perish. But if I do *something*...there's a chance it may end. I must, *must* take that chance. That's what Ryn would have wanted...' Moroda said aloud, her fingers slipping from the wheel.

Looking out to the deck, she could barely see the glow from their weapons, the smoke and ash was so thick. Guilt flashed through her briefly at what she was about to do, then it was gone.

She had to speak with the dragon again. *Convince* her to help.

There was no other way.

Decision made, Moroda pressed another switch on the control panel to lock the sails in place, and found herself running away from the cabin before her mind realised she had come to the conclusion.

In a daze, she made her way down into the depths of the warship, past the loaded guns, past the steaming engines, past the supply storage, and into the cramped cargo bay where *Khanna* lay resting.

With a final breath to steel her determination, she released the hatch holding the cargo doors shut, and clambered aboard Amarah's thief ship. After so long travelling on *Khanna*, the ship was as familiar to her as her ring. Moroda brought Amarah's pirate ship to life and the familiar quiver of *Khanna's* engines purring passed through her. Hurrying to the wheel, each step reaffirming her decision and strengthening her actions, she pulled her ereven sphere from her pocket. It was going to be her guide.

'I'm sure you'll understand, Amarah. I'm sorry.' There was no turning back now, as the cargo doors slowly opened underneath *Khanna*.

The ship dropped like a stone, and Moroda wrestled with levers as she tried to control the dive.

Arillians and other ships flew past her as she shot towards the ground, before she finally opened the correct sails and levelled out her trajectory.

Heart racing, Moroda pushed the engines to full thrust, and headed towards the mountains.

'I TOLD you before that I could not help you.' The dragon snarled at Moroda, lashing her tail like an angry cat. Her scales were vibrant green, gleaming in the low winter sun. Her movements were smooth and graceful, and the scar on her chest already had fresh scales growing over it.

Moroda had hoped against hope the dragon had returned to her lair by now, something the ereven sphere had confirmed, and managed to land *Khanna* in one piece a short way from the cave.

Without Kohl's blizzard blocking the mountainside, she

could actually see where she was going, and it hadn't been too difficult to follow the sphere's navigation and find the dragon resting outside her cave.

From this altitude, the battle raging outside Taban Yul stood out like a dark smudge on the landscape, lit by streaks of lightning every handful of seconds.

'You *can* help. I know you can,' Moroda said, her hood pulled up to protect herself from the chill wind. 'You said yourself that you know when other dragons die, when they are born, when they fight...you all have a connection you can tap into. It's just energy, isn't it?'

The dragon let out another snarl but said nothing.

'So you can find the Sevastos, but you don't want to. I understand you don't want to add to the fighting.' Moroda tried again. 'I just want the Sevastos to protect us. Not its power, like Palom put in those weapons. Not to destroy Aciel and his armies, that would just lead to a never-ending war...I just...want to protect those I love from being taken away from me!'

The dragon snorted.

'I've lost my father, my sister, my home. Anahrik, too...so many friends. How many lives must be lost today?' She fought to keep desperation from her voice, but as things stood, she had no choices left.

Eventually, the dragon said, 'You restored my power so I will not kill you for your insolence.' She got to her feet and strode along the mountain away from Moroda, flexing her wings. 'But you are trying my patience.'

'Archon.' Moroda bowed her head, hoping the use of the honorific would placate the dragon. 'The people of Linaria worship you. You are a *god* to many. Please, I beg you. If there is anything else I can do, just name it!'

'The Sevastos are wanderers. They do not settle.' The dragon said at length, pausing to look out at the fighting outside Taban Yul. 'But they feel the ache I feel. They feel the pain of Linaria acquiring more scars because of this war between you selfish creatures. The life of Linaria *is* a concern to any Sevastos.'

'It's *my* concern, too!'

The dragon laughed, shaking the mountain.

Moroda reached into her cloak pocket and brought out the ereven sphere. 'Archon, this is what I used to find you to seek your guidance as Topeko instructed. He said the dragons would help restore peace and balance to Linaria. Please, help me.'

'Hmm, an ancient sphere?'

'Aciel used it to find and kill other dragons and steal their power. We took it from him, and moved his power back to your stone. I don't want a Sevastos for more destruction and death, as Aciel does. I want to *stop* the war!'

'Your intentions are indeed different to Aciel's. He sought to use my power and that of my brothers and sisters for his own gain, not to help Linaria.' The dragon sighed. 'A Sevastos may end the battle. I do not think it will end the war.'

'What about the fighting?'

'The fighting will cease...But war is not always fighting.'

Moroda stared at the ereven sphere. So close to the dragon, the phoenix feather inside quivered, and the whole sphere vibrated. She turned it in her hand, looking at it closely, but it couldn't point in any direction because she was right beside a dragon—the thing it was designed to find.

Tears threatened at the futility of it all.

Moroda had abandoned her friends in the middle of the battle in the hopes she could stop it in one last, desperate attempt.

She was a silly, naïve girl. A Goldstone with no under-standing of the world and the unfairness everyone endured.

Just like she'd always been. Just like Amarah had said.

Moroda had left Niversai to find out why dragons' behaviour was changing. See if anything could be done to stop it. And it had all spiralled into something else entirely.

She sat on the snow, her cloak covering her legs, and held the sphere to keep her hands warm. Her bare skin was numb in the cold, and she wondered whether it was fitting that she remained on the mountain and froze, before she did anything else stupid.

The dragon lay down, the snow melting where it touched her scales.

Moroda put one hand in the pocket of her cloak, and paused as she felt something sharp against her thumb. Bringing it out, her eyes widened at the thin shard of crystal in her hand.

It was from one of the Sevastos stones back in Berel.

She'd forgotten it had splintered off at her touch. Palom had been with her at the time. She'd been hoping for one last look at the crystals before they'd left the mage city.

Moroda held it up and watched blue and green light emanate from the shard and reflect on the white snow by her feet. She held the ereven sphere in her other hand, and in a heartbeat, another idea hit her.

Moroda twisted the top and bottom halves of the glass sphere, splitting it open and exposing the contents to the cold air.

Clutching the crystal shard, she placed it on top of the phoenix feather, and closed the sphere again.

She shivered.

'Please...please work...' After a moment, it settled, and Moroda felt the sphere grow hot.

'What are you doing?' asked the dragon, but Moroda was too engrossed in the sphere to respond.

'It's just energy. It's just moving energy.' Could she...

464

Would it be possible to *summon* the Sevastos' energy to her, instead of the other way around?

The crystal in her ring was a conduit. The ereven sphere had the ability to seek dragons, and now she had given it a very specific target with the shard. 'It's just energy...'

The wind picked up as she focussed on what she had learned from Topeko and his books, from what she had done when she'd taken the power Aciel had collected, and moved it to another stone.

The dragon raised her head. 'How can you do this? It is not possible?'

Moroda rocked where she sat, feeling her own strength leave her as she searched for the Sevastos's energy, like she had searched for Aciel's energy. Her ring sparkled, throwing out bright light.

Topeko had said there weren't any Sevastos dragons left.

But this dragon had spoken as if there were.

It wasn't long before she learned which one of them was correct.

Energy like nothing she'd imagined washed over her like a waterfall. Like an *ocean*. The power was boundless—it stretched beyond her perception and threatened to devour her.

She understood why the Samolen called them gods.

'It's there! It's so powerful...' Moroda kept her eyes closed, muttering a silent prayer. She didn't know if there were specific words needed, or if it was simply emotion, but she pleaded with every facet of her being for this enormous energy to *notice* her.

For it to come to her.

Topeko had said the five Sevastos of the past had given up their power willingly.

She hoped she would obtain the sixth.

Minutes dragged by as she continued to move the

energy. To beg. To pull. To summon. Her limbs went numb in the snow, her knees locking into place. Occasionally, her mind wandered to the battle outside Taban Yul, but she pulled her attention back.

'It comes.'

Moroda didn't need the dragon's words to know that. She wouldn't be surprised if everyone on the *continent* felt the enormous energy approaching, and the temperature of the sphere in her hands rose to a blistering heat. She dropped it onto the wet ground, and opened her eyes.

A dark silhouette loomed on the horizon, and her mouth went dry. She swallowed, unable to speak, and got to her feet, knees popping painfully.

The silhouette drew closer and closer, crossing leagues of distance every second. It was surrounded by dazzling gold light, dozens of phoenixes flying beside and behind the enormous dragon.

A Sevastos.

Moroda held her breath. The dragon beside her was on her feet, tail lashing, smoke curling from her half-open jaws.

Then, the Sevastos was on top of them—a dragon of immense size. It had deep, silvery-blue scales and black horns, and its enormous wings blotted out the sun. Phoenixes shrieked wildly as they circled the Sevastos, darting down occasionally to swoop through the flames expelling from the dragon's body.

The heat radiating from the group melted the snow across the mountain, leaving the rocks wet and slick.

Words failed Moroda at the sight. Every etiquette and lesson from Berel was lost in an instant.

The dragon beside her bowed her head and spoke with the Sevastos in a language Moroda could not comprehend —guttural noises and rumbling, punctuated with more fire —and after their greeting, she switched back to the common tongue. 'Archon, they never learn. Every time we intervene, they start over again.'

Moroda took a step closer. 'If we don't stop Aciel now, all dragons will suffer! This is about more than me, about people!'

Both dragons ignored her.

'I have not been summoned in many centuries. A gift the Samolen had once. This girl is not of their blood.' When the Sevastos spoke, the mountain shook.

'She has skill. Determination. I do not think it is enough.' The dragon let out a snort of fire.

'I care not for the petty squabbles of people. Too long I have lived above them. Too long has it been since they have worshipped us.' At that, the Sevastos turned his head to look at Moroda for the first time. 'You wish to seal away the bringer of war.' The voice of the Sevastos reverberated through Moroda. 'You have summoned me with old magic, yet you are not a daughter of the Samolen. Commendable.'

Moroda struggled to breathe, and could hardly bring herself to look upon him.

Flames arced from his back, the light vivid and intense.

There was no chance Aciel could stand up to something like *this*.

'I want to stop the death. Of us. Of dragons. Our cities and homes.' Moroda wasn't sure how she kept talking in the presence of something so enormous, so powerful. She balled her hands into fists and thought of Eryn.

'Do you know what you ask?'

Moroda understood. It wasn't a weapon to be used and put away. This was life and death. She nodded.

Fire licked across the Sevastos's wings, an arc as bright as sunlight, as he considered. 'When there are those who understand sacrifice. Who give up what they have for others.

For peace. For balance. Is it not our purpose to bestow strength upon those individuals?'

'Archon, will you give this woman your strength?' The dragon's eyes remained closed as she spoke.

Moroda didn't know if that was out of respect or fear.

'I am old. I have seen much. The Arillian darkness will spread if left unchecked. This woman keeps to the old ways. We can stop the battle without more loss of life.'

The dragon bowed to the Sevastos.

Moroda mirrored the action.

With a deafening roar, the Sevastos spread his wings across the mountain, bathing them in shadow. 'I have felt across the dragons who have seen Aciel. Fought him. Succumbed to him. Been destroyed by his greed for power. To seal this Arillian, I am willing to give you the crystal I have carried for over a thousand years and join my brethren in death. This is my burden.'

'You...you would die...?' Moroda's voice trembled. 'How many Sevastos are left?'

He didn't answer her question, but continued to speak as if he hadn't heard her.

'My crystal will allow you to keep Aciel sealed away. You would not have him destroyed, but sealed away he is no threat, no influence on Linaria. Your own life force will be drained to keep him sealed. Your own life force is the price you must pay to request I sacrifice mine. This is your burden. Will you pay it?'

Moroda forced herself to look at the great creature. Tried to reconcile the shock of a dragon this old, this powerful, along with what he asked of her.

What did she want?

She considered, knowing that time was against her, but not wishing to speak too soon.

The Sevastos had asked her to give up her own life to stop Aciel.

And in the end, it was an easy question to answer.

Moroda clutched her ring, felt the swell of power, of life, on the mountain. In the presence of two dragons, she no longer felt weak. Silly. A woman with no place getting involved in war and the struggle of power.

She was exactly where she needed to be.

And she would do what had to be done.

'If, in death, the lives of everyone I know will be safe... every parent, every child...then I would gladly die.' She took a deep breath and looked at him, his golden eyes a bonfire.

This was it.

There was no going back now.

Moroda nodded. 'I would do anything to end this.'

'So it must be.' The Sevastos tilted his head towards the sky and let out a roar of such intensity, Moroda thought the world would split open. Fire burst from every scale, flames licking up his wings and legs, engulfing his body. The phoenixes scattered as columns of fire shot forth from the dragon, and Moroda covered her head with both arms.

A moment later, the Sevastos dropped to the ground, landing heavily on the mountain. The flames covering his body burned violent purple, and peeled away scale and flesh alike.

Horrified, Moroda jumped back.

'This is what you asked,' the green dragon said, her head low as if in sorrow.

Moroda was sickened. In only a few minutes, there was nothing left of the Sevastos except a blackened skeleton.

Moroda trembled from head to toe, and it took all her strength just to walk over to it. She could not fathom this creature, the strength it held, the suddenness of its arrival and departure. A beast that had lived for countless centuries, a god among people and dragons, had given its life at her request.

She sought its power, true, but did not want more death.

Her cloak flapped around as the wind picked up. It was going to snow again, soon.

'The decision was made willingly. You don't have much time, if you wish to stem the deaths.' The dragon bowed low over the skeleton. 'I did not think the great one would listen to you. You are no Samolen, but you have skill in their ways.'

Moroda ran a hand over the Sevastos' skull, and as she touched the bone, her fingers began to glow. She tried to wrench her hand free, but she could not pull away from the bright, writhing light which enveloped her skin.

Purple and blue, it flared brighter than the *Valta Forinja*. 'What is—?' Fire engulfed her arm and moved to her chest. She squeezed her eyes shut against the glare, bracing for pain, but there was none.

Carefully, she opened one eye and stared down at herself. Purple-blue light swirled on her hand—no, her *ring*.

It glowed a bright violet, and her whole body warmed despite the coldness of the mountain.

She had the power of the Sevastos at her fingertips, and knew what she had to do.

Calm determination washed over her, as everything became clear.

'Moroda. You have no time. The Sevastos sacrificed himself and his power to you. I will take you to the battle to fulfil his wish.'

33

In the midst of the frenetic battle above Taban Yul, Amarah's arms ached from swinging her scythe. Sweat and blood mingled at her temples, and her chest was tight, making every breath painful. Several tornadoes tore through the valley surrounding Taban Yul, ripping into airship sails and emptying the skies. She needed to get her warship out of the way before it, too, went down.

Amarah raced into the cabin, an insult on her tongue for Moroda's slowness to react, when—

The cabin was empty.

Debris from the battle whipped around the warship, clattering onto the glass panels surrounding the cabin like hail. Thunder echoed overhead, rattling the wood and shaking the ship where it hovered. Amarah leaned against the doorframe for support.

Where was Moroda?

She'd left the damned Goldstone at the wheel!

Moroda should have been safe!

Had she been thrown overboard?

Chips of splintered wood and broken glass lay strewn about the cabin floor. They'd taken heavy damage from the

Arillian storms, and Amarah grabbed the wheel, carefully flying her warship away from another raging tornado that swirled towards them. She'd already seen several ships crash, pulled from the sky by Arillian lightning and wind, and had no desire to add her own new ship to the wreckages on the valley below.

Taban Yul itself was under attack by ground forces— troops taken from their own city or across the sea, and forced to fight for Aciel. Everywhere she looked, fighting and screaming filled the skies.

This was the kind of thing she'd run from in the past. Why get involved? Why risk serious injury or death? Especially when it wasn't anything she was personally involved in.

But with her new *Valta Forinja*, she had a real chance of victory.

She didn't *have* to flee when she had the upper hand. *She'd* get to dominate for once.

Amarah had to hand it to Palom, the weapons he had created were nothing short of sensational.

It was the main reason they were still alive in the middle of a fight against hundreds of Arillians. Simply flicking the weapon in the direction of an aggressor sent forth a blast of energy that seemed to do more damage than the blade itself. It had removed the Arillian's flight advantage and levelled the battlefield.

But she was not in a celebratory mood.

Moroda was gone, seemingly without a trace. There was no blood or ripped clothing. There had been no screams— although she'd been so engrossed in fighting that she might have missed that.

For all Amarah could tell, Moroda had simply...*disappeared*.

She wondered whether an Arillian had targeted the

cabin and flown off with her while she and the others were in the thick of fighting. She was barely aware of what was happening five paces away, let alone keeping an eye on the cabin, too.

Most of all, Amarah was terrified her plan to keep Moroda safe had backfired.

Other than the tornadoes sweeping across the valley, there was a lull in the fighting. Several waves of Arillians had retreated, keeping their distance from them and their *Valta Forinja* once it had become apparent the amount of damage they were causing.

Grateful for the breather, she returned to the main deck, where Palom, Morgen, and Kohl were seated. Well, Morgen was seated. The others leaned on their weapons, panting heavily, eyes warily scouring the sky in case more enemies descended upon them.

More Arillians gathered on the edge of the battlefield. It wasn't over yet, not by a long shot, but she was going to take the rest while they had the chance.

'These weapons of yours saved us, Palom!' Morgen was bleeding from a scrape to his cheek, but otherwise seemed uninjured. 'They couldn't get close to us! I can see why these things were so powerful in the war. Need to arm the entire Imperial Guard with them!'

'We need to survive. We are doing this.' Palom massaged his shoulder, and glanced up as Amarah stepped out on deck.

Kohl smoothed his hat, then put it back on his head. 'I wish more Arillians had seen sense and flown off. So many have died today. Needless deaths.'

'They should not have attacked us!' Palom snapped.

'It's *Aciel*!' Frustration edged Kohl's voice. 'None of them *want* to be here. Even if they're afraid, they *can't* flee. Or have you forgotten Aciel's power of compulsion?'

Palom didn't retort.

'You can't fight it,' Amarah said. She knew all too well what Aciel's compulsion felt like. 'But he wants to win, right? If he sees all his followers being cut down, he'll have to retreat. Compulsion or not?'

Kohl laughed bitterly. 'You don't know Aciel. He'll keep pushing them to their deaths, and they'll keep blindly following him.'

'Then we must kill Aciel himself.' Palom growled low.

'Where is he, then? Sorry but all these Arillians look alike. They're too high up to tell them apart,' Morgen asked.

'I didn't see Aciel or his generals.' Kohl sat down beside Morgen, wincing at the movement.

'Know who else I don't see?' Amarah waited until they were looking at her. 'Moroda.'

'Moroda?' Morgen got back to his feet, sword in hand. 'I thought she stayed in the cabin?'

'Well she ain't in there now. Did any of you see an Arillian land? Did one grab her?'

The three shook their heads.

'Did she go below deck? Hide there, perhaps?' Kohl suggested, spreading his wings. He leapt overboard and circled the ship, in a burst of frigid air.

Amarah led Palom and Morgen into the ruined cabin.

'Nothing at all.' Amarah pulled at a lever to adjust one of her sails while they hovered on the edge of the battlefield. 'Damned if I know what happened to her.'

Palom crouched, inspecting the damage in the cabin. He touched the floor with two fingers. 'No blood. I smell her, but faintly.'

Kohl landed by the cabin a moment later. 'Cargo hold doors at the bottom of the ship are open. *Khanna's* gone. She must've fled.'

'On *Khanna*?' Amarah raced out the cabin's rear door

474

and charged down into the hold. 'On *my* ship!' She couldn't believe the cheek of it.

And the Goldstone hadn't said a word?

Amarah threw open the doors to the cargo bay and halted in the entrance. She stared into the empty bay, wind swirling in from the open doors on the belly of the warship. 'Moroda! Dragons above, what are you *thinking*?'

'I don't believe it!' Morgen said, joining Amarah. 'You really did teach her to fly, didn't you?'

Amarah shook with rage and indignation.

'If she's damaged a single panel on *Khanna*...'

'But where would she have gone? Back to Niversai?'

'And how in Rhea's name would she know the way?'

'I don't know. Where else would she go?'

'Damned thief!' Amarah ignored the irony of calling someone *else* a thief.

Amarah had already lost Eryn because she had been too interested in getting out of the palace to warn the Goldstones that Sapora had been planning something.

Now she'd lost Moroda too, because she hadn't been paying attention.

That was *two* lives on her conscience.

'It's Aciel!' Kohl's shout pulled Amarah's attention away from her thoughts, and a wave of panic flooded her at that Arillian being named. She wouldn't soon forget what he'd done to her on Jato's warship.

What if he took control of her again? With the *Valta Forinja* in her grasp, she wouldn't have any control over what she did with it.

He would.

'Don't we just have all the luck?' Amarah muttered, racing back to the deck, taking the narrow steps three at a time. She bit down on a dozen curses as she resurfaced from the hold. She'd been so confident they'd have the upper hand after the bulk of his power had been taken. After Palom had given them these dragon-forged weapons.

But just *hearing* Aciel was there…It terrified her.

'Where is he?' Amarah asked, joining the others and staring up.

Palom pointed.

She followed the gesture, trying to make out details against the dark grey thunderclouds. It took her a moment before she spotted three silhouettes high above the battle-field. They were too far away for her to make out much detail, though she supposed Palom could count how many damned eyelashes they each had, but it was obvious Aciel was there. His white robes and black wings stood out against the armoured Arillians.

And even if she hadn't seen that, the entire atmosphere in the valley had shifted.

They might have had the upper hand with the *Valta Forinja*.

But Aciel was here now.

And his attention was on *her warship*.

Amarah clutched her scythe with both hands. 'He's…he's coming towards us!'

'Must've seen the power of the *Valta Forinja*.' Morgen wiped away sweat with one hand. His other was no longer in a sling, but he didn't have the full range of movement in his shoulder. The *Valta Forinja* had been compensating for his injury, but now, he looked vulnerable.

The three Arillians descended slowly, Aciel and two others, heading straight for her.

Fuck.

She shuffled back, wondering if she should grab the wheel and make a run for it. Her warship didn't have *Khanna's* speed, so outrunning them was unlikely. But damn, what choice did she have?

'Do not be afraid, Amarah. We have *Valta Forinja*. We can kill Aciel here!' Palom's gaze hadn't left the approaching Arillians. There was hunger in that glare.

'I didn't say I was afraid!' Amarah knew it was silly. After everything they'd been through, she could admit fear in front of them. Palom could probably smell it! But her words were an instinctive response. She *was* afraid.

And she was trying to put on her usual, brave face, so her opponents didn't see that.

'Aciel...' A freezing gust of wind accompanied Kohl's words. It made her teeth chatter. 'It's my fault Aciel is here. I should have stopped him a long time ago. When I had the chance.'

Amarah wanted to look at Kohl, to ask what he was talking about, but she didn't want to risk taking her attention off Aciel. Now the three Arillians were closer, she recognised one of the others—Jato. The third she didn't know, but he wore similar armour as Jato. Must have been another general.

She should've killed Aciel when she'd had the chance.

Sapora should've killed Jato.

So many *should haves*.

Kohl spread his wings again, another freezing gust of wind sent forth by his feathers. He bent his knees slightly, feathers fluttering.

'You are going to fly away? Again?' Palom accused.

It was a fair question as far as Amarah was concerned. Jato was *there*. What was to stop him behaving the same way as he had when he'd last seen his daughter?

Kohl didn't take his attention away from the descending Arillians. 'Aciel is the root of it all. My mistakes. Everything that has changed. It's all Aciel.' He blinked, turned his head to look at Amarah, Palom, and Morgen. 'I am going to make him *pay*.'

Thunder roared through the sky as Kohl leapt into the air, waves of icy wind shooting out from his open palms. Amarah hunkered down, protecting her face against the strength of the freezing wind. Kohl's attacks weren't aimed at them, thank Rhea, but she hadn't realised how powerful he was.

Come to think of it, she hadn't known Arillians to have any sort of ice powers other than Kohl.

Why was he, as strong as he was, so...pitiful?

Whatever his reasons, at least he'd decided to fight back. Aciel and his generals were getting closer to her warship by the second. But they were out of range of their *Valta Forinja*.

Kohl was the only one able to keep them at bay. He raised his hand and sent out another blast of icy wind. 'Aciel!' His attacks bit into the trio and scattered them.

'Kohl, you fool. You had your chance to live.' Aciel raised his arms, both hands free now he no longer carried his cane. 'Your life and legacy ends here.'

The two Arillians clashed, their attacks sending shockwaves out in a thunderous surge. Aciel was faster, dodging most of Kohl's icy blasts, but he was not powerful enough to do any real damage to Kohl.

'Attack him...' Aciel's voice echoed in Amarah's head. 'Attack him...'

She dropped to one knee, eyes tightly shut. Fought his will with everything she had.

'Attack him.'

Aciel's voice was all-encompassing.

And Amarah could not resist it.

The same numbing sensation as before filled her limbs, somehow deadening her.

How did he have that ability? Moroda had taken his stolen power, hadn't she? Was he really that powerful on his own?

Energy pulsed through her scythe, blue flames erupting from the blade. She gritted her teeth, but Aciel's command forced her to turn. Widen her stance. Raise her weapon.

In her peripheral vision, she saw Palom and Morgen lining up their swords, too. Both burned with blue fire, embers bouncing from their edges.

She wanted to scream. Yell at them to stop. Yell at *herself*!

Either side of them, Aciel's two generals landed on deck. Even from several paces away, Amarah could see Jato's smug smirk. Dragons above, she wanted to slice that woman's head off!

Kohl and Aciel swooped towards the warship, constantly moving as they battled. It meant she couldn't properly aim her strike. Couldn't fulfil Aciel's orders.

She fought his command with every fibre of her being, but there was no strength in her limbs.

'You're a coward, Aciel. You've never been able to fight for yourself!' Kohl roared, more icy wind rolling off him. 'Stand and fight me! Leave them out of this!'

Amarah struck. Her scythe sent a wave of blue energy directly ahead.

Kohl summoned an icicle the length of his arm, tapered and bladed, like the one she'd seen in Burian forest. He threw it at the approaching energy.

When they connected, the explosion flung her to the deck.

'Coward? You're one to talk, Kohl. *You* fled our home-land. *You* left Jato!' Aciel darted close to Kohl and grabbed his cloak with both hands. 'Who is the real coward?'

Kohl let out a guttural shout, freezing the air around him as Aciel responded with another wave of electricity. Sparks erupted from their bodies and several bolts of lightning launched in multiple directions. He whirled round and grabbed Aciel's collar, pulling him close. 'Without your compulsion, you're *nothing*!' Holding on to Aciel, Kohl flipped over and dived towards the ground. Aciel fought back viciously, punching and blasting bolts of electrical energy at point blank range.

In the violence of their fight, Aciel released his hold on Amarah, and she let out a ragged, gasping breath.

Before she could get back to her feet, Jato approached, palms raised towards her.

'I'm *so* glad we found you again.' Jato's voice was almost musical.

The Arillian was taller than Amarah remembered. More imposing in thicker armour.

'You keep terrible company. Fraternising with traitors and snakes.' Jato sneered.

Amarah snorted. Some people were just filled with hate. Nothing could be done about that. She'd have to cut Jato down to size.

She turned her head slightly, saw Palom and Morgen battling with the other general, vicious winds cutting into the wooden deck like knives.

'You'll regret what you did to Aciel.'

Amarah tightened her grip on her *Valta Forinja*. 'You'll regret tracking *me* down!' She flicked the blade of her scythe towards the Arillian, a rush of energy surging forward. Amarah leapt to her feet and charged, spinning her blade like a carriage wheel. Sparks and energy skittered along the deck, before it sliced into Jato's armour and forced her back.

Jato bore the brunt of her attacks, then dodged, using her wings to move faster. She raised one palm and sent a short burst of lightning through Amarah's thigh.

Amarah yelped and dropped to one knee. The strength of that one blast of lightning took her by surprise. She'd expected pain, but not for it to completely deaden her leg.

'Now I have you where I want you.' Jato flapped her

wings lazily, hovering above her. She sent wave after wave of attacks, raining lightning down on Amarah, and cutting through to the skin. Jato splayed both palms open, summoning up a ball of electricity that crackled and spat like a raging fire.

Amarah gritted her teeth, bringing her scythe across her chest to defend herself.

Before Jato could attack, a flash of blue-green energy knocked her out of the sky. She disappeared over the edge of the warship and plummeted to the ground.

'Back on your feet, Amarah.' Morgen grabbed her by the elbow and hauled her up.

'Great shot, Morgen.' Amarah winced.

'We can't lose you, too.'

'So...kind...of you to say.' Amarah could hardly believe an officer of the Imperial Guard had her back. 'Past crimes forgiven, right?'

Morgen turned back to the far side of the deck, where Palom battled the second general.

'Let's finish this.' Clutching his sword, Morgen ran to join Palom in the fray.

By the time Amarah had enough feeling in her leg to hobble over to them, the Arillian had fled beyond the range of their *Valta Forinja*, earning them another breather. 'Good work.' Her chest was still tight, and blood dripped down her breeches from Jato's attacks, but she was in one piece.

'Amarah, land ship! Kohl has Aciel on ground! I will rip him apart!' Palom roared. He leant over the side rail, light creeping along his skin as he prepared to transform.

'Careful, Palom. He can control you!' Morgen said, his sword at the ready.

This time, Amarah didn't hesitate. She'd seen what the weapons could do against Aciel's generals. They needed to push their attack while they had the upper hand. Who knew how long Kohl could keep him down.

She hurried to the wheel as quickly as she could, leaving a trail of blood in her wake.

'Hold on!' Amarah pulled back her sails and engaged the throttles. The sheer weight of the vessel enabled them to drop at speed—she pulled up the nose just as it was about to kiss the ground, allowing the tiger to leap overboard and sprint towards the two Arillians locked in combat.

Palom was a streak of orange and black, but Aciel deflected Palom's lunge with a bolt of lightning. The force of it sent Palom flying backwards, and he crumpled to the ground in a daze.

'Palom!' Morgen cried.

So low to the ground, Amarah's ship was in more danger than ever. Arillian reinforcements swarmed the upper deck now that their leader was under direct attack. They blasted the ship with lightning and wind, bringing it fully to the ground. Amarah let go of the wheel and sails, allowing the ship to crash land.

Then, they turned their attention to the sails—tearing through the fabric with savage winds.

Amarah screamed, grabbed her scythe and raced out. One slash sent Arillians careening away. A second drove them from her sails, most of which flapped uselessly.

With a grunt, she joined Morgen, their backs against each other as they faced their enemies.

'Never thought I'd be fighting with an officer in the Imperial Guard!'

'Or I with a notorious sky pirate! We'll need to have a long chat with my captains after this, Amarah.'

She laughed despite the fear and anger running through her. 'To discuss my reward, I hope? You wouldn't have made it out of Corhaven if it weren't for me!'

Together, they sent out blasts of energy from their *Valta Forinja*. Scythe and sword, blue fire kept Arillians at bay, knocking back bolts of lightning and absorbing cripplingly powerful gusts of wind.

Now they were on the ground, other troops charged towards the warship, several clambering up the sides and joining in the brawl. Some were the Imperial Guard of Taban Yul. Others were soldiers under Aciel's compulsion.

Their war cries were deafening. Chaos ensued, and with so many people on both sides of the fight wearing similar colours, Amarah didn't know who to strike.

The Imperial Guard had always been her enemy, but Morgen was changing her mind on that.

She used her scythe to send shockwaves around herself and her ship, sending people flying backwards and away. Hurricane-force winds kept debris whipping through the air, and Amarah had to defend herself against chunks of wood, broken armour, and lost weapons as much as Arillian attacks.

Most of the tornadoes that had been a threat were concentrated on the far side of the battle. She wondered if Aciel was trying to keep them away from him so he wouldn't be caught in the devastation.

Occasionally, she saw a flash of orange fur as Palom fought in his true form on the ground beside the warship. Ice punctuated most breaths, so she knew Palom and Kohl at least were both fighting.

Together, they kept Aciel too busy to take control of her —and she used every second of freedom she had.

Then, everything stopped.

Arillians hovered in place, lightning bolts dissipating mid-strike.

Ground troops shivered to a halt, as if held down by something invisible.

Amarah looked around, eyes wide. 'What...?'

Shock and unease careened through the area—through the Arillians in the air and the troops on the ground.

'It's the dragon from the mountain!' Morgen exclaimed.

Amarah raised her scythe, ready to defend herself. 'I don't believe it!'

'She...she changed her mind? She's here to help us?'

Morgen's breathing was ragged, but Amarah heard the elation in his voice.

Across the emptying skies, the dragon flew closer, its bright green scales dazzling even without sunlight breaking through the heavy storm clouds.

Smoke rose from burned airships, and many wreckages littered the valley. Taban Yul glistened behind the carnage, a shining city of wealth and strength, in juxtaposition to the scorched battlegrounds. Ground troops saw to their injured and dead, but as they began to notice the dragon, many stopped to look up, raising their shields in defence.

Amarah could understand their wariness. There'd been many dragon attacks since Aciel had been on the warpath. If this one had decided its place in the war was to burn the city instead of helping them, they wouldn't have much of a chance.

She backed away, slowly heading to steps on the side of her ship. If this field was about to become an inferno, she needed to get away.

'Wait. Someone's on the dragon's back!' Morgen squinted. Then he staggered. 'Dragons above, is that *Moroda*?'

Morgen's words froze Amarah in place. '*What*?' If it wasn't Moroda escaping on *Khanna*, it was the Goldstone riding on the back of a dragon—how much stranger was this day going to get?

Then she realised.

Khanna must be somewhere on the mountain. Amarah tried not to think about her ship as a smoking husk abandoned in the snow.

Before she could give her pride and joy any more thought, Moroda lit up like a beacon. Light of all colours—blue, pink, yellow, green, red—poured from her as if *she* was a *Valta Forinja*. The ground trembled like a quake, and Amarah immediately grabbed onto the main mast to stay on her feet.

Brighter than a thousand suns, Moroda's light forced away the black clouds above the battlefield in a single breath. It called a halt to the fighting, rooting everyone in place.

Shielding their eyes, Arillians and Imperials alike turned away from the light as it enveloped everything below.

The beam of light poured towards the ground, violet flames following every particle.

It was heading straight for Aciel, pinned in place by Kohl and Palom.

Amarah watched as long as she dared, watched until the pain in her eyes was too much to bear, then squeezed them shut as an explosion shook the ground and a dragon roared.

She clutched onto the mast with both hands as the aftershocks tore through her and the ship, holding on as tightly as she could. She didn't know how long the eruption lasted. Couldn't feel her own heartbeat, the tremors were so great.

By the time the quaking stopped, Amarah was trembling, her breathing coming in short, sharp gasps.

'Amarah?' Morgen's voice grabbed her attention.

Amarah pulled herself up to her feet, using the mast for balance. She was amazed the wooden pillar remained in one piece.

Thick smoke rolled over everything, churned up from the power of the explosion.

'I'm okay.' Amarah coughed, waving her hand in front of her face, trying to clear her vision.

People spoke in low voices, muttered, whimpered, called for one another. Fear and shock filled the valley like fog.

When the dust settled, Amarah's mouth dropped open.

A pillar of crystal easily as tall as the Sevastos stones of Berel sat on the edge of the field as if it had sprouted from the ground. Pale violet and glinting in the sunshine now the clouds had been dispersed, Amarah stared up at it, utterly lost for words.

'Moroda!' Palom shouted, having transformed back in the explosion's aftermath.

Amarah approached the crystal—barely twenty paces from her damaged warship, and less than two hundred paces from the exterior wall of Taban Yul—and her fingers trembled.

What did it mean?

Where was Aciel? Moroda?

The dragon she'd flown in on circled above, roaring as if in great pain.

She looked more closely at the crystal and realised there were two dark smudges *inside* it, the details too distorted by the violet light to make out, but they looked...like people.

Amarah stared so hard at the crystal that she didn't notice the dragon swoop down until she landed on the scorched grass. The dragon bowed her head to the crystal, letting out a guttural snarl.

As if the spell was broken, the Arillians who had been hovering overhead scattered. Commanding shouts and screams of fright echoed as they flew away—higher and away from the valley.

Few looked back.

Troops shook their heads, fell to their hands and knees, and cried out in anguish.

'Aciel's spell and hold over them has been broken, it seems.' Kohl limped over to her, his cloak shredded. 'It's over.'

Voice unable to work, Amarah turned to the dragon, expressionless. She didn't understand what had happened. Moroda had been there, with the dragon.

Had that light been some Samolen magic?

But the crystal looked identical to those in Berel.

A Sevastos?

'It's over?' Morgen shivered, watching the remaining Arillians drop their weapons and fly off. There wasn't so much as a rumble of thunder from all their movements. 'Amarah? You all right?'

'What happened?' Palom approached, sword held high, blue light shimmering around it.

The dragon looked at them and snarled at Palom until he sheathed his sword. 'She called a Sevastos.'

Amarah's legs were weak, much of her strength gone. She used her scythe as a crutch and stepped back from the enormous crystal. It emitted a soft light, reminding her of a candle.

Kohl reached out a hand and pressed his palm against the stone. His arm trembled. 'Moroda. What did you do?' Tears spilled down his scarred face. 'You didn't want any more deaths, but didn't care what happened to you? If you died?'

Amarah still wasn't following. 'Where is Moroda?'

'She harnessed the Sevastos's power,' the dragon said.

'How?' Palom asked. Too weak to stand any longer, he sank to the ground.

'*Sacrifice.* Do you not listen to what your Samolen teach of lore, dragons, and our powers?' The dragon's voice was cold. 'I suppose you are only interested in the strength we can give to your weapons and nothing else, thief of stolen power. But you will understand sacrifice soon enough if you continue to use them. You are much the same as Aciel. *You* should be dead for misusing our power. You stole it as much as Aciel did. Took our strength and paid *nothing* for it.'

Palom shuffled backwards.

The dragon flexed her wings. 'Payment must always be made. Moroda understood this. It is why this power is clean. Pure. Yours...' She let out another snarl.

Amarah flinched at the dragon's harsh words. She looked down at her own scythe. If not for this weapon, she wouldn't have survived the battle, let alone held the Arillains off long enough before this ended it.

Clearly the dragon was upset with their *Valta Forinja*, but she didn't see why it was such a bad thing. But what Amarah didn't understand was the dragon's words on *sacrifice*?

She looked around as Morgen circled the pillar, more Ittallan soldiers in tow, all investigating the new addition to the valley outside Taban Yul.

Where was Moroda?

Kohl said she was dead, but there was no body? Had he been mistaken?

She limped forwards, closer to the shining crystal, close enough to touch it. It hurt to look at directly, but she squinted anyway.

The two smudges had more detail now she was practically pressing her nose against the crystal, and she realised they were...two dark silhouettes.

'Oh...shit.'

Moroda and Aciel were both *inside* the crystal.

More troops gathered, conversation breaking out as they saw to their wounded, or stared at the crystal in awe.

Many soldiers erupted into cheers and stamped their

feet at the realisation their adversaries had fled, that the fighting was finished.

The dragon spat a flame into the air. 'The Sevastos gave her his power and it went into her Samolen ring.'

'Moroda...' Amarah whispered.

She pressed one palm to the enormous crystal. It was all that remained of a Sevastos's power.

Moroda was lost.

'Her life force went into this magic, as payment for the Sevastos's death. You people cause so much damage to Linaria.'

But no one was listening to the dragon. No one appeared afraid of it, either. Their celebrations had already begun. Nothing else mattered.

'We must report our great victory to the palace!'

'Wielders of the *Valta Forinja*! You will be heroes for all the ages to come!'

'The Sevastos gave his power to us! The Ittallan are blessed!'

Imperial soldiers praised them, and chatter broke out through those gathered.

One soldier shook Morgen's hand and pulled him to his feet. Palom, too, was helped up.

Amarah stared at the crystal, numb.

'We must get the wounded back to the city. You and your weapons have saved us. Val Sharis is forever indebted to you!'

34

The palace had been redecorated. Palom had no idea how they'd managed to change everything so quickly, but after what had happened at the winter ball, he supposed the stewards had jumped to attention for fear they'd be killed if they didn't obey. Damn that Sapora for inciting so much fear in the Ittallan.

Coloured banners and fabric bunting streaked along the walls. Flags had been raised at each tower not just in the palace, but across all of Taban Yul.

Despite the celebrations, Palom's mood was low.

How could he celebrate when they'd lost so much? Anahrik. Eryn. Moroda.

People he'd sworn to protect. Anahrik had been like his brother, and he'd failed him.

Palom kept the greatsword in a holder strapped across his back—he didn't ever want to let the weapon out of his sight—and it seemed to pulse in time with his emotions.

For all the power of the *Valta Forinja*, it hadn't been enough to save them.

Crowds had gathered in the streets of Taban Yul, dressed in their finery, waving banners, flags, and anything else they could get their hands on. Trumpets and horns blared in a cacophony of noise and fanfare. Not only was the Arillian threat defeated, but it had been put down by *their city*.

Strange how people deflected blame and responsibility when things went wrong, but clamoured to take credit for every success.

Palom glanced down at himself and grimaced. Blood from the battle stained his tunic. They'd been kept with the Imperial Guard in their camp set up on the city's outskirts and interrogated by several captains—even one of the Council members. Though their wounds had been seen to, it had taken three days before they were allowed to leave.

As much as Palom wanted to get away and be alone to process everything he'd experienced, they'd been taken to the palace, escorted by the Imperial Guard every step of the way. Morgen and Amarah were with him, of course, but he barely took note of their conversation.

Kohl had been treated with suspicion, of course, and wasn't permitted in the palace. Amarah had spoken to him in a hushed voice, and he'd stood to the side, aloof as ever. The two had promised to speak after their business in the palace was finished, but Palom didn't care for whatever the pirate and the traitor were concocting. Though he would have loved nothing more than to see the Arillian in chains, the boiling anger he'd felt after Anahrik and Eryn's deaths was gone.

Unfortunately, so was his motivation for much of anything else.

He followed the Imperial Guard through the decorated hallways, hardly glancing up at the bright red and gold patterns adorning every wall. Once they had their audience with Princess Isa and the rest of the council, he would be free to leave.

At least, he hoped.

He didn't understand why he had to be there in person. What was the point of all the interrogations, otherwise? If all they wanted was to thank them personally, a messenger would have done the job without inconveniencing him.

All he wanted was to be rid of the crowds. The attention.

Anahrik would have lapped it up. He'd have said the right things, smiled at the right people. Laughed and joked about what they'd been through, turned it into a fabulous story, with all the right embellishments. Anahrik had always been a master of the crowds—could talk his way out of any situation. If he hadn't loved speed so much, Palom wouldn't have been surprised if Anahrik's *meraki* had given him the form of a parrot.

Just that thought set a pang of intense pain through his chest. It should have been a happy thought. One he could think of fondly. But it just reminded him of loss.

Of what could have been, and would never be.

Amarah walked behind him, scythe twirling. He'd always been astounded at how brazen she was, happily remaining armed even while on her way to speak with royalty.

Morgen brought up the rear. Though Palom had been in the depths of despair since the end of the battle, he'd noticed how quiet the young officer had grown. As if he'd withdrawn into himself, a dark cloud hovering above his head that hadn't shifted in the slightest.

But he would be fine.

He had the rest of the Imperial Guard for support.

Kohl had his Arillian brethren.

Amarah no doubt had thieves and sky pirate colleagues.

Palom had no one—aside from those living whom he had failed, and he doubted they'd be interested in seeing him again. Perhaps forging the *Valta Forinja* might reopen those relationships. But he wasn't hopeful.

'Announcing the heroes' arrival!' bellowed a steward in fine blue robes.

Palom barely gave him a glance as they were ushered through a pair of double doors. Anise was pungent in the room. Fennel bisque. One of the Ittallan's seasonal delicacies given the plant's scarcity. Princess Isa was really pulling out all the stops for this ceremony.

Palace staff, soldiers of the Imperial Guard, and other citizens—he assumed wealthy ones—filled the enormous hall. Probably Goldstones.

Just like—

He stopped himself before he thought too much about Eryn and Moroda's fate.

A patrol had been set up outside Taban Yul, keeping watch over the enormous crystal, and the two people trapped inside it—Aciel and Moroda. While it wasn't exactly death, it certainly wasn't life, either.

He pushed his emotions down and forced himself to pay attention. He'd probably have to speak soon, and the whole thing would take longer if he misheard or said the wrong thing.

The captain that had been leading them came to a halt and saluted.

A long table had been set up, with several members of the council seated—Princess Isa among them, though she was on the far left, rather than front and centre, as he'd expected.

Before he could consider any further, Amarah leaned towards him and whispered, 'I never properly thanked you for the scythe. Wonder how much money they'll give us.'

Palom frowned. 'What money?'

She gave him a lopsided grin and winked, before straightening up as one of the stewards cleared their throat awkwardly.

493

'Esteemed members of the council, may I present the wielders of the *Valta Forinja*, as requested.'

Palom exhaled slowly through his nose. At least the rest of Val Sharis would remember him for these weapons, not for the people he'd let die. It was a small comfort.

One member of the council, an aged man with a neatly trimmed white beard, stood up. 'In recognition for your services to not just Val Sharis, but to all of Linaria, the council has decided on suitable rewards.'

Perhaps Amarah was thinking along the right lines, then.

'Morgen. You shall be promoted to captain with imme-diate effect. We'll transport you across the Sea of Nami, where you may continue your duties in Niversai.'

Morgen saluted, but said nothing, his expression dark.

'Amarah. It has been...*agreed* that you will be pardoned of all previous crimes for which you have been accused. Your airship, *Khanna*, may fly freely in Val Sharis's skies in perpetuity.'

'Palom. For your bravery and—'

'What about funeral?' Though it was disrespectful to interrupt, he found he didn't care.

The old man stuttered. 'The...funeral?'

Palom took a step forward and the Imperial Guard stationed behind the table tensed. One even grabbed the hilt of his sword.

'Funeral for Anahrik. Moroda. Eryn. People who died fighting war against Aciel for *you*.' He couldn't keep the bitterness from his voice.

Again, the man stammered, glancing down at his ream of parchment.

Princess Isa stood up, her gaze cool. 'A procession will take place in a few days in South Galeo. Everyone we have lost will be laid to rest in the mausoleum.'

'I wish to be part of this. I wish to carry...' Palom couldn't get the words out.

The council man shook his head, cheeks reddening. 'That is most inappropriate. Why, you aren't a member of the Guard, and this is following war! You should—'

'Of course you may. It's the least we can do,' Isa spoke over him.

Palom's shoulders sagged as the princess granted his request.

Now the most important matter had been attended to, he could relax. His mind churned, thinking about the procession to come. About the mausoleum. He owed it to Anahrik to carry his litter to his final resting place.

But the mausoleum in South Galeo was also the resting place of...

Palom blinked. Time had passed, and he swayed on his feet, unaware of the conversation that had rattled around him. Through the window, the sun seemed much lower. Isa was standing in front of him, placing a weighted purse in his hands and thanking him once again for everything he had done. 'You are more than welcome to food before you leave.' Isa gestured to the large soup pot, fennel and tomatoes bubbling within.

'I can...go?' Palom asked, unsure.

She offered him a pitying look, then nodded. 'Details of the funeral will be made public soon. Come to the palace the evening before. I'll make sure you're part of it.'

Dumbly, he nodded, thanking her, though he was sure he stumbled over his words.

As he left the palace, he tried to focus his thoughts. He just needed to get through the next few days. Then he could figure out what he was going to do. Without Anahrik, he was lost, like a kite with its string cut.

Anahrik had always come up with plans. New ideas. Exciting opportunities.

He'd already have next season's best sellers dreamt up before Palom had finished forging this season's stock.

Even Moroda had been a quick-thinker. Both with the dragon in the cave, and her ability to harness a Sevastos.

Blue skies and glittering streets dazzled him as he made his way down a wide staircase, leading from one of the palace's higher doorways. A burst of cold air accosted him, and he snapped out of his stupor in time to see Kohl waiting.

Rage built, and his sword burned in kind.

'I guess...I guess this is it?' Morgen lingered on the bottom step, his eyes downcast.

'You are returning to Niversai. Is good thing.' Palom offered as much encouragement as he could—Morgen had been away from home far too long.

'Yeah...'

'Come on, Morgen. You got yourself a promotion! Purse of gold from the princess, luxury flight back to Corhaven, probably a bigger salary too. What's not to like?' Amarah laughed, her spirits far higher than anyone else's.

Morgen shook his head, mouth working, but he seemed to think better of what he'd been about to say, and decided to keep quiet.

'What's *wrong* with you two?' Amarah asked, looking between Morgen and Palom.

'We lost people. Did you forget this?' Palom was irritated by her mirth.

'Yeah, we did. That's life. Moping about it won't help.'

'I am not *moping*. I am *grieving*. There is difference.'

She brushed dust from her shoulder. 'Fine. You wallow. See where it gets you. As for me, I'm moving forward. I got a goal now and that's the best way to keep you sharp.'

Palom snorted. 'Goal? More stealing from people?'

She narrowed her eyes. 'I'm heading north as it happens. Seeing what I can learn. Try and fix what can be fixed.'

Palom should have known better than to expect loyalty from a sky pirate.

But Morgen approached her. 'What's north?'

'Potentially something that can help. If there's a way to get Moroda outta that crystal, I'm finding it.' Amarah's voice left no room for argument.

'I didn't know it was possible!' Morgen gasped.

Amarah laughed. 'It's amazing how much you can learn from people when you *talk* to 'em. Kohl was the one who gave me the idea.'

Palom glared at the Arillian, who remained out of earshot. 'He is not talking to *me*.'

'Probably because you threatened to bite his head off the first chance you had.'

Palom supposed that was true.

Morgen sighed. 'I wish I could come with you. But I can't ignore my orders. I've been away from Niversai far too long, there's no excuses anymore.'

A week ago, Palom would have travelled to the ends of Linaria to help those he'd promised to protect.

But he wasn't that person anymore.

There was too much broken in himself that he needed to fix. Too many people in Val Sharis that he needed to reconcile with.

He didn't trust himself.

'Why are you really going, Amarah?' Palom asked. He wondered if she was just looking for more treasures to squirrel away.

She looked at him, wide eyed and eyebrows raised. 'Might be a chance to bring Moroda back. After everything she did, I owe her that.'

Palom wasn't sure he followed the sky pirate's thinking. But she worked by her own code. There was probably more meaning to her decision than he could see. And if she wanted to do that, who was he to dissuade her? 'Good luck.'

'Thanks. We'll need it.'

'We?' Palom really needed to pay more attention to the conversations going on around him. He'd been so wrapped up in his own grief and thoughts of the funeral and getting back in touch with Lathri, that he hadn't absorbed much information.

'Well how else do you think I'm gonna get there? Kohl's providing the escort. Arillians have more power than storms and ice, apparently. Something might be there that can help her.'

'Arillian...magic?'

'Well, you Ittallan have your *meraki*, don't you? Varkain have some version of that, too. Arillians have more secrets on their floating islands. Whatever treasures they have, I'm gonna dig up. Plus, Aciel is in the crystal too. They might be willing to help figure out a way to crack it open.'

'You want to bring Aciel back?'

Amarah laughed. 'Don't be ridiculous. If I can open that thing, I'll have this ready and waiting to stop Aciel before he breathes a single word.' She raised her scythe and a flame of blue energy flashed for a moment.

His heart ached at the sight. His own sword remained in its holder at his back, but it was always ready for the next battle.

'Take care, Palom. My ship to Corhaven will be ready soon, and I can't be late.' Morgen offered Palom his hand. 'Thank you for everything.'

Palom shook it. 'You, too.'

Morgen winced at Palom's grip, then pulled his hand

free. 'Amarah. Keep out of trouble, please. Don't know how long I can cover for you in Niversai.'

She grinned. 'No need to worry about that. I hope not to be anywhere near Corhaven for a while.'

They held each other's gazes for a moment longer than Palom thought was necessary, then Morgen retreated with a short wave. He nodded towards Kohl, who watched from several paces away, hat low and cloak covering his wings.

Kohl tapped his hat in response.

'Take care.' Morgen headed off.

Palom watched him leave, sadness and relief both washing over him.

This was it.

His journey with these strangers—who had become allies, even friends—was finished.

'What're you gonna do, Palom? Swan around and enjoy all the free food people are throwing at you?' Amarah's cackle was grating rather than endearing, and Palom turned away from her.

'Be wary of Kohl. I will let him go now, but next time I will not hold back.'

She nodded, the grin wiped from her face. 'I know. I got the scythe. Don't think anyone'll be getting the better of me for a *long* time.'

He shrugged, making his way down the street, away from the palace, and deeper into the city. He had his workshop to rebuild after the failed *Valta Forinja* efforts. He had Lathri to get back in touch with. He had a life to live, with Sapora as his ruler. He had to cope with the loss of Anahrik. Of his friends.

It was too much.

'I have business in Taban Yul. After that? We will see,' he said over his shoulder.

Amarah took his dismissive response in her stride. 'Well,

if you need a ride on *Khanna* anywhere, you let me know. After this scythe, I think I can fly you to a few places, no charge. I owe you.'

Palom stopped and looked back at her. Remembered their first meeting, when she and Anahrik had insulted each other. How silly that had been.

And how long ago. 'Fare well, Amarah.'

'And you.'

Palom headed deeper into Taban Yul while the city cele-brated, his footsteps heavier than they'd been in years. There was little future for him left after the mess he'd made of everything.

So, he would need to dredge up his past and see if anything could be salvaged.

The shadows of dusk crept across the marble streets, and his *Valta Forinja* flashed brightly.

35

'My King, you have a visitor. A Samolen.' One of the Cerastes bowed low, having entered the large, inner-room of the keep where Sapora dined with his family.

Torches burned brightly and thick woollen rugs covered the ground, bringing warmth and colour. It was clean and comfortable enough, though a far cry from the opulence of Taban Yul's palace.

Four Cerastes stood guard at the door, all in matching livery, spears glinting.

'A Samolen?' Sapora repeated, glancing up from his plate. It had been just over a week since he'd returned to his homeland, and this was the first time he'd been able to sit down and eat a meal at his leisure. But non-Varkain were rare in Sereth. A Samolen would probably be safer than most, but it was curious that one had decided to visit.

It seemed he was fated to never have a moment's rest. 'Send him through.'

Now he wore the crown, those seated with him ate only when he did. They, too, paused their meals, and kept wary eyes on the visitor as he was brought in.

Sapora found it peculiar how he could control when Tacio ate. When his *father* ate.

At the sight of the Samolen, Sapora smiled.

'King Sapora. May I offer you my felicitations on your new title.' Topeko bowed to the table as he entered the inner keep, ever the epitome of respect. Even so far from his homeland, the warmth emitted from the mage filled the room.

Although Topeko was nothing but polite and respectful, Sapora could hear his quickened heart rate, scent the fear in the air. 'Thank you, Topeko. It is most kind of you to travel all this way, and rather unexpected. A letter would have been perfectly acceptable.'

'New kings in Sereth do not come about often, and I had the pleasure of meeting you before. I wished to be personal in my congratulations.' Topeko kept his attention only on Sapora. 'May I humbly request a private word?'

Sapora considered as he drank deeply from his cup.

His people were watching him as closely as Topeko, and he had no intention of appearing weak considering the trials he'd endured to claim his crown. 'We may not. You can speak freely here.'

A flicker of annoyance passed across Topeko's features, then it was gone. 'I am...I am sure you have heard about the end of the war with Aciel?'

'Indeed.' Sapora acknowledged.

'Would you believe a Sevastos aided us?'

'Truly?'

Sapora's attention sharpened. He'd heard reports of such a thing, but hadn't believed them. Why would a Sevastos involve itself? He'd assumed his scouts had been confused, or simply exaggerated matters they did not fully understand.

But Topeko had no reason to lie.

'Truly. At least, the power of one. The beast itself was not present. They say a woman summoned it. She arrived on the back of a dragon and sealed Aciel away in a pillar of crystal.' Topeko shifted his weight.

Sapora didn't need to think very hard to consider Moroda. He could not imagine Eryn or Amarah taking it upon themselves to speak to the dragons or find a Sevastos. Nor was anyone else in Taban Yul interested or experienced enough in Samolen lore to achieve such a result.

It had to be Moroda.

Quite *how*, he wasn't sure, but she did have a knack for ideas and understanding theory.

Sapora considered the implications. If a Sevastos had willingly sacrificed itself to give Moroda power, she would have paid a hefty price for it. All five previous Sevastos had been the same, that's what Topeko had said about the balance of power in Linaria. It wasn't something that could be used indefinitely.

Sapora took another sip of his drink. 'You must be proud of your student.'

'What a student she would have made if she had studied with me at the university!'

Topeko's smile faded. 'There is a crystal outside the gates to Taban Yul, identical to the five we have in Berel.'

'Interesting. I shall see for myself when I return to the city.' In truth, he was curious about what the crystal would look like. Aciel was trapped within. Would he be able to sense that?

Would Aciel be able to sense the outside?

Topeko risked a glance at the other Varkain in the room before speaking again, more hesitantly and somehow more politely than before. 'You...did not send any Cerastes to aid the Ittallan in their defence of Taban Yul? A city *you* rule?'

Sapora didn't appreciate the accusation. He hadn't

thought Aciel would move to attack so soon, and he hadn't planned on leaving Isa undefended.

However, her victory—even aided by a dragon—had shown her resilience. 'We Varkain are well protected by our land. I do not like hiding, like a rat, but I am unwilling to sacrifice myself or my soldiers in a fight we cannot win. I'd seen what Aciel could do. And I had faith the Imperial Guard would thwart him, as they have always done with Arillians.'

'King Sapora, there is more to come—I fear there will be a bloody battle between Arillians and dragons. It is the *dragons* that will end up burning the world and reducing all peoples to ash. From dragon-fire begun, from dragon-fire undone. You will not remain safe from fire, even in your tunnels.'

Sapora's patience for the Samolen was beginning to run thin.

'Spare me your prophecies, Topeko. The war is already over, by your own admission. Tell me. Why did you really visit Sereth? To spread misery? Get us to leave the safety of our homes and fight back in case the Arillians try to avenge Aciel? I've just got hold of my kingdom. Surely you do not expect me to risk it all on day one?'

Topeko waited a moment, his cheek jewels glinting in the torchlight. 'Apologies if I have caused any offence. I only came to understand the new king's stance on Arillians in the future.'

Sapora smirked.

Topeko had come to see whether Sapora would wage war, like Vasil had before him. Like Aciel had done. Now his visit made sense. 'Arillians have always bemoaned their status in Linaria. Complaining about their unfair treatment and banishment from the main continents.'

Topeko's cheek jewels dulled.

'Whinging how they've been shunned and mistreated. Fussing and howling about how much they are owed by the people of Linaria...' Sapora turned his gaze to the others present.

His Cerastes.

His brother.

'So, they fought back, tried to take what they thought was theirs.' He continued on, glancing at Topeko every so often. 'How dare anyone speak ill of Arillians? They have the gift of flight, of *Rhea herself*. Doesn't that make them better than everyone else? Prove they're owed more? That's what they all shrieked. Aciel most of all.'

Topeko gaped. 'King Sapora—'

'Life is unfair. The Varkain know that more than anyone. And I detest people who complain about it, yet do nothing to improve what they have. For his willingness to try, I give Aciel a little respect.'

At that, Tacio let out a low hiss.

Sapora ignored him.

'But Aciel was misguided. The Arillians *had* their time. Their chance. They ruined the harmony of Linaria in forcing this war, and we Varkain—left to slink in caves and hide out of sight—are going to fix his mess.'

'Then...you will not go after them?'

'Aciel has been taken care of. I have two countries to rule and plenty to clean up. Reports of dragon attacks are becoming more frequent above ground. The balance of power in Linaria *must* be restored.'

Topeko's shoulders dropped and a bead of sweat trickled down his temple. 'If there is anything the Samolen can do to help preserve peace, you need only ask.'

Sapora smiled broadly, his fangs glinting. 'Of course.'

∽

In the deep tunnels of Timin Rah, Sapora followed one of the Valendrin, keeping himself at arm's length. The blood mage was, like others of his caste, thin and pale, and vaguely repulsive.

Sapora had spent several hours in discussion with Vasil and his most trusted confidants. Information was shared freely, and for the first time, Sapora felt his father look at him as an equal.

It wasn't something he thought he'd ever get used to, but he was enjoying it.

While it lasted.

One point had cropped up that Sapora dwelled on longer than any other. Over decades, several tunnels in Timin Rah had collapsed or been permanently shut off. Mostly, it was due to age, lack of maintenance, or a tremor from the distant volcano, Mount Kozue.

But one had apparently been removed from maps and records without a trace.

He wanted to see for himself, and apparently it was deep within the district of Timin Rah given to the Valendrin and their practices. Somewhere even Vasil refused to set foot.

Sapora could see why, and though he did not enjoy his decision to come here, he did not regret it.

He'd left Tacio and the others at the keep, and elected to make the trip alone, though he wondered whether Tacio would have refused, even if he'd asked.

He followed the blood mage deeper into the labyrinth. Incense, chanting, and all manner of bottled liquids filled the caves and chambers they passed. Several stared deep into mirrors—enhanced by their magic, the mirrors allowed them to see and speak with others across Linaria. A network of eyes and ears, and something Sapora wished to make immediate use of.

In the tunnels of Sereth, they were hidden.

Safe.

But they were also isolated.

They made their way down a flight of stairs, crudely carved into the earth, and Sapora took great care where he stepped. This was a far cry from the pristine tunnels most Varkain lived in. This was primitive, crude, and seeped with old blood. Darkness pressed around them as they descended.

The air thickened, turned heavy. Still, the Valendrin continued on.

Still, Sapora followed.

He wondered what secrets this much reviled and revered caste of Varkain had kept buried so deep. He would need to appoint a Valendrin to his own entourage. He wanted nothing hidden, now he had power. And he did not care who he obtained his information from.

Vasil preferred to work only with pure-blooded Varkain of good standing.

Sapora had learned that usefulness could come from anywhere. He did not judge a person based on their birth or family. Only on their actions.

And he needed every scrap of strength he could find if he was to elevate the Varkain from the darkness and into Linaria's light.

Something trembled underfoot, like the breaths of an enormous creature.

'We are near Mount Kozue?' Sapora asked, half-expecting rivers of lava to be swimming through the rock down here.

'We are. But that is not what you sense.'

Sapora frowned.

None of the Varkain had ever felt the ground tremble like this. Was it too deep for the population of Sereth to feel?

'If there are more tunnels at risk of collapse, should we not abandon Timin Rah?'

The Valendrin smiled. 'Oh no. It is quite safe.'

Another tremble rushed through the tunnel, and Sapora leaned on the wall for support. 'Are you certain? I'm not sure I trust your senses. They're dulled by too much blood.'

The Valendrin could easily be Sapora's great-great-grandfather, he was so old. But he moved with ease, though his steps were slow. His smile did not fade—a darkness in his eyes that made Sapora shudder—and he produced a small, silver key from his outer coat. 'I am glad we have some...fresh blood in our royal leadership.'

Something about the way the Valendrin spoke made Sapora suppress another shudder. 'You would be the first to be glad of it. Most Varkain were happy with Vasil.'

The Valendrin chuckled. 'Indeed. Varkain do not like change. Even Vasil's mother who ruled before him wanted nothing to do with us. A shame that so many traditions are dying out.'

Sapora had no idea what the blood mage was mumbling about. 'Just show me what is down here. If it is a pile of corpses, I have no interest—'

'In truth, my liege, we do not know. What lies down here is from our most ancient history. There are a few of our order with such knowledge, and even then it is old. Contra-dictory. What is agreed upon is the fact there is power down here, though it has been long since sealed.'

'Why didn't you unseal it and look?'

'Because it can only be unsealed by royalty. As I said, Vasil would not come here. We have not had any royalty come to the depths of our district to study and learn from us since the time of Prince Karekis!'

Sapora knew his histories well. Karekis had been one of the earliest Varkain rulers some five thousand years prior.

He wondered what the Valendrin had been like then, at the height of their power and standing. Now, they were relegated to glorified healers and advisors, and shunned by most Varkain. 'How do I unseal it?'

The Valendrin held up the silver key. 'With your blood, my liege. And a stone from your crown.'

He shouldn't have been surprised. The idea of it repulsed him, but he understood there was power in blood, and his crown would prove his right to rule.

If he was to rise above Vasil's reign, he had to take whatever tools were made available to him.

Sapora offered the Valendrin his hand, watched as his skin was cut, his blood pooling from the small wound. In his other hand, he removed the circlet atop his head and held it out.

The Valendrin wiped the key in the collected droplets, staining the silver bright red. Then, he took the crown and turned to a part of the wall Sapora hadn't noticed as particularly interesting. He chanted something in the old tongue.

Every hair on Sapora's head stood up at the words.

Then, a door materialised in the rock wall. Had it been hidden by some sort of illusion? He wanted to find out what else the Valendrin had in their districts. What else they were capable of.

Though perhaps he'd never return to the rest of Timin Rah, let alone the surface, if he allowed himself to see how deep their district went.

He shook away the thoughts as the Valendrin pushed the bloodied key into the lock and turned it with a booming click.

Heat like nothing Sapora had ever felt accosted him. His skin tightened as sweat appeared at his hairline. Burning light rolled out from the open door in a furious blast, so bright Sapora could not look upon it.

'My...my liege!' Voice full of rapt awe, the Valendrin sank to the ground in the doorway, body trembling.

Hardly able to breathe, Sapora looked upon the deepest cavern of Timin Rah; upon a sleeping dragon, with gold-encrusted scales.

The heat emanating from the beast had to be hot enough to melt iron. The texture of the blackened walls was almost liquid—superheated rock which cooled occasionally enough to solidify once again.

The dragon filled the vast cavern with both its body and tail. Occasional bursts of light and flame licked along its back, though it slumbered. Its heart beat was slow and steady.

Sapora's mouth fell open.

It could only be one thing. A *Sevastos*.

And it was *his*.

The Valendrin began to tremble, his skin steaming from the heat. 'My liege. We...we must retreat before we burn!'

Sapora wasn't listening.

He could now see his path to glory.

To a future where the Varkain reigned supreme—no longer shunned or hidden away. No longer looked upon with disgust and fear.

There would be no more hurled insults and terrified flinching. Never again.

'I will prepare a victory for the Varkain the likes of which has never been seen before.' He voiced his thoughts, more to himself than the Valendrin.

There were always more secrets to unearth, more strength to accumulate.

And his reign was just beginning.

The cavern shook again, sending more tremors up the walls as the dragon exhaled a long, slow breath.

Rock and soil crumbled from the ceiling, dust scattering

down. It melted and evaporated in the intense heat with a searing whoosh.

Topeko's warning echoed in his mind, but Sapora dismissed it.

'From dragon-flame begun, from dragon-flame undone. In the end, everything burns.'

End